Praise for *Breath of Ea*

"The book as a whole strikes a nervy balance between easy-going charm and suspense. . . . As brisk as Cato's plot is, it's also straightforwardly simple. But she embroiders it richly with gorgeous period setpieces, imaginative speculation and the charismatic Ingrid herself, a hero-coming-into-her-own full of gumption and dimension. . . . Cato's exhaustive research of the time and place gives the book texture and grit, and she hasn't whitewashed what was a very problematic chapter of America's history."

—NPR

"The acclaimed Cato creates an alternate early 20th-century San Francisco of stunning detail. Drawing on the power struggles of the refugees and women's work, this vivid reality will keep readers intrigued to the very end."

—*Library Journal* (starred review)

"Readers in search of steampunk and alt-history can find them here charged with magic. . . . A strong cast and an unconventional approach to alternate history and magic . . . [in] this extraordinary world."

—*Locus*

"With an interesting mix of steampunk, alternate history and urban fantasy, this mystery and slow-building romance—first in Cato's new series—is excitingly different. Her marvelous star is multi-faceted and her co-stars are colorful. Her fantastical fiction is unique."

—RT Book Reviews

"While the set-pieces are often spectacular and fantastic, the world-building is the real show-stopping effort. This is not just a dirigible ride for the fun of it (though it *is* fun), but a journey with meaning and purpose."

—B&N Sci Fi/Fantasy Blog

"Cato . . . begins a new steampunk fantasy series with supernatural creatures, action-packed adventure, mystery, humor, a touch of romance, and more to come."

—*Booklist* (starred review)

"Taking on the realism of the ugly parts of society and history make this novel a winner."

—*SFRevu*

"Cato cleverly brings her colorful Barbary Coast–era San Francisco to life, highlighting the neglected perspectives of the outsiders and the dispossessed who made up the majority of its populace."

—*Publishers Weekly*

"*Breath of Earth* is that rare gem, a thought-provoking, imaginative adventure of the highest order, chock full of wonder as well as heart-wrenching what-ifs. It's reminiscent of Jules Verne at his best, with brilliant characters who linger in the mind and heart. Bravo!"

—Julie E. Czerneda, author of the Clan Chronicles

"Beth Cato gives steampunk a magical, global twist in an action-packed adventure that keeps the pages turning in anticipation. And if you don't fall in love with Ingrid Carmichael after reading this, you have no soul."

—Michael J. Martinez, author of *MJ-12: Inception* and *The Daedalus Incident*

CALL OF FIRE

ALSO BY BETH CATO

Breath of Earth

The Clockwork Dagger

The Clockwork Crown

Deep Roots

Wings of Sorrow and Bone: A Novella

"The Deepest Poison: A Short Story"

"Final Flight: A Short Story"

CALL OF FIRE

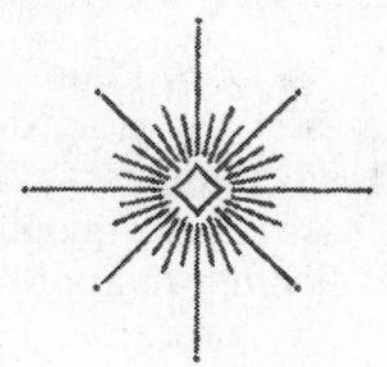

BETH CATO

This is a work of fiction. Names, characters, places, and incidents are products of the author's imagination or are used fictitiously and are not to be construed as real. Any resemblance to actual events, locales, organizations, or persons, living or dead, is entirely coincidental.

HarperCollins books may be purchased for educational, business, or sales promotional use. For information, please e-mail the Special Markets Department at SPsales@harpercollins.com.

FIRST EDITION

Map and interior book design by Paula Russell Szafranski

Library of Congress Cataloging-in-Publication Data has been applied for.

ISBN 978-0-06-242211-8

17 18 19 20 21 LSC 10 9 8 7 6 5 4 3 2 1

To Sue, Mel, Mary, and Paul,

for offering me a welcome

escape in the big tent

“The fiery trial through which we pass, will light us down, in honor or dishonor, to the latest generation.”

—Abraham Lincoln
Annual Message to Congress
December 1, 1862

CASCADIAN AMERICA

Seattle

Mount Rainier

Portland

San Francisco

CALL OF FIRE

CHAPTER 1

Thursday, April 19, 1906

If Ingrid Carmichael closed her eyes, her thoughts immediately drifted to her beloved San Francisco as she last knew it: a city ravaged by earthquakes, the ruins afire, with the unfurled blue energy of the earth coiling up her legs in a turbulent fog.

She sat in one of the pilot's chairs on the airship *Palmetto Bug* and sipped coffee from a lidded mug. The stuff tasted foul enough to scour pipes clean, but the caffeine kept her eyes pried as wide open as a china doll's, which was exactly what she needed.

Between Ingrid's feet sat the simple pine box that her mentor, Mr. Sakaguchi, had asked her to recover. He had told her that the letters inside would explain why she must flee the city before something terrible happened.

Unfortunately, she had not been able to leave fast enough.

Her estranged father had caused the destruction of San

Francisco. Ingrid had pulled in enough energy to mitigate the attack, and it almost killed her. Even so, guilt and regret persisted, stubborn as nettles in cloth. She loved San Francisco. It had been her home. Now it lay in rubble, buried in ashes.

Her thumb caressed the edges of the letters on her lap as she looked out the glass that spanned the front of the cabin. Pine trees coated seemingly endless mountain ridges. A few distant peaks still carried snow. Sporadic trails of smoke denoted settlements. No blue energy fogged the ground as it had around San Francisco Bay.

The *Palmetto Bug* had flown for a full day now. Ingrid surmised that they had crossed into Oregon. Cy had said that they should arrive in Portland that night.

"Goddamn it." Fenris scowled in his pilot's chair a foot away. He stared at the dashboard dials the way Ingrid would look at a large spider.

"What?" she asked.

"When I used to imagine the *Palmetto Bug*'s maiden flight, I thought it would be something—I don't know—*pleasant*. Like a trip to the salvage yards down in San Jose. A day-trip. A chance to test the vessel and tweak things afterward. Not this." He waved a hand toward the wilderness below. "A prolonged flight over nothingness, not a damned mooring mast in sight."

"Do you think we're going to crash?" Ingrid tucked the letters in their box again and sat up straight. "If we get everyone together, I can—"

Fenris raised an eyebrow, cutting her off. "If we were going to crash, I'd just announce, 'We're going to crash.' Simple and effective."

"Good to know." Adrenaline and caffeine had mingled together in Ingrid's blood, making her even more jittery and anxious. Not that she had been steady at all over the past day. Mystical and mysterious as her powers might be, the repercussions manifested in very physical—and damned annoying—forms. Even if Fenris had said they were going to crash, she wasn't sure she should—or could—hold the energy to protect them.

"That said," Fenris continued, "go rouse Cy. I need to talk to him."

Ingrid locked her mug into a holder built at foot level of the dashboard, then pushed herself up off the arms of the upholstered wooden chair. She felt Fenris's scrutiny, his worry, as he waited for her to show signs of frailty. She set her jaw and made her rubbery legs move like normal, one hand to the wall as she entered the narrow central corridor of the airship. Her stocking feet whispered against the tatami matting.

Her left hand kept the pine box tucked close to her ribs. She needed to discuss the contents with Lee—a talk that had to come sooner rather than later.

The *Palmetto Bug* was a Sprite-class airship designed to fit up to four passengers, though not in comfort. The entire gondola was about thirty feet in length from control cabin to engine room. Just outside the cockpit was a large floor hatch with stairs that folded flat; Ingrid didn't like stepping on grates or manhole lids—her mother had raised her to be skeptical of such infrastructure in San Francisco—so she took mincing steps around this potential opening as well.

Just past the hatch was the kitchenette of the craft. It consisted of a packed pantry of boxed and canned foods or other things that could be eaten with minimal preparation, as a lone stove burner was their only means to heat food on board. Within hours of being under way, Ingrid had realized that the coffee percolator had a permanent home there, so it was best to eat straight out of the cupboard.

The thought of food made her pause. She had been relentlessly hungry over the past day as her body recovered. It was appalling, really. She felt like a sumo wrestler before a bout.

Ingrid slid up the pantry door. Fenris had made it clear that the situation in the cabin wasn't an emergency. Awakening Cy would wait a minute more.

None of the cabinets opened outward to impede movement within the limited space in the corridor. High-sided boxes and elasticized straps secured food in place as a precaution against turbulence. An entire shelf was devoted to fine liquor that they had raided from Mr. Thornton's airship, thinking that the bottles might prove useful to sell.

Her fingers glanced over boxed crackers and canned chicken. She pulled out a parcel wrapped in parchment and twine, and she sniffed it to guess the contents.

"That's hard cheese."

Ingrid looked up in surprise. Heat fluttered in her chest. Cy leaned against the wall a few feet away. His button-up blue cotton shirt hung crooked on his lanky form, the tails partially tucked into brown trousers. Pince-nez sat atop his rather long nose. He smiled at her, his brown eyes kind.

"You can cut into that block, if you like, but we always need some cheese handy in case gremlins latch on to the ship. The critters aren't as attracted to orichalcum as they are to silver, but they still like to cause mischief, and that's a bad thing in flight." His voice stayed at a low rumble out of respect for those still sleeping nearby.

"The cheese is bait, then?"

He nodded, and she noticed his jaw was lightly covered with a fine scruff that was redder than his brown hair. "I chuck cheese out a window and gremlins dive for it like a wyvern on sheep." He grinned. "Sometimes I wonder if gremlins've trained people to do that very thing, just so they get cheese." His southern accent was sweet enough to flavor a pitcher of tea.

Ingrid closed the cupboard. She was too self-conscious about her terrible hunger to grab anything with Cy right there. Which was silly, really, considering how the man had seen her slathered in blood, gore, and manure.

"Did you sleep well?" she murmured.

"Well enough." He worked his shoulders, quirking his neck to either side as he frowned. Cy stood at about six and a half feet, and he certainly didn't fit well into the small, stacked sleeping racks on board.

Ingrid wanted to feel the tightness of his shoulder muscles beneath her hands. She wanted to feel a lot more than that, actually. The memory of kissing Cy brought a magma-like flare to her body.

She swallowed, her throat dry. This was neither the time nor the place to be lusting after Cy, not with Lee and Fenris in such close quarters. She leaned against the wall, partly to give her weakened legs a break, partly to create distance between them. "Fenris wanted me to fetch you. Something about the ship is aggravating him."

Cy snorted softly. "Everything aggravates Fenris like a woolen union suit. I'll see what the matter is." His hand grazed her shoulder as he sidled past. She turned to watch him walk toward the cockpit. Even rumpled, his trousers fit him in a fine way.

As soon as he left, Ingrid slid open the pantry again and secured the pine box on a high shelf. From her eye level, she grabbed a box of British digestive biscuits, more salvage from the late Mr. Thornton's airship. The British-born warden had never disguised his deep passion for India, a place Britannia was currently bombing with civilized efficiency to quell rebellion. But Ingrid had never suspected that Mr. Thornton had joined the modern incarnation of the Thuggees to ruthlessly fight for India's independence. Current bestselling dime novels liked to romanticize Thuggees as dark-skinned pagans with weighted scarves in hand to strangle their victims, carrying on the legacy of the reputed cult of Kali that had existed earlier in the nineteenth century. In reality, the name had been fully appropriated by pasty-skinned Brits with natty suits and Oxford and Cambridge egos.

San Francisco had become their testing ground for a new brand of warfare. Four days ago Mr. Thornton had orchestrated an explosion at the Cordilleran Auxiliary, killing almost everyone Ingrid knew. She and her mentor, Mr. Sakaguchi, would have died as well if she hadn't spontaneously created a strange pressure-wave bubble to keep them safe in the debris.

She had thought things couldn't get worse than that. How little she knew.

Ingrid moved to sink onto the bunk vacated by Cy, the biscuit tin on her lap. He had tugged the sheets straight but the mattress still carried some of his warmth. In the rack above, Lee made soft noises as he slept.

Directly across from her, their one unexpected passenger, Miss Victoria Rossi, remained utterly still in the bottom bunk. She hadn't awakened since Papa, flushed with earth energy, had tossed her the way a temperamental child might fling a doll.

Miss Rossi and Mr. Thornton had been lovers and partners in their plot to create an earthquake. Miss Rossi's goals had been twofold: vengeance against San Francisco, and a chance to provoke the Hidden One within the San Andreas Fault to emerge and be immortalized by her camera lens. Papa injured Miss Rossi before she had the chance to witness the massive two-headed snake that had reared up from the fault line in Olema. Tragic justice, that.

Miss Rossi had yet to make a sound. When they had

carried her onto the ship, her body had been bruised and bloodied, both of her legs broken, and worst of all, her spine hadn't rested at the right angle.

Ingrid leaned forward and tugged back the curtains that offered a modicum of privacy to each bunk. Miss Rossi lay curled on her side, facing the corridor. Her tumultuous black hair framed her face as if she posed for a Pre-Raphaelite artist. Purple bruises, puffed like pillows, encircled her eyes. Her chapped lips gaped open.

"I want you to know that even though I hate you, I still don't wish for you to die," Ingrid whispered, her voice wobbly with unspent emotion. "There's too much on Papa already. He killed Mr. Thornton and that other man. He tried to kill me, too." She touched her neck. Her throat was still raw from when Papa choked her with his invisible grip. He said if he had known about her power, he would have smothered her to death as a child. She believed him.

"We'll be in Portland soon, Miss Rossi. We'll get you to a doctor." She touched Miss Rossi's hand. It was cold.

Ingrid recoiled with a slight cry then lunged forward to press her hand to Miss Rossi's cheek. It was likewise cold and stiff.

"Ing?" Lee's muffled voice came from above.

"Lee, you need to get up." Ingrid gripped the wall to pull herself upright again. "Cy?" she called. Then she saw he was already walking their way, his expression grim.

"Ingrid, we have a mite of a problem. Lee? Glad to see you're awake. We need to palaver."

"Yes, we do." Emotion squeezed Ingrid's throat, as if Papa had hold of her again. "Miss Rossi's dead."

"A dead woman on board. That's just dandy." Fenris remained in his pilot's chair. The cabin glass showed the same view as before, with forested mountains stretching to a cloudy horizon. "I suppose the plan to quiz her for more information is out unless someone knows how to conduct a séance."

"I knew mediums in Chinatown." Lee sat on one of the wooden benches that flanked the door to the control cabin; Ingrid had claimed the other seat, though by Cy's frown, he would have much rather she had taken the plush copilot's chair. "But the way Chinatown was when we left, the mediums might need mediums." The joke fell flat even for him.

Cy angled to look at each of them in turn. "It would have helped matters to question Miss Rossi, true—"

"'Helped'?" Lee echoed. "*Helped* is putting it mildly. She's the only one who could've given us any information at this point about the attack on the auxiliary and the attack on the city. Both of which, I might remind you, are being blamed on the Chinese. On *me*."

He ran a hand through his wild black hair and released a huffy breath. Ingrid nudged his shoulder with her knuckles. His grin for her was thin.

The allied forces of Japan and the United States, known as the Unified Pacific, had worked together for over a decade to subjugate the Chinese people. Many refugees had fled to America, but the Land of Liberty had not granted them refuge.

In public, Lee Fong had been a meek errand boy for Mr. Sakaguchi, in every way subservient to his Japanese master. In private, Lee was fully educated and treated with outright fondness.

Ingrid had thought this was simply part of Mr. Sakaguchi's kind nature—he was dangerously outspoken on behalf of the Chinese people—but things were more complicated than she had ever realized.

Lee Fong, the boy she had engaged in tickle wars with, was in fact the only surviving child of China's emperor Qixiang. Mr. Sakaguchi had known the truth and had nurtured Lee as he kept him hidden from both American and Japanese forces.

"We can't take Miss Rossi to authorities in Portland. It brings too much attention to us." Cy's brows scrunched together. "Much as I'd prefer to treat her body with dignity, our circumstances make that a challenge."

"I can argue about how much dignity she should be granted, considering the hell she caused. This woman wandered all over San Francisco taking pictures of the city in its final days so she could sell the prints later, remember?" Fenris scowled over his shoulder.

"What if we find a mooring mast before Portland?" Ingrid asked. "We can dock long enough to bury her and speak some words."

"Mooring masts also mean civilization. A docked airship will draw attention and people will talk, especially if a dead woman's involved. We can't risk that," said Cy.

No, they couldn't. Not with the Unified Pacific and Ambassador Blum after them.

"Dignity." Lee worked the word as if he had something stuck between his teeth. "Miss Rossi's actions say a great deal about her soul. She'll be judged. She might even become a ghost. I hope she's tormented for all eternity, quite honestly, but it's only right for us to treat her body with respect as long as it doesn't endanger us."

Cy nodded at Lee. "Wisely said. I think that leaves us one option. We need to drop her from the air. Maybe into a lake."

"Bodies float," Fenris said. "We need to weigh her down. We don't have much deadweight aboard—pardon the expression." His lips quirked in a split-second smile.

Cy thought for a moment, and then his expression twisted in disgust. "Well. We can seal bilge waste in buckets. It's not exactly respectful, but it would weigh her down."

"Sounds appropriate to me," said Fenris.

Ingrid shook her head in disbelief of the whole conversation. "Where's the dignity in that?"

"It's a better fate than she would have given any of us," said Cy.

Ingrid wanted to argue for some other means of disposal, but nothing came to mind. She sighed, resigned. "I'll wrap up her body best as I can."

"Since I made the suggestion, it's only right that I take on bucket duty," Cy said.

"I can help," Lee added, tone quiet.

Fenris sighed. "And I can fly my poor beleaguered airship, who in her two days of functionality has been shot, repaired, and hosted a dead woman who might possibly become a ghost. I'd also like to remind you that I had important revelations of my own before this problem with a corpse cropped up."

Cy froze as he started to stand. "That's right. Sorry."

Fenris flicked a wrist over his shoulder. "It's not as though the issues are *that* dire. Yet. Some of the dial readings don't feel accurate based on other data. Our viewing windows and mirrors at the back keep frosting over. The vents must not be angled quite right. And I think the ballast weight isn't quite balanced because—"

A squeak of alarm escaped from Lee's throat.

Cy held up a hand. "That's enough, Fenris. They get it."

Fenris grunted. "When we moor in Portland, we'll need to stay for a few days. I know, I know, it's not ideal with the UP on our tails, but the city has a good stockpile of parts. We shouldn't need to wait for anything like we might in some Podunk town."

"Will these repairs completely prevent the ship from flight?" Ingrid couldn't bear the thought of being stuck, of being as vulnerable as a kappa without water in its crown. "Blum's going to come after me. You know she will."

The combined power of Japan and America was governed by twelve ambassadors. Most of them remained unknown to the public, while others, like Theodore Roosevelt, were darlings of the daily newspapers. Ambassador Blum was not a public figure—nor was she human. In the brief time that Blum had held Ingrid captive in San Francisco, the ambassador had taken care to demonstrate that she was a kitsune, a Japanese fox spirit. A very powerful one, judging by the way she emanated magic. With each century of life, a kitsune gained new tails and new human forms that she could don at will. Ingrid had encountered Blum in the form of an elderly Japanese woman, while Cy had once known her as a beautiful, young redhead.

"I'll do what I can to keep the *Bug* operational in case we need to vamoose. I don't relish the idea of being a sitting duck either, you know. Blum's a big reason why I made the *Bug* in the first place. She'd like to get her hands—paws—on Cy again, too."

With reason. Cy was a brilliant inventor. As a teenager, he had designed the Durendal tank, one of the Unified Pacific's greatest assets in the wars against the Spanish Empire and now China. He had deserted the Army & Airship Corps, become an avowed pacifist, and had spent almost half his life on the run so that his skills could never again be used to create weapons of mass murder. Not to mention Blum had apparently delighted in flirting with Cy in the brief time they had known each other.

Cy cleared his throat. "Enough about Blum. We'll stay on the move."

Ingrid welcomed the subject change. She was repulsed by the very idea of Cy and Blum acting friendly, even though she knew that he had believed Blum to be a normal human at the time.

"You're not alone, Ingrid. We're right here with you," Cy

said, misreading the dismay on her face. "We'll outfox that old fox." The fierceness in his eyes made her forget the faint brush of jealousy and want to crush her lips against his instead.

"That's right. Why hang alone when you can hang as a group?" Fenris mimicked pulling a noose at his neck.

Ingrid couldn't help laughing, as horrible as the joke was. The truth was, she'd never be lucky enough to die in Blum's possession. No, she'd be treated like Papa was while in Unified Pacific custody: brought to the brink of death time and again in order to agitate Hidden Ones and level whole cities.

As she worked her way down the hallway to prepare Miss Rossi's body, Ingrid promised herself that she'd never be abused as Papa was. She'd make certain that she died first.

CHAPTER 2

FRIDAY, APRIL 20, 1906

Rooftops across Portland gleamed in the morning light. The heart of the city clung to the bends of the Willamette River, with buildings and roads stretching into the green hills at all sides and spreading north to the wide cut of the Columbia. Farther north still, Mount St. Helens squatted, a snow-capped dome. To the east, Mount Hood stood dominant.

But Ingrid's gaze was focused downtown, where black plumes rose high into the sky.

"Is it like San Francisco all over again?" she hoarsely whispered.

"I don't think so, Ing. I traveled here with Mr. Sakaguchi once a few years ago. That smoke looks like it's from their Chinatown." Lee spoke up from the other bench seat. "It doesn't seem like the fire spread very far."

"Yes." Cy was at the rudder wheel, as he had been much of the night. Fenris's steady diet of coffee couldn't fully eradicate the need for sleep, despite his efforts. "That looks about right. We lived in Seattle for a while and came down here more than once. Portland used to treat their Chinese better than most cities. They didn't even confine them to a set area back then. As the war's gone on, well . . ." Cy's voice trailed off.

The Japanese alliance with America had existed since the brief War Between the States in the 1860s, when Japanese airship technology enabled the Union to crush the fledging Confederacy; the Unified Pacific gained true cohesion in the 1890s as America joined with the Japanese to dominate China. American hatred of the Chinese had evolved with the rising death tolls of subsequent generations of young men.

"Mr. Sakaguchi might be down there, caught in the cross fire," she murmured.

Lee shot her a glance. "Uncle Moon will take care of him."

"He might heal Mr. Sakaguchi if he's injured, yes, but forgive me for not placing too much trust in your uncle," she snapped, her worry for Mr. Sakaguchi making her voice sharper than she intended. Lee said nothing more.

After Mr. Sakaguchi survived the auxiliary explosion in San Francisco, a sniper had attacked him in his home. Desperate to save her ojisan, Ingrid had begged Lee to take Mr. Sakaguchi into Chinatown to a powerful *lingqi* doctor. She knew it was risky for a Japanese man to be in the grotto, much less an esteemed geomancer, but at the time she had no idea Uncle Moon actually led one of the *tongs* that had filled the power vacuum left by the fall of the Chinese government. When the *tongs* fled the city before the earthquake, they had taken Mr. Sakaguchi along as a hostage.

Wui Seng Tong would demand that Mr. Sakaguchi use geomancy to transfer earth energy to kermanite to power Chinese machines and airships. He wouldn't. He had long refused to fill any kermanite that directly powered the war effort for either side.

Ingrid wondered how long the *tongs* would tolerate an uncooperative Japanese man in their midst. The Chinese were fleeing for their lives, after all. Mr. Sakaguchi would be a burden.

The airship swooped lower to follow the Willamette River northward. Ships flecked the water. Along the river stood an airship dock with rows of tall mooring masts like lighthouses of exposed steel. Dozens of towers were spaced out on what seemed to be an island that connected to the river's eastern bank by a small land bridge.

Cy adjusted two levers in the dashboard. The engine noise shifted to become more guttural.

"We're mooring." Fenris leaned in the doorway, arms crossed. He had a small, straight figure, his brown skin pale enough to make him socially acceptable. His wardrobe consisted of oil-stained cotton shirts and brown dungarees.

"Yep." Cy didn't turn. His focus was on an empty tower just below. Two boys raced up the metal staircase to the top and beckoned the *Bug* forward.

The *Palmetto Bug* hovered closer, closer, the engine noise dropping to a mere purr. The red ball atop the mooring tower loomed close, as if Ingrid could open up a window and tap it. A small lurch shook the craft and the engine noise wound down to nothing.

"There. Welcome to Portland." Cy planted his hands on his lap and looked back at Ingrid, as if seeking approval. She gave him a small smile; his eyes brightened in response. Cy beckoned to Fenris. "There's already hot coffee in the pot. Maybe you can be somewhat pleasant in discourse with other folks here."

Fenris muttered something indecipherable as he turned away.

Cy stood and stretched as much as he could in the confined space. "I'll get us set up here and find out the scuttlebutt. That shouldn't take too long. You both need to stay aboard." His gaze flicked between Ingrid and Lee.

"For now," Ingrid said. Cy shot her a look as he continued down the hallway, pausing only to tug on his shoes.

She understood his caution about letting her wander the city, even if the need for it rankled her. Her deep brown skin, inherited from Papa, caused folks to label her everything from Cherokee to Mexican. San Francisco was probably more tolerant of her than many places because the population abounded with new immigrants from all over the world. She knew that wasn't the case in Cascadia, where the demographics favored Japanese and Anglo-Saxons.

Cy yanked open the hatch. Heavy metal clanged and the stairs jangled free. "Hey there! G'morning!" he called. "Fine sunny day up here . . ." His voice faded with his footsteps.

Cy had a graceful way with people; he was slick as butter on a hot cast-iron skillet.

Lee remained in place and stared out the glass with a frown.

"Hey," Ingrid said softly, nudging him. "You seem to still be up in the clouds."

"I'm trying to figure out how to handle this. I haven't been outside of San Francisco on my own, you know. With reason."

She studied him. He wore a white button-up shirt, the paper collar fresh, and dungarees like he would wear most every day. Lee had the foresight to bring clothes aboard for both himself and Ingrid. This had been a very good thing since the gorgeous dress she last wore in San Francisco had been coated with manure, blood, and unidentified filth. They had stuffed it into a furnace before they departed California.

"Other than Wui Seng Tong, do you think you might know anyone else around here?" she asked.

"Maybe. Depends on how many other Chinese came this way from California. I don't think I know anyone who lives here."

"Well, here's my suggestion: don't wear your brassard." Her words scared her a bit, but at the same time the suggestion felt right. In public, all Chinese were required to wear yellow cloth on an upper arm that bore the kanji for Shina, as well as carry an identification booklet. To do otherwise was sedition.

"When you speak in Japanese on the phone, people think you are Japanese," she continued. "You're as fluent as I am."

"Ah yes, I'm very good at saying 'moshi moshi.'"

That made Ingrid laugh. Those words were the standard Japanese greeting via telephone, akin to saying hello. According to mythology, kitsune couldn't pronounce the syllables in "moshi moshi." Hence its use as a phone greeting; if the person on the other end couldn't reply in turn, they might not be human.

"I should say that to Blum sometime, see if she can reply." She smiled at Lee. "Think about this. You know how to act Japanese."

"That's true." He looked thoughtful. "You know what? It could work. I knew too many people in San Francisco to ever get away with such a masquerade there, but here, maybe."

"These clothes are clean and look like something a working-class Japanese boy might wear into town, too. You just have to carry yourself in a different way." If anyone noticed his bruised face, the slight discoloration could be readily excused as a martial arts injury.

They stopped talking as Fenris grumbled into the hallway and clomped down the stairs. Outside, a large staircase wheeled closer. Ingrid recalled seeing a similar structure in Fenris and Cy's workshop.

"A proper Japanese boy shouldn't be wandering downtown alone on a school day either," Lee said.

"Of course. You need a nanny. It's a different sort of play-acting than being a secretary, but I think I can manage."

She and Lee grinned at each other. Their subterfuge might be unlawful, but it certainly was titillating.

Not only could they search for Mr. Sakaguchi here, but maybe Ingrid could find out more about Papa as well. Judging by his correspondence, he had lived in Portland for years. Maybe someone here would have the answers they were desperately seeking.

Ingrid might be on the run from Ambassador Blum, but this was a strategic retreat. Information was ammunition, and she was determined to be well armed when the battle resumed.

"Ingrid? Lee?" Cy's voice carried up the stairs as he boarded. "Pardon the interruption. I want to talk with you both, but I need to disconnect some things right quick. Do you mind following me?"

They walked to the engine compartment at the very back of the ship. Ingrid glanced around. This portion of the airship was less than ten feet across, maybe five feet long, and was crammed with tangled pipes, wires, and gadgetry. A few of the larger tanks looked big enough to hold a person.

The only part of the machinery that she could name with certainty was the kermanite crystal that acted as the primary power source for the *Bug*. She had filled that rock herself just a few days before. It awed her to think that Fenris had assembled much of the engine, including a portion of the hull, over the course of a single night. She could stare at this mechanical jumble for a lifetime and she'd never understand how it functioned.

Cy turned a valve. By his somber expression, he did not

have good news. "The smoke is indeed from Chinatown. A block of buildings burned to the ground last night. The Chinese here've been jailed for their own safety."

Lee inhaled with a hiss. "Their own safety? Like hell."

"Therefore," Cy continued, "it's best for you to stay aboard, Lee. I can ask around to see if Mr. Sakaguchi has been locked away with the Chinese, since he could be unconscious from that gunshot wound, or he might have been coerced to stay quiet—"

"No. No." Lee shook his head violently, tousling his black hair. "The Chinese won't talk to you. The police? If you slip them enough money, they'll claim a giant octopus can sing opera. I need to do this. The two of us have a plan, see? I'm going to be Japanese today. Boku wa kawaii nihonjin desu ne?"

Concern created wrinkles in Cy's forehead. "I don't like it. You're too important, Lee. For you to wander around town—"

"Anything we do has risks," interrupted Ingrid. "Even meeting with Mr. Roosevelt. We know he was Mr. Sakaguchi's friend, but we have no idea if we can trust him beyond that."

The Mr. Roosevelt Ingrid had known since childhood was an affable man who delighted in regaling his companions with the same old stories time and again and guffawing in laughter all the while. She most often lurked nearby and read books while he and Mr. Sakaguchi socialized, fetching drinks and snacks as requested. If he engaged in any personal conversations with her, the subject matter involved the book she was reading at the time; Roosevelt was a voracious reader with an astonishing memory. But he had never once let on that he knew the truth of her geomantic heritage—meaning he was a man who could casually conceal secrets.

She continued, "Even if we can trust Mr. Roosevelt, we don't know about the people around him, but we must approach him nevertheless. We'll be smart about it. We know the dangers involved."

Lee offered a small nod of agreement.

"I need to help Fenris start work here and then get some shut-eye, if I can. Work on the airship has to be our highest priority. We can always find Roosevelt later, if need be." Cy shook his head as he unfastened some bolts. "I'm not keen on the two of you wandering around town, but I'm not going to lock you up in the *Bug* either."

"Good. That would not be well received," said Ingrid, her tone cool at the very idea that he would do such a thing. Worry clouded Cy's eyes as Ingrid sidled past, and she softened. She knew he fervently disagreed with their errand, but he also had the sense to keep his counsel. "Cy, please don't fuss over us."

"Assuredly, I will worry. You're like a kitten set loose in a room with fresh paint."

Lee snorted. "I won't argue with that." Ingrid shot him a glare.

"Well, then, Cy, if you need to find me, look for the trail of mayhem and paw prints, though we do plan to find our own way back."

Cy's smile created warm crinkles around his eyes. "You

do that, Ingrid. I'll leave out a saucer of milk for you, just in case."

Lee made a soft gagging noise and pressed past them to return to the cockpit. Ingrid was suddenly aware of the strange quiet surrounding them after days of engine noise. The nearby bunks were empty, too. She and Cy had some semblance of privacy for once. Cy seemed to realize it as well. His gaze averted as he flexed his neck and shoulders.

"Your neck's bothering you?" she asked.

"I'm not about to complain."

"No, you wouldn't do something so ungentlemanly. Would you like me to give you a little massage?"

Ingrid could see the refusal poised on his lips, so she stepped closer. Their bodies almost touched. "Please? Maybe it'll help some. I promise I won't besmirch your honor. Not today."

A smile lit his face again. "No promises about tomorrow?"

"Absolutely none."

Cy sidestepped out of the engine compartment and faced a top rack. Ingrid had never given a massage in her life, but she supposed this was as good a time as any to learn. She positioned her hands and thumbs where his neck met his shoulders. Through the thin cloth, his muscles resembled hard knots. She worked in her thumbs. Cy grunted and braced himself against the copper rail.

"Is this helping or hurting?" she asked, easing up some.

"Both, in all truth." He flinched. "But that doesn't mean I want you to stop. I like your touch."

"And I like touching you." She kept her tone light as she eased her fingers beneath his collar best as she could. The task would certainly be easier if he took his shirt off, but she knew he wouldn't do such a thing, as much as she might want him to. "I think your left side is the tightest." She pressed harder there, her right hand gripping his other shoulder.

An exaggerated cough rang out from down the way. "I'm going to the top of the tower for a few minutes while you, er, finish up here." Lee's feet pattered down the stairs.

Ingrid's cheeks flamed. She loosened her hold on Cy. "I forgot he was still here."

"Well, he's gone now." Cy twisted around. Ingrid had time for a small gasp of surprise and then his lips met hers, his kiss strong and tender all at once. Their bodies melted together, his form solid against her. Ingrid didn't know what it was about Cy, but she could happily kiss him forever and a day.

Lee's and Fenris's voices carried up the hatch, muffled but close.

Ingrid reluctantly pulled away from Cy, but his broad hands remained on her waist, his fingers sprawled downward against the generous curve of her hips. The firm pressure of his touch made her yearn to press against him again, to feel more of him.

He cleared his throat. "I'd best get to work before Fenris comes after me. And you—"

"I'll be careful as I can be," she finished.

His eyes searched hers in a silent plea for her well-being, and he stepped away.

Lee seemed bouncy and bright in a way he hadn't been in days. They left the port and walked through a high gate bearing the name SWAN ISLAND. A paved walkway took them along a neck of land to reach a bus stop along the frontage road.

A few other men idled in wait as well, older men with the heavy bodies and deep scowls that Ingrid associated with dockworkers. They didn't cast Lee a second glance; with his head held high and yellow armband absent, he was nondescript. Just another Japanese boy. Their study of Ingrid was not so discreet. She kept her posture prim as she fidgeted with the lip of her dress pocket.

Ingrid hadn't been on land for two days. When they left Olema, a blue miasma of unleashed energy had still covered the ground. She hadn't been able to bear contact with the surface for long, as her fatigued body would have continued to pull in energy and made her even more ill.

It was almost eerie to be on regular earth. No blue sheen. No warm energy lapping her ankles in a tide only she could see. Portland was seismically active, true, but there were a few geomancers stationed here to balance and harvest the energy flow. She blinked back tears of relief. She felt safe here; a misleading feeling, she knew, with Blum after her, but at least the earth didn't threaten to quake right now. That was one less threat to contend with.

A rusty and rumbling bus arrived in a matter of minutes. Ingrid and Lee sat side by side as the transport roared south. It was easy to spy downtown Portland across the river. Smoke trailed to the heavens like a banner.

"It's nice to sit like this," murmured Lee, fingers brushing the worn leather seat. She could tell he was making a concerted effort to play his part; his vigilance was more subtle than hers, and he kept his gaze up, not on the floor, as was appropriate for subservient Chinese.

"I wish that kind of freedom wasn't so extraordinary," Ingrid muttered. She acted out her own role as she kept her posture both attentive and meek. His knuckles tapped the side of her knee in a silent apology. Her skin color and gender would never allow for such liberty. "Did you decide where we should go first, Master Sato?" They had agreed on the common Japanese name for Lee to use for this trip.

"I want to see what happened to their Chinatown." He made no effort to lower his voice. "It looks like a lot of smoke."

One of the other passengers leaned closer. "Not enough in my opinion. Fire stopped all too soon. Didn't burn out all the rats."

"Well, they could hardly let all of downtown burn," said his companion. "You know how these fires get. One woman burns an egg for breakfast, and suddenly half the town is gone."

Lee faced forward, his outward expression one of excitement. Only Ingrid noticed how his hands clenched together as if to strangle someone.

"That fire is the last place we need to go," Ingrid said. "It's not an appropriate place for you."

"A woman would say that!" One of the men leaned

against their seat. "You want to see what burned? We can take you there. Give you a proper tour of the town." His buddy chortled.

"That won't be necessary," Ingrid said, her voice like ice. That made the men laugh even more. "You've seen this kind of thing before in San Francisco," she whispered to Lee. "You know what you'll see. You know the kind of people who will congregate there."

Photographers. Looters. Men cheering and toasting the destruction. Lee offered her a small nod, his demeanor now more Chinese than Japanese.

"Then where should we go?" he muttered.

"I can't believe they locked up all the Chinese. Heaven forbid the residents here wash their own clothes or cook their own food. All of civilization would collapse." At that, Lee snorted. "We'll wander about as tourists do. We'll find someone to talk to."

The bus followed the river and passed a massive rail yard and, after a few miles, finally crossed the Willamette River and into downtown. In the time it took for them to leave Swan Island, clouds had swept over the sky. The air carried a distinct scent of rain, though it was different than in San Francisco. It didn't bring along the briny odor of the ocean.

"We need coats," Lee muttered. He sat taller, fully assuming his role again. "I wish I'd thought to grab some in San Francisco."

"I'm glad you managed to grab me clothes and boots at all or I'd be walking around like a newfangled nudist," she whispered. She wore a westernized take on a kimono, the fabric deep purple. The sleeves puffed out at the elbow and tapered at the cuff. An obi-style cloth belt accentuated the waist of her thick hourglass figure. The dress overall was a bit baggy, like the others Lee had grabbed for her, but she couldn't gripe.

Most important, the dress included pockets. Ingrid had taken care to bring a handful of empty kermanite from their stash on the ship. If an earthquake struck, she needed the rocks handy to take in excess energy so that her lingering power sickness didn't worsen.

Lee glanced at Ingrid with an arched eyebrow. "I'm sure Cy would have lent you clothes again."

She muffled a laugh. "Yes, that would have made a good impression in Portland."

A few minutes later, they disembarked and stood beneath an awning for a moment to gain their bearings. The business district bustled on a Friday morning; paved roadways hosted autocars, horse-drawn vehicles, and bicycles aplenty. Brick buildings stood two and three floors in height, the architecture blending stark American fronts with Japanese-style curved roofs. Flags flanked entrance doors, the forty-five stars on the American flag set just higher than the Japanese rising sun. Others had affixed a third flag, the diagonal blend of the Unified Pacific.

Ingrid wondered aloud where Mr. Roosevelt might be in the area, if he was still here at all. She purchased a newspaper and handed it to Lee, as was appropriate for her subservient role, and waited impatiently as he scanned the headlines. The whole front page was devoted to the devastation in San Francisco and the hunt for the villainous Chinese who had somehow committed the deed. Lee quickly skipped several pages forward.

"Yes, there's mention of T.R. He's in negotiations with some trade organizations here through tomorrow."

"Does it mention if he'll meet with the public?" He often did so in San Francisco.

"No . . . yes. Not today. By appointment only, it says. Few time slots available. Sign up at a police station on Front Street on Saturday. Front is that way." He motioned back toward the river. A slow drizzle began to fall, and he held the paper overhead.

Front Street! Papa had mentioned it in his correspondence to Mr. Sakaguchi. Excitement surged in her veins.

The rain fell harder. "Master Sato, that newspaper won't be useful for long. There's a haberdasher across the way," she said respectfully, keeping up their charade.

"Hai!" He led the way, a swagger to his step.

The smell of smoke tainted the air. It put her in mind of San Francisco as she last saw it: those crosshatched lines that demarcated block after block of charred and crumbled masonry, the skyscrapers afire like torches held toward heaven. She grimaced and pushed the thoughts away. Portland was not San Francisco.

She welcomed the chance to step inside the shop and out of the rain. The chemical sharpness of starched clothes and sachets of lavender cleansed her senses. A cheery piano tune rang from a Marconi on a back table.

A few minutes later, Lee wore a lined oil slicker and a tweed flat cap that accentuated his youth. They continued down the street to a shop that catered to women of modest means. Lee made a show of treating his beloved nanny for her birthday, which delighted the older women who ran the store. Ingrid left adorned in a black hooded slicker of her own and a few headbands, and Lee had been provided with a handful of candied plums as if he were an adorable toddler, not fifteen years of age.

"Don't enjoy your acting gig too much," Ingrid murmured.

"Who knows when I'll get to play the benevolent master again?" He paused to bow to an elderly Japanese man in natty attire. "Ohayou gozaimasu."

She felt a pang in her heart to see Lee walk down the street with such freedom and confidence. It didn't seem right or fair that it was only possible as part of a masquerade.

She glanced around. No one walked close to them. She could chance asking Lee the questions that had been on her mind ever since she discovered his real identity. "Lee, I've been wondering about Uncle Moon. He's not related to you by blood, is he?"

"No. It's like how you call Mr. Sakaguchi your ojisan. 'Uncle' is an honorific."

"Why is he called Moon? It seems odd for someone so . . . traditional to use an English name." Speaking in Chinese was illegal, but names were commonly regarded as exceptions to the rule.

Lee casually looked around before answering, his voice low. "He came to America a long time ago and became fully westernized as he taught *lingqi*. I once saw a picture of him from back then. He had a normal head of hair and wore a seersucker suit." He shook his head, still in disbelief. "He changed his name to something that was easier for white people to say. *Lingqi* is believed to be part of yin nature, which is connected to the moon. Hence that name."

Ingrid nodded for him to continue.

"When the war started . . ." Lee sighed. "He kept the English name the way someone keeps a scar uncovered for all the world to see, Ing. He's said he'll only answer to his old name when China belongs to the Chinese again."

She wasn't sure what to say to that. Rain thrummed on the sidewalk canopies. Above the increased noise and bustle of street traffic, she heard a beautiful bell-like sound that made her think of the wind chimes that Mama made from scrap and hung in their yard years ago. Ingrid smiled and looked around to find the source of the noise. As she did, she was startled by a flash of gold a block away and across the street. Along with it, she felt a tingle of magic—strange magic. In Mr. Sakaguchi's backyard, pixies in close proximity had caused a vaguely similar sensation, but this one carried with it a profound sense of coziness, the relief that came with being in sight of home after a long day of work at the auxiliary.

Ingrid shook herself from the reverie and grabbed Lee's arm. "Did you see that?"

"See what? Ing?"

She dodged pedestrians and paused at the corner. The

policeman-operated traffic light almost instantly let them cross.

"What did you see?" Lee kept pace alongside her.

"I don't know." She stopped where she had seen the flash. Through the window, a Japanese shopkeeper bowed and spoke with customers. Ingrid whirled around to get her bearings.

The tintinnabulation rang in her ears again, haunting and sweet at the same time. This time, the ensuing rush of magic smelled ever so faintly like the French cologne that Mr. Sakaguchi wore for special occasions. Grief froze her for a moment, and then she took off in pursuit of the sound. She heard Lee's surprised cry behind her, but she didn't slow. As she rounded the corner, she saw the glimmer again some distance up the street.

Then the presence of magic was gone, again. Panting for breath, she leaned on a wooden post. A white couple cast her an odd look as they pushed by her and into a shop.

"Do you mind telling me what's going on?" Lee caught up to her, a scowl on his face. "I thought we weren't going to come to the burned part of town."

Ingrid turned on her heel. Sure enough, the full square block beyond them had been reduced to bricks and rubble, while other nearby buildings looked well scorched. Lee moved closer. The rain had quenched the smoke. Chinese men and women wandered through the destruction with long boards or rakes in hand. Curious folks, mostly whites, hovered at the edges of the street. A few policemen in distinct caps stood back as overseers. No Unified Pacific soldiers were present.

"We shouldn't be here," Ingrid murmured.

"I know that! *You* led us straight here. What were you chasing?"

She opened and closed her mouth without any sound escaping. A flash of light? The sound of bells? "I don't know," she said finally. "We need to be especially cautious."

"Since we're here, I'm going to make a friend," Lee whispered, and ambled directly toward a policeman. Ingrid started to yank him back by the arm but stopped herself. Frowning beneath her hood, she followed him. What part of *be especially cautious* had he not understood?

"Ohayou gozaimasu." Lee deeply bowed to the white policeman.

"Ohayou," the red-haired policeman replied with a short bow. He was older, his Japanese clumsy.

"I just landed in Portland. I heard part of Chinatown burned but I wanted to see it for myself. What happened? Did anyone die?"

Water dripped in a steady stream from the officer's brim. "Not that we've found so far, lad. Lot of injuries, though."

"Burns?" Lee's eyes were wide with innocent wonder.

"No. Injuries didn't come from the fire. A mob awaited the Chinese as they escaped the building. A few were shot, most of 'em were well beaten. Folks here made it quite clear how welcome the Chinese are in the city of Portland."

Ingrid pressed her arms against her torso as she tried to contain her horror. Lee's acting was worthy of the stage as he continued to feign eagerness for news. Or maybe the officer's revelation simply didn't surprise him.

Lee motioned toward the haggard figures in the rubble. They wore no raincoats. Their sodden and stained cotton work clothes drowned their slim bodies.

"I thought all the chankoro were locked up?" Lee asked. Ingrid had to stop herself from flinching at the foul epithet he so casually used.

"Most are. Folks in town were worried that traps might be set up in the buildings, though. It's the sort of thing they do in China. These volunteers are walking through in a grid pattern to make sure it's safe. If they find some gaps to the basement, better for them to fall through than any of our people. We'll clean up the block soon as we know it's safe, build something proper there."

Lee's smile slipped ever so slightly, but he caught himself. "Interesting."

A clutch of white women attired in black approached the officer. Two figures at the back held aloft tall umbrellas.

"Excuse me, sir," said an elderly woman, "I'm Miriam Bonhoff—"

"Oh. Yes. You're the Quakers." The policeman sounded bored. "I was told you might show up."

"It's lunchtime. We brought some food and blankets—"

"Certainly, certainly." He motioned to another officer. "Call the Chinese out."

A whistle split the air.

The drenched Chinese—mostly women and old men—dropped rags to mark their spots and hobbled toward the street at a glacial pace. Their faces, pale and bared to the chilly spring rain, bore dark bruises and fresh red cuts. The Quaker women waved them over. A few white men hauled steaming kettles closer.

Ingrid had known that groups like the Quakers had helped black slaves escape to freedom decades before on the Underground Railroad. But she hadn't seen with her own eyes the good work that they were doing now. She wanted to hug these kind people, thank them, but knew that if she did, there was too much danger involved, for her and for them.

"Damned Lincoln lovers!" someone shouted. Lincoln had devoted his late-life work to securing rights and safe havens for Chinese refugees.

"What's with them pigtails getting free food?" called one of the white men playing audience. "Half the canneries are shut! Help the people who deserve it!" Other men grunted agreement.

"Oh, shut it," snapped the red-haired officer. "Half your money goes to Billy's Bar." At that, others burst out in laughter.

"This is my chance," Lee murmured, his gaze on the Chinese people in line for soup, his voice so tight Ingrid barely understood him.

"They might give you away," she whispered. She suddenly wished she did hold a smidgen of earth energy in order to act in their defense. She also worried at her endurance if she and Lee needed to run.

"I have to try." He walked toward an older Chinese

woman standing off by herself. Two of the Quakers approached him as if to defend the woman, but she waved them back to confront Lee on her own.

Ingrid's head snapped up as she heard the chime again, so soft that it was almost lost amid the clamor of the crowd. She glanced around, trying to spot where it was coming from. She was ready this time when the golden flare appeared on the far side of the rubble. The presence of magic was faint, like the scent of cooked rice from a kitchen window. Her mouth watered in response, leaving her genuinely discomfited by her own reaction.

She wanted out of here; if she had her druthers, she'd haul Lee back to the *Bug* straightaway. But he was close to getting the answers they so desperately needed. And now—she also wanted to know what the hell was going on with this magical presence.

Slowly, she walked around the periphery of the burned building while keeping an eye on Lee. The rain lightened but continued to fall. Beyond the ruins, mud and random debris created a swamp where once there had been a garden with thick heads of cabbage and tangled beds of strawberries. A gnarled pine tree curled to one side like an overgrown bonsai. She gingerly stepped over a plank fence that had been knocked flat and partially burned. The garden smelled of greenery and fresh mud. Her heart racing, she looked around, though she half expected the sound of chimes to lure her onward again.

Heat prickled against her skin.

She stood straighter. This wasn't the heat of earth magic.

And it wasn't what she had felt from the flash that had guided her here. All the hair on the back of her neck stood up as she moved toward the gnarled pine, feeling the intensity of the magic grow stronger with every step.

The earth at the tree's roots was particularly muddy, as if it had been freshly turned. She moved without thinking, reaching for a charred piece of plank.

Mud slurped and slid away as she dug; she tried to appear nonchalant, a bored nanny killing time as she waited for her charge—but she knew she didn't have much time before someone became suspicious.

About a foot down, the wood struck something solid. She worked the plank to one side and pried at the object. With an obscene sucking sound, the mystery item came loose and poked to the top of the muddy puddle. Quick as a wyvern, she grabbed it. The thing was almost the length and breadth of her forearm and in a leather bag. Whatever it was, it absolutely radiated power. She instantly was reminded of how it had felt to stand before the two-headed snake in Olema, the Hidden One.

She stroked the leather casing, her fingers leaving streaks in the gritty mud. She felt an intense longing to know what was inside.

Ingrid glanced up and gasped. Lee was approaching. The police officer walked beside him, his glower as dark as the clouds.

CHAPTER 3

Ingrid angled her body away from the approaching policeman and tucked the leather-wrapped object beneath her coat. She fumbled to find the drawstring at the end and yanked it through her obi. A second later and she had it knotted in place. The rain fell heavier, but not heavy enough to immediately wash mud off the sleeve of her new slicker. She grabbed her digging plank and with a quick swipe knocked a cabbage free just in time.

"Look, Master Sato! We haven't had any fresh vegetables aboard the airship. Don't these cabbages look wonderful? Officer, is it all right if I take one?" She punctuated that with a bright smile.

"Leave it, girl," he snapped, whisking her away with a gesture.

"I'm sorry, Officer," said Lee. "She's always after me to

eat more vegetables, but I didn't think she would start raiding gardens to acquire produce."

Lee's light tone evoked a slight chuckle from the policeman. "You'd be better off at the market. I wouldn't trust anything here. Could be poisoned." At that, Ingrid dropped the cabbage for dramatic effect, though she'd have much rather chucked it at the man's head. "Now move along. This stew may very well start to boil." He jerked his head toward the crowd, expression grim, then moved back that way.

The unearthed object was as warm as a cat against Ingrid's thigh, its presence almost stroking at her senses. What was it? It was not magic, not as she had encountered it. No, this thing felt . . . *holy* was the only way she could think to describe it.

As she followed Lee back to the sidewalk, she wondered if she should put the object back. The Chinese had almost certainly been the ones who buried it, but would they be back here again? Would they be able to take any belongings with them? The officer said the lot would be rebuilt as soon as possible.

Guilt gnawed at her. Ingrid wasn't sure if she was saving something for the sake of the Chinese or thieving from them as so many others did.

"Those people on the street saw you near the vegetables and started complaining," Lee muttered. "I managed to get the officer to come over instead of the mob. What the hell were you doing?"

Ingrid was suddenly grateful for the presence of the surly officer. She glanced back. The Quakers had formed a protective barrier as the Chinese continued to rest and eat. The crowd of onlookers had grown and formed a thick wall of black hats.

The standoff would not end well.

"I found something buried in the garden. Something powerful. That's all I really know. If we can find a park or someplace private, we can unwrap it and see. I don't want to take it all the way to the airship in case you think we should put it back."

Raindrops trickled down Lee's cheeks as he nodded. "I think I saw a park a few blocks this way." He motioned up another street and they started in that direction. "I found out a few things from that woman. Uncle Moon *was* here. Briefly. His group made it out before all this." He jerked his head toward the burned city street.

"How was Mr. Sakaguchi? Was he conscious?"

"I don't know, Ing. Not like I had the chance to ask that much. Uncle Moon has a reputation for his *lingqi,* and he's very recognizable. The woman I spoke with wishes that he was still somewhere close by so that he might be able to visit the prison and heal some of the more gravely injured people."

"Would that even be allow—"

"Of course not." Lee kicked a stone with enough force to send it bouncing across the road. "She's cold and she's soaked and she probably has broken ribs, judging by how she held her side. Others are hurt worse. She has to . . . she has to hope someone will help them, someone other than Quakers who will probably be burned out of the city by the end of the week." He rubbed at his face. The water on his skin wasn't raindrops. "And it's not just here. This is happening everywhere. We just . . . we want a home, you know? Someplace safe. A roof overhead. Food. Family and friends nearby. Is that really too much to ask for?" He looked at his hands as he formed fists. "I feel so useless."

Emotion choked Ingrid's throat and she couldn't speak for a moment. "You'll be able to help them somehow," she said softly.

"Help them. God." He shook his head. "Do you realize what you're saying? It means bringing the full war here to America. My home, the only home I've known. It means the Chinese strike back and everyone suffers for it. Women, children. Those brutes back there who ached to scalp some pigtails. Those Quakers." Lee looked at Ingrid, and she knew he was thinking of her, that she could be hurt or killed, and they were all too aware of what the ripple effects of that might be.

Past the curved rooftops, she could see the tall trees of the park. Pavement ended. They padded through mud that was packed mostly solid. "There's something I need to talk to you about, too. Something important."

"Isn't everything important now?" He sounded too damned old and jaded. Anger and sadness caused her to blink back tears. Lee didn't even need to shave yet. He was a *child*. He shouldn't be carrying this burden.

"This is especially important. To both of us." She shivered, even as the strange object continued to warm the inside of her coat. "Have you ever heard of the Gaia Project?"

"No, I don't think so." They stopped under the dry overhang of a building at the edge of the park. The windows were dark, the structure empty.

Ingrid took a deep breath and she told him about the other bundle of letters that Mr. Sakaguchi had hidden for her—not the ones from Papa. The ones about the Unified Pacific's covert plan to crush China. She explained that Cy was really an Augustus, a scion of the infamous Augustinian Company that developed the best new weapons of war. Cy had known how to disable a Durendal tank because he had designed it, and deserted the Army & Airship Corps when he saw firsthand what devastation it caused. Lee's face turned as impassive as stone.

She confessed that when she and Cy attended the opera the night before the earthquake, it was so they could covertly speak with Cy's father. The two hadn't been together in over a decade. George Augustus had known very little about the Gaia Project, only that it was a weapon that required power from an unrealistically large piece of kermanite.

"Like the kermanite that was stolen by the Thuggees?"

"Yes. That was why they tortured Papa to provoke the terrible earthquake, and also used him to channel the energy from the seism into the stolen kermanite."

"Ingrid, why are you telling me all of this *now*?"

She took a deep breath. "The UP got ahold of Papa in the Hawaiian Vassal States back in January. They took him to China soon after. They . . . used . . . him to start the Gaia Project."

Lee stared at her. "January? You're trying to say that Peking . . . that was him? That was the Unified Pacific? Both those earthquakes?"

She nodded, unable to speak.

Lee leaned on the wall as if suddenly dizzy. "Hundreds of thousands were killed in each quake. If you add in those who died of exposure and starvation afterward . . ."

"Papa caused that. Unwillingly. But he still caused it." Ingrid took a breath. "Lee. If Ambassador Blum catches me, she will use me the same way. I hate telling you this, but you must know. If she finds us, then you need to . . ." She tapped the center of her forehead.

Lee's head jerked up. "What?"

"You know what I mean. You're the only one who can do it. Cy wouldn't be able to. He . . . I . . ." She couldn't say aloud her fantasy of a future with Cy. "Fenris . . . well, Fenris would want to dismantle the whole plan the way he tears apart a machine, try to find some other way—"

"That's not a bad thing!"

"If Blum has me, there's no time to dawdle, no time to analyze. That means it's on you, Lee." She hated the words. She hated throwing an even greater burden on him. "You used Mama's revolver to hold off the gunman after Mr. Sakaguchi was shot. You're carrying that other gun now, I bet. Promise me you can do this."

"Damn it. Don't ask this of me." Grief twisted his face.

"It's only as a last resort."

"And when you died, what would that do to the nearest Hidden One?"

"Papa's pain caused the two-headed snake to experience pain. When the snake ate him, that agony . . . stopped."

"I better have good aim, is that what you're saying?"

"I hope it doesn't come down to this, Lee. I don't want to die."

"Good. I don't want you to die either."

They both exhaled shakily. Ingrid lifted his cap to ruffle his damp hair. He was almost as tall as she. "Do you think this is a good spot to open up that parcel I dug up?" she asked, wanting to change the subject. "Looks like no one's in the park today."

"That's probably because this isn't really a park." Lee motioned around the corner. She looked.

"Well, no one's being buried today." The building they used for shelter must have been the cemetery office or a storage building. Ingrid opened her coat and worked the strap loose from her belt. Mud streaked her skirt down to the ankle; good thing the fabric was dark.

The leather looked like it hadn't been in the ground long. She leaned on the wall for balance as she pulled the drawstring loose and tipped the bag forward. Dirty water gushed out. The object was still stuck inside, yet heat flashed out as if she had opened a furnace. Lee gasped.

"Do you feel that?" he whispered. "The heat and . . . it's like an odd tingle in the air. Do you . . . ?"

Ingrid was astounded. As far as she knew, Lee didn't have any affinity for magic. But if this meant that every person walking by sensed strange heat from the leather bag, they might have a problem.

"I feel it. That's how I knew it was in the ground. It's like being near a fantastic, but not."

Lee laughed. "You can feel fantastics nearby? So *that's* why you always could point out when a unicorn or pooka was being ridden close to us in San Francisco! You told me you had magical horse sense. I almost believed you." He shook his head as he reached for the object.

She pulled it away from him. "Be careful! This thing is searing hot, even through the bag. We don't know what will happen when we pull it out." She couldn't help but think of the policeman's concern about Chinese traps—though Lee knew about Chinese armaments and tactics and he didn't appear concerned. Even so . . .

She tipped the bag again, and this time let the item fall onto the ground. Cloths swaddled the thing; she found an end and pulled upward, letting the rags unwind. A large metal item about the length of a rolling pin plunked onto the mud.

The object resembled the head of a large halberd or spear, similar to the medieval weapons she had seen in Mr. Sakaguchi's books with illustrations by Howard Pyle, but broad and with an odd curve. The base of it had another curve, too, creating a weapon with two crescent points.

A strange animal wail escaped Lee's throat and he fell to his knees, heedless of the mud, his body bowed forward, face to the ground.

Ingrid reached for him, panicked. "Lee? What is it? What's wrong?"

His shoulders shook. He reared back on his knees,

and to her surprise, his grin was exuberant even as tears streamed down his cheeks.

"It's Guan Yu's *guandao*. The real thing. The actual real thing." He squeezed his eyes shut and said something in Chinese, then looked at Ingrid again with pure joy. "You found one of the greatest treasures of China, Ing. This . . . this means everything. With this, we have proof that the Chinese people can survive. Our Mandate of Heaven hasn't been lost."

"Guan Yu?" Ingrid echoed, kneeling next to him. Her memory flicked back to the labyrinthine house Lee had taken her to in San Francisco's Chinatown, and the portraits and statues of a swarthy figure with a halberd in hand. She knew from Mr. Sakaguchi's teachings that Guan Yu was one of the ancient guardians of China, worshiped by a large swath of the Chinese populace of both Taoist and Buddhist faiths. At least, that used to be the case. As with many signature elements of Chinese culture, imagery of Guan Yu and shrines to him were now forbidden.

"This weapon is light as solid orichalcum, but the coloration looks like a mix of metals." Ingrid frowned. The edge was surely sharp enough to slice the protective cloth that had swaddled it, but it hadn't. "I'm trying to remember the old stories. Wasn't Guan Yu's weapon supposed to be heavy?"

"Yes." Lee looked puzzled as well. "You can tell by the curves on the head that it's not a throwing spear. It *should* be very heavy, even if it's not mounted on a shaft. I don't know. There are many stories of Guan Yu. They date back almost two thousand years, and they all say different things. One thing's for sure: this is no ordinary weapon." With reverence, he scooped the blade up, his hands shaking slightly as he dabbed it clean with his coat. "The Green Dragon Crescent Blade can't be in the mud. We need to get this on the airship." He began to gently rewind the cloth. "We can't leave it here. You heard what the cop said. They'll probably start rebuilding that burned lot within the week."

"Whoever hid the *guandao* would want it with you, anyway," Ingrid said. As she watched Lee wrap the blade, she wondered how many artifacts of China were scattered across the world, how many were buried—as with the *guandao*—or dragged around by refugees. Many had likely been looted. The thought depressed her.

"Maybe. Maybe not. I know who I am, what I'm supposed to be, but there's a reason few people know of my ancestry. Some people might die for me. Many more would want me dead."

Ingrid shook her head in disbelief. "The Chinese people are being butchered by the Unified Pacific. Why fight among yourselves, too?"

His motions slowed. "It's never that simple, Ing. You know that. China is huge. Tribes and families have been fighting and killing each other for centuries. God, the nineteenth century alone was a bloodbath. It's impossible to know how many men were killed because they didn't have a proper haircut. A haircut!" He referred to the Manchu queue hairstyle, a shaved forehead and long braid in the back; it had been a mandatory sign of loyalty to the Qing

Empire. Now the meaning had been reversed; the style was worn by Chinese rebels who fought against the UP.

Lee continued, "During his Restoration, Emperor Qixiang tried to unify the Manchu and the Han peoples, declaring them to be equal, but a piece of paper can't erase centuries of subjugation and hatred. It was all too little too late. By then, Japan had Manchukuo and prepared for their full invasion."

Qixiang, the father Lee had never known. The emperor who could have willingly ceded China to Japan and lived out the rest of his life in the Summer Palace. Instead, he had joined the last wave of refugees allowed inside America. He died of smallpox in San Francisco over a decade before. Lee had been born to a loyal concubine about the same time.

"Now the *tongs* are the only leadership we have. We're so scattered, Ing. Even more so with San Francisco gone. We're all just trying to survive, and it's still easier to think in terms of families, instead of trying to see the Chinese as one people." He finished wrapping the ancient weapon and slid it back inside the bag. "But this . . . this is hope. Like encountering the *qilin*."

Ingrid more often heard of *qilin* by their Japanese name of kirin; the Chinese term was not acceptable to use in public. Mr. Sakaguchi had even had a decorative statue of a kirin in their backyard, where it was intended to bring luck to their household.

"What was that like? Does a *qilin* really float?"

The legends said that the creatures' pacifism was such that they floated when they walked over grass so that they wouldn't hurt a single blade. They also only visited those destined to be esteemed rulers or sages; it was said one had visited Confucius's mother before his birth. Some of Mr. Sakaguchi's old books in Japanese ranked kirin as the most powerful of all fantastics and Hidden Ones. It wasn't merely what they could do—it was what their presence *meant*. But they were also largely considered extinct—if they had ever been more than myth at all. Which is why Lee's seeing one was nothing short of remarkable.

"Yes. It hovers just over the ground. Everything about it is celestial." He shook his head in clear awe. "You don't know how much I've wanted to tell you about this, Ing. I've actually seen a *qilin* twice. The first time I was five. Uncle Moon found me in the orphanage, the *qilin* beside me in a cot. He regarded its appearance as confirmation of my identity."

"I understand why you had to keep it a secret," Ingrid said, her voice softened by awe. She knew Lee had been raised by nuns for the first years of his life and felt detached from his Chinese identity for years after that; sometimes, that feeling still plagued him. He beckoned her forward.

Ingrid used the wall to help herself stand, and trailed him into the rain. "And the second time?"

He was quiet a moment. "The day your mother died."

"What?" That was the last thing Ingrid expected him to say.

"I was in the backyard. It was during that awful gap between Mrs. Carmichael's death and Mr. Sakaguchi's arrival home. You weren't fully there. You wouldn't leave her bedroom even though the city had already taken her body. I couldn't get you to talk. Laugh. Eat. Anything. I didn't know what to do. I started questioning everything. Me, as some bridge between China, America, and Japan? As an emperor? How could I help my people when I couldn't help you, someone so dear to me? The *qilin* came and kept me company."

"Does it talk?"

"Yes and no. It . . . chimes. It's impossible to describe."

"You're talking to the woman who communicated in images with a gigantic snake." Ingrid laughed. Then she realized what Lee had said. "It *chimes*?"

"Yes, a little like the sound of bells. I also smelled things, wonderful things, when it was with me, like your mother's cardamom bread right out of the oven. I couldn't help but think of happy memories when it was there." He looked away, his expression wistful.

Ingrid blinked, momentarily stupefied. Apparently, she had been herded through Portland by a *qilin*.

She could understand why it might want them to retrieve the Green Dragon Crescent Blade, but if it had come to Lee before, why had the *qilin* only made its presence known to her this time?

She wanted to tell Lee what happened, but at the same time, it felt wrong for her to have encountered a *qilin* at all. She wasn't sure what to do.

Lee reached out to steady Ingrid as she almost slipped. The *guandao*'s bag bobbed against her. "You're wearing out, Ing. This was too much walking."

As if it were that simple. When she had switched stockings that morning and felt along her legs, she couldn't ignore the abrupt changes that had occurred in her own body over the past few days. Her muscles felt . . . depleted. Slack. As if the near-fatal magic she had held and used in San Francisco had consumed actual body tissue.

That made it all the more important for her to get out and move, to bolster her physical strength. She needed her full vitality to survive the next quake.

"I'm fine," she insisted, but her voice was strained.

"Damn it. Mr. Sakaguchi was right, you know. You're arrogant sometimes." Lee spoke in a fond though exasperated tone that reminded her of Mr. Sakaguchi. "Don't be stupid, too. We passed a Reiki place not far from the clothes shops. We can stop in there."

Anger flushed her cheeks. "No. The bus stop isn't far from there either—"

"Good. You can rest before we continue our walk."

"They might not even serve me, Lee."

"You forget that it's your birthday and that I'm treating my loyal nanny. They had better serve you." He glanced back, his gaze softening. "Seriously, Ing. I might not get another chance for something like this," he whispered. "The one measly advantage with most of the Chinese locked up is that no one can give me away. No rival *tongs* can call me out." He motioned with his chin to the arm where his brassard should be. "Let me do this for you."

Frustrated as she was, she nodded.

The Reiki business was well lit with decorative, kanji-adorned banners on the brick walls. The white receptionist did a double take at the sight of Ingrid but was all smiles as

Lee explained his desire to treat his nanny. Soon enough, the doctor emerged and engaged in pleasant palaver with Lee before walking Ingrid back to a small private room overflowing with the earthy fragrance of fresh seeds.

Mr. Sakaguchi and Mama had always coddled Ingrid and taken her to a Reiki doc if she had the slightest injury; they had simply told her that she couldn't handle pain. She hadn't learned until this past week that they were sheltering her from a dangerous truth: that her pain caused earthquakes.

The Reiki doctor looked to be in her forties, her brown hair streaked with gray. "Since your complaint is fatigue, not a physical injury, you won't need to take off your dress. Sit in the chair and we'll get started."

Ingrid hooked her coat on a rack and exchanged her shoes for slippers. An assistant entered and they set up the appropriate plant seeds for the job. This doctor was a licensed practitioner of Reiki and used only plants. Less reputable businesses drew from living animals, even people, but for much more potent results. That's how Uncle Moon had saved Mr. Sakaguchi's life with his Chinese take on Reiki, *lingqi*.

Ambassador Blum had snapped the necks of baby rabbits and used their ki to mend Ingrid. As loathsome as that healing had been, the power of Blum's work had also saved Ingrid's life through the worst of the earthquake as she struggled with the overwhelming influx of energy.

The doctor twirled her hand over a mound of seeds as if swirling invisible cream. An assistant stood close by. Just as Ingrid could see the blue energy of the earth, ki doctors could see and manipulate the colors of life.

"Are you recovering from influenza?" asked the doc. "We had a terrible season here."

"Something like that." The lingering symptoms were similar, in any case.

"Now relax. Breathe deeply. Let your ki be at peace. Open your body to be healed."

Ingrid allowed her shoulders to relax into the high back of the chair and breathed in to fill her lungs. The doctor hummed, then made a small choking sound.

"Your colors. That's . . . interesting. No, continue to relax." The doctor continued to coax energy from the seeds and draw it to Ingrid. The seeds' ki caressed her skin like a breath.

"What do you see?"

"When you were sick, did you almost die? Were you healed by . . . a different sort of doctor?" By the way the doctor hedged her words, she wasn't referring to standard Pasteurian physicians either.

Could the doctor actually see evidence of Blum's dark Reiki? Ingrid resolved to play dumb. "I was very sick. I'm not sure who my employer called to tend to me."

"I see. Your ki is very unbalanced. Miss Harold, can you fetch another bin of the class-three seeds?" The assistant left, the door closing behind her, and the doctor faced Ingrid, her arms crossed over her chest. "I've worked Reiki for fifteen years. I've seen a lot. Your ki isn't just out of balance, it's *stained.* I've heard that dark Reiki can do that, but this . . . this . . ." She shook her head. A loose strand from her bun whipped her cheeks. "Was it voodoo? Something pagan? Whatever it is you people do."

You people. People with Ingrid's skin tone. Ingrid clutched the chair arms, heat rising to her cheeks. If she had held any power, the chair would have broken beneath her grip.

"That kind of energy regenerates you for a longer time than licensed Reiki, that's true," the doctor continued, "but it's like . . . ghosts become part of you for a while. I have trouble believing that a good Japanese family would meddle with this sort of thing." She gestured toward the front office, where Lee was waiting. "I'm telling you this as a favor. If you want to keep your job, you should tend to both your body and your soul."

"That's very generous of you." Years of secretarial work in the auxiliary had taught Ingrid how to grin through seething rage. She stood. With a few abrupt kicks, she shed her slippers and shoved on her boots. Her legs felt a little stronger, but maybe that was from sitting down rather than the brief whiff of floral Reiki. "I'll take my stained ki elsewhere then, thank you." The door opened, and the assistant stepped back as Ingrid walked forward.

"Young woman, I'm not done—"

"Yes, you are." It would've been nice if her body had the help of Reiki to heal faster, but it wasn't worth listening to this tripe. Ingrid shrugged on her coat and walked herself out.

Lee jumped to his feet as she emerged. He took in her mood in an instant. He gave the receptionist a cheery farewell and waited to speak again until they were outside and walking toward the bus stop.

"What happened in there?" he asked in a low voice.

"Patronizing unpleasantness." She hunched her shoulders, making it quite clear she was unwilling to say more.

The doctor's attitude aggravated her, but the assumption that she *wanted* Blum's healing bothered her even more. Ingrid had been handcuffed and stabbed! She didn't want those rabbits to die, for Blum's dark, horrible power to flood her body. And now to hear that the macabre healing continued to stain her even days later . . .

Ingrid felt sick. She felt *violated.* How long would this taint linger in her life energy?

It was still helping her to recover from her power sickness, too, and likely was the only reason she wasn't bedbound on the ship. It appalled her that she should be grateful to Blum in some way.

"We should grab fresh food to take back to the airship, Master Sato," she said, her voice tight. As much as she wanted to explore Front Street, now was not the time.

"Yes. It'll be good to get this on board, too." The leather bag swayed in his grip.

No passersby seemed attracted to the *guandao.* No one else seemed to sense it as Ingrid and Lee could.

"Let's keep that item a secret for now," she said. "Just in case." Not that she didn't trust Cy or Fenris, but an artifact of such importance was priceless to both the Chinese and the Unified Pacific. The fewer who knew of it, the better.

"That's a good idea," said Lee.

Behind them, loud yells rang out, dozens of people in a terrible chorus. Ingrid glanced back. She couldn't see anything amiss in the past few blocks, but she recognized the source of the noise. It came from the vicinity of the burned building.

"Should we—" Ingrid started to say.

"It's a riot." Lee spoke in a raw whisper. "We can't stop it. We can't save anyone. If we turn around, we only endanger ourselves." He clutched the *guandao* closer to his body. His posture stayed upright as he walked faster, his Japanese-boy act still in place except for the glimmer of tears in his eyes.

CHAPTER 4

SATURDAY, APRIL 21, 1906

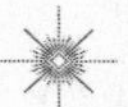

"How are repairs proceeding?" Ingrid murmured. She had awakened to find Fenris fussing about the engine room; he dinged on metal like a drunken musician. She stood in the hallway in her stocking feet. Not far behind her, she could hear Cy's soft breaths as he continued to sleep. He and Lee might very well sleep through Kingdom Come.

Weak morning light leaked through the cockpit glass down the way. Cy had insisted they all stay aboard the airship at night for safety's sake, as there weren't any decent inns within convenient walking distance of Swan Island.

"Repairs are gliding along like a snail in a footrace." Fenris propped his goggles onto his forehead. "The majority of the work is done. The *Bug* can fly now, if she must, but I won't *like* how she flies."

"How long would it take to reach that esteemed approval level?"

"Another solid two or three days, maybe. Depends on how much Cy can pitch in. You're stealing him away for part of today and that will slow things down." Fenris pressed down with all the weight in his slender frame to make a valve turn.

"She's hardly stealing me away." Cy swung his legs into the hallway, his tall form hunched over so that his head didn't strike the top bunk. "I need to head to downtown, anyway. We need laundry done and more food." Ingrid couldn't help but notice that he was wearing nothing but cotton drawers and a loose shirt. One pant leg had rolled up to expose his hairy calf. She felt herself flushing with the sudden, intense wish that more of his skin was visible.

"Normal-people needs. Bah." Fenris dismissed the notion with a wave.

"I can help with repairs." Lee's hoarse voice came from the bunk above the mattressless rack. Metal rings rattled as he pushed open the privacy curtain. Ingrid knew why he wanted to stay on the ship. He had quietly told her that he didn't want to be apart from the *guandao,* and he certainly didn't want to carry it away from the dock unnecessarily.

Ingrid had a hunch that he didn't want to continue with the subterfuge of being Japanese either. Or find out what happened to the Chinese people and Quakers caught in the riot.

"Ah yes. *Help.* Which means training and explaining as I go. That will slow me down, too." Still, Fenris didn't seem too displeased to have a new volunteer.

"If all goes well, we won't be gone long," Cy said, stretching out his legs. A knee popped.

"Oh yes, because things always go well for us. Like a kraken taking up mountain climbing."

Ingrid and Cy shuffled around in the confined space to attend to their morning toilet rituals. She brushed against him on occasion. He acted perfectly polite, hands to himself, but when he was close, all she could think about was that magnificent, all-too-brief kiss the day before. She could have growled in frustration.

Only when Ingrid and Cy were ready did Lee emerge from his bunk, his black hair spiked on one side and flattened on the other.

"Here." Lee shoved his gun toward Ingrid. "I'll feel better if you have this." She opened her mouth to argue with him and remind him of his promise the day before. He shook his head. "Yeah. I remember what you said, but you're going to be out there surrounded by people. You need this."

"I have my Tesla rod as well, miss." The telescoping metal rod dangled at Cy's hip, ready to extend and deliver an electric shock on contact.

Lee gave Cy a tight nod. The two of them had engaged in a private talk the prior evening. It seemed that Lee had come to a grudging understanding about Cy's background as an Augustus and a weapons engineer.

A few minutes later, Ingrid and Cy set off. About half the mooring masts were filled today; other airships were blips against a gray smear of sky that poured rain. They sloshed through a veritable minefield of puddles.

"I wish I could carry that," Cy muttered.

Ingrid had a waxed canvas bag full of laundry hefted over her shoulder. "We can't attract that sort of attention. I'm obviously a servant. I need to do my job." The societal expectation bothered her; the actual work did not, especially since she felt a bit stronger today. Maybe the Reiki and exercise had helped her to recover some muscle. "Don't glower so much, Cy. It doesn't suit you."

At that, a warm smile creased his cheeks. "Much as I like the company aboard, the confines are awfully cramped after a time. It's a pleasure to be in the open air with just you."

Her smile strained her cheeks as she resisted the urge to giggle. "I've been wanting to ask. Where did you get that milk yesterday?" Cy'd been true to his word. Ingrid had returned with Lee to find a saucer of milk at the top of the mooring mast.

"I do believe the original source was a cow, though I didn't taste to be sure." He grinned.

"I didn't either. I carried it down the mast to share with other felines at the port."

"Quite generous of you, Miss Ingrid." His teasing tone was going to undo her one of these days.

As they rode the bus, Ingrid had to remind herself that she was in public and was expected to act a certain way. It was so easy to converse with Cy—easy to laugh, to flirt, to behave as though the tight corsets of propriety didn't exist. But they did. Cy didn't exactly act appropriately for a man in town with his female servant either. A grin kept teasing the corners of his mouth as he gave her little side glances.

They disembarked in downtown and found the nearest laundry. Roaring fans of the kermanite-run dryers made the place as loud as an airship dock. The flustered proprietress said they were shorthanded with their Chinese staff gone and it'd take a full day to get their clothes done. Cy produced more money from his pocket, and suddenly their clothes would be clean and dry in three hours.

As they left, he lingered at the edge of the porch and assessed the street, then Ingrid.

"How does the earth feel to you here?" he quietly asked.

"Calm. I can tell there are geomancers nearby to hold the energy in check. There's no blue on the ground. It's how San Francisco used to be, back before."

"Good. Tell me, Miss Ingrid. What geomantic Hidden Ones are said to be around Cascadia? I only know the aerial fantastics. Seen wyverns and thunderbirds from a distance a time or two."

She stayed quiet a moment as people passed by speaking in fast Japanese. "Native tribes tell tales of two-headed snakes in fault lines as far north as Vancouver Island. Then there are the volcanoes. Mount St. Helens and Mount Hood were boldly visible from the air yesterday, and Mount Tabor is a cinder cone right here in the city."

Cy looked troubled. "What manner of creature can live in a volcano?" He hopped down to the street. Ingrid followed.

"A god," she said. That took him aback. "That's only one

way to describe that sort of Hidden One. As Mr. Sakaguchi used to explain it, language evolves, and not always in the best way. Native-told tales describe the entities as gods, spirits, or elders, then Christian missionaries transcribed their stories and the Hidden Ones became demons. Volcanoes fit in well with the whole idea of fire and brimstone, after all. No matter what names these Hidden Ones have, though, they do tend to be fickle."

"My father wondered if the Gaia Project could trigger an eruption." Cy was quiet a moment. "He's been on my mind a lot."

"Of course he is, Cy." Ingrid longed to give his arm a sympathetic squeeze. "He knew something terrible was afoot in San Francisco. Surely he left before the earthquake."

"When I spoke with Reddy that night, I told him to get Father out of there." Reddy was George Augustus's manservant, an elderly black man who clearly doted on Cy. "Father knows I need to keep my identity hidden from the UP. He wouldn't linger in the city, knowing soldiers were nosing around close by. He wouldn't want to help them add two plus two." Cy didn't sound convinced of his own argument.

Ingrid subtly tapped his elbow with hers. "We'll keep an eye on the papers. The headlines yesterday said it was awfully chaotic down there with fires still burning and refugees scattered in camps all over. Your father's one of the most powerful men of industry in the world. He'll earn a mention." A positive one, she prayed.

Cy nodded. Rain dripped from the brim of his brown derby hat.

"Returning to the subject of volcanoes," Ingrid said, her voice soft. "I think it's a valid concern. A terrifying concern. Last week I compiled a portfolio on the current eruption of Vesuvius in preparation for the wardens' discussion on the matter. I had to analyze how many people had died, how many were estimated to die, how many were refugees, how many geomancers were needed to offset the eruption. I gathered photographs forwarded by other auxiliaries. I felt so . . . detached from everything. An eruption is beautiful when viewed in black and white."

"We'll do everything we can to keep you safe," he said softly.

"I know, but you can only do so much. An autocar could veer onto this sidewalk. A tile could blow loose from a roof." She motioned above.

"Try to keep positive for your own sake, too."

"That's another reason to find Mr. Sakaguchi. He's the sort of optimist who can stand in the middle of a tornado and be grateful for the brisk wind." She smiled at the thought of him.

"We'll find him. Have faith."

Faith. Mama hadn't raised Ingrid to be the churchgoing sort, and she hardly knew what to believe now. In her brief talk with Papa, he had referred to himself and Ingrid as being like gods of old, gods that would be abused by any people who knew of their true power.

Lee's gun weighed down her coat pocket. She'd asked

him to aim true if he had to shoot her. She wondered how steady her hand would be if she held the barrel to her own skull.

Cy's steps slowed. The Front Street Police Station was just ahead. "There's a lot of risk just walking in that door to sign up to see Roosevelt," he murmured. "Far as we know, Blum has distributed wanted posters for you across the whole west."

"An officer looked me in the face yesterday and didn't recognize me."

"Things can change in a day. I'd rather you wait out here. If I can see Roosevelt right away, I'll fetch you."

She took a steadying breath and nodded. "I'll wait right over here." She motioned to an alcove to one side of the door.

His gaze raked over her as if to memorize her features, and he hopped up the stairs and inside.

Ingrid took shelter, her hood pulled as far forward as possible without blinding her. People walked by with baskets of vegetables and baby carriages and wheeled carts of goods. She studied everyone, her hands in her pockets. The gun was cold against her right knuckle, while kermanite clinked softly against the fingers of her left hand. She heard no chimes and sensed no presence as she had the day before. It seemed like the *qilin* were satisfied that they had recovered the Crescent Blade.

A brick building across the way wore a painted advertisement for Genghis Khan Cigars. The colorful figure anachronistically wore full samurai armor. Ingrid snorted softly. Mr. Sakaguchi called that sort of thing a "realignment of history." Japan had taken many figures from mainland Asia, like Genghis Khan and even Confucius, and rewritten history to make them native Japanese who traveled abroad. After all, it simply wasn't possible for primitive peoples of Mongolian or Chinese origin to do such extraordinary things. They *had* to be Japanese.

The rain slowed and stopped. A sudden burst of sun made her squint at the glare, so she was startled as Cy rejoined her. "T.R.'s not in. So they say." He jerked his head, and he and Ingrid walked on. "I jotted a note that I have something of vital importance to the Cordilleran Auxiliary and Warden Sakaguchi. The officer said Roosevelt's in meetings all morning, so I shouldn't expect anything for hours, if I hear back at all. I left our mast number to receive a reply."

"But if he does turn us in, that leads the UP back to all of us," she whispered with a slight surge of panic.

"I know, but if I rented a mailbox, we wouldn't be able to get a reply from him tomorrow. As we discussed yesterday, every action we take carries a risk." He tapped his elbow against hers.

Cy was right, of course. It was just one of the myriad dangers they faced. And speaking of risk . . . "The letters from Papa said he stayed at a boardinghouse here in Portland for some years," Ingrid said quietly. "At one point, he mentions it's on Front Street and that he has a favorite tavern nearby called Edgar's Coin." She had spent an hour the night before skimming over Mr. Sakaguchi's deciphered text to double-check the exact reference.

Cy arched an eyebrow. "I know he wrote in code, but that seems foolishly specific."

"It was in one of his more recent letters. He'd been hiding successfully for about twenty years. Maybe he became careless, took the freedom for granted."

"I've been living the same kind of life for a dozen years now. I try not to give in to that carelessness, but yes. It is a real risk."

Ingrid recalled that Cy said he'd used a full alias for years but finally decided to go by his middle name of Cypress. She wondered now if that had been foolish of him, but she also understood his need to be true to himself. "I thought we could visit this boardinghouse. Maybe someone there knew him, or he left something behind."

"What name did he go by here?"

She bowed her shoulders. "I have no idea."

"We can still take a gander at the place. I think I recall the tavern you mention. Its sign is prominent down the way."

"Thank you, Cy. It might not come to anything, I know . . ."

"Your father wronged you greatly, but you still want and need to understand who he was. If this errand'll help, it needs doing," he said gently.

And with those words he reminded her of why she had fallen in love with him so very quickly. Ingrid was glad he walked a step ahead of her so he couldn't see the raw emotion in her face.

Edgar's Coin proved to be an easy landmark to locate. The three-story structure featured a placard out front with a coin upon a large spindle. In the wind, the coin spun to reveal carved heads on both sides. The disreputable nature of the place was obvious, too. At that hour on a Saturday, grungy men lined the wraparound porch and jabbered without a care for the sensitive ears of passersby. Tobacco smoke created ground-level fog.

Ingrid and Cy paced up and down the block to find the nearest boardinghouse. The tenement was one of many wooden structures squeezed between the street and the river. The front steps creaked underfoot in a way that screamed for Ingrid to move fast or the weathered wood might well collapse. Dense metal banging noises carried from a nearby shop while dogs barked in an incessant chorus.

Beside the front door was a small sign, easy to miss from the street, with letters in sloppy black paint: BOARDINGHOUSE SOPHIA STONE PROPIETER.

"Pro-pie-ter. Does that mean she makes pies?" Ingrid asked, giggling. Spelling errors were an endless source of delight to her.

"This isn't the most pleasant of neighborhoods, but pie could be a redeeming factor. As my father would say, the only way to make pie more holy is to serve it at Communion."

Ingrid snorted softly. Fitting wisdom from an Alabama family. "I bet you'd like Mama's recipe for dry apple pie. It converted Mr. Sakaguchi to the ways of pie. If we ever get a decent kitchen for a time, I'll make it for you."

Cy flashed her a grin as he held the door wide. "All I can say to that is 'Amen.'"

There was a staircase directly ahead; a parlor wrapped around it. Echoes caused Ingrid to glance upward as she pushed back her hood. The ceiling stretched up high, a second-story railing forming an almost complete circle above. A few male voices carried from another room. No one emerged to greet them.

"What do you reckon to do?" Cy asked, voice low. He held his hat in his hands.

"Ask if anyone remembers a man who looked a lot like me? He lived here off and on for ten years. He only left last year. Someone has to know him."

"Papa? Papa!" a girl's voice screeched from above. By the time Ingrid glanced up, all she spied was a blur of movement. Feet pounded down the stairs. The girl leaped to a stop before them. She was young with creamy brown skin, a stick figure in calico and stained white stockings. A mismatched bow in kimono fabric was almost bigger than her head.

"Oh." The girl stared at Ingrid. "You're a woman. Up there, I saw the top of your head, and your skin, and I thought . . ."

Ingrid didn't know what to think.

A nearby door squawked as it swung open. "Mirabelle, what fuss you causing?" The woman carried a damp rag and a scowl that could stop a galloping horse. She looked between Ingrid and the girl and stood even straighter. "Jesus, Mary, and Joseph. *You*. You're Ingrid Carmichael."

Ingrid glanced at Cy; his expression was grim. She knew by how he stood that he was ready to grab his Tesla rod if a threat emerged. "I am. And you are?"

"I'm Sophia Stone. That's my girl Mirabelle. My other girl Casey's cleaning rooms upstairs. Never expected to see your face waltz in my door." Her laugh reminded Ingrid of a barking harbor seal. "I'm your stepma."

CHAPTER 5

"My stepmother?" Ingrid blurted. "No. You can't be, he couldn't—"

"He could and he did." The woman barked out another laugh. "Come along. We need to sit and chat a time."

Ingrid's legs went wobbly as if her energy sickness had suddenly worsened. Cy's broad hand rested at the small of her back to help her stay upright. She took in a deep breath, willed her legs to behave, and followed the woman around the stairs.

Papa. Another wife. Two daughters. Mr. Sakaguchi had told her that Papa hadn't behaved with discretion during his marriage with Mama, but Ingrid hadn't considered *this*. The letters gave no hint. She wouldn't have expected the man to stay celibate, but a whole other family?

And a new surname of Stone. If Papa had a sense of

humor like Ingrid, maybe that was his idea of a joke—a reference to kermanite.

"You're my sister?" Mirabelle trotted alongside her, her face softened with awe. Ingrid looked at the girl and saw her younger self. That same black, bushy hair that refused to be tamed by any comb. That walnut-toned skin. Brown eyes lined with thick lashes. Broad lips.

"I suppose I am. You didn't know about me?" she asked.

Mirabelle shook her head. Her mother unlocked a door with a large skeleton key, then motioned the rest of them forward.

Cy stopped at the door, his hat to his chest. "Pardon, but I should introduce myself. I'm Cy Jennings, a friend of Miss Carmichael."

Mrs. Stone flicked her gaze over him. "I'm sure you are. Girl, bring in two chairs, then go back to work."

"But, Ma—" Mirabelle quailed at her mother's glare and retreated.

This was obviously Mrs. Stone's private room. The Western-style furnishings were modest yet well kept, the bed made. A side table hosted a chipped china vase and a drooping rose. Mirabelle carried in a chair almost as tall as herself, and Cy took hold and brought it the rest of the way inside.

Mrs. Stone faced Ingrid, her arms crossed over a generous chest. Ingrid's mama had been tall and thickly curved. Her Irish, Norwegian, and Swedish heritage had been clear in her wheat-colored hair and skin as pale as Jefferson Davis's ghost. Mrs. Stone's face was a bit different, but her body, her hair, her complexion . . . good God. Papa must have liked a certain type.

Cy set down another chair and Mirabelle left, the door closing behind her. Mrs. Stone motioned them to sit as she fumbled in a drawer. Ingrid obliged, if only to rest her legs. Cy was more hesitant, as a lady remained standing.

"You want to know how I knew you?" Mrs. Stone flung a card onto the side table by Ingrid. "Here."

Ingrid recognized it in an instant. "That was taken on my sixteenth birthday," she said as she picked it up. She'd posed in Miss Rossi's studio next door to the Cordilleran Auxiliary. The colors were rendered in sepia, but she recalled her pride in her sea-green dress in a very current kimono cut. Her hair was knotted in place by sticks, pins, and prayers that the style defy gravity long enough for Miss Rossi to get some decent shots.

"I have all sorts of his nonsense stuffed in this drawer." Mrs. Stone swirled her hand around, objects rustling and jangling. "You seen him? Did he tell you to come here? Last time he left, he said he was never coming back. That he stayed as long as he needed to stay."

Ingrid had no idea how to tell the woman that her husband was dead. Cy caught her eye, then leaned forward on his knees. "Ma'am, we hate to bear bad news, but he's passed on."

Mrs. Stone barked out a laugh. "'Course he has. Was bound to happen. I figured it'd be his liver with the way he drank. Not like he did much else around here."

"Mirabelle and your other girl, they were close to him?"

Ingrid wasn't sure how to feel. She knew Papa was an unpleasant man, but at the same time, he had stayed with *this* family. They knew him. She'd been with him for a matter of minutes and he almost murdered her. And she had directed a two-headed snake to kill him.

"Close? No one was as close to him as a bottle. Those girls adored him just the same, the way fools do. The way I did, ages ago." She snorted. "He went by Abram Stone here, so you know. That's the only way I knew him for years, but as he drank more, he talked more. He said he had another daughter down in California but that the dalliance with the mother was well over." Anger flushed Ingrid's cheeks, but if Mrs. Stone noticed, she didn't care. "You saw him, then? Or did he call?"

"I saw him briefly, at the end," Ingrid managed to say. "Did he . . . did you know he could . . ."

"The geomancy? Well, sure." Mrs. Stone shrugged. Ingrid gawked, stunned that she spoke of the subject so readily. "That's the only way he brought some money in. Sitting on his arse, siphoning energy from the earth to fill those rocks, selling 'em or trading 'em away."

Being a geomancer in Portland would have offered a covert way to make a living, to idle in the shadows of other official geomancers in the area.

She thought of Mirabelle again. Ingrid had inherited powers no other woman was known to possess. What if her half-sisters shared the same legacy?

"Mrs. Stone, how old are your girls?" Ingrid asked.

"Mirabelle's seven. Casey is nine. Our two boys, God rest

'em, would have been eight and ten this year." She crossed herself.

Brothers? Ingrid felt a mix of awe and acute grief.

"My sympathies, ma'am." Cy glanced at Ingrid, concerned. "Did they pass as babies?"

"No. My boys were both six when they went. Dead in their sleep, just like in the old prayer."

If I should die before I wake, I pray the Lord my soul to take. A cold sensation crept through Ingrid's veins. Papa had said that if he had known about her geomancy, he would have come down to California and smothered her in her cot. Six was the prime age for geomancy to manifest itself in a slim percentage of the populace. She'd been a tad younger than that when she had first taken in energy, and almost died of a fever that no Reiki or Pasteurian doctor could cure. Only kermanite could pull away her high temperature; it wasn't until she was older that she began to vent power when she was angry.

If Mirabelle and Casey were geomancers, it would be evident by now. Had Papa suspected that his geomancy might carry through his female line, and stayed here long enough to make sure the girls were normal? Something Papa had said implied that his mother might have been a geomancer, too.

"I don't know much at all about Papa or his kin," Ingrid said, speaking slowly. "Did he ever say anything about his parents? His mother?"

"He grew up in Hawaii, a wild urchin. I know that much. He never said a thing about his father. Not sure if he knew who the man was. His mother, he'd have to get truly soused to speak of her, and when he did, she was a figure of worship. The most beautiful woman he'd ever seen. A spirit or kami or some such. Her name was . . . Bucket? Pail?"

"Pele?" The word choked out of Ingrid's throat. Had Papa really said *Pele* was his mother?

"Something like that." Mrs. Stone's lips curled. "He'd say she made him who he was. One time I answered him that she must have been a lazy lout, too. He backhanded me and never mentioned her again."

Mrs. Stone touched her cheek, flinching at the memory, and her expression shifted. Hardened. "You sure look a lot like him, even more 'n my girls. You want something, don't you?"

"We just want information, that's all—" started Ingrid.

"Is it about money? Most always is, isn't it?" She assessed their clothes, contempt like sparks in her eyes. "I don't have much to my own name but my place and my girls, and Abram near took it all. He almost gambled my house away time 'n again. He drank my profits, ate my boarders' food, ran off good customers by thieving from rooms. It was a sweet mercy of heaven the day he left. The girls mourn him like a lost cat, and I keep telling them the truth of it. You want to know Abram Carmichael's legacy?" She spun on her heel and reached into the drawer again. "This!"

Mrs. Stone flung dark pebbles at Ingrid. A few rocks struck her, but most pinged against the table.

Cy jumped to his feet. "Now, ma'am—"

"Don't you 'ma'am' me, boy. This is my place. I aim to keep it best as I can for my girls."

Ingrid picked up the rocks. They were darkened kermanite, each about the size of a fingernail; as a battery, they were the right size for flashlights and other small devices.

These useless rocks had been fully drained of power and turned almost black . . . but they didn't look normal at all. Ingrid picked up each of the shards on the table and studied them in turn. Kermanite was fragile and would completely split under pressure, not crack like this. It certainly wouldn't *melt* around the fissures like in these pieces.

"What did this kermanite power?" Ingrid asked. "How—"

"Hell if I know, hell if I care. You want more of it?" Mrs. Stone flung a small drawstring bag down on the table. The contents chimed together. "Here. Take that. That's your inheritance. Useless rocks. Take the picture, too, or I'll just burn it."

Cy grabbed the photograph and the bag as Ingrid stood. "We didn't come here for anything," she said. "I just wanted to see where he lived—"

"Now you have. So get. Don't bother me and my girls none after this. We might be *kin* but we're not *family*."

Ingrid and Cy didn't need further encouragement to leave. Cy shut the front door behind them. Tepid sunlight glinted through the clouds.

"Well," he said. "That had more twists than an opera."

"You didn't even get a close look at that kermanite yet." She started to hold up her fist, where she still held two shards, but he shook his head.

"Let's get off the street first. You're shaky, Miss Ingrid. Let's get some food in you."

"I *am* stronger," she said as they slowly began to walk north.

"I know you are, but I also know how the events of Wednesday taxed your body. It's a miracle you're alive at all."

"Hey. Hey!" called a soft voice. Ingrid glanced up to find Mirabelle crouched on the second-story balcony. "I heard Ma yelling." Tears streaked the girl's face.

"You heard more than the yelling, didn't you?" asked Ingrid.

"Ma doesn't know that voices carry really well if you lay by the vent in the room above hers. Papa's really dead?"

Ingrid nodded.

Mirabelle blinked fast. "I know what Ma says. Papa was a bad man, but he was still Papa. Sometimes he was nice. He'd buy us lumps of sugar and at Christmas once he gave me a doll and the eyes opened and shut when she tilted back. I loved that doll till Casey broke it."

Ingrid had to take a risk. "Mirabelle, do earthquakes make you or your sister feel sick?" she asked in a low voice.

The question didn't seem to surprise Mirabelle. She immediately shook her head. "Not us. Just our brothers. When Casey and me were sad about them dying, Papa whispered that it was magic that killed them, that it was best that they were gone to Jesus while their souls were still pure as snow. He said that, but he doesn't even believe in Jesus. Didn't. Does that mean he's gone to hell?" Her voice choked.

Ingrid felt cold and awful as she thought *yes*. "I'm sorry, Mirabelle. Our papa wasn't a nice man, but you're right. He was still our father. It's okay to miss him and miss those good times."

Mirabelle glanced at the open door behind her. "I need to finish my rooms. Will you come back someday?" Hope brightened eyes that looked so much like Ingrid's own.

"I'll try," she said, feeling like a liar. "Tell your sister that I wish I got to meet her."

"Hai." With a quick flash of a gap-toothed smile, she was gone, the door closed.

"Ingrid, what she said. Your father. Do you think he . . . ?"

"I know he did. He killed those two little boys just as he would have killed me if he had known about my power." Her whisper was barely audible.

"Let's find a proper place to sit." Cy took her by the elbow and guided her along. Tears blurred her vision.

She squeezed her fists. The clutched kermanite pieces stabbed the softness of her right palm. The earth responded with a mere breath of power. It wasn't enough to affect her body temperature, but she shivered all the same.

CHAPTER 6

Soup was said to be good for the soul, and perhaps there was some truth to that. Ingrid and Cy sat at a miso shop and drank from their bowls. She closed her eyes and let the fragrant broth fill her senses. The rain had returned and pattered on the eaves and sloshed beneath wheels on the street. She could almost pretend this was a rainy-day lunch interlude with Mr. Sakaguchi at their favorite miso place on Battery, that he was safe and musing over a newspaper article, that all of the wardens were alive and San Francisco still fully intact in its cowl of fog.

"I worry for those girls." Cy set down his bowl with a soft clunk.

Ingrid opened her eyes. Her circumstances might be dire these days, but she kept excellent company. "So do I, but what can we do? We can't bring them with us, and even if we left some money, do you think it would be used for their benefit?"

Cy used his chopsticks to pluck up a noodle. His entire face was skewed in a frown, his pince-nez still spotted with droplets. Ingrid took another long sip of soup and stared out the window.

With the port so near, the restaurants here catered to a diverse clientele, but even so Cy and Ingrid were a white man and a woman of color on a lunch outing together. She found it best to not gaze at their fellow diners with their raised eyebrows and pursed lips. Their table was fairly private, at least.

An old Catholic church stood across the way. It looked gray as the clouds above, the stained-glass panes like compressed rainbows.

Ingrid prodded at her pork. Her favorite meat of all, one that usually made her salivate like a bulldog, and today she could scarcely stomach it. "In Olema, Papa said we were like gods and goddesses. I think he was including his mother in that statement. If his mother had power, that would explain why he stayed around Portland long enough for his daughters to reach manifestation age. Certainly no one else would have expected geomancy in girls."

"You wondered before about why your father bothered to continue exchanging letters with Mr. Sakaguchi for so many years. Maybe he was monitoring your maturation, too."

That was a sobering thought: that Papa had never cared

about Ingrid, but only checked in on her progress in case she needed to be eliminated.

Cy set aside his empty bowl. "What was the name that Mrs. Stone mentioned, that of a spirit? Was your grandmother some kind of earth fantastic, like a dryad?"

Ingrid choked and coughed a piece of radish into her hand. "Sorry. That . . . I did not need to imagine a man and a sentient-tree woman engaged in *those* sorts of relations." She tucked the errant vegetable into her napkin.

"I didn't intend for you to envision such a thing." He blushed.

"Let's just say my imagination needs little provocation." At that, his cheeks took on an even deeper shade of red. "Pele isn't a dryad, if that's really who she was talking about. As for Hawaii . . . It makes sense for Papa to have come from there. Warden Kealoha used to call me his *hanai* niece because we looked similar." She blinked back sudden tears. Dear Mr. Kealoha. He had been Mr. Sakaguchi's closest friend—his only friend, after the split with Mr. Roosevelt. She'd loved him like another uncle.

"Ingrid." Cy's soft voice coaxed her from bittersweet memories. "What is Pele?"

"An ancient goddess of volcanoes."

"And, perhaps, she's your grandmother."

"She couldn't possibly be my . . . No." Her brow furrowed as she shook her head.

"You're denying that possibility because she's so powerful?"

"No. Yes. I don't know." The very idea of being descended

from an actual *goddess* made Ingrid's fingers tremble so much that she gave up on her chopsticks. "People still worship Pele there, though most of the old Hawaiian ways are discouraged if not outlawed. I suppose you could say Pele is not very hidden as a Hidden One. People still report seeing her from time to time. She demands acknowledgment. But really, Mrs. Stone wasn't sure of the name. Maybe there's another minor entity in Hawaii with a name more similar to 'bucket.'"

"You can talk to fantastics like the selkies and the big snake. That points to kinship with something more than human. A goddess sounds closer to the truth than a mere dryad."

"Papa didn't speak with the big snake. I can only guess that he couldn't talk to yokai, but he certainly passed that skill along to me." Ingrid sighed. "I wish I were more like Mama in a lot of ways. It'd sure make my life easier."

"I didn't have the pleasure of meeting your mother, but from what I've heard you and Lee say, you inherited a great deal from her." Cy bent over the table to speak lower, as a few other folks had started to gab at the nearby window. "Maybe your father had *too much* of that ancient power in him. Your mama raised you, and she raised you right, but she brought into your blood what might be most important of all: your humanity. She was and is your saving grace, Ingrid."

She closed her eyes for a moment to absorb his words and take solace in his presence. "Thank you for that," she whispered.

Cy pushed himself away from the table. "I figure it's high

time we head back to the *Bug*. It makes me feel itchy to be away too long. Shall we go?"

The laundry shop was almost empty. Ingrid double-checked their clothes to ensure that everything was present and clean, and repacked their laundry bag. She had just drawn the bag shut when a man burst into the business.

"Charlotte! Charlotte, did you hear? Gold's been discovered in Baranov!"

"Gold's been discovered in a bear's what?" yelled the woman behind the counter. The clothes dryers roared behind her.

"Gold! Like in California in '48, but up north!" The older man hobbled forward. "News just hit town! An airship loaded with gold landed in Seattle, and there's a naval steamer on the way with more!"

Ingrid shouldered the hefty bag. It was about as long as her torso.

"Ingrid." Cy's voice sounded strange. "This is bad. We need to go."

"What you telling me this for?" the woman yelled at the man as Ingrid and Cy exited the shop. "You can't be thinking to actually—you are, you ninny—"

The street was eerily quiet after the racket inside, and the mood had shifted in a matter of minutes. Few people ambled by. Several wagons tore by at a gallop. Out of nowhere, an autocar zoomed the other way, a hand heavy on the horn.

"Cy, what . . . ?"

"Run." Cy plucked the bag from her grip and set off. Ingrid followed, though she felt the strain in her legs within a mere dozen feet. Panting, she forced herself along. They dodged pedestrians and overexcited dogs and rounded the corner to the bus stop. Men mobbed the area.

"It's as bad as I feared. Good Lord!" He spun in place. "Gold fever."

Ingrid was a San Francisco girl raised on images of the 1849 Gold Rush. The population stampede had made San Francisco a powerful city, but not at first. Men, overcome by visions of wealth, fled from their families and jobs. Entire cargo ships rotted in the harbor, fully abandoned by their crews. More ships arrived, loaded with fools and dreams. Folks soon realized that staying in the city and selling goods to the miners could produce greater wealth, but that level of rationality likely wouldn't come into play here in Portland for weeks yet.

"There's going to be a riot at the airship dock," she said through gasps.

"The dock, the naval port, any means folks can use to get to Baranov." Cy squinted to the north, as if he could see through buildings and around the bend in the Willamette to Swan Island. "We can't wait for the bus with that mob. Come on. We have to move fast. And pray."

Swan Island had to be a good four miles away, but Ingrid wasn't about to complain. She pushed herself to move at Cy's speed, her eyes on the skies above in case she could recognize the *Bug*. Some airships drifted on high, but most looked to be Pegasus or Behemoth class by the sizes of their envelopes.

Fenris and Lee didn't have any weapons available other

than tools and parts and a kitchen knife. If men rushed the ship, what could they do?

Fight back. Be taken captive. Get injured. Die.

Ingrid made herself walk faster, weakness be damned. "That man said the gold was found in Baranov, right?"

"Yes." Cy huffed for breath.

"Blum mentioned Baranov more than once. She said it was why she'd been on the West Coast at all. She made it sound like some sort of big, important project."

Cy gave her a sharp look. "Baranov is a big place."

"What are the odds of it being mentioned in such significant ways in one week? You said yourself that Blum is involved in everything."

He said nothing more, but his expression was troubled.

From Mr. Sakaguchi's geography lessons, Ingrid knew that Baranov was far to the north, a sizable chunk of land that had been a Russian territory for centuries. Independently, it was of no great consequence. But Russia had recently tussled with Japan over railway rights in Manchukuo in northern China, and the conflict had expanded to include gun battles between fishing boats in the Sea of Japan. That had increased concerns over Baranov—that its location was perfect as a base for Russian incursions into Canada or Cascadian America.

How would the discovery of gold alter those concerns?

Ingrid and Cy started across a two-lane bridge over the river. All vehicles rushed to the far side of the Willamette; none drove back to Portland. It was as if they were traveling toward Swan Island and into a bottomless pit.

"Might need to abandon our laundry. This bag's heavy." Sweat sheened Cy's skin.

"Promise me we'll only leave it as a last resort. I only have the one other dress, and I'd rather not go gallivanting into the wilderness without a spare pair of knickers."

He burst out in laughter. "Knickers? Really?"

"It's a much funnier word than something like 'unmentionables,' isn't it? And 'unmentionables' is such a contradictory term, since it's being mentioned!"

He panted for breath. "Even under these dire circumstances, you have a way with enlightening conversation. And about women's underthings, no less."

An autocar roared past, squealed to a stop, then backed up. Rubber burned. Cy dropped the clothes bag and unhooked his Tesla rod. With a flick of his wrist, the rod extended to full length. The blue tip sparkled; in that mode, it'd provide a fierce electric shock to anyone it touched.

Ingrid clenched the pistol in her pocket. Her fingers trembled, and she desperately hoped their survival didn't depend on her aim.

"Gomen nasai! Don't shoot!" The driver's-side door popped open and a gloved hand waved in the air. "Mr. Jennings! It's me, Fujiwara!" His head briefly popped into view; he wore a bowler hat.

Cy let the Tesla rod collapse as he dashed forward. "Mr. Fujiwara!"

"Come on, you and the woman get in!"

"Who—" Ingrid started to ask.

"He's moored at the mast next to ours." Cy flung wide the

back passenger door, tossed in their bag, and then he and Ingrid threw themselves inside. The car lurched forward as she slammed the door and flopped over onto Cy. As he sat up, he pulled her upright as well. The little car roared over the bridge at an alarming speed. Ingrid clutched the seat in front of her.

"Damn ugly business!" Mr. Fujiwara said. "You think our ships will still be there?"

"God help us, I hope so," said Cy.

"Thank goodness you had a car," said Ingrid.

Mr. Fujiwara laughed, the tone almost maniacal. "Yeah. I had an extra set of keys to show the driver." He held up his right hand. Blood stained the knuckles of the white glove. He grabbed the wheel again to turn hard onto the frontage road.

Cy gave her knee a discreet squeeze, as if she needed a reminder to withhold comment. This wasn't a time to argue over morality, not when Fenris and Lee needed them. Not when they needed to skedaddle from here before all hell broke loose.

The rail yard blurred by. Ingrid could see the tips of the southernmost masts at Swan Island. Many were vacated. She felt a lurch of panic and clutched the seat harder. Fenris and Lee had to be okay. They had to be.

She felt the slight burble of the energy that she had absorbed in Portland; it wouldn't even be enough to crack a teacup in her hand. She needed to be capable of her own offense and defense.

Stopped cars clogged the road ahead. As they drove

closer, Ingrid realized they had been abandoned. Doors were left wide open. Some vehicles were still running, exhaust creating small clouds of gray.

Mr. Fujiwara pulled the car off to one side. "This is as far as we can get, it seems."

"Domo arigatou gozaimasu," said Ingrid as she popped open the door. Cy echoed her. Mr. Fujiwara leaped from the vehicle and granted them a tip of his bowler hat as he waded into the tight knot of cars.

Cy shouldered the canvas bag. "Let's assess the situation before we get too close."

They wound through the autocars, their bodies hunkered over. Men's voices overlapped—angry, chaotic, insistent. Ingrid glanced over car hoods and through windows, and ascertained that the mob was trapped on the narrow land bridge leading to Swan Island.

"The staff must have dropped the metal gate, but who knows how many men made it through first?" Cy muttered. "Could try to swim it. The lagoon between this road and the island looks to be about a hundred feet wide. No idea how deep it is, though."

Ingrid searched her pocket for the sharpest of the dark kermanite chips. With that in her fist, she rolled up her coat sleeve, then the loose sleeve of her dress beneath. Cy glanced back just as she brought the shard to her forearm.

"No, Ingrid!"

She drew the edge along the tender skin on the underside of her arm. Not too near the veins; pain was her intent, after all, not suicide. She pressed hard, biting her lip as she choked back a screech. The earth teased her with a faint and brief blue fog. She yanked down her sleeves again and wiped her bloodied hand on her coat.

She formed a fist to inflict more pain in the muscle, but as much as it hurt, the energy draw was pathetic. She barely felt any heat.

"Damn it. This is why the Thuggees killed everyone in the auxiliary before the quake. This very reason. The local geomancers are like a wall. I'd have to really hurt myself to get a reaction from the earth." She wasn't sure whether to laugh or weep. "Maybe this is enough to throw us over the water and the fence, though." That effort might pull too much energy from her body, too, not that she would voice this to Cy.

"Which won't do us a lick of good if the *Bug*'s been nabbed or damaged, Ingrid!" For the first time she could recall, Cy looked at her with outright anger. His hands curled over her fists as if he could protect her from herself. To her surprise, he was trembling. "You can't do this to yourself. Your body's still struggling to get well. This up-and-down flow of power's too dangerous. Your magic will eat you alive."

He was genuinely terrified for her sake. She gently pulled her hands back to her sides. "Everything is dangerous right now." Gunshots split the air. Men yelled. More car doors slammed nearby as newcomers joined the fray. She warily eyed the mob through a window. "Let's try to get a different view. Maybe enough of the other airships have left for us to see our mast."

"You worry me, Ingrid." Cy's jaw was set.

"Well, I worry over you, and Lee, and Fenris, and that cramped airship we're calling home."

"Don't let Fenris hear you say a critical word about his baby." He paused. "Though I think one of these days I'll wake up on board and my head will be permanently angled to one side. I'd rather sleep in a chair than in those coffin-like racks."

Ingrid shot him a quick grin.

They worked their way through the haphazardly parked cars. More men ran by. "Almost everyone in the mob looks to be an older white man."

"That doesn't surprise me. Most Japanese men around here wouldn't think to drop their obligations and dash off in pursuit of fortune. It's not the Bushido way."

Cy and Ingrid reached the edge of the road along the water basin. Ingrid gasped and pointed. "There's someone in the water."

He dropped the clothes bag and half slid down the gravel slope to meet the other man at the water's edge. The white-haired fellow coughed and choked between torrents of Japanese epithets aimed at belligerent Americans.

"Mr. Ito." Cy bobbed his head, the closest he could come to a bow while still on the slope. He extended a hand. "Mr. Fujiwara provided us a ride here. He was trying to get back to your ship."

Mr. Ito squinted. "Ah! Mr. Jennings!" His English was heavily accented. "He will have no luck there. Our ship is gone! The thieves, they threw me out!" He waved a hand to the sky. "Your ship is gone, too."

CHAPTER 7

Gone? The *Palmetto Bug* was gone? The world wobbled around her. Where were Lee and Fenris?

"What happened?" Ingrid snapped.

Mr. Ito slipped on the slope. Cy reached to help and almost slid headfirst into the water. Both men flailed to find their footing. Mr. Ito's errant fist whacked Cy's face. Cy landed on his backside, but he had finally managed to grip Mr. Ito's arm. They staggered up the embankment.

"Gomen nasai, Mr. Jennings!" Mr. Ito panted. "I did not mean to . . ."

"It was an accident, sir. Pay it no mind."

"You said our airship is gone?" Ingrid repeated, staring at Cy. His glasses were missing. Damn it all, the man would be blind as a worm. Cy glanced back at the slope with a dismissive shrug.

"Hai! Group of men rushed aboard, unmoored it. I did not

see what happened next." Mr. Ito frowned at Ingrid and then focused on Cy again. "I thought I was safe with the hatch closed but they broke through. As it took off, they threw me out!"

What sort of horrible people threw an unarmed, innocent man off an airship in flight? Anger caused a small spike of pain in her arm. She couldn't see anyone else in the water. Could Lee swim? Chinese hadn't been allowed to use public pools or beaches around San Francisco, though he had surprised her with other skills recently. She doubted Fenris could swim either—he was likely averse to an activity that might reveal his slight natural curves to others.

"Let's get under cover again," Cy said, motioning them toward the cars. "Did you see if both our companions were aboard when they took our ship?"

Ingrid grabbed the bag and winced at her injury.

"Hai! Both men. Outside work was done. Stairs gone." Mr. Ito granted Cy a quick bow and headed toward the mob. "I must find Mr. Fujiwara! Domo arigatou gozaimasu."

"Cy, what are we going to do?" murmured Ingrid.

"I don't know. Lord have mercy, but I don't know." More cars squealed to a stop at the northern access to the dock. Gunshots caused both Cy and Ingrid to drop to a crouch between cars. Feet pounded past them close by.

Cy motioned her to stay put as he removed his hat. He tugged a switchblade from his pocket and slipped the blade along the lining of his hat.

"What are you . . . ?" asked Ingrid.

"A trick I learned a few years back, from one of Mr.

Roosevelt's books, actually. When he was on the battlefield, he kept spare pairs of glasses sewn into his hat." He pried his fingers into the cloth lining and pulled out a small parcel wrapped in a rag. Another pair of pince-nez emerged. He planted them on the arch of his nose and grinned. "A gentleman is never without a hat, after all."

"What a marvel!" she said. "How many glasses do you have there?"

"Another pair, and more on the *Bug*."

"I guess it'd be prudent to avoid being smacked in the face again."

"I must say, 'get smacked in the face' is never something I add to my daily to-do list." He adjusted the derby hat on his head again.

"Run! Run!" a man screamed. More gunshots punched the air. Cy and Ingrid hunkered lower.

One thing was clear: they had to get away from here. Cy immediately led the way back through the cars, heading to the northern perimeter of the airship dock. Ingrid heard footsteps behind her. Someone grabbed the clothes bag, yanking her to a stop. She turned, in the process pulling the bag from a man's grip. He was a stocky fellow with a face like lumpy bread dough that'd been dropped on a filthy floor.

"Gimme your money." He brandished a Tesla rod of his own.

She heard Cy shuffle behind her, likely drawing his own rod, but the space was narrow and he couldn't defend her on this end. She didn't need him to.

"Of course." She reached for her pocket, but she didn't go

for the gun. Instead, she whirled around, using her sliver of power to bash the man with the loaded laundry bag. His head met the trunk of an autocar with a satisfying crunch. She brought the bag down on his legs and used the blunt force to send him flying backward. His back and head struck the car on the other side. He slid to the ground, limp, as she brought up the bag again.

"Ingrid! I think that's enough! Leave him be," Cy yelled.

She was panting heavily. Hot blood drained down her raised arm, trickling to the armpit. "You're right. This is clean laundry. I don't want his blood to soak through the bag."

More gunshots. More men running to the dock, away from the dock. Cy spared the time to grab the fallen man's Tesla rod and motioned Ingrid forward. "Look for a running car, or one with keys left in the ignition!"

A man was sobbing nearby. Other voices overlapped. "We should get on a ship for Seattle—"

"Let's get more of the boys and come back—"

"Gold! They say there's so much gold in a vein up there, it's like a river! All a man's got to do is stake a claim—"

"Carmichael!" A voice boomed over the chaos.

Ingrid couldn't help but look up. An elegant autocar was idling in the empty road past the tangle of abandoned cars. A man stood by an open door, his hands cupped to his mouth. He saw Ingrid looking his way and waved.

"Cy. Cy!" She grabbed him by the coattails. "That man! I know him! He's Siegfried, he works for Roosevelt!" As a secretary for the Cordilleran, she had come to know many of the most powerful men in the world by the companionship of their servants.

Cy and Ingrid ran for the car. Siegfried flung open a back door. Ingrid threw the laundry bag into the dark interior, then herself. Cy's warm body landed beside hers. The instant he slammed the door shut, the driver hit the gas. The car reversed with a roar and made a tight turn away.

Distinct, familiar laughter brayed from feet away. Two plush seats faced each other within the autocar, the seat across from them occupied. "Dee-lighted to see you alive and well, Miss Carmichael." Theodore Roosevelt embraced their thick laundry bag with both arms, his grin broad and brilliant.

Ingrid had always been a bit intimidated by Mr. Roosevelt; within the small space of the autocar, she was even more acutely aware of his dominating presence. Two hundred pounds of muscle were packed onto his small frame. The walrus-like thickness of his neck strained his collar while a tailored black jacket accentuated his broad shoulders. At a glance, anyone would know he was an athlete in top physical form, though no one would accuse him of being good-looking. His stiff brown hair was parted high and was clipped unflatteringly short, emphasizing the largeness of his head. A glossy bowler hat sat on the seat beside him. Lights inset in the roof and sides of the car seemed to be angled to set him aglow.

"It's good to see you, too, sir." Ingrid bowed.

Against the canvas bag, it was easy to see the large signet ring of an ambassador on Roosevelt's left hand. It looked just like the one worn by Blum. Ingrid sensed its enchantment like buzzing bumblebees. The ring afforded its wearer incredible protection against injury. It could only be removed by a quorum of the Twelve Ambassadors.

Siegfried and the other men must have seen that Cy carried two Tesla rods but no one expressed concern, and with reason. Those rings were said to be among the most powerful artifacts in the world due to their nearly impervious level of shielding.

"Pardon me, sir." Cy bobbed his head in apology. He set his hat on his lap and pulled away the laundry bag to rest at their feet.

Roosevelt squinted at him. Both men wore pince-nez. "Do I know you, sir?"

"My name's Cy Jennings, Mr. Roosevelt, sir." He seemed uncharacteristically nervous, and justifiably. Mr. Roosevelt undoubtedly knew his father, George Augustus, and had likely heard of Cy. After all, he had been the brilliant inventor of the Durendal who tragically died in an airship crash. Or so the newspapers said. Cy had spent the past dozen years as a deserter from the military; here before him was a man who deemed military service akin to godliness.

Roosevelt also had a memory as keen as Excalibur's blade. He memorized whole books during a single reading, and recalled faces and names years after brief meetings.

Ingrid weighed what to say. Secrets seemed to be the

currency of the day. They needed Roosevelt as an ally, but they couldn't tell him everything. Certainly nothing about Cy's true identity. The presence of the three men in the front seat, their heads visible through a small window, only complicated things more.

"Sir, Mr. Sakaguchi advised us to go to you. But what we need to say should be for your ears only."

"You're concerned about my men. I trust them with my life, Miss Carmichael."

"Begging your pardon, sir, but our lives are substantially more fragile than yours." She certainly felt her own frailty now. Exertion and adrenaline were causing her whole body to tremble. She pressed her knees together to steady herself.

Mr. Roosevelt's arms sprawled against the back of his seat as he fixed his level gaze on her. "I trust them with the very welfare of the United States of America. They hear secrets but do not repeat them. What you wish to say, they may very well already know." He tapped on the glass. Two of the men tilted their heads. "Gentlemen, did you already know Miss Ingrid Carmichael here is the only known woman geomancer in the world, and one of titanic skill?"

"Yessir," said all three men in a slightly offbeat chorus.

Indignation caused Ingrid to open and close her mouth several times without being able to form coherent speech. She'd certainly never been privy to the late-night conversations between Mr. Sakaguchi and Mr. Roosevelt, so it was *possible* that Siegfried had been in attendance for those talks. He had been a regular fixture with Mr. Roosevelt, though he often ended up in the kitchen, where he knew Mama usually had cookies or pies of which he could partake.

These other men, though . . . they were strangers. Strangers who had also kept counsel well enough that Blum hadn't suspected anything about Ingrid's power until the events of the past week.

Ingrid didn't like her hand being forced like this, but she also knew there was no time to dawdle. If she and Cy couldn't trust Roosevelt and his men, they were already as good as damned.

"Sir, our airship's gone, nabbed by gold rushers. Lee Fong was on board."

"Lee Fong?" Mr. Roosevelt's eyes narrowed. "You *know*."

So much weight in that one word. "Yes. We both do."

Mr. Roosevelt tapped on the window again. "We are done with Portland! We must fly straightaway. These airship thieves will likely fly toward Seattle."

"Understood, sir!" barked the driver. The car made a hard right turn. Ingrid viewed blurring trees through the tinted side windows and estimated that they drove to the east.

"My airship is moored at the ranch I am staying at nearby. It's vital that I maintain my distance from Mr. Sakaguchi and his concerns, Miss Carmichael. That includes *you*. In light of these circumstances, however, I must make an exception. I will assist in your pursuit of this airship. In return, I need to hear from your lips what befell Mr. Sakaguchi and San Francisco." His face reddened. "This fool business with Baranov has such wretched timing."

"Ambassador Blum engineered this gold rush in Baranov, didn't she?" asked Ingrid. Better to delve into someone else's secrets before exposing more of their own.

It was odd to feel Roosevelt's intense scrutiny on her. She had enjoyed his after-dinner stories as a child but she usually interacted with him in a more menial role.

"Baranov is Miss Blum's idea of a grand diversion. Russia has wandered into Manchukuo and disrupted the railroad. That entity is run by one of the most powerful corporations in Japan—"

"South Manchukuo Railway, the main rival of Augustinian," added Cy.

"Indeed." Roosevelt studied Cy for a moment then continued: "This past winter was hard on Russia. The czar's coffers are low, as is soldier morale in the motherland and abroad. Our people have known about gold in Baranov for some time. Miss Blum delayed the announcement of its discovery until now, springtime—"

"To lure mass desertions to Baranov. Russia will execute any soldiers who abandon their posts, and either kill or imprison their families as well." Cy grimaced.

"The ones who don't die in the effort to reach the Baranov interior, yes," said Roosevelt. "The gold isn't conveniently located at the coast. It's a dangerous and long trek, one unfriendly to airship and man alike. A good bit of gold is just across the border in the Yukon as well. It will likewise distract the Canadians and Brits."

"And plenty of Americans, too," said Ingrid.

"The sorts of Americans that Miss Blum deems to be

past their period of prime use as soldiers. I assure you, *I* don't agree with her assessment. Many of these men are fathers and still contribute to society in other useful ways, but I doubt it will surprise you that Miss Blum doesn't readily accept my counsel."

Ingrid shook her head. "What a horrible political ploy."

"But brilliant all the same," added Cy softly.

"Such plots are Miss Blum's hallmark. You're now part of her grand web as well, Miss Carmichael. She has scoured the ruins of San Francisco for you the past few days. She is convinced that Mr. Sakaguchi now works against Japan and is in league with a *tong.* She'll see him executed, and rejoice in that. She doesn't tolerate disloyalty to Japan."

"Whereas your loyalty is to America," Ingrid murmured.

At that, Mr. Roosevelt dipped his head. "Thus is the nature of the Unified Pacific: we combine our militaries, our resources, yet the representation is not equal, nor is the sacrifice. I vowed to fight for America and what is right, and indeed I will fight!" The spark in his eyes could light fires.

"That's a dangerous position to take, isn't it, sir?" asked Cy. "A common man would be jailed for saying such, but as an ambassador, you take a different risk. It's not the first you've taken either. You might have publicly ceased your friendship with Mr. Sakaguchi, but you still fought to keep him free these past months while Japan was well aware he'd lied about Abram Carmichael's death."

"You are privy to a great deal of information for a man who is a stranger to me."

Ingrid didn't like the way Mr. Roosevelt was regarding

Cy. "I wouldn't be alive without the help of Mr. Jennings and Mr. Fenris Braun, sir. Mr. Braun is aboard the airship with Lee."

The autocar's horn blared, and Ingrid swayed as the driver made another tight turn. The engine roared as the car accelerated.

"Fenris!" Mr. Roosevelt laughed, all teeth, and an instant later his face went utterly sober.

"Unfettered will fare the Fenris Wolf
And ravaged the realm of men,
Ere that cometh a kingly prince
As good, to stand in his stead."

He grinned again. "A piece of the poem 'Hákonarmál.' A tenth-century work. I should hope this Fenris of yours is not intent on destroying the world in the manner of his namesake. There's already a queue for that privilege."

"Our Fenris doesn't tolerate long waits in line, so it's all well and good for us that he favors construction over destruction," said Cy. "He's my business partner in our machinist business. We ran a shop South of the Slot in San Francisco. I met Miss Ingrid this Sunday past when I dropped by the auxiliary to buy some kermanite."

"Easter Sunday. The auxiliary explosion." Roosevelt's hands knotted together. "I read a report penned by one Captain Sutcliff that said Miss Carmichael credited Thuggees with the attack. The press has joyously blamed the Chinese for the explosion and many wish to blame them for the earthquake as well, though they aren't sure *how* to do so. In any case, it validates the flimsy logic of many men who wish to treat the Chinese as less than human." He sighed. "I hope Lee manages to stay hidden aboard this airship. I shudder to think of what those louts would do to a Chinese boy."

Ingrid nodded, her throat dry. Fenris and Lee could be in danger even if they weren't physically attacked. The thieves might be inexperienced with airships, or bad weather might arise, or the state of the *Bug*'s repairs could have catastrophic consequences. Possible disasters were infinite.

Roosevelt stared out the window, into the distance. "If any semblance of China as a people and a culture is to survive these next few years, Lee Fong is our hope to lead it. Millions of bright lights are being extinguished. That boy is a spark in the deepest, blackest night. He is hope for people who have little else."

Ingrid thought of the *qilin* and the *guandao* as she met Mr. Roosevelt's gaze. "What is he to you, sir?"

"Redemption."

CHAPTER 8

Mr. Roosevelt shifted in his seat. He reminded Ingrid of the youngest boys at the auxiliary, the six- and seven-year-olds who struggled to sit still in hard wooden chairs for hours on end. Roosevelt had that same relentless energy.

"Redemption," Ingrid echoed. She clutched her injured arm to her side.

"I have written numerous books on the subject of war, from my first treatise on naval and airship strategies when I was almost your age, Miss Carmichael, to the book published this past Christmas on my campaigns against Spanish-held domains. I believe war to be an agent of change. It is an opportunity for a superior people to guide the less advantaged to the light of civilization. China is a nation with a storied past that refused to move forward in time. This past century, they have destroyed themselves through corruption, vice, and rebellion."

Cy leaned forward on his knees. "If China of the nineteenth century was an ill man, Mr. Roosevelt, then he was a man pinned down in bed by a dozen different nations, each forcing a different poison down his throat."

"Ha! I see why you have this Mr. Jennings as a companion. He and Mr. Sakaguchi would get along like beef and beer. Yes, certainly. China was vulnerable and other world powers circled it like vultures. Japan and the Unified Pacific first and foremost. This . . . this is where we have fallen astray." He had begun to speak faster and faster. From past observation, Ingrid knew that if Mr. Roosevelt had freedom to move, he would pace as he spoke. It's what happened when he fell into pedagogue mode. "As Americans, as the most privileged nation on this earth, it is our *duty* to be stewards to our backward brethren, to enable them to rise and stand with us, side by side. That is what I have worked to do on native reservations across the west, and among the lost souls of the Philippines."

The dark-skinned, the pagan, the Catholic. Ingrid suppressed a sigh. Roosevelt could be very selective in what he chose to see from his high pedestal.

"Yet in the most rebellious parts of China, beneath Miss Blum's direction, the Unified Pacific has initiated the policy of Sankō Sakusen!" The Three Alls Policy: kill all, burn all, loot all. She knew American military units followed their own less brutal yet still ruthless code, General Order 100. "This goes against everything America stands for, and yet this war is powered by American lives and resources." Roosevelt practically snarled. "Meanwhile, Japanese settlement continues in both China and America. Japanese populations dominate our most affluent cities. Japanese language is taught alongside English in our schools. We are losing our identities as Americans, and that's exactly what Miss Blum wants."

"Why does she care?" asked Ingrid. "She's not even human."

Mr. Roosevelt's eyes widened in surprise.

"She made sure that I knew, sir. I think she gave me every hint except for showing her tails. How many does she even have? Do you know?"

"I know better than to ask any woman her age, especially if that woman is a kitsune. She has spoken of Tokugawa and Nobunaga as contemporaries, and knowing her particular brand of honesty, I believe her."

Blum was oddly honest, true, though it wasn't a positive character trait in her case. Mr. Sakaguchi had always counseled Ingrid against using moralistic and hyperbolic labels like "evil" to describe actions, but Blum was the closest thing to evil that she had ever encountered.

"Oda Nobunaga and Tokugawa Ieyasu? That'd make Ambassador Blum at least four hundred years old. Four tails. Lord have mercy. No wonder she has such magical might. I feel a fool for assuming that she was close to my own age, but I imagine she relishes such deceit." Cy shook his head.

"It's all a game to her," said Ingrid. A sort of seduction, really, not that she had the gall to speak the word aloud in reference to Cy and Blum.

Cy looked to Roosevelt. "You never hear of other fantastics seeking out her kind of human political clout."

"No, and that's what makes Miss Blum so dangerous, and it gets to the heart of your 'why' question, Miss Carmichael. To elaborate on your metaphor, politics are the greatest game in the human realm. A chessboard where a single pawn equates to billions of people. It is a game that involves wit and perseverance, but Ambassador Blum's greatest asset is her patience. She believes in the *holiness* of Japan, that its superiority goes even deeper than the emperor tracing his lineage to the goddess Amaterasu. For many centuries, Japan's culture, language, and religions looked to China as an inspiration and ideal. Miss Blum has enabled Japan to be the upstart child and put the elderly parent in its place, and she's having *fun* doing so."

"Other fantastic tricksters manipulate people on a whim," Ingrid said softly. "You're saying Ambassador Blum is willing to set up her pieces and wait *centuries* to see the results."

"That's it exactly, Miss Carmichael. She delights in the long game, in the pursuit, in being foiled and reworking her strategy. She's at her most dangerous when she respects her opponent, and she respects *you*."

"Aren't I the lucky one?" said Ingrid. She felt Cy brush her side as a reminder that she wasn't alone.

The autocar slowed. Roosevelt peered out the window. "Ah! We are here at last."

They'd driven deeper into the hills. The window showed

tall pines, thick bushes, and a gorgeous lodge of hewn logs. Mr. Roosevelt bounded from the car the instant the door was opened for him.

"Siegfried! Rally the crew. We must depart immediately. Immediately! Seamus—"

"I'll pack your things, sir, and see to the rest."

"Excellent!"

Ingrid started to open her door only to be intercepted by one of the other men. He gave her a nod as he opened the door wide. She stepped out, followed by Cy. The place seemed almost devoid of people. In the distance, she heard the sounds of horses and chickens, and plentiful birds in the nearby pines. The air smelled gloriously fresh, in stark contrast to the scent of smoke that had haunted her these past few days.

Across the yard from the lodge, a large airship was moored to a mast far taller than any nearby trees. The orichalcum belly of the craft shone like a fresh penny, the curvaceous shape of it reminiscent of an illustration of a Spanish galleon from a book about eighteenth-century pirates. The envelope had the mottled coloration of antique paper. The whole thing screamed of opulence.

Roosevelt whirled to face Ingrid and Cy. "Clean up best as you can. There'll be food aplenty aboard. My *Bucephalus* is fast—"

"Pegasus class is fast, sure," said Cy, "but the great weight'll slow it down, too. Our *Palmetto Bug* is a heavily modified Sprite. If our thieves know what they're doing, they'll make it to Seattle hours ahead of your ship. Mr.

Roosevelt. Sir." Cy offered a bashful bob of his head as he donned his battered hat.

Ingrid knew Fenris would have said very similar words had he been present, though without the softness and smile at the end. He and Cy were so very alike in some ways. Oh, Fenris. Ingrid desperately wanted him to be safe and sound.

Mr. Roosevelt barked out a laugh. "We'll see about that! Siegfried! Round up the men. The race begins!" He pointed at Ingrid as he walked away. "Once we're aboard, I want the full details of what happened since this Sunday past."

"Of course, sir."

Maybe reciting the awful events of the past week would distract her from thinking of what terrible things might befall Fenris and Lee, if they were even still alive.

Cy's smooth ways and easy smile convinced a member of the household staff to let him and Ingrid briefly speak in private in one of the first-floor rooms. The way Cy handled the matter, it didn't even come across as improper.

Once they were alone, he motioned to Ingrid's sleeve. "Let's get that properly bandaged now. There's no telling when we'll be alone like this again." He opened up the laundry bag, pulled out one of his newly whitened shirts, and started to shred it. "Please don't ever hurt yourself like that again." She couldn't see his face, but the pleading in his tone tore at her heart.

"I can't promise that." She flinched as she tugged her sleeve away from the wound. Bleeding began anew. "I can't bear to feel defenseless or useless. I need to do *something*."

In response to her pain, a blue miasma flared along the ground, its warmth lapping her skin. She eyed a set of prisms hanging in the window but they didn't even jostle, nor did Cy notice anything amiss. Being farther away from Portland and its resident geomancers enabled her pain to agitate the earth just a tad.

"That *something* might kill you one of these days," he muttered. "I wish we could wash this cut. There's no time." He began to wind cloth around her arm, his moves confident. He'd done this sort of thing before.

"I don't like how T.R. talked about my power in front of his guards," she whispered. "I tried to keep the conversation away from us while in the car, but that's not going to work on his airship. He wants to know everything, and I'm not sure how much is safe to tell him, especially with more people around."

Still bent over, Cy glanced above the lenses of his glasses. "You did just fine. Get him to talk, especially about Blum. We need to know her weaknesses."

Ingrid gritted her teeth as Cy pulled the bandage tight, even as she welcomed another tiny well of energy. "The old tales say a kitsune's hoshi no tama is supposed to contain part of its soul. Blum wears hers as a pendant. If we could steal or destroy that, perhaps we could prevent her from changing forms." She thought a moment. "Stories also say kitsune hate dogs and dogs hate kitsune, but she's so powerful that when she simply bared her teeth at the tosa inu at the police station back home, the big dogs whimpered like they'd been kicked."

"A four-tailed kitsune or worse. Christ." Cy tied off the bandage and his hand trailed down to close over her fingers. "A difficult creature to kill, even without an ambassador's ring."

She reared back slightly but kept her hand in his. "I'm surprised to hear you talk of killing, Cy."

"I'm a pacifist. Blum is against peace. She has killed billions and damaged the lives of far more. She won't stop. She won't be reasoned with. She won't ever concede defeat in this game." Exhaustion weighed his features. He looked older than his twenty-seven years. "I want to go home someday, Ingrid. I want to go to Wedowee. I want to see my mother there in the garden painting her calla lilies. I want to see my father smoking his pipe as he reads in the evening. Maggie . . . I want to see Maggie's grave and cuss and holler at her for dying and leaving me a twin apart."

Ingrid could think of nothing to say, so she gripped his hand between both of hers. He closed his eyes for a moment, regaining his composure, then brought her left hand to his lips. His kiss to her knuckles was soft but she felt it like a spark on her skin.

"I'm sorry to ramble in such a way," he said. "Grief itches at me. I have to hope that if we can get Blum, maybe we can stop this war. Ease my pain, and that of so many others who have suffered. It sounds grandiose, I know . . ."

"It sounds suicidal, really. But as you like to point out, we're in this together," Ingrid said in a perky tone. "Just so you know, when I told you that I'd try to bring about world peace, I didn't intend to be so literal and prompt about it." It seemed like she'd known Cy Jennings for years, not a mere six days.

He smiled at her, warm crinkles lining his brown eyes. "You're a woman of action. Just please, take care. Don't purposely try to pull in power. It breaks my heart to think of how close you came to death in San Francisco. I don't want to repeat that."

Arguing over this would do no good; neither of their minds would change. It's not as if she wanted to die, or to struggle through this accursed fatigue. She just wanted—needed—to be *useful*. To not be dismissed as weak-minded, frail, and feminine, as she had been for so many years.

Men's voices carried down the hallway. Ingrid pulled her hand free. "The airship should be ready."

"Yes." Worry flickered across his face, and she knew he was thinking of Fenris. Lee as well, she was sure, but it was only right that Fenris be central in his concern. Ingrid hoped that Fenris was guarding his tongue for once and that the thieves had no reason to see beneath his clothes.

Ingrid touched Cy's sandpaper-bristled jaw long enough to provoke a smile, and together they exited the room.

After a lifetime of ground travel, Ingrid in the past week had boarded three very different airships. The *Palmetto Bug* was still shiny and new, built as it was of refurbished parts and odds and ends; Mr. Thornton's ground lander airship had been like a mobile version of a gentleman's den, all dark woods and the reek of tobacco.

Mr. Roosevelt's *Bucephalus* was something else entirely.

As a Pegasus class, the gondola was taller, the feel of it more spacious and narrow at the same time. Light cherrywood paneling, ubiquitous orichalcum, and a thick burgundy carpet underfoot made the space warm and yet masculine. Ingrid ached to pry off her boots and let her feet sink into the carpet, but that'd never do in such company. There was certainly no Japanese-style footwear etiquette to be found here.

Besides Roosevelt and his three men, there were five airship crewmen. None seemed flustered at the abruptness of their departure as they brusquely went about their duties. Ingrid and Cy were advised to stay midship, which included a kitchenette, lavatory, and a miniature parlor with plush chairs and a rather well-stocked liquor cabinet.

Ingrid let her body drop into a velvet-upholstered chair. Cy lurked at one of the porthole windows a minute longer and then sat in the chair beside her. He frowned at the liquor cabinet and switched seats to face her. Ingrid recalled how he said his father had fought the drink.

"Well! The race is under way." Mr. Roosevelt entered the parlor with the vivaciousness of a child coming home from school. Ingrid and Cy stood, and they all sat down again at the same time. "We'll see if we can catch this Sprite of yours."

Ingrid heard voices and footsteps in the hallway. Privacy was impossible here.

"I'm curious," said Cy. "You don't normally see a Pegasus gunship remodeled to look like . . . a pleasure boat, but surely the armaments haven't been completely removed?"

"Certainly not. As an ambassador, I must have a conveyance that serves both social and defensive purposes. Augustinian does masterful work." Cy showed no reaction to the mention of his father's company. "Now, Miss Carmichael, I must know the truth of the events in San Francisco this week. Truth untainted by a fox spirit's oversight."

As Ingrid spoke, she kept an eye on Cy, waiting for him to make a sign that she was saying too much. He remained quiet for the most part, his posture attentive. Ingrid explained what happened at the Cordilleran Auxiliary, how Mr. Thornton had feigned illness and exited before the explosion ripped apart the building and killed all the wardens, students, and staff but for her and Mr. Sakaguchi. Mr. Roosevelt accepted her creation of an energy-shield bubble with a thoughtful nod.

He was much more intrigued by the news of the massive chunk of kermanite that had been stolen by the Thuggees. His eyes gleamed behind his spectacles. "Aha! In this I can outwit Miss Blum. Now I know the very place from which it departed the Bay Area, and the sort of vehicle required. The crystal would almost certainly be aboard a train in order to move any great distance."

"If the kermanite is recovered, what happens next?" asked Cy.

"Abram Carmichael couldn't have filled kermanite of that size, not even in a quake of that magnitude. Certainly, the size of the tremblor indicates that he wasn't in constant contact with the rock or he would have died. I would guess that he was unconscious, likely drugged." He glanced between them. "The Gaia Project, as you are aware, has been under way for many months now, long before this single chunk of kermanite was recovered. It'll prove very useful, certainly, but a new engineer on the project found a way to chain together other unusually large pieces of kermanite. When your father was in China, Miss Carmichael, he worked to fill those other rocks."

"How big were they, sir?" she asked.

"The size of that laundry bag of yours, though not of that shape, of course." Kermanite tended to fragment into finger-sized or smaller pieces, so that bulk was indeed unusual.

Cy frowned, his fingers steepled against his mouth. "Which leads to the mystery overhanging all of this, Mr. Roosevelt. What single device needs that sort of power? What is the Gaia Project actually creating?"

"It won't be a secret for much longer, so I shall tell you—"

"Why?" interrupted Ingrid. His forthrightness set her ill at ease. "Why tell us so much?"

At that, Mr. Roosevelt granted her one of his trademark grins, his teeth boldly white and broad in contrast to his dark mustache. "A sensible question. I am telling you as a sign of respect and trust. I know you, Miss Carmichael. I've watched you grow into a young woman, and I know that you're *more* than a woman. More than most men, too. You are . . . uniquely qualified."

"Am I like a Marine to you, sir? A force to be . . . deployed?"

"In a sense, yes, though you're of a covert nature. Anyone looking at you sees a mere servant, a secretary, and yet you're highly educated, intelligent, and a geomancer of profound skill. Most soldiers are akin to bludgeons; you're a scalpel, Miss Carmichael. You can cut where others cannot."

Damn it. Roosevelt was no better than Blum, really. To him, Ingrid simply served a different function.

"And you, Mr. Jennings. I didn't know you from Adam before today. Are you the bludgeon to guard the scalpel?" He laughed. Ingrid shot Cy a worried look, but he looked thoughtful. "As I said, it won't be a secret much longer, but if some anonymous tip were to arrive at the offices of the newspapers in Seattle, I could be fairly sure of the source."

"So telling us is also a test," Ingrid said softly.

Mr. Roosevelt acknowledged this with a dip of his head. "With that said, I will inform you that the Gaia Project is creating a flying citadel. The likes of which has never been seen before. It will be shielded and armed, and transport a full ten thousand soldiers while flying at the speed of a Behemoth-class airship." Delight shone in his eyes, even as Cy shrank back in his seat. "It's being built in Atlanta as we speak."

"Ten thousand! That means that many deaths if the citadel crashes, not to mention the damage such a device could cause to the ground." Cy looked physically ill.

"If this is Ambassador Blum's pet project, shouldn't it be *stopped*?" asked Ingrid.

"Certainly, Miss Blum has orchestrated it. She wants the citadel overseas to finalize matters in China and to quell the encroachment of both Britannia and Russia. She intends for this citadel to be used specifically for the benefit of Japan." His face reddened as he scowled.

Of course Roosevelt wanted this magnificent weapon to stay in America. Ingrid didn't need to ask Cy what he thought of the matter. He was certainly opposed to the citadel's very existence. Mr. Sakaguchi would feel the same.

Ingrid wasn't sure how to feel. If it could be used for America's defense, that would be the better option, but who was most likely to conduct a widespread attack on American soil now?

The Chinese.

Who would make an ideal figurehead for such an effort, if he was still alive?

Lee.

"Pardon me. I think I need something to eat and drink," she said as she stood. Mr. Roosevelt and Cy immediately stood as well. She masked a grimace at both the pain in her arm and the quivering in her legs. A tiny fever lingered in her veins, too. Maybe only about ninety-nine degrees, but that was enough to worsen her fatigue.

She could use kermanite to drain the energy away. It's what Cy would want. She just couldn't make herself reach into her pocket. Some power was better than none, consequences be damned.

"Can I help, Miss Ingrid?" Cy asked. He phrased the question casually enough, but she knew he was worried about her.

"I'm fine. The kitchenette is across the hallway. You men continue your conversation, please."

Two guards stood in the hallway, Siegfried and another man. She murmured greetings to them as she passed.

The kitchenette's food stores sat in contained boxes and trays like on the *Bug,* but here they also stocked fresh fruit. She grabbed two oranges and a box of rye crackers. She stood by the window as she spiraled the peels from the oranges and scarfed down the fruit in minutes, then followed it with the crackers.

She wasn't satiated, but the snack would have to suffice for now. Roosevelt said the staff would serve up a basic supper in the evening; they wouldn't dock in Seattle until sometime during the night.

Ingrid wondered what damage had really been done to her body back in San Francisco. By holding magic as she did right now, how much was she setting back her recovery?

Mr. Roosevelt and Cy had said very little since she stepped aside. The guards murmured among themselves. Everything seemed peaceful. But still something caused Ingrid's attention to jerk to the porthole window. Something felt *wrong.* She rubbed at her ears as if bothered by a sudden pressure change.

The scenery below looked much like that of southern Oregon. Trees, mountains, and scattered little lakes that reminded her of Miss Rossi's awful grave. Ingrid breathed in, focusing. This peculiar sensation wasn't like the magic of the earth. She was reminded of being in proximity to selkies in the ocean, of how their distinct power needled her skin and made her tongue taste brine.

She didn't taste anything remotely like the ocean up on high in the *Bucephalus,* though. Instead, she heard a sudden, sharp whistle of wind, though no breeze stirred the cabin.

She dashed to the parlor. “Cy, Mr. Roosevelt, something is—”

Klaxons began to blare, the sound aggravating the increasing ache within her ears. The vessel tilted, sending Ingrid stumbling forward. Cy stood up in time to catch her as his back met with the wall.

“Sir!” The tinny voice came from a speaker above. “We’re under attack from a thunderbird, a sizable one, we may not be able to evade—”

The ship rocked again, this time sending Ingrid backward into Cy’s former chair. Cy landed over her, his body braced on the chair arms. Mr. Roosevelt waited a few seconds for the ship to stabilize then rushed away. The airship rumbled again. Ingrid felt momentarily weightless as the ship dropped in elevation, her stomach slow to catch up to the rest of her body. She put a hand to Cy’s shoulder. Barely any power thrummed in her body, but if the ship was going down, she’d pull whatever energy she could to form a bubble and keep them both alive.

Foreign emotions flickered through Ingrid’s consciousness, the sensation of powerful wings like a ghost in her mind. “The thunderbird is angry,” she whispered.

CHAPTER 9

Klaxons continued to blare throughout the opulent airship. The vessel swayed to and fro, dropped in elevation again, then surged up. Ingrid's stomach didn't know quite which way to go.

"Guests, please restrain yourselves until advised otherwise," said the voice over the speaker. The man sounded impressively cool-headed considering that they were being attacked by a massive, legendary bird.

"Cy, do thunderbirds usually—"

"Sometimes they attack like this, especially in spring. I'm going to the cabin. I might be able to help."

"Do you think that perhaps my magic . . . Maybe the bird senses me here, as if I'm invading its territory." She didn't want to say much more. She doubted anyone was eavesdropping in the thick of an attack, but still.

His brow furrowed. "Like with the selkies? I don't know,

and now's not the time to dwell on it." He walked away with a wide stride and caught himself on the doorway as the *Bucephalus* lurched.

"Cy, I need to stay close, just in case."

He opened his mouth as if to argue then granted her a small nod. Ingrid followed him into the hall. After a few unsteady steps, she dropped to her knees and crawled. Her shoulder cracked against a doorway.

"Good thing I'm not on the ground," she muttered to herself, wincing. They had better not be on the ground anytime soon either. This Pegasus class with its tapered gondola wouldn't meet the dirt with any sort of grace.

The ship shook violently and she swore she heard the booms of a storm. That didn't make a lick of sense—the skies had been clear when she looked out the window minutes before. Ignoring the pain in her shoulder and arm, she crawled to the control cabin.

Ingrid recognized the back of Mr. Roosevelt's head in a central chair. Beyond him, the curved cabin window stretched from waist height to the ceiling and granted an extraordinary yet awful view. Clouds boiled around them, the world rendered an impenetrable gray. Thunder cracked and caused the airship to shudder.

"Two points abaft the beam, starboard side," called a man. Two more crewmen echoed the statement. To Ingrid's surprise, she heard the patter of gunfire. She crawled to just inside the cabin. The craft bulged out to either side, like the eyes of a frog, each side with a gunners' station. Cy was strapping himself into the one on the right side, while

Siegfried was already in the left. She'd seen such technology in newsreels but never in person.

It said a great deal about the seriousness of the situation for Cy to take a gun in hand.

She glanced back at the control cabin window in time to see a flash of gold and red in the mist ahead, an outstretched wing as large as the *Bucephalus*. She gasped as its rage blew into her like a tornado.

The crew continued to call out positions as the thunderbird circled them. A bolt of lightning seared her vision, the clap of thunder instantaneous and deafening. Gunfire drummed all around her. Roosevelt's shoulders moved in a way that revealed that he controlled a gun from his position in the center of the room.

"I believe it to be a *Brontoraptor occidentalis,*" said Mr. Roosevelt, "in contrast to the *maximus* found in southern climes. These in particular are known for their relentless pursuit of prey. There'll be no outflying this one, I fear."

Die. Die. Die.

The clear statement walloped Ingrid across the head as the thunderbird fully emerged from its nest of storms. She had seen Miss Rossi's black-and-white postcards of thunderbirds, but the images did the creatures no justice. The creature resembled a hawk or eagle, a magnificent bird of prey, with a curved golden beak and eyes as intense as the sun. Feathers were colored in a range of earth tones—gold, red, brown—each vivid and almost aglow. The thunderbird soared hundreds of yards away, yet its palpable presence created a sort of wind-tunnel sensation within her head.

She could see why the thunderbird was venerated among the native tribes of Cascadia. This wasn't simply a magical creature. It was . . . raw majesty. Something ancient and incomprehensible.

The broad wings flapped, and lightning cracked again. The ship dipped. Ingrid's hands and knees remained suspended in air for one second, two, then she smacked the floor with a soft grunt. Blue sky was visible for all of an instant and then the clouds coiled around them anew.

The thunderbird cried. It was a sound terrible and sad, gripping her emotions like the plaintive wail of bagpipes. If the others felt it so poignantly, she couldn't tell. The crew's full concentration was on getting them out alive.

Maybe the thunderbird could get out of this alive, too.

Ingrid crawled down the short side passage to Cy. There were no straps to secure herself, so she shamelessly wrapped her body around his right leg, her own legs braced against the orichalcum plating of the lower wall.

"It's angry. It knows humans are on board and it wants us to die," she said.

Cy cocked his head toward her; he had donned a leather cap with thick padding over the ears. Thunder crackled from the starboard side as the crew called out more positions. "Are you able to talk with it?" Gunfire pattered.

"I'm about to try. I keep getting flashes of emotion, but I don't think it's *trying* to speak with me. Its rage is carried by its power, like a leaf on a breeze."

Brown and gold flashed through the clouds. Cy fired his gun. She cringed at the loudness and pressed her forehead against his knee. Closing her eyes, she breathed in and out as if in meditation, and let her awareness expand beyond the ship. Her sense of terror dissipated, replaced by the emptiness of Zen. *Mu*. Nothingness. She made herself a hollow vessel, one receptive to whatever came.

The thunderbird's might buffeted against her; its very magic, its essence, rivaled hers. Ingrid didn't let the horrible pressure dissuade her. She breathed and tried to ignore the eerie roar in her ears, the stench of ozone strong.

Stop, she thought at it, and imagined a sapling utterly still, a wide river unmoving.

Rage lashed her. Emotion thrummed along the length of every feather. *Die, die, die.*

Ingrid repeated the imagery. The anger faded, only a touch, tinted by a sense of surprise. The thunderbird hadn't known that Ingrid, a representative of earth's magic, was there in its realm. Damn it—would its awareness of her presence provoke an even more violent attack?

She imagined a full view of herself, her hands faced outward in a universal gesture of helplessness. She meant no harm.

A feeling that she could only describe as *indignant* flashed at her. She saw a high mountain peak. A nest formed of whole trees, dried and uprooted and woven together like a basket. In the middle: a broken egg leaking fluid. Dips in the nest marked the places where other eggs had been.

GONE. Grief lashed Ingrid like a hurricane-force wind. The nest still stank of humans; the thunderbird would kill humans. She didn't differentiate between one person and another.

"People stole her eggs," she said aloud to Cy. Her voice sounded far away, maybe because her spirit was far from its home.

Ingrid reminded herself that this was still a bird, revered and ancient as it was. Like the two-headed snake, this mother wasn't sentient in a human way.

She presented the image of herself again, her hands empty. She didn't take the eggs. She didn't know where they were. She let her own sense of grief creep into her power, let it say that she knew about the loss of home, of family. That she was sorry.

GONE. Rage blasted into the silence. The thunderbird didn't care that Ingrid didn't have the eggs. To this bird, the loss of the eggs was a fait accompli, her hatchlings dead. More images flickered by, showing spring and snow and a rotating swirl of stars to mark the passage of time, the nest empty through it all. The laying of eggs was a rare event. Blessed. Holy.

The ship trembled and bounced. Thunder crashed around them. Tears slid down Ingrid's cheeks as she shivered and pressed closer to Cy.

She imagined the thunderbird dying and spiraling to earth. She didn't hold back her reaction to that thought: intense sadness that the nest would now be completely empty. That the skies would be empty.

Her nose fiercely tingled from electricity, the pressure in

her head intensifying. A boom rocked the ship and popped her ears. Then nothing.

The prickling rage was gone.

The thunderbird was dead. Her absence left a sudden gaping hole in Ingrid's awareness of the world.

Ingrid felt numb as she untangled her limbs from around Cy's leg. He flung back the restraints on his lap and chest, and tossed aside the protective cap. The back of his hand touched her forehead. "Lord Almighty, you're like ice." With both hands, he stroked her face, his eyes searching hers. Far in the background, she heard whoops from the crew. The window before them revealed dissipating clouds and a painfully bright blue afternoon sky.

Ingrid leaned into Cy's touch. Bone-deep exhaustion weighed her down, but his presence both uplifted and grounded her.

"Talk to me. Are you in there?" Cy tilted up her chin.

"Mostly. I think." Her voice rasped, her throat parched as if her body had directly felt the magical vortex around the thunderbird. "The thunderbird is dead. I tried to get her to stop, but she was too angry. I couldn't . . . I couldn't make her understand." Grief swept through her again.

"Ingrid." His voice dropped to a whisper. "We can't let Roosevelt and the crew know about this particular skill of yours. Can you get up and walk?"

"You're right." Sheer grit and aggravation empowered her to rise to both feet. She leaned on the chair's back. "I'll be damned if I let them think I'm some lily-livered female in need of smelling salts after that."

A smile brightened Cy's face, even as worry lingered in his eyes. "Watch your pride, Ingrid. Better to let them underestimate you than for them to know what you're truly capable of."

"You. Jennings. Miss Carmichael." Siegfried's gruff voice carried down the short corridor. "Come on out of there. We need to bring in the guns."

Ingrid leaned on the wall to walk. She hoped that the recent turbulence affected some of the men, too, so that maybe her unsteadiness looked normal. As she reached the main corridor, she heard a mechanical whirring sound behind her. The gunner's nest had retracted about five feet into the ship to create only the slightest bulge. She couldn't see what happened to the gun but it must have folded away somehow; she hadn't noticed any exposed weapons when she viewed the ship from outside. Augustinian had outdone themselves with this ship design.

"Our position is noted? Excellent!" Mr. Roosevelt's high voice carried. "As soon as we land in Seattle, deploy the Sprite to return here and guard the thunderbird until the wagon arrives for the body—"

"Excuse me." Ingrid stalked into the control cabin. "Mr. Roosevelt, you're going after the thunderbird?"

She knew very well about his obsession with birds. Mr. Sakaguchi had several specimens that Roosevelt had shot and stuffed himself. The very idea that the thunderbird would become some . . . some . . . *ornament* caused hot anger to chase away the coldness in her skin.

Mr. Roosevelt turned to face her. He held his glasses in

his hand as he wiped his sweat-soaked face with a handkerchief. "Yes, as soon as is feasible. God forgive us for the necessity to kill a creature of such power and beauty! We should forget the eagle as the symbol of America and summon up the imagery of the thunderbird as tribes have done for centuries. They have the right of it." A fervent, patriotic gleam lit his eyes. "If other men find the bird's body, Miss Carmichael, it'll be dismembered, the feathers individually sold for fool's talismans, the meat peddled with the promise of eternal youth and divine power!" His voice rose along with his fist. "I won't have it! If a man were starving, yes, let him eat such a creature, but I won't see it carved up and used to steal away the funds of the desperate, like some poor medieval farmer buying the proclaimed bones of a saint."

Stunned, humbled, Ingrid felt her anger evaporate. "What will you do with it, then, sir?"

"Brontoraptor occidentalis," he said again, this time pronouncing the Latin like a benediction. "A new natural history museum is being built in Seattle. A creature of such glory will be preserved for all to appreciate."

Ingrid pictured the map of Cascadia she had viewed, time and again, in one of Mr. Sakaguchi's texts on Hidden Ones. "We're flying over the home of the Yakama tribe, correct? They lived with thunderbirds for a long time. Perhaps they would have some thoughts on the matter."

"Pagan thoughts," muttered one of the men. Another chortled.

"It's my understanding that most of them have been moved to work in canneries," said Roosevelt. He dismissed the suggestion with a wave of his hand as he turned to another man. "Make sure that the wagon team knows to . . ."

She recognized the light pressure of Cy's hand on her back. She let him guide her down the hall to the parlor. Her feet stumbled some, as did her thoughts. Roosevelt's contradictory nature infuriated her. Or it would have, if she weren't so blasted tired. She knew how he and Mr. Sakaguchi would argue sometimes, their voices piercing the ceiling to where she slept on the floor above. Oh, Ojisan. He would grieve for the thunderbird, too. He would understand, if he were here.

As Cy helped her to sit, she was reminded that she was still quite fortunate in her current companions. "My suggestion was reasonable, wasn't it?" She tried not to sound whiny. "And they laughed at it. Dismissed the idea out of hand."

"Of course it was reasonable, Ingrid. More than that, it was respectful." He drew the shades on the windows, creating cozy dimness. He moved stiffly, not willing to meet her gaze.

"Cy, what is it?"

"When I first went to the control cabin as the attack started, the crew was making note of fires down below. Large ones, newly started. They could've been started by lightning from the bird, or caused by other airships that the thunderbird downed."

"Oh." Ingrid sank deeper into the chair. "You mean, there's a chance that the thunderbird might have taken down the *Palmetto Bug*."

He was quiet for a moment, running his hand over his

jaw. "This is the heading it'd take if it was flying directly toward Seattle on the way to Baranov."

There had already been the risk of the airship going down elsewhere if Fenris were injured, if the thieves were inept, if a scuffle occurred on board. But this . . . Ingrid couldn't bear the thought, and not simply for what it'd mean for the fate of Mr. Sakaguchi and so many Chinese here and abroad. She couldn't imagine the world without Fenris's acerbic wit and miraculous mechanical feats, and Lee with his boundless curiosity and bright grins.

"There's no proof, Cy. We'll find them in Seattle. We must. We'll search every airship dock. You said you used to live there, right? You know your way around?"

"More or less."

"See? Roosevelt will drop us off and pretend he doesn't know us. We'll find Fenris and Lee. We can pass word along to Roosevelt that we found Lee, and figure out what we do from there. God willing, we'll find Mr. Sakaguchi in Seattle, too."

Cy sank into the chair across the way, his head in his hands. He stared at the window, silent.

Ingrid stood and made two tentative steps to reach his chair. He tilted up his face to meet hers. His bristled jaw scraped her tender skin as they kissed. This wasn't a passionate kiss, but one that affirmed her presence, her support. When they broke apart, she desperately wanted to say something inspired, something helpful, even though she knew she'd likely muck it up.

"I'm not a natural optimist, Cy," she said shakily, her

words slow. "Mr. Sakaguchi was always the one with aggravating good cheer in my family. I need you. I need you to help me stay uplifted during this fight. I need someone to be my hope in this awful world."

"I won't lie to you, Ingrid."

"I'm not asking you to lie to me. But you're not being honest with yourself either. There's no proof that they crashed here or anywhere else. We've all stayed alive so far amid ridiculous odds."

The look in his eyes changed. Ingrid kissed him again, this time drawing a soft moan from his throat. "That was a mighty fine St. Crispin's Day speech," he murmured.

"You said not a minute ago that you wouldn't lie to me, and now you compare my words to Shakespeare? Hyperbole on *that* scale is pretty close to a lie." She gave him a gentle kick in the shins.

"If any ship could outrun a thunderbird, it'd be the *Bug*." Cy nodded, more like his old self. "I'm sorry to vex you like that. These recent days have been as pleasant as chugging castor oil." He motioned her back. "You rest up. I can bring you some food."

Ingrid wasn't about to argue with that. "Food sounds divine." She really needed to warm up, too. She'd obviously used up her stored earth power and started to pull from her own body's energy again. She'd likely suffer for that tomorrow, and for days to come.

The damage wouldn't be permanent, though. She was young and strong. Given some time to recuperate, she'd bounce back. Cy was fussing for nothing.

Ingrid sat back in her chair, considered propriety for a moment, then slipped off her shoes. She tucked her knees up close. Apparently she hadn't masked her shivers very well, as Cy grabbed a blanket from a rack and tucked it around her. He started to rummage in the food pantry. Roosevelt and the rest of the crew were busy for now. This was a good chance to rest, if she could.

"Lee and Fenris are alive and we'll find them," she murmured to herself. She almost believed it.

CHAPTER 10

SUNDAY, APRIL 22, 1906

There was no miasma or sign of agitation in the earth of Seattle, but the potential for disaster was visible, gorgeous, and unnerving.

Ingrid had seen many photographs of Mount Rainier over the years. Most any geomancy textbook featured an image or two. For a time, when she was young, she confused it with Mount Fuji in Japan. Both mountains dominated skylines above their cities. Mr. Sakaguchi had told her back then that the cities themselves were quite different. "If you're confused, look to the roofs," he said.

That advice would be ineffectual now. After recent fires, Seattle had been built anew. From her vantage point near the top of Queen Anne Hill, in one of Mr. Roosevelt's sitting rooms, the city looked distinctly Japanese with many curved, red-tiled roofs peppering a landscape abundant in trees and greenery. Beyond it all, Mount Rainier loomed, a giant with a thick white cap of snow.

"It's quite a sight, isn't it?" murmured Cy as he stepped alongside her. Coffee steam curled into his face. He breathed it in with a delighted sigh. Ingrid would never understand how he could willingly tolerate the stuff. For her, it would forever be a drink of desperation.

"I knew it was big but it's so . . . *much*."

"The shift of engine noise caused me to wake up as we approached the city last night. All that snow up there glowed, even with it being a new moon." He sipped from his mug.

The *Bucephalus* had docked at around three in the morning. Ingrid had roused long enough to stagger down the private mooring mast and into a house lit by low electric lights. She had a vague memory of Cy telling her he was sleeping in the room next door and to give the wall a good thump if she needed him, but then she fell into a glorious bed and remembered nothing more until the sun woke her.

The more that magic physically depleted her, the more her body acted like that of a somnolent teenage boy.

Not only was it damned annoying, but it was foolhardy. She needed to be alert. Her wits had been as thick as a straw-tick mattress last night. Blum herself could have stood in the doorway and Ingrid would have moved as swiftly as a tortoise.

Cy set down his coffee long enough to fill a plate from the small private breakfast spread a maid had set up in the rather sterile sitting room. Ingrid guessed that they'd been bunked in an empty servants' wing of the household. Only one maid had interacted with them, which Ingrid found comforting. The fewer people who saw them here, the better.

Cy piled up three biscuits, each already split and bleeding butter, and a thick cut of ham. A banana—a sign of luxury as sure as gold—curved like a smile on one side of the plate.

"What's the full story on Mount Rainier's Hidden One?" he asked as he began to eat.

"This mountain is home to a powerful spirit originally called Tacoma. That was the name for the mountain itself, too, until . . . well." She summarized the ways of white settlement with a tired shrug. "Tales say that tribes wouldn't travel above the snow line. There was said to be a lake of fire up there, and intruders weren't welcome. Tacoma only wished to see family." She drank from her cup of green tea and eyed the ham on Cy's plate. She'd already eaten, but the slab of meat still looked tempting. "Maybe when I have my own house someday, I should get a lake of fire to keep people away."

"I don't think it'd work. Get a lake of fire, and soon enough you'll have salesmen coming around offering new and improved lakes of fire."

"True." She snorted and looked out on Seattle. Was Tacoma some kind of relation to her? The idea was strange, yet the more she thought of Pele as her grandmother, the more the idea felt *right*. Ingrid had known from her earliest years that Mama and Mr. Sakaguchi loved her, and yet she had never known quite how to view herself in relation to them. She was set apart by her skin, the texture of her hair, the way she channeled energy. She never fit in; that's why she used to joke that she was like a fantastic. Now that had turned out to be the truth, though the divine aspect was difficult to comprehend or accept.

She pulled her gaze from the mountain to the city below. All she could hope was that it now housed Fenris and Lee, and maybe Mr. Sakaguchi, too.

Someone knocked on the door. Before either she or Cy could turn, it opened to admit Mr. Roosevelt. He was neatly attired in a pin-striped brown suit. "Please continue to eat and drink. I cannot stay for long; I'm due at the Rainier Club on the half hour. I hope everything in my household has met with your approval?"

Ingrid and Cy murmured gratitude as Mr. Roosevelt joined them at the window.

"I will pursue the stolen kermanite," he said without preamble. "I still would like to know how Abram Carmichael went from presumed dead in Unified Pacific custody in China to Thuggee hands in San Francisco. There are rumors of alliances between Chinese and Indian rebels, but if the Chinese knew what Mr. Carmichael could do, I don't see him being handed away."

"That assumes the exchange was a willing one," Ingrid pointed out. Her father had been a cruel and unpleasant man, but he hadn't deserved to be tortured and passed around like that.

"True. Political alliances these days resemble hungry

dogs gathered at a food dish. A single snap, a growl, and suddenly good playmates are in a deadly melee." He began to pace, his motion causing the sheer curtains to sway. "If you cannot find Lee Fong, send a message to my house here. Say the fire has gone out. Find him, say the opposite." He pulled a thick envelope from inside his jacket. "You trust this man with your life?" He looked between Ingrid and Cy.

"I meant what I said before. I wouldn't have survived the earthquake without him."

"If I find out her trust is misplaced, I'll attend to you personally, Mr. Jennings." Mr. Roosevelt handed the envelope to Cy. Ingrid grimaced. *Of course* Mr. Roosevelt passed it to the only man present. "Here are addresses. No context included. If you must get hold of me elsewhere in the country, visit these places, or write them. The people are mine. They will contact me and will also supply you with money, within reason. I must leave here for San Francisco later today. The refugee crisis is being handled by fool mugwumps."

Cy opened and shut his mouth. Ingrid's heart ached. She knew that he desperately wanted to ask after his father.

"What about Ambassador Blum, sir?" she asked.

At that, Mr. Roosevelt sighed. "You're prey to her, young Miss Carmichael. Even more, you're a fellow member of the fair sex, a woman of power at a disadvantage in a man's world. She often mourns the lack of women like her. I'm afraid for you. I'm afraid that her respect for you will bring you all the more woe."

Ingrid compressed her lips. Roosevelt's respect for her

invited different sorts of woe, not that he could see that. Still, he was far preferable to Blum.

"I will discreetly help you however I can," Roosevelt continued. "I am firmly of the belief that you should not be abused as your father was."

Cy angled his body forward. "Pardon me, sir, but what would you see happen with Miss Carmichael?"

Mr. Roosevelt considered Cy for a moment. "I would see her in a place where her pain couldn't provoke the earth, but where she might know contemplation, happiness, and a sense of worth."

The answer felt almost too . . . politically pretty. Like something intended to please Mr. Sakaguchi. Cy accepted it with a neutral expression and a tiny nod.

"I don't intend to go down without a fight," said Ingrid.

"Which leads us to another matter, that of my dear friend Nobuo." Mr. Roosevelt looked between Ingrid and Cy, his knuckles rapping on a side table. "If I can unravel this Thuggee conspiracy, we can remove the perception of guilt that has tarnished his reputation since the auxiliary explosion. You mentioned before that Lee intends to use himself to negotiate for Mr. Sakaguchi's release. I mulled this matter over for some time. Lee cannot carry through with this plot." Roosevelt raised a hand to request silence. "Lee Fong cannot go to the Chinese now. His people are in full diaspora since San Francisco, and they are militarizing. If he were placed in any leadership role now, that would harm his reputation later on, when, if all goes well, he will step forward as a diplomat."

"I beg your pardon, sir, but the Chinese are militarizing because they're being butchered for simply *existing.*" Ingrid was increasingly irritated by Roosevelt's idea of "help."

"Do you *want* Lee to have a gun shoved in his hands, for him to open fire on American people?" Mr. Roosevelt's face reddened.

"Lee *is* American. He was born here, same as you or me." She levelly met his gaze. "I don't want him being put in that position either, but what do you expect him to do? Go off with me to this hypothetical seismically dead place to keep me company while I experience contemplation and happiness? As if we'll be happy with the knowledge that we've abandoned Mr. Sakaguchi to die. You know that's what will happen. The Chinese are fighting to survive. They can't drag around a useless Japanese geomancer indefinitely. They'll kill him."

"Mr. Sakaguchi would not want Lee to risk himself this way. Lee must be the higher priority here."

"I do appreciate the help you've offered, for getting us to Seattle, but you're asking an awful lot of us while you stay in the shadows," Ingrid said softly.

"I ask a great deal of you because of your unique capabilities." He looked at Ingrid, not Cy, as he spoke. "You have proven yourself competent and you keep America's interests in mind. I cannot send soldiers in pursuit of Lee, not without provoking undesired questions and escalating tensions with the Chinese."

"That is true," Cy added. "But there are still inherent

risks with putting Ingrid in places where she might be hurt. I'll do whatever I can to keep her safe, but I can only do so much." His words carried his frustration.

"Do you want me to place guards on Miss Carmichael?" Mr. Roosevelt shook his head. "Would that encourage Lee Fong to come with you? Would that truly make you feel *safer*?"

"No," Ingrid said in a small voice. "I wouldn't trust them." *Nor am I sure I can trust you,* she thought.

"Do what you can to find Lee Fong while keeping yourself safe, and then immediately retreat from the public eye and let me know of your whereabouts. Your coloration sets you apart, and Miss Blum will have agents in search of you."

"I'm fairly well aware of my coloration and how I stand out at this point in my life, Mr. Roosevelt."

To her surprise, he leaned down to give her an avuncular kiss on the cheek. "You're a credit to your dear departed mother and to your adoptive father, Miss Carmichael. Stay the course! I'll depart the household. Wait awhile longer, then exit through the alley. Mary will show you." He briefly clasped Cy's hand. "Godspeed." With that, he left.

With Roosevelt gone, the room felt empty, quiet. Ingrid nudged the faithful laundry bag with her foot. "Discreet help is better than no help, but damn it, why must everything be so complicated? Abandoning Mr. Sakaguchi . . ." She shook her head, tears in her eyes.

"Don't think ahead that much. We need to find Lee and Fenris first, or we have no way to negotiate for Mr. Sakaguchi at all." Cy ran his hand through his hair. "Seattle's grown in the past few years. We have a lot of ground to cover."

"We'll find them, Cy."

He nodded. The affirmation didn't reach his eyes.

The pleasant weather Ingrid admired from the window had shifted to a chilly drizzle by the time they departed. The housekeeper, Mary, supplied them with lunch for later and an old hardback luggage case to replace the conspicuous laundry bag.

"I suppose Fenris and Lee will be happy to see us for the laundry alone," she said. "I hope they appreciate the effort we're going through to make the delivery."

"Fenris doesn't notice if anything is stained or dirty. He'd live in the same clothes for a year and a day, if he could."

"If I could have asked for anything more at the house this morning, it would have been a bath, but that can wait. I don't mind stinking if we can find Fenris and Lee all the faster."

"Maybe that can still work out today. The idea of a bath appeals to me as well." He said it innocently enough, but Ingrid gave him a little side eye as they rode the Counterbalance down the steep slope of Queen Anne Hill toward downtown.

The mechanism was ingenious: in order for the electric cars to safely go up and down the hill, at either end of the ride the attendant would hook up the car to a sixteen-ton weight attached to the cable. That weight would travel in the opposite direction of the passenger car.

She was grateful that Cy had a pleasant distraction for a few minutes. He had obviously been on the electric cars before but he still took in the device with a boyish smile as they clanked downhill.

Downtown featured signs in both English and Japanese. Considering the niceness of the area, the streets smelled foul and there was a surprising amount of garbage about. As Ingrid and Cy worked their way closer to the largest ports at Elliott Bay, the pedestrian demographics shifted to the less affluent and more white. Other women of color were about town, too. Many carried baskets of groceries for themselves or employers. White women and children wore their Sunday best as they whirred past in rickshaws pulled by dark-skinned men.

With a start, Ingrid realized they were wearing their Sunday best because it was *Sunday*. She stopped and leaned against a brick building. Rain droplets pattered on the back of her hood.

"Ingrid?" Cy quietly asked. "Is it a . . . ?"

"No. Not a seism," she whispered. "It just struck me that it's Sunday. It's been a week since the auxiliary, since all this started. It feels like a lifetime."

"Probably because if you were a cat, you would have burned through a life or three. We're almost to one of the larger docks in the area. You'll get a chance to rest while I make queries."

Trash was decomposing in the gutters. She covered her mouth and fought the urge to gag as they walked along one particularly foul block. Other people wore cloth masks over their faces.

"I wonder why the garbage hasn't been picked up," Cy muttered.

The tall spires of the airship dock emerged from behind the buildings. As Ingrid and Cy approached, the noise of the engines escalated like the buzz of a million confined bees. This dock featured only small-class airships; the massive port for freight haulers and troop transports was down the way.

Signs lined the fence around a large, sturdy gate. Some of the words wept inky trails from the rain.

BARANOV TRANSIT. SIGN UP HERE.

RECRUITING MEN FOR BARANOV! STRONG AND YOUNG!

YUKON NEEDS WOMEN—GOOD PAY.

AIRSHIPS NEED CREWS! OTHER MEN RAN OFF AFTER GOLD! SEEKING MEN FOR CONTINENTAL ROUTES . . .

Cy bent his head close to hers. "Follow me closely and don't make eye contact, if you can help it."

"I'm no fool. I can imagine what sorts of jobs for women net good pay up in Baranov."

Cy arched an eyebrow at her as he moved toward a knot of men. Ingrid hung back a few feet and scrutinized the board.

"Oh, you poor dear." Ingrid felt a light touch at her elbow. An old woman had shuffled beside her, her skin frail white. Her attire consisted of a corseted, bustled modified kimono paired with a broad straw hat. Massive silk flowers on the brim had gone limp in the rain. "I can't help you with the Japanese—I'm old like that—but I can read the English for you."

She looked to see where Ingrid might have been gazing last. "If you're wanting passage to Baranov, look for this letter here." She traced a large-painted *B* with a gloved finger and the following letters as well. "It's a tough life up there, though. Dragons, they say, and bears." She shuddered. "Men up there could certainly use the influence of more good, Christian women. You're of faith, aren't you, dear? Have you known missionaries?"

Ingrid ground her teeth together. "I was born in America, ma'am, I—"

"Were you? How wonderful! Bless your heart. So many are turning Buddhist these days." She patted Ingrid's elbow again. "Well, remember to look for those letters. I'm glad I was able to help." At that, she shuffled away again.

Ingrid stared after her, flushed and frustrated. She knew from experience that it wasn't worth the effort to correct the woman's misperceptions. Straight-out bigots were often easier to deal with than well-meaning idiots. The woman would certainly be pleased with herself the rest of the day because of her good deed.

She stepped closer to Cy as he talked to man after man and explained the tale of his stolen airship. All agreed that, of course, the overwhelmed local authorities couldn't be trusted to track down the lost ship, but no one present had sighted a modified Sprite like the *Bug*.

Some men close by looked to be police, but a sly inspection

of their colorful badges revealed that they were militiamen who were also affiliated with local lumber unions. Ingrid sidled away. Labor unions actively agitated citizens to act aggressively against the Chinese or anyone else who could be construed as a job-thieving foreigner. She'd endured harassment from their ilk in San Francisco a time or two.

It didn't take long for Cy to get them access to the port. The news of gold had brought a wave of airship thefts here, too, but it seemed this port had been readier to defend itself. Only confirmed owners and passengers were being allowed inside.

Cy walked the long pavement beneath the airships. It took mere minutes to confirm that the *Bug* wasn't present.

"On to the next," he said to Ingrid, making an effort to not sound as bleak as the weather.

They took another electric car line south to a more industrial area. This port looked to hold only about ten masts. Ingrid was perplexed. "I'm surprised airship docks are so scattered around the city. In San Francisco, that wasn't allowed. Too much risk of crashes and explosions."

"That risk is very present here as well, certainly, but docks exist where they are because of how fast the city's grown over the past ten years. There was no cohesive city plan when it started out. When I was here last, they were excavating all of Denny Hill and using that dirt to infill marshy areas in Elliott Bay."

"They moved an entire *hill*? One the size of these other hills around?"

"Not as big as Queen Anne, but it was quite an effort.

Anytime there's a fire, the city rebuilds and shuffles things around. Give it another few years, and all these parcel docks on hilltops and industrial neighborhoods will be pushed toward the fringes of the city."

Haphazard barriers reinforced the dock's gate. Yet again, entrepreneurs were lurking here to take advantage of those wanting to fly north. A large group of men negotiated to earn their transit to Baranov as indentured servants.

Ingrid lurked behind Cy and listened, wary, as she kept her eyes cast downward. Folks had been complaining about the inadequate rickshaw transportation in downtown since Seattle's Chinatown had been locked down on Tuesday. It turned out that the whole district was blockaded, no one going in or out. Laundries were shut down, clothes locked away. Garbage hadn't been picked up in almost a week; well, that explained the refuse. Other woes were aplenty: houses were going uncleaned, children were without their nannies, factories without cheap labor.

It boggled her mind. She'd been jesting in Portland when she said civilization would collapse without Chinese labor. In Seattle, the joke had become reality.

Cy was finally able to penetrate the conversation long enough to talk to the man in charge and ascertain that no Sprites were moored inside.

"Those small ships are what thieves want. Not these big 'uns that need a large crew and more know-how." He gestured over his shoulder as he chewed tobacco. "Had some thieves land here earlier, too. Drunk as skunks. We had fun dragging them in to the station house." His grin showed brown teeth. "We provided some justice of our own."

"Good. I'm glad to hear of it. Much obliged for your time, sir," said Cy. He turned to Ingrid. "To the next port, then?" His hands were shoved deep in his coat pockets, his face drawn beneath his derby hat.

Another port, then another. Some Sprite classes were moored and under heavy security, but not the *Bug*. Cy accumulated lists of other possible moorages farther out: Bremerton, Everett, Tacoma. Maybe the thieves had pressed on to Bellingham right at the Canadian border. Maybe they opted for a different route entirely and followed the rain shadow of the Cascades. Maybe the ship crashed just out of Portland. Maybe the thieves already docked and departed. Maybe the thunderbird had downed it; word of the berserker bird the previous day had spread as well, though no one had confirmation whether it had taken down any airships.

Every "maybe" drove Cy deeper into his depressed shell.

Ingrid would have been equally dispirited, but her relentless hunger reminded her of lunch. Cy accepted the suggestion to take a break, though he obviously had no appetite. He bit into the cold chicken and biscuits packed by Roosevelt's maid and acted like he was chewing through sun-bleached newspaper, while Ingrid found the meal plain yet delicious.

They ate beside a street-side shrine. Such constructions had become more common in recent years around San Francisco as well. Rain dribbled on some of the stone idols. Ingrid noted the presence of several kitsune; foxes were said to carry messages to the kami Inari. Ingrid had trouble believing someone like Blum would ever be a mundane courier.

Cy seemed to barely notice where they were. He stared into the rain, likely envisioning the next dock and the next dead end. Ingrid realized that if she weren't here, Cy would rove like a machine. Not sleeping, not eating. Doing everything he could to find his dearest friend, the only family he kept when he left everything else behind.

"Cy. Cy." She tugged on his coat sleeve to get his attention. "Is there anywhere else they could have taken the *Bug* if they landed in Seattle?"

He stood with his angular nose in profile, his brown hair damp and curly at his neck. "I don't know. Fenris would still have to moor somewhere first and hire folks to lead the *Bug* under cover. We've been to all the closest docks. No one has said a thing."

"Maybe you're underestimating Fenris. He knows the *Bug* can't stay at a public dock, not with all this fuss about Baranov. He knows how to pay people to stay quiet. He's seen you do that plenty of times over the years, right? Lee will help, too. He may not know how to pilot an airship, but he was a jack-of-all-trades for Mr. Sakaguchi."

"You think someone might have lied to me about the *Bug*?"

"I hope someone has! I do! Because if they lie to you, maybe they'll lie to Blum's people if they nose around. It'll keep us all the safer. Trust in Fenris. Where would he go if he piloted?"

For a moment, Cy seemed to turn to stone like the nearby statues, but then he slowly nodded. "There's an old skating rink we once rented maybe a half mile away, back when we were starting to accumulate orichalcum for the *Bug*. It'd have enough space to house the ship, just barely."

"A half mile's nothing after all the walking we've done." She hooked his arm and dragged him into the dismal drizzle, the suitcase wheels smacking through a puddle at her heels. She hated lying about how weary she felt, but she wasn't about to idle somewhere while he searched on his own.

"Someone else might be renting the rink now. Or it mighta been torn down. It's not a bad neighborhood, and the place was quite the eyesore."

It grieved her to hear Cy sound so negative. She needed to summon up another St. Crispin's Day speech. "Maybe the rink's now being used to stable a blessing of unicorns. Maybe it holds a scale model of the whole city of Atlantis. I'm sick to death of maybes! This whole week has been a cesspool of maybes and suspicions." She stopped with a grimace. The spiel had certainly sounded more effective in her head.

Cy was quiet for another block. A few other pedestrians dashed along beneath black umbrellas, their chatter in Japanese.

"Maybe I'm in love with you," he said.

Ingrid's stride faltered but she didn't stop moving. "Maybe that maybe isn't so bad."

"Maybe I appreciate your company under the wide variety of unpleasantness we've been dealt this past week. You set a fine standard right away, pointing a gun at me and soon after offering to lend me my favorite book by Twain."

"Maybe I should become a librarian with a harsh policy on overdue books."

"Maybe that'd be a good side trade along with the geomancy."

"Maybe I love you, too," she said. "Because when you're deep in sorrow, it breaks my heart. I want to do anything I can to bring a smile to your face again."

Cy stopped walking. His hand rose, his thumb brushing her cheek. For a moment, she thought he might kiss her in public, for all of the world to see, but he remained still. His brown eyes smoldered with a combination of lust, love, and adoration. Despite the cold, dreary day, Ingrid felt inexplicably warm. She leaned into his touch, and his face creased in a smile.

"I reckon there aren't really any maybes in how we feel about each other," he said softly.

"I reckon not." Her voice was husky in a way quite unfamiliar to her ears.

With shy, giddy glances at each other, they continued their walk. They passed a small lot of airship mooring masts that they had already checked. The same ships hovered at the tops of the towers, their envelopes pale against the gray sky.

She felt Cy deflate again as he looked away. She squeezed his cold hand, and a tepid smile returned to his face. "We keep on going."

"Your company is the sun on a day like this, Ingrid."

They made a couple more turns onto a broad street with sparse trees and few electric lines. Tall Victorian-style houses flanked the way, which made the curved roof of the old rink stand out even more. The wide building was surrounded by a newfangled chain-link fence.

"How did you even find this place?" she asked.

"Would you believe that I have a fondness for roller-skating?"

Ingrid laughed, surprised. "Really?"

"Yes, indeed. I'm not much for sports overall. Baseball's a good way to fall asleep, and horse racing interests me if it's more about the horses than the money. Skating, I can do. It's science and grace all together. My academy had a team back in the day. I did fair to middling. I skated here when this place was still open years ago. Came back months later and found it was shut down and for rent. I made the call, and that was that. It worked well as a shop space."

"I've never been skating. Mama never would have let me do something that dangerous." Ingrid made a face. All those years Mama and Mr. Sakaguchi treated her like an invalid while they hid from her the true repercussions of her pain.

"Well, maybe one day soon I can wrap you in pillows and get skates on your feet, but right now . . ." Cy stopped before a broad gate bound in place by a hefty lock, which he examined in his hand. "This has been opened recently after staying locked for a while. Look at the scratch marks." Ingrid couldn't see much of anything. Cy stalked on, more spring in his step than he'd had in hours. Tired as she was, she had to scurry to catch up.

He stopped at another, smaller gate. He assessed the lock, squinting, then took a step back. He kicked, his heel striking the lock hard. The fence clanged and rattled as the lock dropped to the ground in several pieces. "This brand's cheap. Easy to break," he said, almost apologetic.

"That may be, but how'd you learn to do that?" Ingrid couldn't disguise her admiration.

"Practice. The past decade has taught me numerous skills." He opened the gate just wide enough to admit them through and pulled it to again. Puddles were scattered along the uneven brick pavement.

He didn't head for the broad double doors at the front but to the back, where a metal sign for EMPLOYEE DOOR had lost most of its letters to read YEE OOR instead.

Cy used the toe of a boot to point to the ground before the door. The bricks showed fresh crescent scrapes. Cy unholstered his Tesla rod and knocked on the door in a rat-tat-tat rhythm. The crystal tip on hollow metal sounded as loud as a war drum. He motioned Ingrid back and to one side while he stayed in a central place visible to the door's peephole. Ingrid tensed.

The door pushed open with a small screech of metal on bricks.

"Ing!" Lee cried as he flung himself at her. She caught him with both arms, the suitcase splashing into a puddle at her heels. He pressed his head to her shoulder as she hugged him tight, rocking in place. Lee was here. He was okay.

"Let's get out of the rain. Where's Fenris?" The horrible tension in Cy's voice was gone.

"Working on the airship, of course. How the hell did you get to Seattle?" asked Lee in return.

"Wasn't the *Bug* commandeered? How did you get past the thunderbird?" asked Ingrid. She grabbed hold of the case again and rolled it inside. Cy stared out into the bleary late-afternoon light to study the street for a moment before he shut and locked the door.

"I don't think we were followed," he said.

"What thunderbird?" asked Lee. Even spoken in a normal tone, the words echoed across the cavernous space.

Cy and Fenris's old warehouse in San Francisco had been crammed with all manner of metal detritus from customer orders and their own projects. This building had to be roughly the same square footage, and yet it was wide open, with the exception of a counter and enclosed office on the far side.

The *Palmetto Bug* dominated the open space like a lone thundercloud over high prairie. Cy was right in his estimate that it barely fit in the building. It had been anchored with the gondola about ten feet off the ground, with about the same clearance from the top of the envelope to the metal struts of the ceiling. Ladders flanked the airship at all sides, and other items were scattered around the base. Dim illumination shone down through skylights that looked to be smothered with debris.

"Well, I suppose it's good we'll hear if someone is coming," muttered Cy as he looked around. "I swear the echo's worse than it used to be. Maybe it's because more of us are here." They walked to the airship, where Fenris was lying on his belly as he worked on what looked to be a stub wing from the *Bug*. The orichalcum casing had been removed, revealing a jumble of wire innards.

Fenris's head tilted to take in their arrival. "What took you so damn long?"

"It's a long walk from Portland, in case you didn't realize. Next time don't leave us behind." Cy stood over him, arms crossed.

"I'll be sure to tell that to armed brigands the next time they take over my ship. 'Oh no! Don't leave yet. Cy and Ingrid decided to picnic during a riot. Again.' I'm sure they'll be sympathetic."

"Armed?" asked Cy.

"Are you hurt?" Ingrid asked. Fenris looked the same as always, his clothes stained, goggles permanently adhered to his head. Lee's clothes were soiled as well but he appeared fine. The last of his bruises from San Francisco had faded away.

"Is it story time?" Fenris sighed. "You never have good timing. Here, let me finish getting this wire in so I know where I left off."

"As if you'd forget," said Cy.

"I didn't say I'd forget, just that it needed finishing. There." Fenris pushed himself to sit upright, cross-legged. "I don't suppose you brought any food, did you?"

"Here." Ingrid unlatched the suitcase and tossed a shirt at Fenris. "Chew on that."

"Mother-of-pearl buttons. Delicious." He dropped it to one side.

With a huff, Ingrid snatched up the shirt and folded it again. "That is—was—clean. Show a little gratitude for your laundry delivery service. We've spent the past day in dread that you were both dead." Cy pulled over an old crate for her to sit on while he claimed another.

Lee dropped to the floor near Ingrid's legs, his eyes anxious as he studied her. "We were just as worried, you know. I wanted to fly back to Portland, but Fenris said we had to stay put or we'd end up chasing each other in circles."

"What happened at Swan Island?" Cy asked, his eyes on the stub wing and everything else about the airship. Even to Ingrid's untrained eye, it was obvious that the *Palmetto Bug* wasn't able to fly at this point. There'd be no quick exit from Seattle.

"We were both on board when we heard the fuss. I looked out the cabin window and saw men rush the ships nearest the entrance," said Lee. "One pilot tried to unmoor, but he was exposed at the top of the mast and he was shot. When I saw that, I yelled at Fenris that we needed to hide."

Fenris shrugged his slim shoulders. "That's what we did. I propped open one of the hydro tanks and we hopped in."

"While he complained the whole time that he'd have to scrub the whole thing later so that our filth didn't gum up the system," added Lee.

"And I did scrub it out first thing this morning. As I was saying, we hopped into the tank. The cold water stood about waist-high. Lee pulled the dome lid so that it looked shut on the corridor side but didn't suffocate us. A minute later, the brutes were on board."

"Four guys. An unlucky number—for them, anyway. They unmoored within a few minutes. We couldn't hear them talking in the cabin, but once the ship was under way, they started ransacking it."

"Ransacking?" Ingrid asked with a pang. "I have a pine box on board from Mr. Sakaguchi—"

"It's still there, Ing. Nothing's gone." The fact that Lee said this meant he had likely read the contents, too. Ingrid was all the more glad that she'd had the chance to talk with him in Portland. "They didn't care about letters. They wanted money, food, jewelry, anything valuable." His eyes gleamed. "That's when they found Mr. Thornton's scotch collection."

Fenris's grin was wicked. "For a brief time, they considered the value of selling those amber bottles, but in the end they decided it was prudent to taste test at least one."

"Dear God. I see where this is going." Cy groaned. "Don't tell me they pickled themselves."

"Why, of course they did!" Fenris cackled. "Men of that caliber are accustomed to watered-down swill from saloons. They discovered the majesty of fine imported whiskey! They discovered *culture*!"

"Soon followed by the discovery of liver poisoning?" Ingrid asked.

"Well," said Lee, "we have three sealed bottles left. Not that they drank all the rest. A good bit spilled."

"Three bottles left?" Her jaw dropped. "Only *three*?"

"The pilot partook as well," Cy stated.

"Of course the pilot partook. You don't expect him to abstain during such a cultural opportunity, do you?" said Fenris.

Lee leaned forward. "The pilot had the sense to set the *Bug* in a hover when they all decided it was time to go to the Land of Nod. We waited a little while, crawled out of the tank, tied them up, then dragged them onto the empty rack. These men were such good friends that they spent the rest of the ride retching all over each other." His eyes sparkled with mirth. "Mind you, I wasn't laughing when I cleaned up that area earlier, but it's hilarious in hindsight."

"What did you do once you landed?" asked Cy.

Fenris shrugged. "As soon as the stairs were down, I told the mast staff what happened. God's honest truth. They were delighted to haul those foul carcasses off the ship and to the nearest police precinct. The staff'd had similar thefts at their dock, so they enjoyed a chance to witness some comeuppance."

"We heard talk about drunken airship thieves, but I never would have connected the story to the *Palmetto Bug*." Cy shook his head. "That tale's going to become a bigger legend than those bicycle mechanics who pretended to make a flying machine powered without kermanite. I bet we'll hear it in every port from here to the Azores in the coming years."

Fenris didn't seem displeased. "See, Cy? I didn't do so badly without you, did I?"

Cy's grin was fond. "You did just fine."

"You never saw a thunderbird yesterday afternoon, then?" asked Ingrid.

"No. The erstwhile pilot decided to take a more scenic route toward the coast. I'm guessing we missed a bit of fun?" asked Fenris.

Cy croaked out a laugh and rubbed his face with both hands. "You might say that."

CHAPTER 11

Fenris resumed work on the wing as Cy and Ingrid told their adventure of the past day. Lee expressed disappointment at missing out on the thunderbird, which earned him a solid kick in the shins from Ingrid. As if Lee needed to be present during yet another near-death scrape!

Fenris confirmed that since leaving Portland, he had still not completed maintenance work on the *Palmetto Bug*. The stub wing wasn't running efficiently—perhaps due to a bird strike—which was why he was cleaning that out. Fortunately, this incident occurred on the approach to Seattle, so Fenris was at the rudder wheel and quickly brought the airship down.

"It's late on a Sunday, but the local docks are all busy, thanks to this Baranov business. I can make a run for parts. That'll give Fenris plenty to do overnight. I'll haul in some food and cleaning supplies as well." Cy stretched, his form long and lanky. "Whereas my plans for overnight involve sleep in an honest-to-goodness bed. That inn across the way was pleasant enough a few years back. I'll see if they have any vacancies."

"As glorious as that sounds, is it wise for us to be away from the airship overnight? We just reunited," said Ingrid.

"*I'm* not leaving my ship," said Fenris.

"I can rig up some alarms around the building as a precaution. We'd be close, Ingrid. Besides, trying to sleep while Fenris works is like trying to nap during a fairy reel, and this building gets bitter cold at night."

Lee stood, hands in his pockets. "I need to go into Seattle to look for Uncle Moon. I know I have to be careful, Ing, so you don't have to say it. But I'm going."

She bit her lip. She needed to talk to Lee in private.

"The mood out there's like the pressure before a boiler blows," said Cy. "Scuttlebutt at the docks said that Chinatown is walled off. We saw for ourselves that the streets are guarded by local police and some militia formed out of local union workers. You know how most of them regard the Chinese." Lee acknowledged this with a grim nod. Cy continued: "No Chinese are working or walking out in public. Any seen will be arrested for their own safety." Distaste twisted his face.

"I can play Japanese again, at least until I'm in Chinatown."

"But how will you even get in?" asked Ingrid. She crossed her arms and fought the urge to say more. The original goal of flying here had been to find Mr. Sakaguchi. She knew all along that would involve danger, but damn it, she had just been reunited with Lee. She wanted to keep him close and safe.

"Oh, trust me. There are ways. I've heard talk over the years about an underground to Seattle. The city burned and they built on top of the ruins. Besides, for a young and cocky Japanese man, there are reasons to sneak into Chinatown. Stupid reasons, sure, but at my age, that's to be expected."

"You're no fool, Lee, but that's a treacherous walk ahead of you." Cy extended a hand, and Lee firmly gripped it. "I'll be setting an alarm on the door here as a precaution. If no one answers at a knock, just wait around for us. Don't make Ingrid worry too much, you hear? And thanks for taking care of Fenris this past day."

Lee waved the words away. "Ah, he's a good sort. I'll see you later on."

Cy nodded to both of them and walked out. Not far away, Fenris worked on the stub wing and occasionally groused to himself. He'd rigged a sling and pulley from the ceiling to help him haul larger parts. The whole setup struck Ingrid as haphazard and it made her nervous to watch.

"It's actually kinda fun to go up there," Lee said, following her gaze to the ladder into the cabin. "It's anchored down to the floor in about a dozen spots, you see. The airship doesn't move around much."

"Much." She shook her head, a loose strand of hair lashing her cheek. "I think I prefer a standard mooring mast, thank you."

"You have no sense of adventure!" At that, they looked at each other and burst out laughing.

Fenris began to bang on metal. Loudly. Ingrid cringed. "Maybe we can find a quieter place to talk?"

"Sure. Over in the office." Lee picked up a kermanite lantern and turned it on as they entered the room at the far side of the rink.

Stark white walls reflected the blue-toned light of the lantern. A long wooden counter lined the wall just inside. Three wooden chairs looked as if they'd survived a vicious beaver attack. Ingrid gingerly sat down. The chair squawked a little but held her weight. Lee dropped into a chair to face her, his elbows on his thighs.

"Talk. I need to get out while there's still daylight."

Ingrid took in a deep breath. This close to Lee in a confined space, she could smell the vinegar that he'd used to clean the *Bug*. "Roosevelt knows who you are. That's why he was willing to drop everything and escort us to Seattle."

Lee absorbed this news with stoicism that surprised her. "You found me. Now what?"

"Roosevelt didn't think you should try to make contact with Uncle Moon or try to—"

"Like hell. What, every Chinese person I know is supposed to think I *died* in San Francisco? How is that supposed to help things?" Lee shook his head in disgust. "And we leave Mr. Sakaguchi with them, too? If he doesn't fill kermanite, they'll kill him. And if he fills kermanite, he's betraying everything he is. I once saw him light incense and pray after our autocar struck a *cat*."

"I know, I know. He's not going to help the Chinese. I don't agree with Roosevelt, but I hate the risk you're taking. Roosevelt considers you an . . . investment. He wants to keep you safe."

"Safe." Lee laughed bitterly. "Like how Portland and Seattle keep their Chinese safe? Lock them in jail, starve them, attack anyone who shows kindness? It's all for the good of the Unified Pacific, right?"

"I get the sense that Roosevelt would unravel the UP if he could. I've heard him and Mr. Sakaguchi discuss that often enough, the steady way that Japan has integrated itself into American society. It's a different method of invasion." She tilted her head to one side, frowning. "Roosevelt works for what he sees as the American cause. I think he views you as an ideal mediator for the Chinese people because you're American born, educated in a Japanese household. He just doesn't want you to be *too* Chinese."

"That sounds about right. Chinese, but not too Chinese." Lee rolled his eyes. "Mr. Sakaguchi often told me that I had to earn my destiny. I had to live up to the promise of the *qilin*'s presence."

"Lee, you were all of ten when you moved into our house. *Ten*." She couldn't disguise how appalled she was. "How could they ask you to be the representative of your people?"

"How could they not?" he retorted. "As if being ten meant that I was a child, that I was *innocent*. The nuns had me working the wash tubs ten hours a day when I was just four. I saw other children beaten and burned. I saw a man lynched when I was six. So yeah, when Uncle Moon told me that I was the son of Qixiang and I was destined to save the Chinese, I willingly took on that burden. I relished it. It meant that I could *do something,* not just wait for death to come because some angry stranger rode me down in the street or a master took a whip to me because I dared to touch his books. That maybe when I did die, it would serve a purpose."

Ingrid bowed her head, chastened. Lee sighed, his voice softening. "It's not as though you were given a choice either. Here you are, the woman geomancer who can talk to thunderbirds and selkies and who knows what else. We have different sorts of powers, different legacies, and we're caught up in a war. We have to fight in our own ways."

"Fight how?" The direction of this conversation was making her feel physically ill.

He suddenly looked much older than fifteen years. "Tactics are not that straightforward. The Chinese are at a disadvantage. We need to seize any opportunity we can, strike where the enemy is vulnerable. Somehow my people have to survive."

"My God. You're already planning to do exactly what Roosevelt doesn't want you to do. Who is the enemy to you, Lee? America, Japan . . . ?"

Lee maintained an even gaze on her. "The Chinese can't run forever as our numbers dwindle away to nothing. We have to make a stand."

"The Chinese are being blamed for San Francisco. Would you have attacked there, if you could?" She hated using the word "you" to talk about Lee like this, as if a line were being drawn between them. She hated that he wouldn't identify his enemies. That she might become his enemy, if she wasn't already.

"Ing, do you really want to discuss this?"

No! she wanted to shout. Instead, she stood and paced. Her legs were rubbery, but she needed to move. "I want to understand. I want . . . I want to always be your friend, Lee. I love you. You know that, right?" He nodded, his eyes glistening. "I hate that we're in this position, that this chaos has been engineered by people who moved us all like pawns. Mr. Roosevelt. Mr. Sakaguchi. Ambassador Blum in particular. She worked toward this war with China for *centuries*."

"Hatred of Blum is something we hold in common. You said you talked to Roosevelt about her. What did you learn?"

She explained about Blum's assumed age and might, her grudge against China, and the intention of the Gaia Project.

"A flying citadel. That would be fantastic if it wasn't intended to kill me." He drummed his fingers on the table. "Everything goes back to Blum. It's almost impressive, really, when you consider how women are treated in Japan. Things have improved there as more American influence has crept into society, but still."

Ingrid nodded. Mr. Sakaguchi said it had never sat well with him, even as a child, to see women treated as objects, good only for entertainment or caring for children. She wondered how a kitsune had conquered such an insurmountable cultural wall, but for Blum, that was likely all part of the fun.

Lee continued: "Things are awful enough here in the States. I know how *you're* treated a lot of the time."

"Yes." She thought of the old woman at the dock earlier, and suddenly was reminded of what Mrs. Stone said about Papa being from Hawaii. Natives of the vassal state islands suffered through a special sort of hell not unlike what the Chinese endured. Hawaiians were forbidden to speak or write in the native tongue. Many labored for whites or Japanese overlords on fruit and sugar plantations, or in other subservient roles.

Ingrid wasn't quite sure how to absorb this as part of her identity yet. In a way, it was easier to accept a possible connection to Pele because of their bond through geomancy. She couldn't relate to what Hawaiians endured on a daily basis. She'd been born in Oklahoma Territory to a mother who was blond and white, raised in San Francisco in a privileged Japanese household from age five. That place was her home; the bay fog ran in her veins as sure as blood.

Lee stood. "Ing, before I go—the *guandao.* It's in the pantry near your box of letters."

"I'm guessing you read them?" she asked, trying to reel in her wandering thoughts.

"I did. I had to distract myself somehow during the last part of the flight as those men retched. But listen. I had a lot of time to think about the *guandao.* The meaning of it. What it might mean going forward. I might not come back—"

"Don't talk like that!"

"Please, Ing. Let me finish." He took a deep breath. "I don't know what to expect in Seattle's Chinatown. I don't know which *tongs* are fighting for dominance here with these refugees coming in. I don't know if Uncle Moon is there with Mr. Sakaguchi. Even if Uncle *is* around, my task won't be easy. I'm trying to bargain for Mr. Sakaguchi using myself as the chip. That . . . that's not a very strong position to take. They'll already have me there. It's not as if you or Cy can do this, though. It's on me."

"Meaning, you walk in the door, they capture you, and there might not be a negotiation." Roosevelt had likely already understood that. "But 'capture' might be too strong a word. You want to be with them."

"It's where I belong."

"I guess you feel like traveling with us is too easy these days, huh?" Ingrid tried to keep her tone light, but she felt a piercing ache deep within her chest. "The Chinese are in constant peril, after all. Here, we just have the occasional riot or thunderbird attack."

"Aw, Ing."

She could beg him to stay. It might keep Lee there, for a while, but she didn't want to think what the guilt and confinement would do to him.

"No. No. I get that you need to be with them, that you need to support the Chinese in a direct way." She released a huff of breath. "It's just, even with everything we've endured this week, it's meant so much to have you here, to know you're okay. Pure selfishness on my part, I know, but you're my family." She blinked back tears, and his eyes looked moist as well. "When you go to Uncle Moon . . . what kind of reception will you get?"

Would Lee risk death, even walking in the door? It was a silly question, and she couldn't even give voice to it. These days, he risked death no matter what he did.

Lee sighed. "Uncle will be furious that I didn't leave San Francisco with them. Some of the others will be angry, too, for other reasons. Some hate me for being too American. Others think I'm a traitor because I respect Mr. Sakaguchi as my teacher. I'm not going to be greeted with hugs." He shrugged.

"No. That's an American response for sure." Her throat clenched with worry. "What about the *guandao,* Lee? Do you want to take it with you?"

Emotions flickered across his face. Longing. Sadness. Frustration. "I considered that, but no. Holding that piece of history, it was easy to think that it was found because of *me.* That it fit in with the *qilin* and the Chinese's desperate hope for our own kind of savior. The fact is, you found the Green Dragon Crescent Blade, Ing. Not me. If I don't come back, carry the *guandao* onward. I hope it will help someone else."

He grabbed her hand and squeezed, and she pulled him into a hug. "We'll procrastinate until it's midnight and that won't make it any easier for us to say good-bye. Just go, Lee. And please try to come back soon."

"I'll try to get word to you in a way that won't endanger you, just so you know I'm not . . ."

No, no, Ingrid wouldn't fill in that blank. "Please. Some word would be better than none at all." She released him and wiped a tear from her cheek. "Damn it, I hate crying. Go, Lee, or I'll kick you out."

"I'm going. See you soon, Ing." He lingered at the door then pushed himself away. A minute later, she heard the door clang on the far side of the building.

"Goddamn it." Ingrid paced the confines of the small room. She wanted to feel more hopeful at this point. She and Cy had been reunited with Fenris and Lee. Maybe, maybe, Ojisan was here in the city. Roosevelt had helped them and promised more help, limited as it was. Blum hadn't caught up to them yet.

But now Lee was off to do something dangerous by himself. Ingrid was left as custodian of an ancient Chinese artifact. The *Bug* wasn't functional.

Images of San Francisco flashed through her brain. That destruction could happen all over again. And there was the very real danger Mount Rainier presented—that it might decide to erupt if Ingrid were in significant pain.

She thought of the smoke. The fire. The boiling blue miasma. The bodies. Humans. Horses. The screaming cattle. She inhaled, as if she could smell the awfulness anew.

Ingrid wanted to hit something. Actually, no—she wanted to shatter something. Mr. Sakaguchi used to claim that she engaged in warfare on dishes because of the many pitchers and cups she cracked when she was holding power and peeved at one thing or another. She had hated the added expense for him and the auxiliary, but at the same time she had relished those small displays of power.

Now she dared not expend any energy like that. She plunged her fists into the slicker's pockets, as if the cloth could hold her frustration in check. Jagged objects grated against her right hand. Frowning, she pulled forth Papa's marred kermanite. She scooted a chair close to the lantern and bowed her head to study the rocks.

The darkness inside the kermanite indicated that power had been fully withdrawn, but how? The cracks in each stone were significant. Kermanite fragmented easily, but it was also more durable once it held earth energy.

If a mechanic wasn't paying attention to the color of the kermanite and left it installed in a device too long, the attempted power draw *might* make the stone crack. When that happened, the kermanite simply became a dead battery, and the mechanical device stopped working. That tended to be a bad thing if the device in question was an airship that was under way.

That kind of power draw didn't cause kermanite to melt, though. Ingrid had never seen the like, and she'd handled a lot of kermanite as secretary at the auxiliary. Heard plenty of stories, too. Old earth wardens and adepts gossiped worse than any women she'd ever met.

Ingrid pressed her thumb over a crystal and tilted it toward the light. The blemish actually resembled a fingerprint a bit larger than her own, as if a hand was clenching the crystal.

All of her life she'd heard the boys in training at the auxiliary repeat their lessons. Hyperthermia, hypothermia, the dangers of energy sickness. The necessity of always carrying kermanite in case of an earthquake. The fact that kermanite took in energy to capacity, and that was it. A geomancer filled stones, and only machines could draw the energy away.

Papa'd had dozens of stones like this. Had he been able to pull out the stored power? Could Ingrid do the same? In truth, she'd never tried because in her head it was impossible. Just like how she'd never formed a shielding bubble until the previous Sunday when she instinctively knew she had to protect herself and Mr. Sakaguchi as the auxiliary exploded.

Ingrid had already-filled kermanite on board the *Palmetto Bug*. She would need to fetch the stones later, or ask Cy to grab them for her. Climbing that precarious ladder was too much for her right now.

Carrying the lantern, she returned to the main floor to where Fenris was working. "What are you doing now?" she asked.

Fenris squatted beneath the airship as he sorted through metal parts. "Plotting where I can find a remote cave so that I can build things without constant interruptions."

"That would make it difficult to get parts and supplies."

He waved away the logic. "I could make occasional trips to a town to stock up. Now let me guess. You want to help me work on the *Bug* even though you know nothing about airships or machinery. Right?"

"No, I planned to randomly throw bolts at you to make sure you're awake and alert." Ingrid set down the lantern and crossed her arms over her chest. "Of course I want to help! I'm sorry if I'm a nuisance, but if I'm idle I start thinking about San Francisco and . . ." She shook her head. She hadn't wanted to mention that. "If the thieves happened to leave any books on board, I'll read, but I would prefer to be useful in some way."

"I don't think our thieves were of an erudite nature. I liberated them of any other useful belongings, but they didn't have—"

"You stole from them, Fenris? Really? You didn't mention *that* in front of Cy."

"Of course I didn't. That's because I'm not an idiot. He probably would hunt them down in jail so he could return a few coins and pocket lint."

"Speaking of pockets." Ingrid pulled out a few pieces of Papa's blemished kermanite. "Have you ever seen stones melted like this?"

"Huh. I think you know more about kermanite than me." Fenris frowned and lowered a magnifying lens on his goggles. He tilted the kermanite toward the nearest lamp and stared down his nose at it.

"Geomancers are like any other consumer when it comes to the actual usage of the rocks, though we might hear more news and gossip on the subject."

"This is odd, the way it's cracked and melted. And that swirl . . . it actually looks like a fingerprint."

"I thought so, but . . ."

"Yeah, it's pretty clear when the rocks are magnified. None of these show signs of being fastened into any kind of machine either. There should be tiny scratches where the clasps and cap fit on. Those sorts of marks might be invisible to the eye, especially on chunks this small, but I'd see them if they existed. Where'd you get this?"

"They belonged to my father. We forgot to mention that along with everything else that happened in the past day.

I went with Cy to the boardinghouse where Papa lived in Portland, and found out he had a wife, more children, and a drawerful of kermanite like this." She accepted the crystals from Fenris and dropped them into her pocket again.

The thought of her siblings still hurt. She wanted to help those girls. She wished there could be justice for her murdered brothers, too, but Papa was dead. What more could be done?

"Damn." Fenris's brow furrowed. He was quiet for a moment. "The kermanite is interesting. I'd suggest an experiment, but you're not holding any power right now, are you?"

"No. I used up what I had, and more, to talk to the thunderbird yesterday."

"Ah. *And more*. Yes, I've read about that, how geomancers who see earth's miasma also have the knack to drop their own life energy into kermanite. Jesus. I thought *I* stressed Cy. If he starts losing his hair, at least I know it's not my fault."

"Oh, shush." Ingrid rolled her eyes, even as she cringed in guilt over the danger and strain she'd brought on Cy. "Tell me, what can I do to help?"

Fenris sat up, hands on his hips. "Well, since you're so eager to volunteer, the tatami from the hallway needs a vinegar wash. It's already pulled out over there. There should be enough vinegar left to get it done. If you don't mind, of course, I—"

"I'm a housekeeper's daughter and a housekeeper in my own right. I know what to do." Ingrid pulled off her coat and tossed it over a crate. She noticed the spare Tesla rod on the ground nearby, and took a second look at the box she had sat on. Fenris had scorched identifying marks into the wood. "I didn't know a Tesla rod could be used as a brand like that."

"It's all in how the power inside is channeled, but I don't think I have to explain that sort of thing to *you*."

"I'm sorry if I'm being too much of a distraction. I can stay quiet, if you like."

Fenris shot her a haughty glare as he returned to his mechanical odds and ends. "I'll have you know, I'm capable of working and talking at the same time."

Ingrid smiled to herself and gathered her supplies to start work.

CHAPTER 12

When Cy returned a short time later, he found Ingrid kneeling on rags as she used another scrap cloth to work the stench out of the tatami. She stiffly rose, leaning on a crate for balance.

"Do you need help bringing in supplies?" she asked. "I'm just about done with the floor mat, though it needs to hang up to dry."

"Did you get my parts?" called Fenris from inside the *Bug*.

Cy leaned to shout into the hatch above. "Yes! Every one of them, by some miracle. Seems folks decided that if their airships couldn't make the flight to Baranov, there was money to be made in busting them down for scrap. I grabbed food stocks, too, and new bedding for that rack." He nodded to Ingrid. "I'd be much obliged for your help, too. I have a borrowed cart at the side door."

Ingrid spent the next few minutes hauling parcels indoors. Cy had bought a veritable tower of goods, and at a glance, she wondered at how everything could fit inside the airship. She trusted Cy and Fenris to find a way. With much of the scotch gone, there was certainly more space in the pantry.

Panting slightly, she wiped her hands on her skirts. "Since you bought everything Fenris needs, how long do you think the repairs will take?"

Cy readjusted his glasses on his nose. "The stub wing is on again, but there are still numerous minor repairs and matters of cleanliness. Might take a day, maybe two, if Fenris works at his usual rate."

"Which he shouldn't be, really, considering how he was injured last week. Didn't that Pasteurian say that Fenris should take it easy for a month?"

Cy snorted. "If you can find a way to convince Fenris to take it easy, without complete sedation, do let me know. Fussing over him just makes him more obstinate. He's worse than a mule."

"I can hear you," called Fenris, singsong. "I should add, you've made very similar comments about Ingrid there, though I don't think you mentioned a mule."

"I'm flattered," she said, grinning as Cy flushed.

"Don't try to get me in trouble, Fenris."

"If I wanted to get you in real trouble, I'd rig up a whirlyfly to record and play back your exact words, but I'm rather busy right now." Metal clanged and echoed from inside the craft.

Cy shook his head in exasperation. "Something to look forward to later, I suppose."

Ingrid stared at her wrinkled, vinegar-fragrant hands. "Cy, you mentioned before about a hotel across the street . . . ?"

"Of course. I should've told you about that first thing. I booked us a room. A two-room suite, actually. I hope you don't mind . . . I mean, I didn't wish to imply—"

"That's the wisest thing for security's sake. I'm not keen on being alone. We slept in chairs a few feet apart last night, you might recall."

Oh, she loved how he blushed. "There's a different sort of intimacy implied in sleeping fully clothed in chairs in a shared space aboard a small airship, and in booking a private suite at an inn."

"Indeed there is," she said, low enough that Fenris couldn't hear. "I will have you know, it's been two days since we first landed in Portland."

His brows scrunched together. "Meaning?"

"Your honor may very well be at stake."

"Oh. Yes. The besmirching." Cy's cheeks turned pinker as he laughed, but then his expression sobered. "I have given the matter some thought."

"Have you, now?"

"I have. And being with you, experiencing that special sort of closeness . . . I only see honor in that." His voice was soft, his gaze averted. "I don't wish to pressure you in any such way, though. Too many other men . . ." He shook his head.

"You're not like most men, Cy, and I'm glad for it." His respect for her had been apparent from the moment they first met, and now that she thought about it, that trait was what made him so appealing from that instant, too.

The intelligent spark in his eye and his luscious drawl hadn't hurt either.

While Ingrid grabbed her few extra clothes and toiletries, Cy rigged up his alarm system for the doors. He completed the installation as they exited.

"There. That'll belt out a loud noise if anyone other than us tries to enter. That should give Fenris time to grab a Tesla rod, and we can scamper over from across the street. The noise won't make us any new friends in the neighborhood, but it'll keep us alive."

Ingrid studied the door. Only a smidgen of wire was visible around the doorway. "Maybe we'll find Lee lurking around here when we return." She had to say it. She had to hope.

"Yes. It troubles me mightily to think of him going into Chinatown under such circumstances. Roosevelt's advice had merit."

"It does, but there was no easy choice here." She couldn't say aloud that Lee had already chosen a distinct course of action.

Ingrid pulled up her hood even though the rain had stopped. The prospect of a hot bath awaited, and if the inn staff refused to let her inside because of her complexion . . . well, she might be inclined to break things even though she wasn't holding any power.

Her concern didn't come to fruition. The establishment consisted of several narrow Victorian town houses painted in cheery blue and connected by covered walkways. Cy brought her up back stairs that seemed all too convenient for clandestine hotel shenanigans.

"I'm glad you booked a room on an upper floor," she said. It would take a significant quake to transmit power to an upper level.

Ingrid couldn't see Mount Rainier in the dark with so many buildings around, but she couldn't forget its presence. She wondered if that was entirely paranoia on her part, or if she could really sense the mountain's power even with a fully staffed auxiliary nearby. Or maybe the truth was a mix of both.

"Not just a room, but the whole floor. That's how the suites are set up here," he said, and opened the door.

The heady perfume of roses met her as she took in the appearance of the small sitting room. It was frippery and feminine in a gaudy English way, with boldly patterned floral wallpaper, excessive amounts of lace, and heavy furniture that would do well to block a door. The getabako by the door looked out of place, but she was happy to pause and take off her boots.

Cy was more hesitant to change to slippers.

"You never did take off your shoes last night, did you?" she asked.

Cy shrugged. "Old habits. It's best to be ready to run. I did take a brief bath earlier."

The hotel slippers for women were too small for Ingrid's

broad feet, and the men's slippers too long, so she continued her investigation of the suite in her stockings.

The bedrooms were decorated in the same garish style with heavy four-poster beds and pillow piles that surely had come straight from heaven. Her aching muscles begged to burrow into those layers of feather-stuffed goodness. Maybe she could sleep well here, truly sleep, and for a while forget about San Francisco and Blum and Lee and all the dangers around them.

Her immediate plans, however, didn't involve much relaxation. They had privacy. They weren't in imminent peril for once. If Cy was waiting for her to make the first move . . . well, she wouldn't let him wait long.

The windows of both bedrooms overlooked the street and the former skating rink beyond. She drew the curtains closed. Cy shrugged off a new yet worn leather coat he'd acquired in the past few hours. It suited him.

She noted his gun was now holstered near his waist, not far from the Tesla rod he had taken from their would-be attacker in Portland. The sight caused a lurch of sadness in her chest. He abhorred violence, but now he knew to anticipate it.

"Bath?" she asked, imbuing the word with days' worth of longing.

He motioned to an unopened door. "I'll be right out here."

"Try to relax, Cy." The man had been so reluctant even to take off his shoes; she'd need to provide extra incentives for him to shed the rest of his gear.

She closed the door behind her, a giddy smile lighting

her face. The space was small, the tub only a step away. She propped a foot on the porcelain edge and began to work off her stockings.

"Truth be told, I'm not sure I remember how to relax after this past week," Cy said through the door. "I figure if we stayed in the *Bug,* I'd be worked up about Lee and everything else. Plus, sleep would be impossible. A big advantage of being in a private space is that Fenris can work all night long."

"I suppose sleeping with our ears plugged wouldn't help our alertness."

Ingrid turned on the water to let it heat and continued to undress. Her discarded stockings curled on the tile floor like an old snakeskin. What a mercy, to feel air directly on her legs! A moment later, her dress, camisole, and brassiere joined the heap on the floor. A small part of her mind nagged her to fold everything properly, but the wiser portion noted the delightful steam that quickly filled the chamber. To hell with proper folding!

She left her hair coiled up in a bun as she stepped into the water. Hair washing would come later. She removed the bandage from her arm, too. The Reiki in her system had certainly sped the healing; the cut was a sealed pink welt, only sensitive if she applied pressure.

Ingrid scooted down in the wide tub. Hot water flowed to her shoulders and she couldn't help a blissful sigh. However, she couldn't lollygag; she had *plans.* She shut off the water and reached for the washcloth and soap.

"Did you have any more news as you went about your errands?" She spoke loudly to make sure he heard.

"No. A mercy, that. No mention of ambassadors in the evening headlines." Cy's voice was clear; he stood on the other side of the door. "All the talk is gold, gold, gold. How to get to it, how to get it out of the ground, and how to wheedle more money from miners as they travel north."

"The disaster in San Francisco is forgotten all too quickly." She scrubbed in savage strokes.

"People can only take so much awful at once. Blum's gold rush gives people hope. It's a fool's hope, to be sure, but drowning folks will cling to anything to stay afloat."

Ingrid sat up and worked the sopping cloth over her legs. As she looked at her nude form, there was no denying that she'd lost some weight in the past few days. Magic had depleted her very body—a disturbing thought, and not one to dwell on right now.

She stood and instantly wanted to plop down again and absorb more heat, but she reached for the towel instead. The water could be drained later. She dried herself and tucked the towel around her body as she stepped to the door. "Are you still out there?"

"Yes." His voice was a low rumble right on the other side. "Did you get out of the tub already?"

"Can you help me?"

Hesitant pressure on the door handle made it twitch, but it didn't open. "What do you need?"

She leaned on the handle and took a deep breath to steel her resolve. "You." She opened the door a crack.

"Me, Ingrid?" He peered through the opening.

"You. I'm wondering if you can distract me in a pleasant way for a while."

Through the gap, she saw Cy blink rapidly, his throat bobbing as he swallowed. "Oh."

At that encouragement, she pushed the door open. Cy stepped back. He wore an expression of calm rapture as he took in the full sight of her in a mere towel.

Ingrid looked down at herself and wondered what he really saw in her, what he'd seen from the first time they met on the Cordilleran Auxiliary steps. She adjusted the towel over the generous curve of her breasts. Naughty pulp novels made seduction look so easy. A kiss here, a moan there, and next thing the couple knew, suspenders and stays were undone and passion occurred in sly euphemisms.

Truth was, her anxious heart thrummed like a Porterman engine at full power. She was desperately, horribly afraid that he still might balk and refuse her in a gentlemanly way, and leave her ashamed to face him for the rest of forever. Or even worse, that something might happen in the building across the way while they dared to take this respite. That's how their luck had worked over the past week, like a leprechaun's curse.

"You mentioned that you've thought about this," Ingrid said. "I hope that it wasn't just in terms of honor, but about especially pleasant things." She shakily giggled. "Good grief, I can barely talk."

"Maybe you shouldn't speak, then."

With a single long stride, Cy cupped her jaw and brought

her lips to his. His touch sent a spiral of heat straight through her core. The rough skin of his thumb stroked her cheek as he tucked a stray tendril of hair behind her ear. She pulled back enough to gaze into his eyes, her breath rapid.

"I'd like to think I know what I'm doing here, but I'm relying on a score of purple novels that no proper lady should've ever read and my own rather active imagination."

"Good." His voice was hoarse. "Most of what I know is by hearsay from men who would be judged a mite crude."

Ingrid was surprised by his confession. "So you're saying, you've never . . . ? Not that it would change my mind if you had."

She'd heard enough talk at the auxiliary to know how most men—most adults—were, and if Cy had some experience, it wouldn't have been a bad thing. The thought of learning along with him, though, held a special sort of appeal.

Cy coughed. "I wasn't raised to consider women as casual acquaintances on such a basis, and being on the run these past years hasn't provided a good foundation for a permanent relationship. Not when my very name is a lie."

"I think the nom de guerre of Jennings suits you, really. 'Augustus' does sound a bit pretentious."

He laughed. "My grandfather was a Smith by birth. Pretension was his intent, harkening to the glories of old Rome and all."

Ingrid gnawed on her lip. "Since you're here with me right now, I take that to mean that you're interested in a permanent relationship with me?"

"Yes." His smile created crinkles around his eyes. "It's a good motivation to stay alive and free, I think. We do need to give consideration, however, to . . . er, consequences. Especially considering the magical strain on your body of late." His brow furrowed.

Ingrid bit her lip, unsure what exactly to say. "My body's never been normal in that way." She shrugged, and if not for her hand at her chest, she would have lost the towel. "I've never had a monthly. A good thing, really, considering the pain some women describe. If earthquakes had coincided with my cycle, I imagine I would have figured out more about my geomantic powers back in my teen years." She frowned in thought. "I suppose I sound rather blasé about it, but I came to terms with the matter a long time ago."

She shouldn't have been surprised that Cy brought up the general subject. This *was* a proper adult discussion to have, but now she fretted that she'd spoiled their moment together.

Cy's brow remained furrowed. "That's a relief as far as my immediate concerns, but I can't help but feel sad as well. To have no possibility of bearing children can be devastating for some folks."

"I never dwelled on that as a child. My body is what it is. I hope . . . I hope this isn't a problem?" Nervousness crept into her voice.

"I think your body is quite fine." His voice softened as he touched her cheek again. She shivered. "I want you to be safe and well."

Ingrid caught an edge of hesitation there. *Safe* could

imply many different things. Damn it all, but this was proceeding at a sloth's pace.

She tugged at the towel. It dropped upon her feet.

Cy made a small strangled sound. "It seems your towel fell, Ingrid."

She looked down as if surprised. "My goodness. You're right. Gravity's working." She met his eye again. He had an expression she had never encountered before. He looked . . . intent. "Cy. I'm standing here naked and terrified witless. Please make it plain that you really do want me and I'm not making a total—"

His arms wrapped around her waist and he lifted her up. Her legs barely had time to grip him and then she impacted on the bed with a gasp of breath. Her thighs didn't relinquish their hold. He propped himself up on one arm. His fingertips traced over her cheek and jaw, and down the width of her lips. She kissed his thumb and gave it the slightest nip.

"Ingrid, never doubt for an instant that I want you. You're the smartest, most troublesome woman I've ever had the joy to meet, and your body . . ." His fingers trailed down her neck as his gaze went downward. "You're beautiful," he whispered.

She gave a shaky laugh and eyed his shirt. "Our situation seems a bit unequal."

He sat up on his knees and began to work his buttons. "You're right. This won't do."

Ingrid reached for his waist. "Would you like some help?"

His brown eyes practically smoldered. "Please." He shrugged and his suspenders draped to his hips.

Ingrid's fingers clumsily worked at his trouser buttons. "Should we continue with the good manners? Will that help things along? What if I say, 'please touch me, Cy'? Will you touch me?"

"You might need to be more specific."

"I think," she said, just before their lips met in another breath-stealing kiss, "that I can be very specific."

CHAPTER 13

Monday, April 23, 1906

Ingrid woke often in the night. It was odd yet wonderful to share a bed with someone. Cy tossed and turned, his body free to move after enduring the coffin-like racks aboard the *Bug*. She didn't mind the frequent awakenings. It gave her more opportunities to simply enjoy his presence. She stroked the long line of his nose. The tenderness of his earlobes. The bristles along his jaw. He looked different without his glasses on, as if the proportions of his face were slightly off-kilter.

She felt different, too. Powerful in a new, extraordinary way. She also experienced a profound sense of coziness. Not simply because of the bed, though that was a wonder unto itself, but through exploring this new sort of intimacy with Cy. He felt *right*. And she felt right with him.

Cy slept clothed as a matter of readiness. Ingrid couldn't

argue with that, though she didn't fully dress herself either. Basic underclothes sufficed. They also were conveniently easy to strip off again in the middle of the night as she studied Cy again and suddenly found him staring back. Their lips met with a kiss as hot as earth's magic, and the temperature only elevated from there.

Good God, but that man could kiss. And more. Judging by Cy's reactions, Ingrid didn't think she did too badly herself either. They settled into the blankets again afterward, Ingrid fitted against his backside like a spoon. She embraced him with one arm, her hand on his chest. His body was warm if somewhat sweaty, his heartbeat strong beneath her hand. Within a minute he relaxed into the blankets with a mild shudder. Asleep, just like that. Was that a trait of men, she wondered, or something distinct to Cy? She felt like she had a lot to learn.

Smiling, she tucked her face close to his shoulder blade. A week ago, she had luxuriated in simply sleeping in Cy's bed back in his San Francisco workshop. It'd been titillating to be in such an intimate space even without his presence. Now she had him, and a far superior bed. If they managed to stay alive together . . . well, the future showed a lot more promise.

Ingrid woke with her arm stretched out and unbound hair in a veil across her eyes. Her fist clutched the sheets.

No Cy.

She bolted upright in bed. Sun streamed through the

gaps of the curtains. Cy's clothes were no longer folded on a bedside chair. His shoes were gone, too. She pushed herself free of the tangled sheets and winced as she stood. This morning brought a whole new sort of tenderness to her legs and body, though she felt steadier overall.

A note sat on the chair where his clothes had been.

> I hate to leave you alone, but I'd best help with work on the Bug. You're the most beautiful sight I've ever seen, sleeping there, and as much as I'd like to wake you again, I want you to get more rest. Don't leave anything in the room, just in case. I'll bring breakfast to the shop. Love, Cy.

Love. She traced the impressions of the pencil the way she'd explored his body hours before. His affection for her was impressive considering how much hell the man had endured during their brief acquaintance. He seemed only to grow fonder of her. Miracle of miracles.

The gaudy suite looked even more garish in the morning light, and downright intolerable without Cy present. Whoever decorated the room should be counseled regarding their overuse and abuse of lace doilies.

Ingrid tugged on her clothes. She affixed pins and one of her new headbands to keep the wild mess of hair off her neck; maybe later tonight she could return to the suite and wash her hair.

After a quick check to make sure she had everything, she headed across the street. The sun was already tilting toward ten o'clock. She hastened her steps, feeling strangely lazy at being the last to rise and help.

Only when she was at the door could she hear the roar of an airship engine. She hesitated with her hand on the handle, concerned about the alarm, but proceeded inside. The alarm didn't go off; loud as the ship was, it might have drowned out the klaxons, anyway. She locked the door behind her.

The *Palmetto Bug* was still anchored and moored, though most of the ladders and other debris had been moved some distance away. She left her things with the crates and stood on the open floor for a minute, unsure what to do. The engine finally wound down. Ingrid approached as the bottom hatch dropped down and the stairs dangled into space.

"Hey! Cy!" Fenris yelled. He angled his head to peer out.

"He's not in there with you?" Ingrid stood right below the opening.

"No. I booted him out so I could run tests on that stub wing in peace. He was *smiling* too much." Fenris scowled as if to counterbalance that expression.

Did Fenris suspect something was going on between Ingrid and Cy? Did he mind? Ingrid's cheeks flushed. She knew there was nothing romantic between Fenris and Cy—their relationship was downright brotherly—but she didn't want Fenris to feel as though she was trying to steal away Cy's attention and affection. Ingrid hadn't even considered that advancing her relationship with Cy might endanger the deep bond between the two old friends. That was the last thing she wanted to do.

"Oh. Well. Here, I can bring the ladder over so you can get down," she stammered, relieved to find a reason to turn away.

"I can jump to the floor. It's not that bad. But sure, bring the ladder."

The ladder legs scraped the floor as she dragged it over. She lined it up beneath the hatch only to have Fenris order her to move it this way and that to position it just right. Satisfied at last, Fenris twisted his body around and climbed down.

"Has Lee shown up?" she asked.

"Nope. Nothing tripped the alarms during the night either. It's nice to be in a place where I can work unimpeded all day long. No ridiculous noise curfews."

"Heaven forbid that other people need to sleep," Ingrid said, deadpan.

"That's right. Monsters." He shook his head.

"You *have* gotten some sleep, right? My body isn't the only one that needs to heal from injury."

He flapped a hand in the air dismissively. "Some naps. I sleep when I'm tired enough. I don't like being stuck anywhere, even a bed. That was a big reason why I built the *Bug* in the first place. We needed means to go, and go quickly. I sure as hell didn't expect the need to be so sudden."

"Sorry. The next time almost everyone I know is about to be murdered, I'll give you advance notice to make sure that it works with your schedule."

Fenris grunted, which Ingrid imagined was the closest he'd come to an apology. "So. You and Cy?"

Ingrid blinked. "Me and Cy, what?"

"Oh, come on. You two were making moony eyes at each other even when you were both covered in blood and muck. You shared a room last night. You both come in here this morning smiling and practically skipping in bliss, as if life were all sunshine and rainbows and half the world wasn't out to kill or capture us." He gave her a pointed look. "Cy treats me like a glass doll. Don't do the same."

"I . . . I'm not sure what you want me to say. I don't know how . . . I don't want to make things difficult for you two—"

"Stop it. You hate to be coddled. Don't coddle me either." His face twisted in frustration. "You don't have to hide anything from me, or be afraid of hurting my *feelings*. If you want to do *that,* insult my airship, not me."

Ingrid couldn't help but laugh, and even Fenris cracked a smile. "Okay, then. Yes, I enjoyed the night in Cy's company." She ducked her chin, feeling the blush spread across her face.

"Good. You both need that. Hell, we could all be dead tomorrow. You may as well have some fun while you can." He frowned. "Listen. I love Cy. I'm pretty fond of you at this point, too." He grabbed a wrench and pointed it at her. "It's all good and well that you're canoodling, but I'd rather you not do such things on my airship. You'll probably damage something."

"Damage the ship, you mean. I know your priorities." Ingrid grinned. "That's why you broached this topic at all, isn't it?"

"Maybe. Or maybe I want confirmation that Cy finally

has some happiness. He's spent the past dozen years running from his own brilliance and all the deaths he caused because of that damned Durendal tank. The guilt almost undid him, but losing contact with his family is what crushed him most of all." A wave of grief passed over Fenris's face. "If he had stayed in and resisted the A-and-A, told them he wouldn't design anything else, they would have locked him up. He would have lost his family *and* his freedom. He took the least-bad option, but it still cost him the people he loved." Fenris sighed. "You're good for him. When you aren't almost getting him killed."

"Thanks." She snorted. "He didn't leave behind everyone he loves, though. That was clear in how he searched Seattle for you. He would have walked the streets day and night."

"Yes, well, he can be foolish like that." Fenris stiffened and looked away. "I was worried, too." The words were whispered.

An awkward silence stretched out. Ingrid realized that Fenris needed some emotional space, and she took a step back. "Do you know where Cy is now?"

"Last I saw, he was in the office." Fenris waved that way without turning around. "He had food, too."

Food. An excellent idea.

The office was dark. She found the lantern on the counter and turned it on. A newspaper was left sprawled open, but there was no note explaining where he'd gone. It felt odd to not know where he was after being in his presence so much over this past week. She smiled as she touched the coat pocket where she had tucked the letter from their room, taking comfort in its presence.

Several red-and-yellow apples looked as delicious as fruit from fairy land, but she reached past them to a small box packed with kashi-pan. The hand-sized rolls were a deep golden brown with slits in their centers to reveal hints of the fillings inside. She frowned and angled two pastries toward the light. An-pan with adzuki paste was most common in shops, though strawberry jamu-pan was her absolute favorite. These had *something* red inside.

Well, the best way to find out was to try one. She sat down as she bit into a roll. Strawberry jam immediately met her tongue. Had she mentioned to Cy that this was her favorite fruit? Or had he just gotten incredibly lucky? She practically inhaled the roll and considered eating more. Instead, she grabbed a sheet of advertisements and formed a parcel around another one. It just fit in an interior pocket of her coat. She would need to take care that it didn't get smashed.

Ingrid bit into an apple with a satisfyingly juicy crunch as she scanned the headlines of the open newspaper.

TENS OF THOUSANDS DEAD IN SAN FRANCISCO: WHERE WILL CHINAMEN STRIKE NEXT?

SEATTLE CHINATOWN BLOCKADE CONTINUES

TRASH DEBACLE WORSENS: DOCTORS FEAR ILLNESS OUTBREAKS

NEIGHBOR'S WORDS: THE ENEMY IS HERE: WHY IT IS NOT MURDER TO KILL CHINAMEN IN AMERICA

GEORGE AUGUSTUS OF AUGUSTINIAN AMONG SF MISSING

The half-eaten apple dropped to the table with a spatter of pulp and juice. She angled the lantern closer to read the fine text. The snippet was the size of her thumb tip.

She read aloud: "'George Augustus, the charismatic owner and head engineer of Augustinian Corporation of Atlanta, Georgia, is one of the most high-profile businessmen to disappear in the earthquake and conflagration of San Francisco. The sixty-nine-year-old, known worldwide for his brilliance and hospitality, occupied rooms above the famed Quist's Restaurant, which was utterly lost to the flames. The worst is presumed. This concludes over a decade of tragedy for the Augustus family. He is preceded in death by his adult twin children Bartholomew and Magnolia, in separate accidents, and by the loss of his dearly beloved wife, Eva, this past January.'"

Cy's mother was dead? Stunned, she skimmed over the article again, hoping she had misread it, hoping that Cy hadn't been pummeled by such horrific news. The content of the article remained the same. Ingrid racked her brain to remember the conversation she and Cy had at Quist's after the opera. Cy had even brought up his mother that night. Mr. Augustus had been very upset but hadn't said anything about her being deceased.

Now Cy knew his father was presumed dead and his mother *was* dead. Oh God.

"Fenris!" Ingrid yelled. She shut off the lantern and grabbed the newspaper. "Fenris!"

Seconds later, he was there and gasping for breath. Her

tone had squelched any of his usual attitude. "What? What is it?"

"It's Cy. His parents." She shoved the folded page at him. Fenris pried off his goggles and, tossing them onto a crate, took the paper. His lips moved as he read.

His dark eyes met hers. "We need to go. We have to find Cy. Now."

"What, is he going to hurt someone? Himself?"

"No. Not purposely. If it's anything like when he found out about his sister, his first reaction is to go for a walk, then he's going to realize he wants to numb everything horrible he's feeling, and that's going to lead him to a bar where he will get roaring drunk."

Ingrid knew what Cy's family meant to him. How he still mourned the loss of his brilliant twin sister, Maggie, who had practically managed Augustinian up until her death in a laboratory accident a year ago. How fondly he spoke of his parents, of his absolute joy during his brief reunion with his father.

His father. Cy said that George Augustus coped with the stress and guilt of running one of the most acclaimed kermanite-powered weaponry manufacturers in the world by immersing himself in a bottle each night.

"I'm going to secure the *Bug* and we'll lock up the building. We have to find him." Fenris ran a hand through his short black hair, frantically looking around, then scampered up the ladder.

"How will we find him? We're near downtown and the major ports. There must be dozens of bars."

"Hell if I know, but I'm not waiting here and staring at my watch." His footsteps pounded from inside the ship.

Ingrid looked around. "Lee might come back when we're gone. I should leave him a message." She rummaged through a box where she recalled seeing paper and pencils, and found them a minute later. Fenris scurried down the stairs and ladder, a rope in hand.

"Wait!" called Ingrid.

"We can't dawdle—"

"I need to fetch something."

Propelled by adrenaline, she clambered inside the *Bug* and went straight to the pantry. The Green Dragon Crescent Blade was exactly where Lee said it would be. At some point in the past day, he had replaced its water-stiffened pouch with a similar one of stitched leather.

The airship had already been stolen once. Ingrid wouldn't risk leaving the *guandao* in it unattended. She tied the pouch strings to her obi.

She hopped down the stairs and ladder to the rink floor. With a tug, Fenris swung the hatch upward and shut. The rope still swaying, he grabbed the ladder to haul it to the side of the rink.

A minute later they were outside. Fenris rigged the door alarm again and stuffed Ingrid's hasty note in the doorjamb. He squinted in the milky light and adjusted an ill-fitting bowler on his head. The clouds teased of more rain to come.

"Now what?" Fenris stared at Ingrid.

"What do you mean?"

"I've only been between a single airship dock and here, a matter of blocks. Where are the taverns?"

She exhaled in a huff. Of course he wouldn't know which way to go. That would involve stepping outside. "You have your Tesla rod?"

He pulled back his jacket to show the rod pressed against the flat of his hip. "I don't think we'll need to go to those lengths to get Cy back here."

"I'm not worried about him in that regard." She started walking. "The city's filling up with men headed north. It's not even noon on a Monday but I imagine many are already toasting to their future fortunes."

"Oh." He mulled this for a moment. "That won't help matters."

"No. No, it won't."

Frustration fueled her strides. She still didn't want to think Cy would act in such a careless manner, especially after the night they'd had, but she also knew that his reaction wasn't about her. Once he read that article, all the happiness in him must have fizzled away. If she needed any confirmation of the gravity of the situation, all she had to do was look beside her. Fenris had willingly abandoned the *Palmetto Bug* in mid-repair. That said everything.

"You've seen Cy at his happiest. I suppose it's only right to see him at his lowest," said Fenris.

"I'd rather not witness the full range of emotion within a span of hours."

Fenris inclined his head at that. "You have to realize this isn't a common reaction for him. He's not the type to get soused every other day of the week. He might have the occasional beer, but never to excess. He avoids the hard stuff completely."

"He didn't want us to bring aboard the scotch from Mr. Thornton's airship," she murmured. "I argued for it because I knew how much it was worth. He still eyed the bottles as if they were a slumbering rabid dog."

"Exactly. He doesn't even like being in proximity to drinks like that." The sidewalk ahead was a teeming sea of black and brown coats and hats. Ingrid and Fenris's progress slowed as they reached a bottleneck over a narrow bridge. Nearby bodies reeked of cloves and stale sweat and leather. Shoulders and bags bumped against Ingrid.

The path widened and the pedestrians spread out. Fenris continued, his raspy voice low: "Some people make for angry drunks. Some are sad. Some are hilarious. Cy empties out. And that's exactly what he'll want to do right now."

Ingrid blinked back tears. More than anything, she wanted to hold Cy as he grieved and offer what comfort she could.

The taverns across the way were overflowing with men. Many had carpetbags or cases at their feet. They gathered in little knots, jabbering loudly with drinks in hand.

All of Ingrid's survival instincts screamed at her to get away from this place. Few women walked the street. She was conspicuous, and idling would make her even more so. She had little choice, though. If Cy had managed to get sloshed, Fenris would need her help to cart him away.

"Do you want the Tesla rod?" asked Fenris. Tension rang in his voice. Ingrid imagined his survival instincts were even more honed than hers.

"No. It'd look odd for me to carry something like that. Go on. I'll wait here."

Fenris wavered, eyes half shut. "Goddamn it, I hate men. With certain exceptions." His slim shoulders rose as he took in a deep breath. "Drunkards are worst of all."

Ingrid knew Fenris was discomfited by physical contact, so she didn't grab his hand. Instead, she leaned closer. "It will only take a minute for you to check the taverns. Cy is tall. If he's there, you'll find him right away. You'll be in and out, lickity-split."

"Lickity-split." Fenris nodded, licking his dry lips. With that, he dashed across the busy street, dodging people and autocars like a rangy tomcat.

Ingrid sank against the wall in a niche between two rain barrels. She tugged her hood as far forward as possible and folded her arms over her chest, her gaze wary. The *guandao* rested against her body, as heavy and warm as a sleeping cat.

The observation she had made in Portland still held true: the majority of travelers were older white men. They had abandoned their families and jobs, all in pursuit of a foolish dream engineered by a power-hungry kitsune.

If these men even made it to Baranov, how did they expect to be received by the Russians—by the soldiers who guarded the territory, or those who had already deserted in order to stake claims? Rage and sadness mingled together in Ingrid's chest.

A few women walked by, their hats festooned in lace and flowers. Men trailed them like cats after a fishmonger. Ingrid pressed herself even deeper into the wall. She sensed the attention of passing men but no one lingered.

Fenris emerged and trotted her way. An autocar horn blared at him, but he dismissed the noise with a wave of his hand and didn't slow down. He jerked his head to motion Ingrid to walk with him.

"He's not in those taverns, obviously." Fenris's scowl was darker than usual. He walked with fast steps and hunched shoulders. "Those places stink of tobacco smoke and alcohol and men and idiocy. Did anyone bother you out here?"

"No, but other women are getting plenty of attention."

Fenris muttered something indecipherable beneath his breath.

Ingrid's sense of wariness only escalated as Fenris continued to check establishments down another block. She recognized the sound of a slap as another woman berated a man, much to the amusement of his companions.

A man stopped in front of her. "Ko-ni-chi-wa." He broke apart his Japanese syllables the way a toddler crushes a cracker. "You waitin' for someone? You waitin' for me?" He leaned closer.

Ingrid balled her fists and she suddenly wished the earth wasn't quite so calm.

"Well?" The stranger's fermented breath warmed her cheek. "Ow!" He stumbled backward.

"Go sober up in a gutter," snapped Fenris. He brandished the Tesla rod in his hand. It remained enclosed and inactive, but as a stout copper rod, it still packed a wallop. The man scowled and slinked off. "Did I mention I hate drunkards?"

Ingrid almost laughed at that. "You did. Thank you for the help."

Fenris shrugged her words away, his expression dark as he holstered the rod. "I don't like most women either, but you're an exception."

"I'm honored. We do have a habit of going on interesting walks together, don't we?"

"Everyone needs a hobby," said Fenris. "Though I hope this perambulation doesn't conclude with me getting stabbed again. Or with an earthquake here."

"That would get Cy's attention."

Fenris snorted, then held out a hand to halt her. A crowd had gathered on the upward slope ahead.

"Are we near Chinatown?" Ingrid asked, thinking of Lee and what they had seen in Portland. This neighborhood wore a heavier Japanese influence in vibrant red and green paints, sloped roofs, and business signs. The heady scent of frying fish carried from nearby.

"No, I don't think so." Fenris frowned and wavered in place. He clearly wanted to get the hell out of there, but he grimaced and walked on. "We better see what's happening."

They "pardoned" their way deeper into the crowd. A

few folks whooped and cheered. Past the shorter Japanese heads, Ingrid recognized a tall, gangly figure.

"Fenris," she gasped.

He had to duck around two more people to see. "Oh, damn it."

Cy stood in the street, his brown hair ruffled. His hat and coat lay on the dry ground nearby. His fists were raised. Blood ran in thick rivulets from knuckles to elbow. His Tesla rod remained sheathed at his hip. Across from him stood a man as thick and furry as a bear. His rounded face was ruddy, his teeth bared to reveal numerous gaps. Ingrid felt tiny prickles of awareness and studied the man more closely.

A pudgy pixie was dozing on the brim of his hat. Ingrid had never seen a fairy so obese, more like a fleshy caterpillar than the usual stick-thin fairies that gallivanted around gardens. She doubted this one could even fly. No visible iron bound the fairy to the man, but judging by its tameness and condition, it had to be the man's pet. The poor thing.

Behind both men, a woman in a simple red cotton work smock stood with her fists clenched. Her straw hat rested askew over an updo of black hair. Tears streamed down her cheeks, but her eyes were hard.

"She told you no," Cy said.

"It ain't your affair!" yelled the man.

"Goddamn it, Cy *would* get in a stupid, drunken, public fight over a matter of chivalry," growled Fenris. "All the man needs is silver armor and a white stallion." He wedged forward, his elbow jabbing out as he unholstered the Tesla rod again. Ingrid used her height and width to shove through to the perimeter of the audience.

"*I'm* none of your affair," the woman snapped at the brawny man. "I was minding my own business on my way to work and you *grabbed* me." A sewing basket lay on the ground, tipped. She crouched to gather up her scissors and spools of thread that had rolled into crevices in the bricks.

Ingrid stalked into the open circle. "Here, let me help," she said, and began to pick up spools. The woman granted her a strained yet grateful nod. A few men on the outskirts of the crowd began to help as well.

"Fancy meeting you here," Cy said over his shoulder.

"Seemed like a nice time to go for a walk since it's not raining yet." The Tesla rod sizzled as Fenris extended it.

The bearish man wiped his face with his knuckles. "You're not the only one who can get help from friends. Charlie! Godfrey!" he yelled.

Ingrid dropped the last few spools in the woman's box. "Get out of here!" she hissed.

The woman shot her a frown. She stood and strode past Cy to stare down the other man. "You're a lout. If your mother's alive, I pray to God she doesn't know the measure of the man she raised, and if she's already in heaven, every time it rains you should know she weeps over you." Everyone stared in stunned silence, including the gawking brute. The woman brought back her arm and slapped him across the face. Spittle flew. At that, she turned away. The crowd parted like the Red Sea to let her through.

"Charlie! Godfrey!" the man roared. His full attention

turned to Fenris and Cy. He straightened his hat. The pixie hadn't moved. If it wasn't for the buzz of magical energy, Ingrid would have guessed it was dead. Maybe it was drunk.

"We're coming, boss!" someone yelled from up the street.

Ingrid met both Cy's and Fenris's eyes, and with a synchronized nod to one another, they took off at a sprint. Cy hesitated just long enough to grab his hat and coat.

Within some twenty feet, Ingrid was reminded yet again that running was a very bad idea. Her legs burned, her breath huffed. She wasn't physically fit enough to run, anyway, and now the magical exertions of the past week had dropped her endurance to pathetic new lows. Cy and Fenris passed her and slowed to flank her instead, much to her frustration. She glanced back. The man pursued them at an incredible speed for a person of such bulk. His face was scarlet, his hat gone.

"Enough of this," said Fenris. He halted and lashed out with the rod. A brief look of bewilderment passed over the man's face, and then he hit the ground, convulsing and screaming as if he'd been swarmed by wasps.

Cy tugged on Ingrid's arm. Whistles pierced the air. She didn't need another reminder to skedaddle. She clutched an arm to her waist to hold the *guandao* still, and ran. The last thing they wanted was a trip to a local precinct where a bulletin might advertise her name and likeness for Ambassador Blum.

They ran down the next block, slowing as the crowds diminished, and then walked to blend in. Fenris put away the rod. Cy slid on his leather coat, cringing as the sleeves passed over his fists.

"Well, fancy meeting you here," he repeated.

Fenris stopped in his tracks to face him. "Yes. What the hell were you thinking?" he hissed. "Leaving like that. Getting drunk. Starting street fights over some strange woman."

Cy flushed. "I'm not drunk. I haven't had a single drink." He looked between Fenris and Ingrid, his gaze lingering on her.

This certainly wasn't how Ingrid had imagined things would develop after their night together. She simultaneously felt the need to wallop him for dashing off in such a foolish way and a desire to hug him in sympathy for his grief . . . and also wished to take off all his clothes to inspect him for injuries and perhaps help him to forget those wounds as well. While chastising him most strongly.

Ingrid gestured Cy and Fenris into the shelter of an awning. She leaned on the wall. She was *weak,* and suddenly she felt famished as well. That single jamu-pan and a few bites of apple hadn't sufficed.

She felt a sudden spike of fear. Cy had been right to worry about her. Ingrid would need to take extra care not to absorb more earth energy in the next while. Her miserable sprint just now acted as a reminder that being physically strong was far more important than being magically strong.

"You saw the newspaper back at the rink?" Cy's shoulders slumped as he sighed. "Ah, Fenris. Of course you assumed I'd be off to liquor up. Not like I didn't think of it. I would have imbibed, if every place along here wasn't so packed. God Almighty." He rubbed his face. "I may very well be an orphan. I might be twenty-seven, but that still hurts like hellfire."

"Cy, the fact that your father's missing doesn't mean that he's dead," Ingrid said. "It's chaos down in San Francisco right now. There are refugee camps scattered all over and hospitals besides."

"It's not just about my father." Pain carved lines into his face. "It's my mother. How could he not tell me? He looked me in the eye and acted like everything was well at home."

"Bringing up your mother's death would be a bit of a damper during your happy reunion," said Fenris. "Even *I* can see that."

Cy shook his head. "I've been reading the major newspapers these past few months, too. It never even warranted a mention. Like she didn't matter. That she was *just* his wife." He struggled not to cry. "Maggie's death only made the papers because of how she went. Sensational laboratory accident and all."

"Your father was told *you* had died in an airship crash, Cy. You can't trust what people say. Your father might be fine. Don't give up hope." Ingrid lightly touched his sleeve. "Are you hurt?"

"Are you brain-damaged?" muttered Fenris.

"My fists are banged up, that's all. The blood belongs to that brute."

"You should know we've spent the past while scouring these foul blocks in search of your inebriated carcass." Fenris spoke through clenched teeth. "Yes, I get it. You're *grieving*. You needed to *walk*. Well, you needed to keep some goddamn sense." He stepped close to Cy and jabbed a finger at his face. "Don't ever do that to us again. You hear me?"

"I hear you." Cy's voice was small.

"Did your chivalrous action work out some tension?" asked Fenris.

"Yes, actually." Cy rubbed his hands together and winced. "God help me, but it did feel good. Everyone else was waltzing by and pretending not to see how he harassed that woman. I couldn't abide with that."

"Here I thought I was special." Ingrid nudged Fenris. "Does he do this in every city?"

"Usually cats are the bigger issue. It's as if they sense he's an easy mark. I've told him, one of these days he'll lure in a Cat Sidhe and then we'll really be in for a world of grief."

"Instead he brought me home." Ingrid shook her head. "A different sort of grief."

"I am standing right here, you know. I would hardly compare you to a soul-stealing fae feline, Ingrid."

"Now that our immediate crisis has been averted, I really need to continue work on the *Bug*." Fenris fidgeted. "I don't like leaving the ship alone. It's already been stolen once, and now the city's filling up with even more men who are dense and desperate."

"Yes, let's head back, maybe Lee is waiting—" Ingrid took a step and froze.

"Ingrid?" Cy asked, a hand at her elbow.

"Something is off-kilter." The ground didn't exude any blue miasma, but she felt a minuscule shift. She frowned at the wooden boardwalk beneath her feet. As natural material, the planks would readily conduct the earth's energy.

She jerked. There it was again. A twitch. A reverberation in the air, through her feet, like the snap of a rubber band.

"Do you feel an earthquake coming?" asked Cy, looking up. "This place is brick—"

"No. Not a seism. At least, I don't think so. I've never felt anything like this before, it's like . . . ripples of power, but without any visible earth energy."

"You're not hiding an injury, are you?" Fenris scowled, but beneath the frown was genuine concern.

"No." Her exasperation was clear in the one word. "Let's get away from the building. I see trees over there. Maybe I can sense more once I'm on dirt."

The street was dirt as well, but offered no safe place to linger. Bicycles and rickshaws sped by, as did puttering autocars and horse-drawn wagons. They entered an undeveloped area of pines and marshland, a speck of wilderness surrounded by city. Birds sang and fluttered from branch to branch. A few women chatted beneath a larger tree, while men with carpetbags appeared to be setting up a camp.

Ingrid found a deep, grassy spot and crouched. The leather pouch dangled awkwardly beneath her slicker as she pressed her fingertips to the ground.

"Do you see any blue fog?" asked Cy. Fenris, his hands in his pockets, studied the ground as if he expected a crevasse to appear.

"No, it's not like an earthquake. It's like . . . twitches. But not directly from the earth." Another shuddered out. Then another. And another. It felt like . . . released compression. Like the stays on a corset coming undone.

The constraints on earth's energy were being loosened. Twitch by twitch. Life by life.

"It can't be," she whispered. "When the Cordilleran . . ." Cy and Fenris waited, frustration obvious in their expressions as she struggled to find words. "When the Cordilleran Auxiliary blew up, my senses were overwhelmed by the violent explosion and the debris and the strangeness of using my power in such a new way. So much happened at once. Here, I can isolate what I feel."

"What are you saying, Ingrid?" asked Cy.

"How close is the Cascadian Auxiliary?"

"Maybe a half mile east, closer to Lake Washington. Why?"

Ingrid swayed and gripped Cy to stay upright, sheer horror stealing the remaining strength from her legs. "I think the geomancers are being killed, one by one."

CHAPTER 14

"We need a rickshaw," said Cy, and dashed toward the street.

Fenris stood close to Ingrid, arm out in case he needed to grab her. "Is the local Hidden One angry?" he asked, brow furrowed.

"No. But I can feel the geomancers' hold on the energy relinquish, bit by bit." Death by death. She shuddered, sick with dread and horror. "What if the Thuggees are attacking here? They don't have Papa to channel more energy into that kermanite, but . . ." She couldn't bear to finish the sentence.

Fenris grimly nodded. "But they know how to effectively destroy a city."

"Come on!" Cy waved them over to a dented orichalcum cart. Its two rubber-encased wheels stood almost shoulder high to Ingrid.

“Where to?” asked the driver. Beneath a broad sugegasa straw hat, his skin color was similar to Ingrid’s, though cast darker from exposure to the sun. She felt another ping, another death. They couldn’t tarry.

“The Cascadian Auxiliary,” said Cy. He motioned Fenris and Ingrid to climb in first. The cart had tilted forward at rest, but the footboard bent at an angle, granting them a stable surface to step on for boarding.

Ingrid sat in the middle, the pouch adjusted to rest on her lap. Cy climbed in at her right, his hand brushing her thigh. Fenris was pressed tightly against her left side. The structure of the cart didn’t conceal another faint snap of power.

The driver grunted as he pulled the cart upright. A metal bar folded back to rest above their thighs. The man had to be strong as a titan, pulling around people all day long up and down these hills. With a glance at the street, he rolled out into traffic.

The cart bounced along the unpaved roads. Being packed so tightly into the seat prevented the passengers from sliding side to side, but the hard leather cushion provided little comfort. Ingrid gritted her teeth and clenched the bar at her lap. The rickshaw wheels clattered and squeaked as if they might fall off at any and every pothole. The cacophony of the city surrounded them—autocars roaring, horse harnesses jingling, rickshaws clattering. Ingrid eyed the horses in particular. When the earth’s agitation accumulated in San Francisco, even the most docile old cart horses had been rendered half wild with anxiety.

The animals around them trotted and trudged as if it were a normal day. For now.

Cy followed the angle of her gaze as he tugged his hat more firmly onto his head. “The horses’ behavior is a good sign, isn’t it?”

She could scarcely hear him, so she knew the driver would be unable to hear them at all. “For now, yes. It’s not like San Francisco. Not yet. Remember that it took several days for things to escalate there, and that was exacerbated by Papa’s presence.”

If the Thuggees were eliminating the Seattle wardens, did that mean that they actually had another geomancer to act as an energy conduit as Papa had done? Good grief, did Papa have more children elsewhere? He had traveled all over the world as a warden, and even after his presumed death, he hadn’t stayed put in Portland. What if a *child* was about to be tortured to pull in energy to fill the kermanite—with Seattle as collateral damage? She couldn’t help but think of Mirabelle and her murdered brothers.

Ingrid was reminded of the promise she asked Lee to make, too, but he wasn’t here now. What if they had to flee Seattle? Lee said he would try to get word to her, somehow, but . . .

A particularly hard bounce caused her to grip Cy’s knee. She felt an extra lurch of frustration at the sorry turn this day had taken.

“Your gun’s loaded?” she murmured to Cy.

“Certainly. And I have my rod.”

“And I have mine, of course,” added Fenris. The copper

length of it was pinned against Ingrid's thigh and knee. She hadn't noticed before that Fenris was left-handed.

Cy leaned closer. "You know what I want to say."

"You want me to stay behind so I don't risk injury. I know."

"I also don't want you to hurt yourself in order to pull in power."

"That's . . . a last resort. Especially now." The words pounded out, rapid like her heartbeat. She caught Cy's sidelong expression. "The surest way to keep Seattle safe is to keep the other geomancers safe. The problems in San Francisco only emerged when the geomancers were dead and that buffer was gone. *We can't let that happen here.*" The very thought almost broke her down in sobs.

He nodded, clearly unhappy. "What are you carrying there?" He motioned toward the bulge of the Crescent Blade beneath her coat.

She glanced down and realized this was no time to lie—or to fully tell the truth. "An artifact that I found in Portland with Lee. He wouldn't want it left in the airship with no one there."

Cy was plainly curious, but his attention was pulled to a street sign as they zipped by. "We're almost there."

"Have you been inside this auxiliary?" she asked.

"Once, to purchase a variety of smaller kermanite chunks. Didn't wander much. I recall it was a two-story structure." By the gleam in his eye, he was already working on a strategy.

"Yes. It should have classrooms below, and dorm rooms and offices above. They're closed to the public on Mondays, so hopefully there are few other people present." She gasped, doubling over the bar on her lap. More tugs, in quick sequence. Not here, not again. The ground blurred by; there was still no hint of blue mist. "God. Is anyone left alive in there?"

"How many people should be inside?" asked Fenris, keeping his voice low. The rickshaw quieted as the driver huffed and dragged it up a slope.

She closed her eyes to slits and tried to focus through her fear and grief. "Four wardens, maybe around twenty students, and I'm not sure how many adepts. The numbers depend on how many geomancers they sent to San Francisco or elsewhere." She hadn't followed international news in recent days. As far as she knew, Vesuvius was still erupting and geomancers from around the world were still congregated there.

Ingrid wanted to say more but traffic lessened and the street smoothed out. They rolled down a quiet business thoroughfare that fully blended Japanese and American styles, with curved-roof buildings surrounded by pines, vibrant Japanese maples, and green grassy lawns that thinned at the dirt street. The rickshaw stopped and the driver leaned it back. As soon as the bar lifted, Cy quickly handed him a wad of money.

"Much obliged," Cy said, hopping out of the cart. Ingrid and Fenris followed.

Sweat sheened the man's dark skin. "Maido. Do you want me to stay around? Not many other rickshaws come this way on Sundays and Mondays—"

"We'll find our way," Cy said, tipping his hat as he backed away.

The driver didn't seem to pick up on their urgency. "Go a few blocks west," he said, waving that way, "and you'll be on Boren. You'll find some rickshaws and taxi wagons there."

"Domo arigatou," said Cy, his voice tight. The driver hefted up the cart again and rolled down the slope toward downtown. "Damn it all. I should've asked for us to be dropped off a block away. Anyone inside the auxiliary can spot us."

"I don't see a problem." Hands in his pockets, Fenris strolled across the street.

"Fenris," Ingrid hissed. "What—"

"No. He has the right idea," said Cy. "Walk casual." Ingrid's heartbeat raced as she scurried to catch up.

The auxiliary looked downright pretty from the street. Red-shingle siding lined the walls while dark green paint trimmed the windows and the sloped gutters. The steps creaked damply. The porch was empty, the double doors shut. A sign in the window stated, in English and Japanese, that the auxiliary was always in operation but only open to customers five days a week. In the meantime, messages could be left with the central phone operator.

The curtains didn't move. All was quiet. To any other visitor, it might appear normal, but Ingrid knew better. Even on a day like this, the auxiliary should be bustling inside. Trying to keep young boys silent and still for any duration was like trying to prevent a cat from quivering at the sight of a grounded bird.

"It's closed!" Fenris announced loudly. "I guess we'll need to come back tomorrow." With that, the three of them left, walking toward Boren as their driver had advised.

"I think your acting skills could use more nuance," muttered Cy.

"There go my dreams of the opera." Fenris rolled his eyes.

They took shelter behind trees in the yard next door as they watched the auxiliary. Eerie quiet smothered the street. Another death pinged against Ingrid's skin like a plucked guitar string. She pressed her fist to her chest and took in several deep, rattling breaths. Her body ached with the need to sob and scream.

"The deaths are slowing down," she murmured as she wiped a tear from her cheek. "There can't be many more geomancers left inside." The words scratched through her throat like broken glass.

"We'll go in the back. Hopefully this'll go better than when we broke into your house, Ingrid." Cy nodded to her. "It's troublesome how quiet things are. However they're dying, it's not by gunfire or the neighbors would've noticed."

"Thuggees like poison," Ingrid said, thinking of Warden Calhoun's death.

"Let's be honest, *everyone* likes poison these days. I thought poison was interesting before it became downright popular." Fenris wrinkled his nose.

Cy grimaced. "I wish we had gas masks. Could be an aerosol poison, far as we know. The UP's using those in China. We'll vent windows and doors as we go through. If you smell anything odd, run. Maybe that'll be fast enough to prevent damage."

Well, this sounded just dandy.

Cy stood on tiptoe at the fence to scout out the backside of the auxiliary. "There's a cat nosing along the back porch. It looks healthy for now. That's a good sign."

"See? Him and cats," Fenris muttered. He used his Tesla rod to adjust his bowler hat.

Cy didn't spy any traps rigged on the fence, so they went through the gate. The familiarity of the yard's design struck Ingrid like a blow.

The backyard showed a typical auxiliary lesson in progress. Sections of the yard were scraped bare, while others had wooden slats, stacked bricks, and metal platforms. At the slightest quiver of an earthquake, the boys were to run to the backyard and stand on different materials to recognize the distinct ways that energy filtered through each.

Spaced-out small boulders formed a little amphitheater in a back corner. On a fine day like this, many book lessons would probably take place outdoors to allow students ready access to the ground.

The brown tabby cat spotted them and trotted up, yowling. Her belly swayed from the burden of past litters. A cat had lived in the alley behind the Cordilleran Auxiliary, too. Ingrid still hoped that she had somehow survived the explosion, unlikely as it was.

She blinked back tears as she scratched the tabby cat's head.

Cy hopped up onto the back porch while staying low to

avoid the window. A stone kirin statue sat by the back door; it looked a great deal like the one Mr. Sakaguchi kept in his backyard. The dragon-like muzzle was worn smooth by passing hands rubbing it for good luck. Maybe no one had touched it today.

Ingrid gave the kirin a rub as she passed by, and thought of Lee and his *qilin*. She wondered if there was really a difference between the Japanese and Chinese creatures or if it all simply came down to semantics.

"Door's open," Cy murmured. He nudged it wider with his elbow. Ingrid followed Fenris to the porch. She made herself breathe slowly, attuned to the inherent magic of the earth, to the thrum of her own body.

A thought popped into her mind. Maybe she didn't have to hurt herself to pull energy to protect Fenris and Cy.

Maybe, in an emergency, she wouldn't need any initial earth magic. Maybe she could directly pull on her own life force to form a protective bubble or throw someone. She had done it before . . .

She doubted she could sustain such usage for long, but it might just keep them alive. The possible physical repercussions . . . she couldn't dwell on those now.

Ingrid crept inside the building and left the door cracked open. Several wooden quarterstaffs leaned against the doorjamb. Each bō was about Ingrid's height, so she grabbed a shorter jō instead. The staff was about four feet in length, ideal for younger boys to use while drilling in martial arts.

The Cordilleran Auxiliary used them for fitness training as well. Ingrid had watched plenty of sessions but never formally trained—not that she hadn't pleaded with Mr. Sakaguchi for private lessons. He had refused, of course. Back then, she had fumed that it was because she was a girl. Now she realized he had rejected such training because of the risk of injury to her.

It felt good to hold some semblance of a weapon in hand as she took in the strange room. It seemed to be a social space for the boys. A shelf of books held colorful manga. A Marconi radio sat on an end table. The fireplace was dark, wood stacked and ready to one side. The getabako by the door was low to fit beneath the window, the little cubbies lined with shoes.

A dark hallway gaped ahead. Light shone through an open door to the right. Cy crept that way, pistol ready, and pivoted to look inside. He froze. "God Almighty."

Fenris advanced, made a soft gagging sound, and retreated with his knuckles to his mouth. His tortured expression didn't stop Ingrid from peering through the doorway.

It was a classroom full of dead boys. Apprentices, all likely six to eleven years of age, about a dozen of them. The ones nearest to the door were draped over their wood-and-metal chairs like slack dolls. One leaned back, the slit in his throat bared and dark. Farther away from the door, the desks were askew, the bodies tangled on the floor. A gray-haired adept sprawled in front of them, a failed barricade, his body like a practice dummy for cuts. The air stank of iron and piss and worse.

Ingrid choked back a sob, bile rising in her throat. Dead. All of them. Just like the young boys she knew back home.

Cy crouched down. "The boys were corralled together. There must have been more than one attacker to herd them like this. The cuts are thick, chopped."

"As if done with hatchets?" she asked, her voice strangled. "When the *tongs* used to scrap among themselves in San Francisco, before the war, their fighters had a reputation for using hatchets." She shook her head. "For it to be used here seems . . . too blatantly Chinese in method."

"I agree." Cy looked troubled. "If the Chinese *did* try to strike out like this, I'd expect subtlety, misdirection—not an invitation for retaliation."

"There was a Chinese laundry truck outside my auxiliary right before the explosion, too, even though it wasn't laundry day. I think Mr. Thornton was using it to cast blame on the Chinese. The truck really stood out, being there on Easter morning. A lot of people were about."

If the Thuggees were attempting that same sort of misdirection again, the method felt heavy-handed.

Ingrid shook her head. There were more immediate concerns now. "There should be a class of seniors, too. The teenagers."

"Should we check these children for a pulse? Is there a point?" Fenris's voice was unusually soft.

Ingrid made herself breathe deeply despite the smell, despite her horror at being here. She tore her gaze away from the students to the chalkboard. It contained a list of dates and times, the ones at the top fuzzed by time, the lower chalk lines crisp. She recognized some of the dates: notable tremors in Cascadia. She'd had to transcribe notes on the incidents. The bottom date was Saturday the twenty-first. Two days ago, late night. When she and Cy had been on Theodore Roosevelt's airship, the earth had slightly shaken throughout Puget Sound. A perfectly natural event. The earth often shifted, even as Hidden Ones slept.

She glanced at blood-spattered papers on a desk. The boy had been writing a journal of his experiences with hyperthermia. She looked at another desk. They were all working on the same exercise.

"No. They're all dead. They should have been holding energy from an earthquake a few days ago. Part of their lesson." She motioned to the chalkboard, her hand shaking. The apprentices in the Cordilleran had been working on a similar exercise last week. It was one repeated constantly as they trained, as they studied the potential dangers earth magic could create within their young bodies. A lesson Ingrid continued to learn even now. "If they were alive, I'd see a blue fog within them. There's nothing." She looked at the bodies again then away, blinking fast.

Something touched her legs and she barely contained a scream. The cat was twining around her skirts, her mew soft and insistent. Ingrid's heart rampaged.

"Should have closed the back door," Fenris muttered. The cat continued to meow.

"We can't let down our guard. The attackers still might be upstairs." Cy waved them toward the door.

"I haven't heard any noises up there," whispered Ingrid.

"Assume nothing until we've explored the whole place."

Ingrid picked up the cat and awkwardly cradled her

against her chest. The cat purred like a happy motor. "I'll let her out and shut the door."

Fenris and Cy escorted Ingrid through the back room again. She gently set the cat on the porch and shut the door again with a soft click. Muffled mews continued.

They backtracked to the hallway. The next classroom was empty. Beside it was an office, the walls fully shelved and laden with books. A box of record albums had upended, the sleeved contents strewn across the floor in a sinuous arc. A woman lay beneath a shelf, an arm stretched out and a gray feather duster inches away. Her slender neck was almost severed.

Ingrid stared. Mama had been head housekeeper for the Cordilleran Auxiliary, and Ingrid had assisted in those duties her whole life. This dead woman was a stranger, but her loss felt so damned personal.

Two more women were dead in the front entrance, more cleaning implements nearby. With no customers in the building on Monday, it must have been the staff's designated day for deep cleaning.

The kitchen around the corner still had a sink of crackling suds and a stack of dirty plates. Two women curled against each other on the black-and-white parquet floor. Ingrid's stomach writhed and clenched.

Cy led the retreat to the hall. A mahogany staircase started near the front door and coiled to the second story.

"I haven't felt anyone else die," Ingrid whispered.

"I still haven't heard any creaks from upstairs either," said Cy. "Walk slow and easy."

The stairs emitted mild gripes as the three of them trod upward and to another hallway. A door drooped from its hinges, splinters and wood chunks all over the floor. Inside were five beds, and five young men.

Ingrid could envision the scene; the screaming and chaos downstairs. The time to barricade themselves in a dormitory room. To grab weapons. There was a broken hockey stick, a hefty textbook, a bō. Personal books and papers were scattered across the floor along with body parts. These men hadn't merely had their throats slit. They had been brutally hacked apart.

"God," Ingrid whispered as she turned away and retched. She had thought that nothing else could burn itself into her mind as vividly as the destruction of San Francisco, but this, this . . .

They were silent as they congregated in the hallway. Her senses were numb as they continued down the hall.

Another dormitory room was empty, the small bunk beds smartly made. She looked around, automatically engaging in the old habit of counting occupants so she would know how many plates to set for meals. She stopped herself, then frowned.

"How many boys were in the downstairs classroom?" she whispered.

"Ten," said Cy. She wasn't surprised he knew. By the look in his eye, that number, those bodies, had been seared in his memory.

"There are fourteen occupants here." Fenris opened his mouth as if to argue and she waved a hand. "Don't count the beds. There are almost always extra beds in case of guests. Count how many beds have become *homes*." She motioned to the shelves and desks to either side, each of them tidy yet personalized with photographs, knickknacks, and books. Several wall hooks hosted colorful scarfs, weighted ends pulling the cloth straight; she shuddered at the thought of these boys playacting the dime-novel depictions of Thuggees with their scarves as weapons.

"Would youngsters be sent to a place like San Francisco?" murmured Cy.

Ingrid shook her head. "Not the juniors. Of course, they could be out on errands . . ."

Cy pursed his lips, nodding.

Hope. She had to hope that there were survivors, not just for the sake of their loved ones, but for the well-being of all of Seattle.

Cy pushed open the door at the end of the hall. The office held three desks, bookshelves, filing cabinets, and everything else a person would expect in such a place. A few feet inside the room, a silver-haired man lay curled on his side, arms protectively tucked to his knees. Cy touched his shoulder and pulled it toward the floor. The man's body unfolded to reveal an abdomen split into a foul, deep crimson. Ingrid forced her gaze up to his face.

"Warden Watanabe," she whispered.

"Here's another one," muttered Fenris.

Ingrid knew him by his bald spot. "Warden Terrance."

A third man sprawled facedown in front of a wardrobe. She took a step forward and stopped. The slit between the wardrobe doors revealed a deep blue sheen. She motioned to Cy.

"Blue," she whispered, almost giddy. It had to be one of the missing children. She *needed* it to be one of the missing children.

He leaned close to her. "Don't assume the person in there is innocent," he murmured.

Her cheeks flushed. "You can't think . . ."

"A warden killed everyone in your auxiliary. It could happen again." Sympathy shone in his eyes. He angled his gun toward the wardrobe. "Hello! Whoever's in there, we mean no harm, but we're not sure if you're so kindly inclined. Please come out with your hands up."

Something thudded in the wooden enclosure. "I can't!" cried a small voice. "Mr. Springer's dead, and he's *right there*."

Ingrid's heart broke. "Hello! My name's Ingrid. What's your name?" She heard Cy take in a sharp breath as she said her name, and realized she should have lied. Damn it. She had no brain for a life of subterfuge.

"Kenji Morimoto." American born or well Americanized, since he automatically said his surname last.

Ingrid set aside the quarterstaff and grabbed a worn blanket from a nearby chair. She fluffed it out to cover the dead man. "How old are you, Kenji?"

"Eleven. Is everyone else in the building dead?" he asked in a small voice.

Ingrid glanced back at Cy and Fenris, unsure how best to answer. "I covered up Mr. Springer. Can you come out?"

The door popped open a crack, slender fingers on the beveled edge. A boy leaned out; earth energy misted him in blue. His shiny black hair was cropped short, his pale face streaked with tears. He reminded Ingrid a great deal of how Lee looked when he first came to live in Mr. Sakaguchi's household. Kenji wore a green button-up shirt partially tucked into pleated tan trousers. His white-socked feet edged out as he stared at the floor as if it were deep water infested by sharks.

Ingrid walked around the corpse on the floor and reached out to the boy. His slick hands grasped hers like a lifeline and she pulled him free, coats and hanging clothes left swaying in his wake. Tucking his head against her arm, she walked him past the other desk and near a shuttered window. From here he wouldn't be able to see the bodies. She pressed him into a chair, his body limp and pliable as clay, and pivoted the seat to face her and the wall.

"We need more kermanite. He's energy-sick." Ingrid had empty pieces on her, but she also knew that she needed to be selfish for her own health's sake. "Kenji, who has the ready vault keys for this office?"

He blinked at her, swaying. "Mr. Springer. He's an adept and clerk. He promised us ice cream after we vented out the energy. We're supposed to hold it for one more day to make three days total, which is the longest we've ever made it."

Oh God. Ingrid bit her lip to contain her emotions. "Well, I think you should still get ice cream after two days."

Cy deftly searched Mr. Springer's body. After a moment, he held up a ring of jingling keys. Ingrid motioned with her head to the far wall, which contained an inlaid safe. If the kermanite there was inadequate, they could search the wardens; their cuff links or pockets should contain empty chunks. She certainly had no desire to return to the downstairs classroom to check that vault.

The boy started to turn around and Ingrid tugged on the chair arm so that he looked at her again. Across the room, Cy rustled in the vault. Fenris stared at a bookshelf, his arms crossed as if he was casually browsing for reading material.

"Kenji, can you tell us what happened?"

He shivered. Sweat sheened his skin. "There were screams. Lots of screams. Mr. Watanabe tried to use the telephone but the line didn't work. The other boys wanted to run but Mr. Springer shoved me in the wardrobe and told me to be quiet as a kirin. So I was."

Ingrid accepted a pouch from Cy as well as a full water glass he grabbed from a far desk. "Here, Kenji. Let's pull the energy out. Things are bad enough without you feeling like you have influenza, too, right?"

His nod was weak. The poor child had to be running a 102- or 103-degree fever, and had for two days. This would have been a miserable day even without a massacre taking place around him.

She shook the bag until two kermanite pieces fell into her hand. Each was the size of a shelled peanut. "I bet you can fill one of these and you might need the other one, too."

His brow furrowed. "How do you know? You're a woman, and . . ."

"I'm equipped with a functional brain and I know how to use it." She kept her tone gentle and chiding as she pressed kermanite into his palm. Kenji gasped, his back arching and eyes rolling back. Blue roiled and swirled into the kermanite, filling it within seconds. He sagged. She pushed the second piece into his limp hand. As she suspected, his energy cast a permanent smoky swirl into about half of the crystal. She dropped the pieces into her coat pocket.

"We can't stay here much longer," said Cy.

She nodded as she held the water to the boy's lips and helped him drink. "Kenji, can you tell us more about what happened? What did the attackers say?" Maybe, maybe they mentioned something about the large kermanite or their plans. Some information they could pass along to Mr. Roosevelt.

Kenji sagged in the chair, fatigued, as he likely would be for a few more days. However, some clarity had returned to his eyes. "The attackers. Mr. Watanabe locked them out. He tried to reason with them, but they were huge. Strong. The men yelled about San Francisco and the wardens dying there. They said Seattle deserved the same thing because of Baranov."

"They said Baranov? Are you sure?" asked Cy.

"Yes, sir." He glanced back at Cy. "The men, they were Russians. They were mad because of the gold rush. They said foreigners were going to steal all the gold."

"They'll try," Ingrid softly said. That was exactly what Blum intended.

"The Russians said that other Russians were going to

die in fights in Baranov, and that if they survived that and went to Russia, they'd still die, because the czar would blame them for not doing their jobs." He stared into space for a long moment.

"Kenji." Cy got his attention. "Did the Russians say why they came to the auxiliary in particular?"

"To try to destroy Seattle." He said it dully. "The miners going north have to travel through here. They said it'd be a great triumph if an earthquake happened to stop all the travelers. They wanted . . . they wanted everyone here to know why they were being killed."

The facts sank in. Russians had done this, not Thuggees. Maybe they were directed by their government, maybe they acted of their own volition. Whatever their motivation was, the root cause was still Ambassador Blum.

Ingrid rocked in her shoes, her grief striking her anew. The dead boys, the men who died in their defense, the housekeepers and cooks who never had a chance, the cat that kept crying and crying for the people she loved and not understanding why no one came.

Cy's expression was hard. "Kenji, you said there were other boys in here with you. Where'd they go?"

The boy shrank back in the chair. "The Russians took them. Grant, Daisuke, and Tetsu. They took my friends and I didn't do anything. I didn't say anything." He began to shake. "I did what Mr. Springer said. I stayed quiet and still."

"Mr. Springer told you the right thing. You couldn't have stopped those men, Kenji." Ingrid cupped her hand to his jaw. He began to sob.

"They . . . they were going back to their airship to leave. They wanted young geomancers to take home, that they might be worth something. That . . . that . . . we were old enough to not cry, young enough to learn true obedience."

The presence of three young geomancers could make a major difference in stabilizing Seattle. Ingrid and Cy shared a look.

"They'd need a Behemoth-class airship for a direct flight to Russia," said Cy. "That means the main port in Seattle."

"We better hurry," said Ingrid as she stood.

"You . . . you're going after them?" Kenji asked, his voice soft with awe.

"Yes," said Ingrid.

"I saw from upstairs when they pulled up. The Russians had a produce truck with a white canvas back. That's why Trisha let them in. She thought . . . She said . . ." His face crumpled up again.

"You don't have to tell us anything else," said Ingrid. "You've been so brave, Kenji—"

"No, I haven't," he blurted. "I've been cowardly and I dishonored—"

"Don't you dare say you dishonored your family," Fenris snapped. He advanced several steps to lean on the desk beside Kenji. "That old cliché is ground into people like a bootheel crunching a beetle into pavement. You're alive, child. You did *exactly* what was asked of you under horrible, dangerous circumstances. Disobeying your adept would have gotten you killed or kidnapped, which would've left us with no way to find your friends."

The words shocked Kenji as effectively as a slap to the face.

"Is there a home nearby where you go to play? Where you know people?" Ingrid asked, giving Fenris a slight nod of gratitude for his succinct words.

"Hai. Mrs. March's house down at the corner."

"Grab that scarf from the hook, please?" Ingrid motioned to Fenris, taking care to avoid saying his name. "I'm going to cover your eyes, Kenji, so you don't have to see anything else in the building. We'll get you to Mrs. March, and she needs to call the police and report what happened here."

"You can't stay with me?" he whispered as he squeezed her hands.

Hold it together, she told herself. "We have to hurry if we're going to save your friends." She caught the tossed scarf. It was soft wool, the sort a gentleman would wear. "Also, please don't tell the police much about us. We shouldn't be here."

"I'm glad you were," Kenji whispered. He squeezed her hands again.

"I'm glad we were, too," said Ingrid, and wondered if she would ever again sleep without nightmares.

CHAPTER 15

"Never in my life have I seen so many canvas-back trucks," Ingrid said.

She, Cy, and Fenris disembarked from a rickshaw at the southernmost entrance to the largest dock along Elliott Bay. Since this location catered exclusively to larger-class vessels, Cy hadn't included it in their search for the *Palmetto Bug,* and Ingrid was grateful for that. From the entrance alone, she could tell that the dock was huge. Her legs ached in anticipation of the walk to come.

The embarcadero was a creeping glacier of autocars, carriages, rickshaws with both people and goods, and bicycles. Behemoth- and Tiamat-class vessels hovered above like bloated whales, with naval vessels below. A deafening roar descended on all sides. The airships emitted throaty rumbles that reverberated through Ingrid's chest and down through her feet.

The large airships required mooring masts that stretched as high as skyscrapers, with wide buffer space between each station to accommodate for the wind. Automated cranes assisted in loading and unloading pallets of goods with high whines and hoarse grinds of gears. Vehicle wheels rumbled, horns tooted, and everywhere men talked and yelled and whistled.

As luck would have it, it had also begun to rain. This added to the cacophony with the heavy sloshing of wheels through puddles and water pattering on metal and the muffled drumming of droplets on broad airship envelopes.

"We still have an advantage here," said Cy, pressing into the throng of humanity.

"Really? Do tell!" said Fenris.

"If the Russians have the boys simply flung in the back of a truck, they'll need to drive all the way to their ship to try to haul them inside with any secrecy. On foot, we're faster than the street traffic."

"Never mind that the kidnappers were gone from the auxiliary before we even arrived, and drove away in a kermanite-powered vehicle," growled Fenris, shoving past a stevedore. A Behemoth-class airship with a Unified Pacific flag hovered overhead; several Japanese naval transport ships were docked below it.

"Fenris, can you swallow the sarcasm for once?" asked Ingrid. "Please, please, help me entertain the fantasy that the kidnappers are still here."

Fenris cast her a brief, apologetic look.

Cy hesitated a moment to fall into step beside Ingrid. An

autocar horn blared to their right. The potent stink of fish and motor oil almost made Ingrid gag.

"Before I forget, here." He passed her a rounded pouch the size of her fist. By the telltale clinks, she knew it contained kermanite. A glance inside confirmed this, and that the stones were empty.

Cy ducked his head in a way that signaled embarrassment. "Yes, those are from the auxiliary vault."

They briefly separated to allow a rickshaw with a trailer to pass. Ingrid frowned. "I already had the extra stones that you passed along in case Kenji needed them. You can't just empty their vault—"

"Yes, I can. I know the potential of your power, Ingrid, and that you don't want to harm anyone. This is for the public good, and your own. Be mad at me if you want, but I don't regret taking those crystals." His gaze was level, challenging. She gritted her teeth and dropped the pouch into her left waist pocket, where she kept the other empty kermanite.

"Well, well," said Fenris, his voice almost obscured by the horrible noises all around. "Cy, you're stealing things with defiant justification. I never thought I'd see the day."

"I hoped it'd never come to that day." Cy looked up, squinting beneath the low-angled brim of his derby hat. "It's a mercy that the nationalities of these airships are easy to spot from far off. I spy some more UP vessels, plus Japanese and British. There are two Russian ships about a half mile down."

Ingrid recognized the Russian diagonal-centered St. Andrews blue cross on a white background, as it had been a common sight at San Francisco docks as well.

"You're assuming that these Russians are actually serving aboard a Russian ship," said Ingrid.

"Stole the words out of my mouth," said Fenris.

Ingrid eyed a cluster of trucks on the roadway. Kenji had only described the attackers as large, which wasn't particularly helpful to identify the men. Many workers at the dock were of hefty build.

"Most of these ships are managed by Japanese or American crews. With tension as it is between Russia and Japan over Manchukuo, it's unlikely Russians would serve aboard a ship with Unified Pacific flags. These men sound especially nationalistic, too."

Ingrid sucked in a breath as she looked around. "Cy?"

"I see them." His voice was a whisper.

American Army & Airship Corps soldiers swarmed the dock like bees on a hive. They were not in tidy lines either, but scattered as if they were searching for something. Or someone. Ingrid tugged her hood forward and jammed her hands into her pockets. The Crescent Blade was a warm weight between her arm and torso. High security was to be expected here, what with the thefts at the smaller docks around town, but the sheer number of soldiers was daunting to behold.

"They can't be here for us?" asked Fenris, voice low. "If they're here to help look for the boys, they sure arrived awfully fast." Ingrid, Cy, and Fenris had waited near the auxiliary long enough to see Kenji run into the neighbor woman's arms before they had dashed off to find a rickshaw.

"Could be part of a buildup to move against the Chinese," said Cy. Ingrid felt a pang at those words. *Oh, Lee, please be safe.* "Ingrid, it might be best to—"

"I'm not leaving here. I can't. There are a lot of other boys working here at the dock, but I'll know the geomancers by their miasma." She ducked her head lower, going quiet as they passed a soldier.

Ingrid's heart thrummed like the engine of the airship above. *Please, God, let them be searching for the boys, not me.*

The gray cloud cover darkened as the hidden sun crawled toward the horizon.

A crowd of sailors forced Ingrid, Cy, and Fenris to walk single file. A stack of crates had been knocked into the roadway, and men had engaged in a shouting match as they pointed at the flow of traffic. Several soldiers stepped forward to intercede.

Ingrid glanced at the Unified Pacific vessels behind them. One was Behemoth class, the other Tiamat class; both were massive and capable of delivering hundreds of soldiers, though the closer Tiamat was the more likely transport in this case. Behemoths were favored for hauling heavy and large goods rather than people, or for dropping payloads of bombs on enemy cities. Both of the Russian vessels ahead were Behemoths.

"Listen," Cy said, and Fenris and Ingrid gathered as close as they could while still slogging forward. "If we're separated, if any of us is arrested, the others need to make it back to the rink. We all know the local contact addresses from T.R. Keep that in mind, just in case." They nodded; Cy had insisted that they memorize that information after their reunion the day before. "When we find these men—if we find them—we need to move quickly. That means me and Fenris. Ingrid, you have to stay back." Emotion rang clear in his voice. "I'm praying that the men are injured from their scuffles at the auxiliary. Anything to give us an advantage."

Through stacks of boxes, Ingrid watched a truck with a canvas cover back up to one of the Russian mooring masts. Cy and Fenris likewise noticed, all three of them simultaneously taking shelter between stacks of crates. Other vehicles and cargo shielded the backside of the truck from the heavy traffic along the embarcadero.

Sudden prickles of heat flared against Ingrid's skin. She recoiled slightly as something skittered inside the boxes before her. The whole stack was covered by a grayed and stained tarp, the corner edges revealing that the boxes were only about a foot in diameter. Still, there was no telling what sort of fantastic was inside, and she wasn't sure if she wanted to find out.

"Ingrid," said Cy.

Her gaze jerked back to the truck. Two men exited the cab and rounded the vehicle. A man emerged from the back hatch and pushed forward a smaller figure. A burlap bag covered the child's head but that couldn't hide the unmistakable blue of earth energy that emanated from his body.

Another man shoved the child back inside the truck, his arms flailing as he berated his comrade.

"It's them," she gasped.

Cy leaned close to her. She expected some last words of wisdom, a reminder for her to stay back and safe. Instead, his lips crushed against hers in a hungry, desperate kiss that stole away her breath and made her heart speed up even more. He pulled back, a thousand poignant words shining in his eyes, and turned away with a ripple of wet leather.

"Good-bye for a short while," said Fenris, then shrugged. "That seems rather anticlimactic compared to Cy's exit." He scurried to catch up with Cy.

Ingrid hunkered in the narrow gap between stacks. She was relieved that she was well hidden from passing soldiers and other traffic, but at the same time, she was keenly aware that she was cowering. She hated it, this powerlessness, when she knew she could be powerful. *Useful.*

Cy and Fenris ducked and weaved among freight parcels that kept them fairly well concealed until they reached the area immediately around the truck. She bobbed to see around the crates and follow their progress. Her heart pounded out a fierce rhythm. The men had vanished from her line of sight.

She pressed her fist against her mouth, as if she could stifle her panic. She couldn't stand this. Male voices rang from close by, startling her. She tucked her hands inside her pockets and shrank against the crates. Her fingers found very different kermanite in each pocket—the unfilled rocks on the left, and on the right her father's strange blemished stones along with the pieces Kenji had filled. Her thumb stroked the cracked, whorled surface of one of Papa's, then found the filled kermanite. It was warm with power.

Ingrid focused on the crystal and squeezed as if she could smash it like a tomato.

A hundred repetitive auxiliary lessons flooded through her mind, about how kermanite worked, how geomancy worked, how energy flowed along specific proven parameters.

With the pressure of her thumb, she shattered those rules.

Power eddied beneath her touch, warm as scalded milk, then gushed into her hand, her arm, her entire body. She welcomed the increase in temperature with a small, delighted sigh, even as she told herself that she had to take it slow, she didn't want to create pain, that she didn't dare tax her body too much. The kermanite crunched in her grip. She slowly withdrew her hand to shake out a palm coated with splintered and powdered kermanite. Worried, she swiped her hand on her coat, but found that nothing had penetrated her skin. Kermanite could form sharp points, but it seemed that her desire to avoid pain had spontaneously formed a protective barrier over her skin as she took in power.

Ingrid bit her lip to hold back a delirious laugh. She could pull power from filled kermanite! That meant she wouldn't need to hurt herself to pull in power, that she could actually *steal* power from many of the most common machines around. This changed everything—if she could form a protective barrier at will, that meant she could shield herself from injury, too. It made her fully useful again to help Cy, Fenris, and Lee. She could actively assist in saving Mr. Sakaguchi!

Of course, the back-and-forth flow of magic still claimed a mighty toll on her body. She couldn't forget that.

Ingrid peered around the crates but still couldn't see Fenris and Cy, nor could she hear any fuss beyond the usual din of the port. Power sang in her veins. The energy that had made Kenji energy-sick and miserable for days felt to her like the warm exhilaration that came with dashing up several flights of stairs.

Heat still radiated from the crates in front of her, too. She wasn't defenseless now, and she was certainly curious. She eased the tarp up to her eye level.

Sierran sylphs. Gobs of them. They littered the bottom of the cage like bird dung, their bodies gray and limp. She'd encountered a few sylphs like this once at the Cordilleran Auxiliary. Warden Calhoun had brought them in for boasting purposes. "These sylphs are all the rage in Japan," he had said. "Drop them in hot oil and they are cooked within a minute. Gourmands say a Sierran sylph tastes like magic embodied in a single bite, quite a delicacy for anyone, especially a mundane."

He had made sure that everyone knew his handful of sylphs cost more than what most people made in a month of labor, too, and all for a few bites of food. Sierran sylphs weren't simply regarded as a luxury item because of their flavor and their magical-sensory effects, but also because it was a challenge to catch them at all. In nature, they often rendered themselves invisible. Sylphs had to be drugged in order to be caught, and they had to be alive when cooked. Warden Calhoun had been rather enthralled by that fact.

Ingrid regretted what Mr. Calhoun's murder last week had meant for San Francisco, but perhaps it was fitting that he died an excruciating death by arsenic.

Some sort of white crust coated the cage bars; it looked like salt. She pressed her fingertips to the coating and sniffed, and smelling nothing, gave it a quick lick. Yes, it was salt. As if the iron by itself wasn't toxic enough to fairies. She rubbed the bars to take off as much salt as possible and swiped her fingers clean on her wet coat.

The Russians were loudly arguing by their truck, their words indecipherable. Maybe now they were beginning to realize the errors of their horrific murder spree.

With an eye to the truck, Ingrid reached into her interior coat pocket. To her relief, the newspaper packet didn't feel compressed or sticky. With her body bowed to provide cover, the *guandao* tilting to press against her breast, she unfolded the paper to reveal the intact jamu-pan.

"I'll be damned if I let you sylphs be shipped overseas to be some rich man's snack," she muttered. She tore the sweet bread in half, taking care to show both halves to the sylphs in the nearest cages. Ingrid had read a great deal about such fantastics in her youth, and knew food was powerful for fairies. Giving the fae too large a portion implied subservience; too small a portion invited offense. Equal portions implied respect and equality, and marked the initiation of a business transaction.

She took a bite from her half of the jamu-pan, then from the other half tore off a chunk to squeeze between the tightly spaced iron bars. The food landed inside the cage as strawberry-and-yeast-bread goop.

The sylphs were sluggish to stir. A few fluttered toward the food, then more, then they hovered in the form of a shoe-sized cloud. Ingrid gasped in awe of them as their wings unfurled. At a glance, a fully visible sylph could be mistaken for a large gray moth but for the humanoid body attached to speckled wings. The mob descended on the piece of jam-filled bun.

Ingrid's gaze flicked between the truck and more of the cages as she repeated her actions. She rubbed salt from the bars, then made a show of sharing the sweet bread. The captive sylphs gorged themselves on their meager fare. Ingrid licked her fingers clean and wished she had brought more food.

The sylphs, however, didn't require much food to be revived. One instant, they resembled nothing more than ashy leaves—the next, they were a fluttering mass pressed as close to the bars as possible without touching the salted iron. Not a crumb of food remained.

"I hope that gives you enough power to free yourselves," Ingrid whispered. "Maybe you can find your way back home to California, or maybe the nearby Cascades will suffice. I haven't heard of any mountain sylphs here. I know your kind were an invasive species to North America centuries ago, but perhaps you can adapt here without harming—"

She stopped whispering at the sight of Cy creeping along the side of the truck, a Tesla rod extended in his grip. He dashed at the four arguing men. Even with all the noise above and around, Ingrid heard the crack and smack of a Tesla rod striking flesh. One of the men slumped to the ground like a sack of meat. Cy danced back, his coat flaring as another man lunged for him. With a swipe and an electric flash, that man flopped down, too.

Ingrid watched, heart galloping, energy surging as she readied a strike of her own.

Fenris came into view as he clambered onto the truck's back bumper. The old truck bounced with movement. A boy leaned into view. No bag covered his head, and his black hair stood wild. Cy helped him down, then reached for another child, then another. The boys all looked to be Kenji's age, each attired in the same green shirts and tan trousers. They teetered in a cluster, the daze they were in apparent even at a distance.

Fenris hopped out of the truck, lean and graceful. Cy bowed an arm over the boys and pointed, his gestures urgent. Like the sylphs, the boys were slow to start moving, but once they had accumulated momentum, it was crazed.

"Help! Soldiers! Help!" they screamed and waved as they tore toward nearby soldiers.

When Ingrid glanced back at the truck, Fenris and Cy

were gone. She sank into the gap between the crates, trembling with relief. Thank God, thank God. Now she needed to skedaddle, too.

Tingles traveled along her spine like the mincing steps of a spider. She froze. A strange, dank smell flashed in her nose, even stronger than the competing stenches of the port. She recognized the odor. *Ambassador Blum*. It was the scent of the dark Reiki she had used to heal Ingrid's leg, the magic that the ki doc in Portland had said was still staining Ingrid.

Ingrid turned, slowly, in dread that Ambassador Blum would be standing right behind her with a bright smile on her aged face. There were only more crates. She looked past the mountain ranges of parcels destined to cross the ocean, and to the Unified Pacific vessel with an especially prominent rising sun on the side. A figure in black stood at the top of the high mooring mast, skirt rippling in the wind.

Ambassador Blum had arrived in Seattle.

CHAPTER 16

How had Blum managed to arrive at this very moment? What were the odds of such a thing?

And if Ingrid could sense her—was the feeling mutual?

Ingrid shrank into the shadows between the crates as if she could render herself invisible if she were perfectly still.

Memories of the night she spent in Blum's custody flooded through her and threatened to drown her—that initial hope that a woman ambassador might be sympathetic to her plight, might listen to her. The way Captain Sutcliff—that arrogant, pompous officer convinced of Mr. Sakaguchi's complicity with the Chinese—quivered in terror at Blum's arrival. He'd looked at Ingrid and said, in earnest, "God help you."

As the saying goes, God does work in mysterious ways. The earthquake that devastated San Francisco had filtered enough power to Ingrid to enable her escape from the iron cell Blum had secured her in.

Even if Mr. Roosevelt or his men had betrayed them, the timing of Blum's arrival was too peculiar, too alarming. Had Blum prodded the Russians to lash out at local geomancers, and now appeared to oversee the results? That seemed beyond the pale, even for Blum, but the ambassador worked on a centuries-long time frame that Ingrid could scarcely comprehend. Nothing could be put past her.

Ingrid was certain of one thing: she wanted no part in Blum's game.

The sylphs were fluttering like contained fog, clearly agitated. Ingrid wondered if they were drawing on her own emotions or if they sensed Blum's musky power—or both.

She pressed a hand to the crusty iron bars. "I know your wings are used to make ninja attire invisible. Can you hide me? Not just me physically, but my power, my smell? She can't find me!" Her voice shook, as did her grip on the bars.

The sylphs fluttered in place. They showed no sign that they understood anything she said.

Ingrid glanced through the stacks of freight to the mooring mast. Blum was walking down the long, winding staircase. Ingrid sensed it, somehow, the reverberation of her approach like ripples against her skin. She was utterly baffled. Her connection with Blum couldn't be through earth magic—the high metal tower would transmit little geomantic energy, even in a major earthquake.

She whirled around to the sylphs again. She had to communicate with them, and that left one option. Ingrid focused on her power, on the burble of warmth in her veins, and pulled on that heat to reach out to the mobs of sylphs.

She drew on the potency of her own emotion, her own abject terror.

HELP ME, she pleaded. The rapidness of her heart, her escalating fright, poured outward as viscous as motor oil in summer.

Thousands of sylphs quivered.

Ingrid repeated her plea. She didn't try to project her power as a yell, the way she had with the thunderbird—she didn't dare, knowing that Blum was a fantastic as well.

The sylphs' wings thrummed. They were receiving her words, even if they didn't understand. Ingrid didn't dare bludgeon them with power; they were delicate air creatures that could easily be hurt by elemental earth magic. A few crumbs of jamu-pan couldn't undo prolonged starvation in a poisonous iron cage either.

Blum was coming closer, closer.

Was Ingrid already surrounded by soldiers? Or did Blum want the full honor of tracking down her prey? Ingrid battled to control her terror, and she sensed how the sylphs were absorbing her emotion. They fanned their wings in synchrony.

we understand.

It wasn't said in English or Japanese or any language Ingrid could identify, but it came across clearly in the sylphs' collective hum. The sylphs knew empathy, and fear, and despair. They knew something terrible was approaching. They knew what it meant to be prey in the presence of a superior carnivore.

The image of the jamu-pan flashed back to her mind,

this time seen from their eyes. They understood why Ingrid broke the bread as she did. This was a trade, a transaction, one with mutual benefit.

I understand, she replied, her emotion from the heart.

Ingrid pressed her hand against the nearest cage. The iron bars were set scarcely a pinky finger's width apart to prevent tiny fairy kind from squeezing through. The energy within her body roiled and welled as she called it forth, but she concentrated in order to pour out just a dab, like adding cream to a warden's coffee.

The slender iron bars crackled and dimmed to a faint gray. Ingrid provided a physical shove and shattered them completely. Sylphs flooded through a hole almost the size of Ingrid's hand, their gratitude turning the air fragrant with the scent of lavender.

Ingrid moved fast, breaking each cage in sequence. Sylphs fluttered around her in a delighted, buzzing cloud. She wished she could feed and free all of them—she had no idea how many were stacked there, ready to be loaded—but there was no more food and certainly no more time.

Blum was advancing in a swirl of power.

The sylphs knew, too. The cloud expanded around Ingrid, the moth-like wings beating faster, faster. Ingrid's hood blew back, but no rain dappled her face. Fanning wings propelled the water away. Her coat billowed at her knees, strands of hair drifting at her cheeks. Air magic stung her exposed skin like rose thorns, the pain in her face sudden and excruciating. The turbulent fog filled her vision.

Therefore, she didn't see the flare of blue earth energy

even as new warmth caressed her. Her body pulled in power. She feared that the miasma might send the sylphs scattering, but they seemed fine.

Ingrid needed to stop the pain.

Tugging on her power, she attempted a peculiar sort of shield: she needed to numb herself. She needed the air magic to shroud her, but maybe she could stop the pain signals from reaching her brain.

She slowly inhaled and exhaled, and the stinging sensation faded even as the strange air pressure of the fairies' power increased.

Ingrid glanced down. She could still see herself, and felt a surge of panic.

The sylphs laughed like rustling leaves in a breeze. *worry not. we have you. magic will hold until* . . . They paused. *sunset. then, we rest.*

"Here goes nothing," she muttered beneath her breath as she stepped out from among the crates.

While she had been focusing on the caged fairies and Blum, activity on the dock had shifted to controlled chaos. Even more soldiers had swarmed the vicinity. She identified the location of the Russians by the knot of guards around them. More soldiers climbed up and down the mooring mast to the Russian ship as well as the UP vessel. Traffic within the port had descended from creeping progress to a total logjam as soldiers moved crates to completely block vehicle movement. Furious autocar horns and loud male voices made it clear what others thought of this inconvenience.

Ambassador Blum was standing about twenty feet away. Her aura of magic was so thick Ingrid could practically chew it, but she never would have recognized Blum by her physical appearance.

Blum's vivid red hair was braided and coiled into an artful bun topped by an asymmetrical, shallow black hat with a broad rim. Her face was young, her expression distorted in a frown as she listened to a soldier. She could easily pass for near Ingrid's age. She wore black, as she had before, but the fit of her clothes now accentuated a different body. A black peacoat flared back in the wind to show a black corset defining a narrow waist. A high black lace collar pressed against her throat and contrasted with her milky skin. The backside of her coat showed the protrusion of what seemed to be an antiquated bustle, but Ingrid knew that the lump really indicated the presence of at least four large foxtails beneath her clothes.

This was the Blum that Cy knew and had described from the years when he worked on his prototype Durendal. There had been some sort of flirtation between Blum and him back then, but it hadn't progressed very far. Cy hadn't known she was a kitsune. Indeed, he hadn't even known she was an ambassador for months, as she had always worn gloves to hide her signet ring.

As Blum spoke with the soldier, her gaze flicked all around and she tilted up her head as if sniffing. She looked straight at Ingrid and didn't react.

Taking a deep breath to quell her terror, Ingrid moved closer.

Stories about kitsune said that they were able to take a new body every hundred years as a new tail completed its growth. The emphasis was on *take*. Kitsune cleaved a soul from its newly chosen body so they could claim it as their own, stacking the body with old forms as a person might stack a deck of cards. The soul of the body's former inhabitant was set free to be a ghost or to find nirvana or heaven, whatever it willed.

Ingrid wondered if this body, so attractively Irish or Scottish in origin, was Blum's most recent acquisition because she worked more often with the Western world. Maybe the name of "Blum" came along with it.

An Army & Airship Corps captain was speaking with Blum. ". . . completely butchered. I have never seen the like in America, Ambassador."

"All four boys are unharmed, beyond energy sickness?"

"Yes, ma'am. Frightened witless, too, but grateful to be saved. We're still searching for the two men the boys described, and for the woman said to have been at the auxiliary."

Blum licked her lips. "Yes. *Her*."

Ingrid stood a mere five feet away. The heady scent of Blum's magic made her stomach twist at memories she couldn't linger on, not here, not now. Instead, her fear faded to cold, hard defiance. People moved around her, diverted by the intense magic of the fairy fog. An Imperial Japanese officer even walked by, a Murata-to curved saber at his waist.

"I want them found. It's vital to the security of the Unified Pacific. The woman in particular. She's here. She's close, I've known that for hundreds of miles, and yet . . ." Blum frowned, her naturally pink and pert lips making the expression disturbingly attractive. "She's *not*. It's vexing. But intriguing."

Blum wasn't perturbed by Ingrid's having vanished while she was so close.

In fact, Blum looked *ecstatic*.

"We're deploying more soldiers throughout the city, ma'am, and our other ships will arrive within hours." He hesitated. "Reporters are gathering here at the dock and at the auxiliary. Civilians are starting to panic that what happened in San Francisco might happen here as well."

"Good." Her green eyes narrowed to slits. "Fear can be used. Directed. Honed. Captain, issue a report that describes the butchery at the Cascadian Auxiliary and the miracle of how these boys were recovered here at the dock. Describe our soldiers as the heroes who retrieved the poor children as their Chinese kidnappers tried to smuggle them aboard a Russian vessel."

The captain jotted down notes. He seemed to take her revisions to the truth in stride. "Should the Russians be mentioned as complicit in the scheme, ma'am?"

Blum made a thoughtful hum, her gestures and posture reminding Ingrid of the older woman's body that the ambassador had worn before. "Yes. *Yes*. The Chinese used Russian strongmen, mercenaries. That will increase public sentiment against the Russian possession of Baranov as well.

"Build on the known fact that the Chinese are too physically weak to commit such violence themselves, but don't encourage civilian violence against the Chinese here in Seattle. If the fool townspeople take it upon themselves to police the vicinity, they'll likely burn down the whole city again. Assure them that the soldiers have things well in hand without mentioning our timeline, of course. We need to seize Chinatown tonight before Warden Sakaguchi can slip out of its crevices. My sources say his *tong* plans to move onward immediately. His vanishing act has been *inconvenient*. I need to get back to Atlanta to ascertain the full scope of fire damage at the project site."

Mr. Sakaguchi is here. Ingrid felt a mingled wave of relief and terror rush through her, followed by smoldering rage.

"You bitch," she whispered.

Blum froze. Ingrid scarcely breathed. An officer approached Blum with a smart salute. "Ambassador, we have set up an area for your interrogation of the Russian's leader, Kozlov."

"Hmm?" Blum said distractedly as she sniffed the air again.

"Ambassador?"

Blum looked around, expression uncertain, then came to attention again. "Excellent." She dismissed the first officer with a few words and followed the newcomer with crisp strides. Against all wisdom, Ingrid trailed in their wake. A quick glance at the horizon showed a harsh beam of sunlight cutting through the gray clouds. Ingrid dared not linger long, but she couldn't let this opportunity escape. She needed to know what Blum knew.

Soldiers saluted Blum as she passed, their expressions flickering between awe, confusion, and blatant lust. Ingrid doubted many of them even recognized Blum as an ambassador, but they knew she was someone important.

A group of soldiers stood beneath the cover of a long, wall-less structure that seemed to be designed for loading goods. Low stacks of boxes cluttered one end. Overhead, light rain pinged on the corrugated iron roof. Ingrid edged beneath the cover.

Kozlov sat on a wooden shipping box, three soldiers around him with hands on their weapons. He was a huge man, thick as a Minotaur. Blood smeared the skin of his forehead and cheeks and left black patches in his thicket of a brown beard. His dark peacoat undoubtedly hid far more stains. His brow furrowed at the sight of Ambassador Blum. He barked out a laugh, followed by a torrent of Russian words.

Blum clapped her hands and responded in turn. Her Russian was Gatling-gun fast, poetic to the ears. The Russian's jaw fell slack.

"Now that your rather intimate proposal has been rejected, I will speak in my preferred tongue." Blum spoke in Japanese. "As a sailor, you know the language, I assume?"

"I know it." His accent was thick, almost incomprehensible. He blinked, clearly baffled by the woman before him.

"Good!" Blum tugged off her gloves in a graceful move

and extended her right hand. The ambassadorial ring looked an unnatural shade of green. "I assume you know what this means?"

Ingrid shot another worried glance at the western horizon. Damn Blum and her posturing. This was taking too long.

Kozlov's expression shifted from bewilderment to terror. "You're an ambassador. You're *that* one, the fox?"

"Ah, wonderful. My reputation precedes me." She flicked her fingers. The guards around Kozlov stepped back. His wrists were shackled but his ankles were not. He glanced down, taking this in, telegraphing his intent to escape to everyone around.

"Hope. It's beautiful, yet so ephemeral." Blum spun in place, granting Ingrid a quick glance of her smiling face, and then she pounced on Kozlov, agile as a true fox. Her arms were a black blur as she pounded him in the head. His body recoiled left, right, left again, the smacks of flesh on flesh sounding more liquid with each impact. Blum retreated again, as light on her feet as a dancer, her pleated coat elegantly twirling at her hips. Kozlov groaned, the sound prolonged and agonized.

"Who ordered you to attack the Cascadian Auxiliary?" Blum's words were a snarl.

Kozlov's face was blocked from Ingrid's view by Blum's body, but she heard him gurgle as he sat upright again. He started to speak in Russian, and after a pause to spit, switched to Japanese. "No one. No one over me. It was my idea. To try to slow the American invasion of Baranov. This gold rush, it will cause many Russian deaths, much suffering among soldiers."

Ambassador Blum began to pace. The strength of her power buffeted against Ingrid. "Two auxiliaries obliterated in the past week. The Cordilleran branch destroyed by those newfangled Thuggees—in league with the Chinese, of course," she added as an afterthought. "And then there is your gallant plot. You and your comrades may have annihilated the Cascadian Auxiliary's geomancers, but Seattle won't suffer as San Francisco has. I'll make sure of it." She shook her head, her black hat's wide brim bobbing. "You men with your petty plans. *I am the divine wind!*" Her voice grew louder with each word. "You are nothing. You have the life span of a gnat. I will not tolerate further distractions!"

Blum's power flared, the stench of it almost overwhelming. Even the soldiers seemed to sense something, their eyes widening as they shot nervous glances at each other. Blum's form flickered. Her hair darkened, the outline of her figure blurring.

A second later, Blum relaxed and adjusted her hat. Her form stilled. The cloying thickness in the air dissipated enough to allow for easier breathing, but didn't completely leave.

Ingrid's heart clamored in her chest. Around her, the sylphs quivered. *go?*

Soon, Ingrid thought back at them, picturing slight movement of the sun. They accepted this with a reaction she could only describe as grudging.

It's not as though Ingrid had any true desire to stay. Terror had left her mouth parched, her tongue heavy. Her horror was reflected in the face of the brawny Kozlov, which she could now see clearly. He looked as if he had met with a threshing machine. Claw marks carved crimson trails from his cheeks to his jaw, where tufts of his beard were gone. His eyes were swelling up, reduced to mere slits. A knot the size of the ambassadorial ring grew on his blood-streaked forehead.

"We'll get more geomancers here. The Brits owe me," Blum murmured in Japanese as she began pacing again. "I will make them send more adepts from Vancouver. We'll get Sakaguchi in Chinatown tonight, squelch his little insurrection. Perhaps soldiers will finally find my kermanite now that Captain Sutcliff is no longer in command. The crystal isn't quite so vital now, but it will still be useful." She paused in reciting her to-do list to smile. "I'll retrieve my friend Ingrid somewhere around here, too. That might be the only fun to come from all this mess." She giggled, the sound sending a violent chill through Ingrid.

Friend? The very idea almost made her vomit. She stared at the kitsune with a renewed revulsion. Blum was *lonely*. No wonder she chased after Ingrid; to her, it was as if they were children playing some sordid game of hide-and-seek.

Cy was right. Blum needed to die for Ingrid to have any chance of peace, for the world to have any chance. But how? No mortal weapon could harm her while she wore her ambassadorial ring. Her greatest vulnerability had to be her hoshi no tama, the onion-shaped pendant at her neck.

Knowing Blum, though, the pendant would be difficult to access and likely cursed or impenetrable.

No mortal weapon.

Ingrid's hand went to the bundle tied to her waist: the Green Dragon Crescent Blade. She had forgotten about it amid everything else that had happened this afternoon. She motioned for the sylphs to follow her as she stooped down, slipping open her coat so she could work on the knots. If anything could kill Blum, the *guandao* could. Maybe that's what the *qilin* had intended all along.

Sudden heaviness caused her to lurch forward. She barely caught herself on the icy concrete, biting back a yelp of surprise just in time. A few feet away, a nervous soldier glanced in her direction and then back at Blum.

This was the sort of weight she and Lee had expected when they initially unwrapped the *guandao* in Portland. Had the Crescent Blade read her mind, sure as any fantastic? The heat of the artifact felt the same as before. Ingrid fully lowered her body to the ground before the bag or its strings gave out and created a racket that the sylphs could never hide.

Just feet away, Blum spoke with one of the officers as the Russian was hauled to his feet. The interrogation was over. Blum was going to leave—to prepare for an attack on Chinatown.

I need to kill her! she thought at the weapon. *Become lighter again so that I can move!*

The negative backlash boomed through Ingrid like a

banshee screaming in her face. She shuddered, trying not to make a sound that would betray her, terrified of the *guandao,* terrified of being revealed. She craned up her head enough to check on the sylphs. They continued their circuitous paths, unharmed by the reverberations.

Let me use you. Please, she thought at the *guandao* again. This time, the reply unfolded in her mind, a leaden message in a single word.

CARRY.

That was her duty, and only that. The blade would not allow her to wield it.

The weight vanished again. Ingrid relaxed against the floor, shivering. Sweat coursed down her neck as she struggled to keep her heavy breaths quiet. She restrained the urge to burst out in hysterical giggles. How nice of the holy weapon to keep her humble. After all, Ingrid couldn't get uppity just because she had demigod-like geomantic powers. She couldn't assume she could pull Excalibur from the stone, or the Green Dragon Crescent Blade from a leather pouch.

go? There was anxiety in the sylphs' susurrous.

Ingrid needed to get away from this place, from Blum's evil presence. To be warm and dry and safe—or as relatively safe as possible. She worked herself to her feet and shot Blum a final, frustrated glare. She was a horrible, psychotic *thing.* Relentlessly pursuing Mr. Sakaguchi. Using the Chinese as the scapegoat for the auxiliary attack. Treating the deaths of the auxiliary children as inconveniences when, in truth, they were living beings to mourn. But then, what were these few deaths compared to the millions Blum had already caused? As Blum herself had said, people were mere gnats.

And Ingrid knew she would see the ambassador again all too soon.

Anger brought a flare of power to her skin and she consciously struggled to notch it down so that she didn't harm the sylphs as she rushed from the docks. The fairy glamour caused people to unconsciously step aside and grant Ingrid quick passage. The grayness of the clouds had deepened, the look of them causing a sudden spike of homesickness.

She wanted to go home. Her home, back in San Francisco. It had burned down, for all she knew, but she ached for her room. Her bed. Her old life. Her ojisan. Her dear friend Lee.

And she also wanted Cy and Fenris, for the best parts of her new, terrifying life to somehow blend with the old.

Ingrid waited for traffic to stop then crossed the street with a gush of humanity. The sylphs gauzed her vision in gray as they fluttered around her. Every few steps a sylph hovered in front of her face long enough for her to see its joyous smile. Then the sylph would pirouette into the cloud again, its every movement a celebration of freedom.

All of them needed to stay free. The sylphs. Cy. Fenris. Lee.

"Stay with me, we're going to move a little faster," whispered Ingrid. Her feet teetered at the edge of a paved curb, then she hopped out into the street. In two bounding steps, she was gripping the tailgate of a produce delivery truck and hauling herself up into the vehicle. The *guandao* swayed beneath her coat. Ingrid willed strength into her legs. The back of the truck was empty but for canvas bags and stray vegetables that danced as the vehicle passed over frequent potholes. She maintained her grip on the hatch and stared out the back. The truck was driving in the right direction for now, and if that changed, she'd find another ride to get her as close to the rink as possible before sundown.

The sylphs flew faster around her—they relished this increase in speed. Despite her anxiety, Ingrid silently laughed as she wondered what the sylphs would think of freely flying along with an airship—and how Fenris would react, too.

Ingrid's footsteps slowed over the final few blocks, as did the sylphs' flurried flight paths. She didn't simply feel tired, she felt *pathetic,* and that made her grit her teeth and force her muscles to slog onward. It was as though her nerves couldn't quite carry signals all the way to her toes.

The sun fully set as she crossed the crackled pavement to the old rink. Ingrid sensed how the sylphs were wavering, and she told them it was fine. They could rest now. The tension caused by their magic evaporated from around her skin, and she relinquished the grip on her own power.

She didn't feel pain. Instead, she experienced sudden bitter cold. She dropped to one knee, gasping, almost expecting for her breath to fog, though it couldn't have been cooler than fifty degrees on this April night. Her muscles seized as if she'd been dropped into a blizzard.

Someday she would learn the limits of her power and not to expend too much of herself. Today was not that day.

"Apparently, I n-n-numbed my skin a bit too—too effectively," she whispered to the sylphs. They wavered around her, reminding her of seagulls in a hover as they fought a hard wind off the bay.

"Ingrid?" Cy's voice rang from above. She glanced up. Moving her head felt like lifting an iron kettle. Cy's face was visible for an instant in the open rectangular window high above the back door to the rink.

"Hold on, I'm coming!" he shouted, his voice muffled by the brick walls. She remained in a crouch as he burst through the door and dropped down beside her.

"How'd you sneak up like that? I was watching the fence, and then suddenly . . . !" The soles of his shoes scraped on pavement as he backed off, hands up. The sylphs had flared out their wings and begun a high-pitched buzz that could only be described as angry. "I see you made some new friends."

"C-c-c-cold," she stammered. The intense chill in her muscles made it hard to unclench her jaw to talk. She lunged forward to grab his arm. "S-s-sylphs, he's a friend." Though she knew it drained her more, she let the emotion of love flow through her power to the massive . . . flock? Herd? Passel? Mr. Sakaguchi would know.

He would also point to her as a textbook case of hypothermia. Did she have all the symptoms? Drop in heart rate? Likely. Confusion? Maybe? Discerning the symptoms confused her.

The sluggish sylphs withdrew as Cy wrapped both arms

around her. She could have sucked in his warmth like power from an earthquake.

"Dear God, you're like an ice block. Fenris! Fenris, grab blankets from the *Bug*! Hurry!" He wrapped an arm around her waist to help her inside. The heat of the sylphs' presence followed, though their proximity did nothing to physically warm her body.

"No time." She convulsed with shivers and almost collapsed. Cy's grip dragged her forward. "B-B-Blum's here. Almost caught me. Sylphs made me . . . in-in-invisible."

She couldn't see Cy's face, but his grip tightened at the mention of Blum's name. "The *Bug*'s almost ready to go—"

"Won't help. She—she can track me. Sense me from hundreds of miles. I can s-s-s-sense her from within a few hun-hundred feet. Airship . . . not fast enough. Far enough."

"Excuse me?" said Fenris. His shoes pattered on the floor. "What's this about my—"

"Not now, Fenris. Here, Ingrid, on the crate." He positioned her so she could drop down onto the box. She immediately folded over to clutch her own thighs, moaning as she shivered.

"Fen-Fenris. Need filled kermanite." Ingrid managed to lift her head enough to see his stick-thin legs. "I did it. Pulled energy . . . like Papa. Warm me."

"Got it." Those legs vanished as feet clanged on the ladder. "Cy, be ready to catch!"

"Catch what? What are you talking about?"

"Kermanite! You know it's heavy, don't let it fall on your

head!" The words echoed from the hallway of the airship above.

"How close is Blum?" Cy asked her.

Ingrid willed her body to warm up but she felt so damn cold, colder than she'd been after almost drowning in San Francisco Bay, colder than she'd been in her life. Her thoughts moved like gummy honey.

"Dock. Right where we were. Th-th-those soldiers. Hers."

"Here!" called Fenris. Cy grunted. "Is that enough? Ask her!"

"Ingrid?" His hand passed over her forehead and to her hair, coaxing her eyes to rise. He held kermanite the same size and rough shape as a football, the blue hue denoting it as part of the March batch from the Cordilleran Auxiliary. Papa or Mr. Thornton had transmitted energy into it during the San Francisco earthquake.

"Yes," she said, and snaked out her right hand to clutch the crystal. Nothing happened. That took her aback for a moment. Oh. Of course. She'd touched full kermanite thousands of times in her life and never pulled power out, never considered that possibility. She had to focus.

"Work, brain," she muttered as she violently shivered. Her fingertips gouged into the facets as if she were trying to climb a rock wall. She directed the trapped earth energy to enter her body.

There was no gentle transition. One instant, she was as cold as death—the next, her body felt aflame. She screamed, her voice echoing back at her, rippling through her ears and body. Cy pressed the kermanite onto her lap and she folded over it, her hands clasping either end. The world wavered around her as if everything had been rendered into a heat mirage. Black spots dappled her vision. She ached to scream again but panted for breath instead, her heart threatening to burst from her chest.

Cy curled one arm over her back and wrapped the other over her grip on the rock. She felt secured, as if he had sufficient strength to keep her bound in place, even during a tornado.

"I don't think . . . bodies are supposed to go from cold to hot like that," she said, sitting up. Ingrid felt exhausted now, rather than on the verge of death.

Cy kept an arm over her shoulder. She let her hands fall slack as she gazed down at the rock balanced on her lap. The two irregular jagged ends of the kermanite bore melted imprints of her hands. She set her hand into one of the impressions; it was still warm. Ingrid frowned, puzzled that the imprint was larger than her actual hand.

"You were shaking that intensely," Cy said, holding up his own hand and causing it to quiver.

"Oh." She forced her dry throat to swallow.

"About half the energy capacity drained, just like that," muttered Fenris as he crouched to stare at the darkened coloration of the crystal. "Damn. A rock that size would run a large truck for *years*."

She glanced around to check on the sylphs. They had landed in the shadow of the *Palmetto Bug* and resembled a fluffy mass of feathers. She'd need to make sure they were fed again soon.

Ingrid touched her forehead. Her whole body felt swampy. The whiplash from cold to hot had taken place over a span of seconds—and that could have easily killed her, too. If she had focused for a few more moments, she could have ended up at the opposite extreme. Hyperthermia would have cooked her organs in her sack of skin.

But she was alive, for now. Her immediate physical symptoms had been balanced by the kermanite's energy. What was happening inside her body, though? Would she be able to walk tomorrow? Would she even wake up tomorrow—or sleep for days straight?

At what point did these drastic fluctuations cause permanent physical damage?

"Ingrid, I have an idea. Pardon me while I take this." Cy lifted the kermanite from her lap. "Fenris, where's that black paint you found stashed in the building?"

Ingrid blinked and touched the oilcloth of her new rain slicker. A mottled pattern showed where the jagged crystal had rested. Her touch must have made the kermanite heat up as if it were installed in an engine. It had started to melt her coat. She could even smell the foulness now that she had her wits again.

Good God. She could have burned herself, caused an earthquake, and worsened the whole damn cycle.

Fenris dashed away. Cy crouched in front of Ingrid at face level. "Can you walk?"

Grimacing, she stood. Sort of. Cy steadied her. Blood rushed to her head as she took a tentative step. Her scalp erupted with a mad burning sensation; blackness swarmed her vision. It passed in a matter of seconds but she still felt awfully wobbly. "Yes?"

"I have no clue if this'll work, but I reckon we'll find out right quickly one way or the other." Cy helped her to the office, the kermanite chunk tucked against his hip. "Back at Roosevelt's ranch, you mentioned that the old Japanese tales address how dogs and foxes hate each other."

"Yes?" She glanced back as they entered the office. Fenris was running their way, a small pail in his hand.

"I recall one old tale that described how to prevent a kitsune from possessing a person's body. This old woman wrote on her granddaughter's skin—"

Ingrid perked up. "Oh yes! I remember that one. She wrote the Japanese word for dog. 'Inu.' But Blum's not trying to steal my body. God, I hope she's not." Ingrid shivered. Her body was faulty and frustrating, but it was *hers*. She had no desire to be a lost soul.

"Here's the paint." Fenris slid the container onto the long table. It stopped beside Ingrid's half-eaten apple from that morning, which had puckered like an old man's face.

"Names carry power. If the word 'inu' can prevent possession by a kitsune, maybe it'll stop a kitsune from tracking a person, too. I'm no wizard, but if I do the writing, maybe you can help with the magic."

That was a whole mess of maybes. "Yes. Anything. We can't sit and twiddle our thumbs as we wait for her." Ingrid worked off her coat.

"I'll take that as my cue to go." Fenris backed toward the door. "I'll set the door alarms again. Anything else?"

"Yes," said Ingrid. "Are there still rolls in the box there? Those sylphs earned more food—"

"That's what flew in with you? What sort of sylph are we talking about? They're not going to mess with the *Bug,* are they?"

"They're Sierran sylphs, and no, I've never heard anything about them messing with machines. They aren't gremlins. Listen here, Fenris. When you bring out a roll, you *have* to eat half of it yourself. The ratio's important. Tear their half into pieces to distribute it." If Ingrid was about to be captured by Blum, then it was all the more important that the sylphs' kindness be repaid now.

Fenris looked aghast. "Damn it all. A fairy business transaction? You expect me to do this? I'll offend them somehow and we'll have Oberon and his lot out for our blood on top of everything else."

Cy took Fenris by the shoulders and scooted him toward the door. "Oberon's with a different part of fairy kind, but do try to make nice. Equal portions, Fenris." He shut the door and angled the lantern to provide better light.

Ingrid struggled to undo the knots that secured the *guandao* to her waist, but the strings had pulled tight.

"What is this artifact?" Cy asked. He tugged at the knots, frowned, and reached for his knife to cut the bundle free.

"The Green Dragon Crescent Blade of the Chinese god Guan Yu. That's all," she said.

Cy made an odd strangled sound and quickly set the blade on the table as if it were a fragile Tiffany vase. "That's all," he repeated, deadpan.

"It's like a curvy spearhead. I don't suppose you sense any aura around it?" He shook his head. "We'll discuss it more later, if all goes well." She worked off her dress, her fingers clumsy. The old rink building was bitterly cold, and the mild fever she was now running couldn't compensate for that. "I wanted to take my clothes off for you again tonight, but this isn't what I had in mind."

He popped the lid from the paint pail. "To think, it was just last night we shared together. It feels like it's been weeks since then." He cast her a look of dismay and longing. "I'm so sorry for the turn of events this morning, Ingrid. I should've just stayed in bed."

"Considering how the day's gone, we both should have stayed there." She shimmied out of her hose and shivered. "Should I take off everything?"

"No. Keep on your underthings so you stay warmer. I hope we're not too late to throw Blum off your scent. Is there anything I should do as I write?"

"As if I know dog sorcery!"

"You know a hefty bit more about magic than I do."

She wasn't sure whether to laugh or cry at that. Everything she had learned about geomancy over the years had emphasized that a practitioner couldn't personally control the flow of power; it was about being a conduit. In the past week, she had broken all the rules. Maybe now was a good time to rewrite them, literally.

"When I draw on my power to make a bubble, I focus. I imagine the shape and flexibility and what I need it to do. For this . . . try to focus like the grandmother in that old story. Pour your intent and emotion into the kanji. I'll do the same."

Cy dipped his pointer finger into the black paint and pressed his fingertip to the slope of her breast right above her heart. She nodded approval. The heart was a center of power and a good place to start.

犬 was a simple character, like a cross with curved legs and a dot. As his finger dragged black paint to form the first stroke, a horizontal line with blunt ends, Ingrid called on the warmth stirring in her blood. She thought of Ambassador Blum and envisioned a dog powerful enough to make Blum tuck tail, literally and figuratively, and retreat.

Cy's finger stroked downward twice to draw sweeping ends, and as he dabbed the radical onto her skin, warm magic moved through her body. It slithered along her limbs and coiled itself within the kanji, briefly searing her nerves like a cattle brand. Ingrid angled her chin down to see if the magic was actually visible, but the figure was merely black paint against her brown skin.

His eyes flicked to meet hers. "Do you feel anything? Is this working?"

"Maybe, but I don't know. Keep writing. When I get my clothes on and start moving around, the paint's bound to flake away. Better to be redundant."

Cy nodded. "More names, more power." He shifted to her upper arms, inscribing the character on both, then moved to her torso and back. The first iterations of "inu" dried and stiffened her skin.

She tried to repress her cold shivers. Japanese calligraphy was an art form—shodō—and certainly clarity and perfection could only enhance the magic inlaid in a word. Cy's finger strokes were slow and deliberate. Each symbol was about three inches in height, the black paint thick. His intense concentration was evident in his furrowed brow and narrowed eyes. If he could make this magic real by willpower alone, by God, he would.

He knelt at her feet to adorn her thighs and the backs of her calves and stood again. "I'm recalling other stories now, too, like those about the golem in Jewish tales. The word of life adorns the golem's forehead. That might be awkward for you in public, though."

"Near the brain does seem like a good place, but . . ." She wanted to tell him to hell with it. Write "inu" there. But while Blum was the biggest threat against them, death and abuse could also come in other forms, and labeling her face in such a way only invited trouble. She turned around. "Add one more on the back of my neck. My collar and coat should cover that, and the spine has to carry some symbolism."

He braced himself with a hand on her shoulder as he wrote the kanji with four swipes of his finger. Ingrid focused on the motions and was startled at the end when his lips brushed her other shoulder.

"Oh, Cy," she whispered.

His lips rose to kiss her earlobe. "We're in this together. Never forget that. Can you sense that kitsune at all?"

Ingrid leaned as close to him as she dared while the

paint still dried. "No. She's not close right now. Knowing her, part of the fun might be that she can mosey along and catch me nevertheless."

"If she can track you from hundreds of miles away, she must have sensed your whereabouts in those minutes right after the sylphs tuckered out. I imagine we'll soon have soldiers crawling around in our vicinity."

"Damn her to hell and back. She'll probably say she's searching for hidden Chinese or some such nonsense." Ingrid stood, rigid and quivering from cold. "The sylphs hid me while I stood feet away from her at the dock. She was overseeing the matter with the auxiliary and blaming it all on the Chinese. The UP's planning to strike Chinatown tonight with that as their excuse, but Blum knows Mr. Sakaguchi is there. She's after him. More airships are coming in, too. I even saw an Imperial officer."

"An Imperial? Really? By protocol, they're only supposed to be present on American soil in standard ambassadorial or prisoner custodial roles." He went silent for a few breaths. "Ingrid, if Mr. Sakaguchi is placed in Japanese custody . . ."

"I know. I know all too well." Japan assumed guilt until innocence was proven, and quick executions were a hallmark of their justice system. "I don't suppose there was a message from Lee?"

She could tell by Cy's posture that he was about to say something she didn't like. "There hasn't been any sign of him, Ingrid. The note you left was still on the door when we returned."

She opened and closed her mouth, unsure of what to say.

"We have to leave," he said gently. "Blum's hunting for you and we can't rely on the dog sorcery to work or to hold her off for long."

"I know that, damn it, but I can't go. You can't expect me to go. It's not just because of all the hopes that Ojisan and Mr. Roosevelt pinned on him, it's because he's *Lee.* I can't . . . Cy. He promised me he'd get word to me somehow about where he was if he didn't come back. He's going to get word to me. He could even be with Mr. Sakaguchi right now." She said it with conviction.

"How long do you dare wait, Ingrid?" Cy softly asked. "Think of what Lee would want. Think of what your capture would mean to him."

She wavered there, eyes half shut.

If she were tortured, it would shatter Lee, especially if he knew she'd been captured because of him.

If she were tortured, it would be in order to use her as a weapon to shatter Lee's people.

Cy tapped the fresher paint spots on her body, the pressure more clinical than affectionate. "Looks like you're dry. Let's get you clothed before you're chilled through again."

There was a tender intimacy to his fumbling fingers as he did his best to assist her and help preserve the paint that would keep her alive. Despite the care in its application, Ingrid noticed that the paint had already started to crackle. How long would this enchantment hold—if it worked at all? What more could they do? There had to be tattoo artists around who could permanently ink the word onto her skin—it was an abhorrent thought, that permanent label of "dog" upon her skin—but she also knew that tattoos *hurt*. If she had to resort to that, it needed to be done while aloft in an airship or some metal structure high off the ground.

"I really don't know what to do, Cy. I want to wait here for Lee, but I can't wait here for Blum." She shrugged on her coat. Rain suddenly roared on the corrugated iron roof as if in response to her mood.

"I know. There are no easy answers." He reached for her hand and gave it a squeeze.

"How long until the *Bug*'s ready to leave?" she asked.

"Let's check with Fenris. As far as we know, he's determined everything is hopelessly broken again during our time in here."

Tired and scared as Ingrid was, she couldn't help but smile as the sylphs welcomed her to the shadow of the *Palmetto Bug*. They swirled around her like a thick gray ribbon, leaving her momentarily dizzy, and made slight clicking sounds all the while.

"Well," she said, "I think they liked their bread. They even look plumper. How many rolls did he feed them?" She needed to feed herself soon, too.

"Ingrid? Cy?" Fenris called from inside the *Bug*.

"We're out here," said Cy, standing by the ladder. "We need to figure out our plan of action, and fast."

"We have a problem." Fenris climbed down the hatch stairs and with a hop transitioned to the ladder. He faced them, his olive-toned skin strangely blanched. "There's something on board. I don't know what it is. It looks like a dragon, but it's not. It's in the hallway between the racks. It seems like it's on fire but there's no smoke." He looked composed and yet panicked all at once.

Ingrid and Cy stared at Fenris, and then looked at each other. "I need to get up there," she finally said. "Can you help me make the climb?"

Fenris went up first. Ingrid took a deep breath and followed. She kept her gaze on the next rung up and inched her way upward. The transition to the stairs was worst of all, but she knew Cy was right below in case she slipped. At the top, Fenris extended a hand to help her inside. She accepted it with a nod of deep gratitude, knowing all too well how Fenris avoided such contact.

The minute she was on board, heat caressed her skin, and it was like nothing she had felt before. It wasn't the bludgeoning presence of Blum or the thunderbird, or the tingle that warned her of other fantastics in proximity. This felt like the way a harp *sounded*. Gentle. It felt like soft grass against her bare skin, it smelled like honeysuckle on a morning breeze. Ingrid pivoted on her knees to face the being at the far end of the hall.

The creature was the size of a fawn, its slim body formed of shimmering gold scales licked by shallow yellow flames. Its burning was mesmerizing to behold, each flicker scarcely an inch in height. Fenris was right; there was no smoke or sign of fire damage, and the tatami mat it stood on was certainly flammable. Delicately tapered legs led to feathery fetlocks and dainty cloven hooves. The head was like that of a dragon but with two small antlers extending from the forehead. A frilly mane lined the jaw and trailed down its neck. Thickly lashed amber eyes solemnly considered Ingrid.

It was waiting for her. Ingrid knew this as surely as she knew the sun would rise again.

"A kirin," Cy said with a gasp. He pulled himself into the hallway and knelt at Ingrid's side.

"That's a better-known name for it these days, but I have a hunch this one might prefer the term used in its home, by its people," said Ingrid. She crawled forward so she had room to humble herself before a celestial being. "Greetings, *qilin*."

CHAPTER 17

Ingrid peeked to see if the *qilin* acknowledged her, even as she worried that directly gazing upon it was a horrible breach of etiquette. Fantastic creatures were known to be persnickety by nature, and the last thing she wanted was to give offense to a being this powerful, this *incredible*.

To her relief, the *qilin* granted her a regal nod.

"A *qilin* on my airship. Very well." Fenris paused. "What the hell is a *qilin*?"

"One of the most powerful fantastics throughout Asia, ranked alongside dragons and phoenixes." Cy kept his voice low, his gaze humble. "You see their image everywhere, Fenris. There was a statue of one at the auxiliary today. Greetings, *qilin*," he said, louder.

"Oh. Pardon." Fenris cleared his throat. "It—you—looked a bit different depicted as a statue. Boxier. Bulkier—"

"Fenris," growled Cy.

"Yes, well." His knees scuffed on the floor on the other side of the hatch. "It's not going to burn up my airship, is it?" he whispered.

"They rarely attack people in the stories," Ingrid murmured as she sat up, her trembling hands clutched in her lap.

The *qilin* hadn't acknowledged Cy and Fenris at all. Its steady gaze focused on Ingrid.

"We're honored by your visit," Ingrid said, fighting to keep her voice level. If only Lee were here! "I want to make sure I am addressing you correctly. You prefer *qilin,* not kirin?"

"I am *qilin*. I am not my slumbering cousin, though we may utilize the same idols as we view the world." The syllables were accompanied by the gentle sound of chimes. The scent of honeysuckle shifted to rose. Ingrid couldn't help but breathe in deeper. It smelled comforting. Like the little sachets that Mama made to tuck into linen drawers.

"There is only one of you?" At that, the *qilin* nodded. So this was the same being that guided her to the Crescent Blade. The same one who had come to Lee. Ingrid opened her mouth to ask what it meant by sharing idols, but the *qilin* spoke first.

"Ingrid Carmichael." She *felt* her name more than she heard it. She had the sudden, inexplicable need to sob. Not in sadness, but as a catharsis. "The one you know as Lee Fong vowed that word would come to you, and lo, I am here, but not as a mere messenger."

"No," said Ingrid, her voice tight. "There is nothing *mere* about you, *qilin*." Cy shifted to look at her, his expression puzzled, and Ingrid was stunned to realize that she was the only one who could hear the *qilin*'s speech.

"I am a signet. A sign. I am dawn on a deep winter's day." The chimed words carried a poetic melody. "I am a cloud that weeps upon land scarred and poisoned, where the soil is tilled by foreign hands, where my people fertilize earth with their own flesh and bone."

Ingrid thought of propaganda posters put forth about Manchukuo, of smiling Japanese faces and perspective lines of green crops leading to a red rising sun on the horizon. The original Chinese settlers were not depicted. They didn't belong in this new vision of an ancient land.

"Your people are enduring torment here in America, too," Ingrid said. "We are hoping to stop that, but we have no idea how to go about it. Too many have died on all sides."

"I do not want Lee Fong to die," said the *qilin*, the words stoking its flames to flare gold. Its wide eyes narrowed as it scrutinized her. "You possess the heat of *potential,* of the very force of the earth."

"I— Yes. I do. But I don't understand my own potential, *qilin*. My body struggles to contain and use this power."

"If your body could cope with such power, you would not be human. You would be a god, and this is not an era for new gods."

Ingrid flashed back to Papa's words on that very subject. "What is this the time for, then, *qilin*?"

"Peace. Before all is lost, for all people. You are a fulcrum, Ingrid Carmichael. Much is balanced upon you."

Good grief, but the *qilin* spoke like a sphinx, all innuendo and riddles and prophecies. "*Qilin,* where is Lee?"

"Lee Fong is *here*."

Ingrid knew from the weight on the last word that the *qilin* didn't mean within the airship. And as she thought this, her view of the hallway dissolved. Instead of the narrow confines of the *Bug,* she was looking at a muddy street she had never seen before. It seemed real. As if she could step forward and walk right into a puddle.

Fantastics had spoken to Ingrid with images before, images that were like flickering moving pictures on grainy film; this vision was reality in everything but smell. Garbage stood ankle deep along both sides of the street, the bare surface marred by mud, puddles, and deep wheel tracks. Bony chickens pecked at debris. The flanking buildings were tall and mostly wood, fire hazards all, the roofs curved and paint peeling. Disrepair and despair had soaked into the scene as sure as rainwater.

Chinatown. It had a different look and feel from the grotto she had known in San Francisco, yet it was recognizable all the same.

A haphazardly constructed brick-and-log wall blocked off one end of the street. Spikes at the top angled outward. It was no marvel of modern construction, but the effort of terrified people to throw up a barricade to ward away monsters. The angle of her view turned as if she were flying straight up. A map sprawled below. Ingrid recognized Elliott Bay and various airship docks and the lines of streets she couldn't name. She had no idea she'd been so close to

Chinatown all the while. It wasn't even a mile from the old rink building, and was far closer to Blum.

The view dropped again. The *qilin* guided her around corners, twisting and turning along lanes of dirt and waste, only to stop at a three-story building. Its irimoya roof and balconies sagged like old skin.

A statue of a *qilin* listed by a back door. It was cracked almost in half, its gaze cockeyed from the split, its antlers pathetic nubs.

"This is *wrong,*" the *qilin* announced, the words lit by fierce chimes. Ingrid nodded, even though she had no physical presence. A *qilin* statue was placed as a guardian and to grant good luck—and only in appropriate places. It should never be someplace like a gambling or opium den, but at a family home or a temple. "However, the broken reflection of my kind will be your guide. It has shown me this place, and in turn, I show you."

Ingrid filed this away in her memory: these statues truly acted as guardians of property bearing their image, though that didn't mean the domicile had their blessing. Mr. Sakaguchi would be delighted at the knowledge!

"Is Lee there? What do I do?" Ingrid asked.

The vision pivoted to focus on the blue balcony high above the statue. "Fate is not tidy. It is a flash flood in a desert, forcing channels through lowlands and sand. It can be guided, to an extent, but water goes where it will. As does fate."

The view glided through the door and a creepy hallway rendered gray by lack of light and streaks of mold, past a downward stairwell, and to a stark room. In the middle, a wooden chair had been bolted to the floor. Lee sat there. His head was tilted forward, but she could see by the bruises on his cheeks that he'd been beaten again. Ingrid cried out.

Surely Uncle Moon hadn't done this? He could manipulate life energy within a body. If he were to torture someone, he wouldn't leave a bruise.

A blink later, and Ingrid found herself kneeling on the tatami mat within the *Palmetto Bug*. She no longer sat by the hatch, but in the hallway between the racks. The *qilin* gazed at her from inches away. Its thickly lidded eyes blinked but otherwise the creature didn't waver. Its breath was composed of cozy warmth and brilliant jasmine, like the vines Mama once loved in Mr. Sakaguchi's front yard. The heat of the *qilin*'s presence scalded her without pain; it was magical and so much *more,* like the *guandao*. Holy.

"You are energy bound within a fragile vessel. Your actions may allow Lee Fong to live, but you cannot sacrifice yourself in the process or the world will know only more woe."

Ingrid's awe faded, replaced by frustration. "And how should I go about that in a safe and efficient manner, *qilin*? *What am I?*"

"You already know the answer to this question, but you need to hear the confirmation. You are indeed the granddaughter of Pele. Her blood runs molten through your veins. You feel her legacy in the heat of your rage even now."

Ingrid absorbed that answer, breathless. "How can I learn to handle this power?"

"You learn by living. You fail by dying."

"I failed to kill Ambassador Blum earlier today, when I had the opportunity. I could have ended this—"

"You mean well, Ingrid Carmichael." The *qilin*'s invocation of her name caused Ingrid to break out in chills. "But you wield what is yours, and we wield what is ours. You also presume to know the purpose of the *guandao*."

Ingrid bowed her head in acceptance of the rebuke. "Then why did you guide *me* to the Green Dragon Crescent Blade, and not Lee?"

"If he had found the *guandao* blessed by green dragon blood, his arrogance would have caused him to carry it with him. That could not be. It was safest with you on this day, and it will be safest on this ship through the next."

"But that doesn't mean it is guaranteed to be safe here."

"That is correct."

"What do we do about Ambassador Blum in the meantime?"

"Survive her." The *qilin* sounded quite matter-of-fact. It bowed, one leg extended, and as light as a dandelion puff, the *qilin* took to the air and leaped over Ingrid. She turned in time to see it bound over Fenris and Cy and down the hatch. Gone, just like that.

As though a lamp had been extinguished, a sense of full reality returned. The *Palmetto Bug* reeked of vinegar. The lights were low, much of the hallway cast in shadow.

"Damn you and your cryptic answers!" Ingrid yelled after the *qilin*. It was easier to rage with the entity gone. "You tell me I have powers, and a frail body, and your only advice is to survive?" She rocked on her knees and resisted the urge to pulverize something.

She could scream and cry in her very own Garden of Gethsemane, but this changed nothing. She truly was a fantastic—the granddaughter of a goddess—caught in a war between rival fantastics, with millions of lives cast with her as flotsam.

"You know, jeremiads against godlike beings are ill-advised, even if they aren't physically present," said Fenris.

"Ingrid, are you all right?" asked Cy as he scrambled toward her.

"No, I'm not. I'm angry. I'm frustrated. I'm sick of all of this." She swiped tears from her cheeks.

"We couldn't hear anything the *qilin* said to you, but I think we picked up the gist pretty well from your side of the conversation. You know where Lee is?"

"Yes. He's being held captive in Chinatown. I know the building."

"I see." Cy looked contemplative.

Fenris approached at a crawl and passed Ingrid to pat the place where the *qilin* had stood. "I'll be damned. It's like the thing wasn't here at all. Not a mark on the tatami."

"The *qilin* came here for a reason." Ingrid looked around. "Do you have any imagery of a *qilin* on the ship?" She looked at Cy.

"No." He frowned. "Actually, yes. But I only found it when I was making up the beds earlier today." He stood and motioned over to the top bunk where Lee had slept.

Ingrid stepped up a few rungs to peer over the rack. The light was dim. "I don't see anything."

"Go up another rung and look at the back wall."

She did just that, leaning into the gap in the railing and onto the thin mattress. A *qilin* had been carved into the back wall. It was maybe five inches long, the nicks coarse, but it was recognizable. She wondered when Lee had carved it during their journey, and if he had known the power within this action.

She hopped to the floor again, her legs wobbly. The heaviness of her burden weighed on her like an anvil. She sat, knees bent, her face tucked against her skirt. The cloth stank of mustiness and dirt, or maybe everything smelled worse in the absence of the *qilin*. She wanted to curl up in a ball and hide away in a closet, like she used to do as a girl. She wanted to tell the world to go to hell. She wanted, she wanted . . . Lee safe. Mr. Sakaguchi safe. For all of this to stop.

Cy hovered close by, his brow wrinkled in concern. She reached out for him and he was there. His arm wrapped around her shoulder, her head fitting just so against his neck. God, but he felt good and right. She needed this, she needed *him*.

"Tell us what we need to do," he said.

CHAPTER 18

A strange quiet had descended on the city of Seattle. No music blared from windows. No autocars or wagons traversed the streets. People ducked in and out of houses like ghosts in their own neighborhoods. A catfight rang out from an alley, shrill and loud, the crash of a metal trash can like a gunshot. A gentle drizzle fell and pattered in puddles and gutters, the smell of moisture and fireplace smoke strong on the wind.

Curfew had been declared. It didn't need any grand proclamation. Tension carried in the air, sure as electricity.

Ingrid walked arm in arm with Cy. Sylphs surrounded them in a gray halo. She hadn't needed to descend into her power to communicate with them; simply holding up a jamu-pan was enough to elicit a whir of delight from the full hive. Ingrid supposed it was just as well that they worked off the sugar through their magic. If they kept eating bread rolls at this rate, they'd end up as lazy and plump as the pet fairy that street brute had worn on his hat.

It would have been nice to mingle with nighttime carousers or traffic, but instead, she felt utterly conspicuous as they walked along the empty street. Cy didn't appear to be invisible to her eyes either.

The street dipped down as it led to the waterfront. Past the angled roofs, massive Behemoth- and Tiamat-class vessels glowed in a way that made her eyes ache if she looked for more than a few seconds.

"Soldiers," Cy said in a murmur as they passed through an intersection. A block north, troops in Unified Pacific navy blue almost blended in with the night. Electric streetlights showed the shine of hat brims and guns in hand. "Doing a sweep block by block. Looks like they're working east more than south so far."

"Will they give Fenris a hard time?"

"The fact that I paid folks from the police station to accompany the *Bug* to the dock should help matters along." She still couldn't believe his nerve to walk into the precinct like that, but Cy could work miracles with his drawl and easy smile. "Fenris'll need to show his papers, but so long as he doesn't talk too much, he should be able to moor properly and do a complete check-over of the ship. He'll fly up to Edmonds, and we'll meet him there soon enough."

"If the curfew doesn't keep ships grounded," she whispered.

"The opposite." He sounded especially grim as he pointed upward. The pale ovals of airships stood out against the starless sky. "If Blum's moving in on Chinatown, every working airship'll be encouraged to lift off. When Durendals are at work and bombs are being dropped, you don't want airships around. Enchanted helium isn't highly flammable like hydrogen, but sometimes, all it takes is a spark on the breeze striking just the right spot."

"The buildings around here are brick but they're still awfully close together. The whole city could go up." The Chinese would be bound to catch the blame again, too. She shuddered at the memory of San Francisco.

Cy's hand squeezed her waist. "Don't think about that right now, and don't think about San Francisco either."

"Is it that obvious?"

"These past few days, I close my eyes and I see San Francisco again, the way it was when we left. Sometimes, I swear I still smell it." His voice was low and hoarse. "Seeing Manila and Peking years ago did something terrible to me, but they were never places I called *home*. I had empathy, but not intimacy with those cities."

"You used to live here in Seattle, too." Voices carried from farther away. A woman dashed across the street, both hands clasping a hat onto her head.

"I did, and I like the city just fine." He sighed. "Ingrid, here's the way of it. Something awful's about to happen here. It's not our fault. It is what it is. We need to control what we can and get out of here as fast as a dragon after gold."

Ingrid nodded. Control what they can. Not exacerbate the situation. "The energy of the earth hasn't fluctuated yet."

"We're ready as can be if it does."

They'd brought along as much kermanite as they could quietly and conveniently carry. Her coat pockets were filled as full as she dared, with energized kermanite on the right, empty on the left. Cy had more in two old gunnysacks tied to his waist. Over a thousand dollars' worth in all, a wealth of stones that the auxiliary normally would have transported with armed guards.

A dog trotted into the street. It was a German shepherd, black ears erect. It paused a moment then trotted straight for them, tail swaying.

"Cy?" Ingrid whispered.

"Keep walking." Another, smaller dog emerged, a little mongrel more gray than white. It likewise bounced their way with a wagging tail.

"Is this the point where we assume that dog sorcery really did the trick? Dogs typically don't pay me much mind."

"Me neither, though as Fenris loves to mention, cats follow me like I'm a Pied Piper. Come on, dogs, shoo!"

They didn't. Both dogs whined and bounced along at Ingrid's side as if they'd found a new playmate. This required some magic, and fast, before people—soldiers in particular—wondered at the dogs' behavior.

Ingrid partly closed her eyes and focused on the heat writhing in her body. She'd taken care to absorb the rest of the energy from that big chunk of kermanite to make sure she had enough power to shield her skin for another walk with the sylphs.

"Dogs," she whispered. *"Go home."* To her surprise, the words tumbled from her lips with the slightest trace of blue fog. The color dissipated as it stretched toward the dogs. The German shepherd emitted a tiny whine, and then both dogs bolted away.

"Did you see that?" she whispered.

"I saw the dogs leave. Was there something more?"

She might have laughed if she had dared to make loud noise. Her earth magic had somehow melded with the dog sorcery, no question about it. Could she instill that sort of power into other kanji? Would it work with other animals—horses, perhaps, or maybe even fantastics? Why confine possibilities to creatures? The potential was staggering.

A loud engine roared somewhere close by, accompanied by a terrible grinding noise. "A Durendal," Cy muttered. "That's the sound of treads on wet pavement."

"It must be a few blocks away, then." Their street was still dirt; the paved avenues of downtown were north.

"Not far enough away." She felt the tiredness in his words, and knew the exhaustion went far deeper than physical weariness. He loathed the machines that were his legacy.

They both grew silent as more soldiers emerged from buildings on both sides of the street. The soldiers in Unified Pacific blue escorted families carrying carpetbags and birdcages and bundled blankets folded to transport belongings. A businessman carried an entire till. Lights shined from upstairs windows and revealed other people throwing items together, soldiers waving them on.

A wagon lurked in the street, a bored horse in the shafts. Soldiers stewed in wait. Ingrid did a double take—none of them were smoking. Quite odd, considering the popularity of the vice.

“Going to dynamite soon,” Cy said in a hiss. “Firebreak.”

She nodded. These blocks around Chinatown were poor, their residents disposable. The UP had to take precautions so that their offensive on the district didn’t set the whole city aflame.

Ingrid smelled Chinatown before she saw it. The streets throughout Seattle stank of garbage, but here the potency of sweet-sour rot increased exponentially. They rounded a corner to see a building at a dead end ahead. The windows of the brick structure were boarded, and the base of the building mounded with garbage. More had been flung high at the walls—pieces of rotting meat and fruit and unidentified foulness adhering in a spatter. Sticky, foul trails showed where other trash had slid down to join the piles below. A dead dog lay on its side, rib bones exposed and swarming with dark flecks. Farther down was the decaying body of a horse, or part of one. Ingrid tried not to breathe as they hurried past more and more dead animals.

The sheer number was no accident. It was intent.

The city had degraded to medieval-style warfare. Dead animals and disease as weapons against the Chinese. It galled her. This was supposed to be a civilized age, with the Unified Pacific as the pinnacle of technology and education, and yet . . . and yet. She again thought of the Quakers and the Chinese imprisoned in Portland, and forced the memory away.

Cy was right. They had to focus on what they could control in the here and now, or they'd go mad.

The street had been blockaded by broken bricks, lumber, and what looked to be the stacked chassis of a few old autocars. The wall stood a good ten feet in height and sloped outward. The top featured carved wooden spears angled outward. It was impossible to tell who built the wall: the whites and Japanese, or the Chinese, or both, each engaged in a flurried effort to protect themselves from each other.

"The spears are smart," murmured Cy. "I imagine folks were flinging firebombs over the side. Chinese need to stay on guard."

"I expected more guards on this side, too, police or soldiers."

"They're here, though not exposed." He motioned to windows across the way. "Trust me, both sides are watching."

Tension carried in the air, in the darkness, in the suspicious silence of thousands of people awaiting an explosion.

"We need to find a good place to break in," Ingrid whispered, looking around. Their spinning barricade of sylphs was starting to slow down. The long walk and the effort to cloak two people had drained them far too fast. Good thing Cy was packing pastries along with a pistol and Tesla rod.

Dodging trash, they continued along the street and to another brick building against a dead-end alley. It faced a business that looked to be closed, the windows partially boarded and the interior gutted by fire.

"Here," he muttered, motioning to the Chinatown side. "Take care when you push out power. It's hard to know how well built these places are."

"That's a comfort," she muttered as she glanced up. A two-story structure, all brick. She could shield them if the entire wall collapsed, but she couldn't do anything about the noise. Forces on either side of the wall would assume the attack had started, and she and Cy would be right in the middle.

She addressed the sylphs in her mind and felt prickles from their focus on her. Ingrid showed them how she would place her hand on the bricks and vent power, and that they needed to avoid direct contact with her outward hand or the area around it. She didn't want to hurt them.

A happy hum came in the affirmative. They understood.

Cy shifted to unholster the Tesla rod. He planted a quick kiss on Ingrid's cheek and edged back while keeping his left hand on her waist. The elliptical flights of the sylphs adjusted around them.

Ingrid worked her boots forward into the garbage, gagging slightly, and planted a palm against the coarse red bricks.

Power surged in her arm, eager to be unleashed. She breathed in, out. She only needed a small pressure wave. Like the tap of a doctor's hammer on a knee, not a jackhammer. She pushed out energy.

Cracks expanded from her hand with a soft rumble. A small cascade of brick chunks and red powder joined the refuse below. She glanced up. No sign of an imminent collapse—that was good—but damn it, she'd been *too* gentle.

"Try here." Cy motioned a little farther over and down. His pointer finger was still painted black, his knuckles red from the fight earlier in the day. Ingrid moved her hand. This time when she pushed out, several bricks completely crumbled. More cracks appeared, like zigzag lightning bolts.

Cy tugged on her shoulder. "Warn the sylphs that I'm about to kick a few times."

Ingrid passed along the message. The sylphs' trajectory altered. "Do it," she said. "I'm not sure how well they can cover us right now."

Cy kicked. The first impact caused a few bricks to fall inside, but the second kick punched a hole that momentarily snared his foot. Once he was freed, it took a third kick to cave in a portion of the wall some four feet high. Ingrid turned away, smothering coughs against her arm. The dust cleared to reveal pitch-blackness within.

"Oh yes!" She softly clapped her hands.

Cy surmounted the pile of rubble and trash first and offered her a hand to help her over. Debris rumbled and slid beneath them. She hopped into the dark room. Something crackled underfoot and she eased back, terrified the ancient floor might be caving in.

"A chair," said Cy, the words a mere breath. He pulled her forward. More pieces of the brittle chair shattered underfoot and were kicked against a nearby wall. She cringed. Invisible or not, she made for a poor ninja.

They ducked through a doorway, the sylphs a gray smear in the darkness, and into a hallway lit by gaps in the roof far above. This building, like its neighbor across the wall, had been abandoned, and with reason. Scorch marks colored a full wall in black, while the stairway wall wore the words DIE CHANKORO in thick white paint. Nooses swayed from a railing far above. A few had loops that had been cut, the ends dangling unraveled.

Male voices speaking Chinese echoed from another room. Cy guided her near a wall. His head angled downward, his expression worried. She felt a spike of panic—had their footsteps shown in dust on the floor? The light, dim as it was, illuminated a well-worn path through the foyer. She felt a smidgen more at ease. If they were caught, it wouldn't be for that reason.

Two men burst into the room. One hoisted up a lamp. Both held knives. They chattered softly as they moved toward the outer wall. Cy nudged Ingrid, and they dashed through a doorway without a door to the outside.

More male voices approached. Ingrid's first instinct was to duck into the shadows, but Cy nudged her again. He motioned to the sylphs. They had slowed more, their flutters more like those of sparrows than hummingbirds.

Ingrid tried to gauge their location based on the *qilin*'s vision. She nodded Cy forward. They traversed a somewhat paved street that was crackled and sunken in spots. Some of the dips were quite deep. This was likely made ground, like in downtown San Francisco, where dirt was dumped into natural marshland. Such land quickly liquefied during an earthquake.

A baby's cry pierced the night. A woman sang, the melody of a lullaby clear even though the words weren't in English. Speaking any Chinese dialect was punishable by death, as if that law mattered now. Being Chinese was punishable by death.

Men in dark clothes crouched on a balcony that looked to the north, toward downtown and the dock. A garage door cranked open in the building below. A team of men stood there, stripped down to pants. They grabbed hold of a beam and pulled, each man straining and groaning. Some sort of war machine wagon rolled into the open. Ingrid recognized a heavy gun barrel, like the sort shown in illustrations of the War Between the States. A man chanted to keep time as the team of men clutched the tongue of the wagon to inch it toward the wall.

Following the *qilin*'s vision, she led Cy down a block, then turned. Rain began again in earnest. The stench of water and rot carried on the wind; Elliott Bay was close by. Chickens scurried past. A shop window featured rows of herbs whose names were poorly translated into English words. Next door, an open entry revealed a room whose floor was packed with bodies. Ingrid feared they were dead but then a few of the figures shifted. They were sleeping, or trying to. She recalled what Lee had said—refugees from Portland, San Francisco, and other outlying towns had fled this way, too. Vancouver was located just north of the Canadian border and it had a large Chinatown; Britannia wasn't at war with China, but the British didn't welcome the Chinese or treat them well either.

It was all about hope. Walk far enough, maybe someone won't try to kill you there.

Sleeping bodies lined a porch like sardines in a can. Rain dripped from the overhanging roof. Ingrid recognized the next building and walked faster. They rounded another corner and crossed a yard thick with rusted autocar parts, and at last she saw it.

The three-story building leaned inward as if it were hunkering down, drawing its walls closer to keep warm. No people slept on its porch. The shadows in the yard were deep, but couldn't quite hide the cracked *qilin* beside the steps. Ingrid knelt before it and gripped its snout in a reverent request for luck.

She couldn't count how many times she had done the same thing to the kirin statue in her childhood backyard. To think, it had been guarding the house all along. Maybe that's why the assassination attempt on Mr. Sakaguchi had failed. The gunman would have been near the statue in their yard.

Ingrid looked up at the third-floor balcony. The structure seemed as if it might collapse beneath a pigeon's weight, but she knew it provided the best access to Lee. Her bare fingers probed the filled kermanite in her right pocket and squeezed. The crystals dissolved to powder as heat coiled up her arm with a delicious shiver that made it oh so easy to dismiss the consequences that would come later.

"I'm ready," Cy said. His face was grim, the rod telescoped in his grip.

"So am I." She brought her hand to his cheek and her lips found his. It was a hungry, desperate kiss. A good-bye kiss.

With her excess power, she shoved him away, his boots leaving a sleek track in the mud. She willed the sylphs away with him. Cy's mouth gaped in anger and dismay, as if he would yell, and then he vanished. Even though she was expecting it to happen, the immediacy of the illusion came as a shock.

"You'll be safer out here. Hide and feed the sylphs. I'll be back soon," she whispered. Raindrops spattered her cheeks. She crouched and pushed off the muddy ground, her gaze on the balcony high above.

CHAPTER 19

It amazed Ingrid how long the seconds stretched as she sprang from the earth toward the rickety balcony on high. Dark thoughts galloped through her head: *What the hell am I doing? Will that balcony even hold me? Someone can very well shoot me the instant I land!*

She worried for Cy, too. He would be visible as the sylphs rested and ate. She needed to be fast for all their sakes.

Heat drained from her body as she flew up, forming a high arc, and then gravity returned. Ingrid pushed the frantic worries from her mind and fully focused again. Remembering how she softened her jump from the airship in Olema, she imagined a cushion beneath her feet. Gravity dragged her down, but in a kinder, gentler way, as if her feet impacted on a feather pillow instead of splintered floorboards. Her soles tapped down and she straightened, pleased.

That's when the balcony groaned and shuddered. Wood crackled like a gunshot.

She dove for the door. A rusted lock secured the handle to a bar in the doorframe. She shoved power inside the mechanism. The entire metal unit crumbled beneath her touch, the handle draping loosely against her hand. She pushed the door open and slipped inside.

Her skin still held a mild fever, though the magnificent leap had taken a lot out of her. Well, that's why she had more kermanite.

Water dribbled somewhere nearby. She remained utterly quiet except for the mad rampage of her heartbeat. The balcony continued to tenaciously cling to the building—thank God for that. The last thing she needed was to attract attention to the yard where Cy was hiding.

The building creaked but she didn't hear any voices or footsteps racing her way. Maybe it was abandoned, except as a prison for Lee.

Or maybe this was a trap.

That made her pause. A trap for her? No, it couldn't be. No one in Chinatown except Lee knew the truth about her power. Would the *qilin,* peace-loving creature that it was, direct her into a trap? How did that fit into its comparison of fate to a turbulent river?

Whatever the case, she was here, and she didn't intend to leave alone.

Ingrid walked with slow care, wincing at every gripe of the floor and thud of her boots. The place had almost no furniture, and what existed was battered and broken and chewed on. Something scuffled in the darkness, and then a rat the size of her forearm darted across the floor. She shuddered.

The vision the *qilin* had given her remained clear in her mind, as if she were holding a map of the building in her hand. She slipped down the hallway and past a staircase. A painting of a Porterman airship hung crooked on the wall, as if the airship would dive nose-first into the floor. She passed through another room. Filthy blankets lay in heaps on the dark-speckled floor, a strong contrast to the opulent yet degraded details of the architecture: the haphazard wainscoting, the crackled crown molding, and the artful ceiling tiles blotched in gray. Everything stank of dank rot, and Ingrid had a strong desire to escape the place and somehow scour her lungs clean. She continued, step-by-step, her sense of unease increasing.

This place had been a glorious mansion before the dynamics of the city had shifted. Now it was more like a crypt, a building so decrepit that even the most desperate people didn't take refuge beneath its roof.

Through the next doorway, she could see Lee.

He looked as he had in the vision, his body bowed forward with his hands secured behind the chair. His shaggy black hair draped over his face in a short veil. Ingrid hesitated in the doorway. This was too easy. Chinese were known for setting traps for Unified Pacific soldiers, but she had no clear idea what to look for here. Cy would have known. She peered to either side of the door. She didn't see beams of light that might set off an alarm or cause an explosion if the light was blocked. The patchy red carpet, like mange on a feral dog, showed the splintered wooden floor below. Rivulets of water trickled down the wall behind Lee, the rotten wallpaper curling to the floor in sodden sheets.

"Lee," she hissed. His head bobbed like a balloon thrust into water. "Lee!" His head almost lifted high enough to see her. "Lee! It's me! I'm here."

His head jerked up. His cheeks were purple and rounded, his eyes almost squinted shut against the swelling. A gash across his hairline left dried drips of blood down to his eyebrows. The crisp white shirt he'd worn the day before had turned almost as gray and stained as the wallpaper. The knees of his dungarees were brown with grime, his shoes and socks gone.

"Ingrid?" The word was fat and puffy through his swollen lips.

She curved her hands into fists and resisted the urge to run to him. "I'm here, Lee. Oh God. What happened?"

"I decided I wanted a new look. What do you think?" The words were slurred.

"I think I want to shake some sense into your bones then hug everything into place again. Who did this to you?"

He squinted and twitched against his restraints. "Another *tong* grabbed me. They've never made a move against Wui Seng before, but one of their men is really hurt, so they were desperate. They saw me and thought Uncle Moon must be close by, and didn't believe me when I said I didn't know where Uncle was. Not then. My captors connected with him . . . um, a few hours ago. I think." He squinted at the boarded-up window. "Their meeting's supposed to be tonight in an herb shop. He'll heal that man and take me in exchange. What time is it now?"

If Lee was traded to his uncle, as this *tong* planned, Ingrid could use the sylphs to follow along. Maybe Uncle Moon would lead her to Mr. Sakaguchi. But how long would that take? How long did she dare wait? The painted words on her body must be wearing away.

She couldn't wait. Not even if it meant sacrificing Ojisan. God, it hurt to even *think* that.

"I don't know," she said, her voice thick. "It's late. Blum is in Seattle and about to lead an attack on Chinatown. The whole city is holding its breath in wait."

"That ambassador's here?" He sat up straight with a shudder and moan. "You need to go, Ing. You can't be here. If she gets you—"

"Damn it, Lee, I'm already here. Is it safe to walk across the floor to you?"

His attempt to laugh ended in a painful wheeze. "I don't know. My initial memories of this place are a little blurry." He studied the floor, his arms straining from side to side. "Hard to see with my eyes like this."

"Leave it to me. What should I look for?"

"Shallow lumps in the carpet. Could be alarms or devices that could shock you. If you walk slowly, you should be okay."

"Famous last words." She knelt down to get an eye-level view of the carpet. Sure enough, she did spy some bumps in Lee's vicinity. She stood again, lips pursed. She could play it safe and draw on her power to float across the floor, but that might be better to do when she crossed again with Lee. She didn't need to drain herself unnecessarily.

"You don't have to do this, Ing. Really. It's okay to leave me." Lee's tender smile was distorted by his swelled cheeks.

"You know I won't leave you."

"Yeah. You're stupidly stubborn like that sometimes."

"Sometimes," she scoffed, and gently stepped into the room.

"How's your day gone? Miss me?" he asked.

"Oh, you know, pretty normal. Cy found out his father is presumed dead. Almost the entire Cascadian Earth Wardens Auxiliary was slaughtered by Russian sailors angry at the Baranov gold rush fuss, and we had to rescue the apprentices they kidnapped." She took a few more careful steps. "That's when Blum showed up with a lot of soldiers. It turns out she can track me somehow—she can sense me from hundreds of miles away. I only escaped her because I made friends with a hive of Sierran sylphs. They made me invisible. That's how we made it into Chinatown, too."

"We? Who else is here?"

"Cy. He's in the backyard." She stooped again to check the area ahead. It was hard to see in the bleary light, but she did note a few protrusions in the patchy carpet. She altered her path to the right.

"Damn." He sighed. "Is that all I missed?"

"No. The *qilin* spoke to me. It gave me a sort of vision of this place where you were captive, and told me that I needed to rescue you if there was to be any chance for peace."

Lee went very still. "The *qilin spoke* to you?"

"Yes. I . . . I don't even know what to think of it."

"You found the *guandao,* too, Ing." His voice was soft. "That has to mean *something.*"

Yes, it meant that the *qilin* had conscripted her to help Lee stay alive so that he could utilize the Crescent Blade in proper time—something Ingrid would have gladly done without all of this manipulation.

She knelt beside Lee's chair. "I won't go into all the details now, but you need to know the *qilin* really is drawn to the places it's called to guard. This building has a broken *qilin* statue in the backyard."

"Oh. *Oh!* Did the *qilin* speak to you on—"

"The *Palmetto Bug,* yes. Cy pointed out the carving you made."

"I just . . . felt like it needed to be there." Lee bowed his head and murmured something in Chinese. By his tone, it sounded like a prayer.

His injuries looked even more horrible up close. Anger brought a flare of power to her skin. She followed the line of his arms to where his wrists were shackled together in the darkness behind the chair.

"Lee. There are wires here. Something is attached to the underside of your seat."

"Damn. What does it look like?"

"A box about the size of two decks of cards side by side." She stared at the contraption in dismay. "What could it do?"

"Blow us up. Or if we're lucky, it's only an alarm. What color are the wires?"

"Black. I can't even count how many there are in the darkness. What can I do? And don't you dare tell me to leave you."

"You know if you dare me, I'll—"

A voice cried out in Chinese. Ingrid glanced up. A man stood in the doorway, a gun brandished. Lee yelled something back at him as Ingrid called up her power to form a bubble.

The gun fired.

Lee screeched as the bullet struck with a fleshy thump just as Ingrid raised her hand. A second bullet pinged off the protective bubble and cracked into a wall. The man yelled, his voice echoing through the massive house.

"Lee? Lee!" Ingrid leaned forward on her knees. Lee had collapsed over his thighs. She pulled him back by the shoulder far enough to see the expanding crimson across his belly.

A gut wound. *Lee was shot, he was shot, he was shot.* This couldn't happen, this couldn't be right. Lee couldn't die, not here, not now, not because she had been too sluggish to shield him in time.

The man screeched, and more voices called throughout the building. Ingrid had no time to deal with them. In her mind, she kept the bubble formed around herself and Lee, and she pulled her arm down. Another bullet ricocheted away, proof that the shield was holding. She grabbed the side and back of the chair, and calling on her strength, she yanked. The metal bolts snapped away from the aged wood.

With Lee and the chair in her arms, she ran for the window. Something clicked underfoot; a beeping alarm roared in her wake. The bubble bludgeoned through the outer wall with the crunch of wood and clatter of shattering glass, and then they were airborne and sailing from the third story.

The world blurred beneath them, but all too clearly Ingrid saw the Behemoth-class airship above, a rising sun-and-stars upon the side. That distinct, horrible smell flared in her nostrils again. Ambassador Blum was aboard and all too near.

CHAPTER 20

The attack on Chinatown. Ambassador Blum. Lee, bleeding.

Gravity.

Ingrid pushed power through her feet as the ground rapidly neared. She softened their descent, just barely, the impact jarring through both of her feet and sending out a gush of mud. Yells rang out from above. So much for a subtle exit.

"Ingrid!" Cy called from the deep shadows of the fence. "What the—"

"Lee's been shot in the stomach. We have to get him to his uncle. The herb shop." She glanced up to see if anyone was taking aim at her, and the evidence of what she'd done stole away her breath. She'd punched through the brittle wall as if it were tissue paper. Jagged edges marked a hole a solid seven feet in diameter, and she'd broken apart a chunk of the roof as well. Debris littered the yard. Good God, she could have killed Cy with shrapnel.

Her breath rattled. There was no time for doubts, no time for what-ifs. The screech of the alarm and men's yells echoed through the decrepit mansion.

She let the bubble fall and focused to leap again, bounding from the small crater with the chair in her arms. She dashed toward the warm magical presence of the sylphs. They welcomed her with a happily buzzing chorus.

Cy's eyes were wide, dim light reflecting on his pince-nez lenses. "Are you—"

"I'm fine." She gestured to the sylphs. They rose in a fluttering mass, their perkiness evidence of a good meal and some rest. She asked for their aid again, and they were delighted to acquiesce. Their movements were a gray haze in the black night.

Cy reached to help with Lee's chair but she moved past him. "No, come on!" She would have relinquished the burden if possible, but there was no time. Ingrid ran for the alley. Her muscles clenched as she fought the urge to convulsively shiver. Footsteps and yells carried across the yard and gained on them fast.

Ingrid motioned to Cy and they stopped beside a fence. She forced her ragged breaths to be quiet and shallow just as three men tore past them, two toting rifles. More cries rang out around the block. Ingrid wasn't the sole source of the hubbub; the UP airship hovered low overhead. Gunfire popped close by.

The attack was under way.

They remained quiet and still. Ingrid kept a wary eye out in case she needed to call up her shield again.

"Waste of bullets," Cy murmured, panting softly as he glanced at the airship. "That envelope has enchantments to make it almost as impenetrable as orichalcum. At least it's distracting our pursuers." He leaned down. "Are you with us, Lee?"

"Kind of." He barely squeezed out the words. "Hurts bad."

"We'll get you to Uncle Moon." Ingrid reached for the chains at Lee's back, and stopped at the sight of the black wires. "Cy, there's a bomb or something attached to his cuffs. Can you—"

"Yes." They switched spots. Cy crouched to investigate. He pulled a tool from his pocket and worked at the box, his face angled only inches from the refuse. Ingrid leaned to touch both Cy and Lee by their shoulders. She didn't know if she could protect them if the device exploded this close, but by God, she'd try.

Cy muttered to himself. Metal clicked in his hands. More gunfire clattered nearby as the airship thrummed overhead.

"There. The alarm is disarmed. It's a wonder you didn't trigger it when you landed." Cy stood. Ingrid sagged in relief. "I can pick at the lock—"

"No. I can handle that." She gripped the chain at the chair's back, and squeezed. The metal snapped. She shivered, gritting her teeth. "Blum's up there. I can feel her. The painted kanji will wear off soon. The sylphs can't hide me all night either."

Cy helped pull the chain free from Lee's wrists and lap. Lee groaned and sagged forward, but Cy caught him before he tumbled face first into the garbage. Ingrid reached into her pocket and grabbed a handful of kermanite. The energy entered her body in a delightful torrent.

"You're going through rocks faster than any machine," said Cy.

"I know, I know," she muttered. Her extremities felt all wobbly.

"Ing." Lee gasped. "Don't go to Uncle. Not safe for you. He can't know . . . what you do."

"I know the risks."

"Just because . . . *qilin* told you to . . ."

"This isn't about the *qilin*. This isn't about you being some prophesied leader. This is about you. *You*." She stroked the back of his knuckles.

"We could all end up as hostages, or worse," Cy whispered.

"I know the risks," she repeated. "Can you carry Lee? It'll be easier for me to create a bubble if my hands are free." If she'd only shielded him from that bullet a split second faster! She quivered and shoved away the guilt.

If Ingrid and Cy were attacked, which was likely, her powers would be evident. If she were captured, the Chinese, desperate as they were, had reason to be even more ruthless than Ambassador Blum or the Thuggees in exploiting her deviant geomancy. She understood that. But it didn't mean she would comply.

"Lee." She whispered low enough for Cy not to hear. "If I'm captured, remember the promise you made me in Portland. Don't let me be a weapon."

He couldn't speak, but the pain in his red-rimmed eyes only deepened.

More voices rang out nearby, but they didn't dare hide any longer. Lee stank of blood. The sylphs could only hide three of them for a limited time, too. Ingrid gestured with her head. Cy followed, Lee limp in his arms.

The airship roared above. Blum's presence was like the buzz of a mosquito, niggling at Ingrid's senses.

The street was bustling with activity at this late hour. Men, women, and children carried guns and rakes and pipes. Ingrid and Cy wove their way through the masses. Oblivious people parted to allow them passage.

The apothecary shop looked dark inside. They rounded the side of the building. An unusually tall Chinese man stood by an open door as he smoked a cigarette. They sidled past him, Cy taking care to angle Lee's legs to avoid bumping the door.

The store smelled fresh and strange and delightful all at once as the scents of a hundred different herbs and ingredients warred for dominance. Drawers and drying bundles created claustrophobic aisles. Lee's feet struck a scale. It swayed with a slight metallic ding. Ingrid snared some aprons from a hook and passed them to Lee. He was weak, but he tucked the cloths against his belly with a deflated, pain-filled whimper.

Ingrid glanced at the floor. They had left a trail of mud and blood on the swept wooden floor. The door guard only needed to turn around to notice. She desperately hoped Uncle Moon hadn't left. With the crowds outside and the attack imminent, how would they ever find him in time? Sweat soaked her feverish skin.

They hurriedly wandered through an office and a storage room. Voices speaking Chinese carried up a stairwell. Ingrid looked to Cy. His expression was solemn. He'd followed her through hell before, and he was ready to do so again. Lee was silent. The boy's arm dangled limp, his eyes shut, his teeth bared in a grimace.

She gripped the railing to walk downstairs, her legs rubbery and her breath fast. The sylphs continued their flight paths, their motions slowed. She had asked too much of them tonight.

A cluster of fidgeting men waited in the basement, Uncle Moon most prominent of all. Everything about him stood in antithesis to the Unified Pacific and their policies against Chinese garb and culture. He wore a crimson satin suit with a mandarin collar. His forehead was shaved high with the rest of his white hair bound in a tight, rope-like braid that dangled to his waist. Deep wrinkles surrounded his eyes and almost hid the pupils, but Ingrid felt his gaze shift to rest on them.

Uncle Moon called out something in Chinese; he sounded like a creaking door. The armed men around him, all in Western-style suits, suddenly froze.

To Ingrid's surprise, Lee answered, his voice rasping and weak. Ingrid hissed in frustration as she looked between him and Uncle Moon. She needed to know what was going on, damn it! As if to emphasize her ignorance, the hatchet men deployed to surround them. She noticed one of the men was pointing to the floor. She glanced back. A bloody trail led right to where they stood.

Ingrid bent close to Lee's ear while keeping an eye on the men around them. "I'm going to send the sylphs away. Warn them."

"You tell them," he mumbled.

Very well. She took a deep breath and faced Uncle Moon, one hand on Cy's sleeve. "Lee Fong is gravely injured. Sylphs are keeping us invisible. I'm going to send them away now. Please don't fire on us." Her voice quavered. The sylphs seemed to pick up on her agitation, too, or perhaps they loathed being underground and so far from greenery.

The hatchet men looked to Uncle Moon. He nodded. "We will hold fire for now." His diction was as clear as empty kermanite; the only other time Ingrid met him, she thought he knew no English at all. That had undoubtedly been Uncle Moon's intent.

Through her power, she thanked the sylphs and envisioned sharing the jamu-pan. "You can go," she told them, and pictured them flying away.

The sylphs continued to encircle her. Their reply flashed to her. *go where? no home.* Sadness seeped into the words. They really did want to leave the basement, but they were utterly lost.

The men continued to stare in wait. Thinking fast, Ingrid imagined the *Palmetto Bug,* its appearance, its smell. "A home?" she queried.

The reply was a sudden flash of positive emotion, and yet reluctance. The sylphs had been fed near the *Bug*. It was a safe place, a good place, but they didn't want to leave Ingrid in such an obviously dangerous location.

Ingrid released a frustrated huff. Any other time, she would be honored to have such beings imprinted on her, but this wasn't a debate to have now. Lee was *dying*.

"Trees close by? Rest?" she asked them, picturing pine trees she recalled a few blocks outside of Chinatown. Still they wavered. "We can go to the airship together when this is done. There is more bread there." It took everything she had not to plead; as devoted as they were to her, she had to remember these were fairies, not people. She couldn't allow them to dominate the transaction.

The promise of more bread—of more business—did the trick. *soon,* they said in unison before zooming away.

The heat of their magic dissipated, the silence sudden and eerie. The men didn't gasp, but they shifted in place, guns at the ready. Ingrid instantly expanded the protective shield from her skin to encompass both her and Cy. She met Uncle Moon's inscrutable gaze.

A boom shuddered through the air and floor and shivered dust from the ceiling. Everyone glanced up. Gunfire smattered in the distance. The full Unified Pacific bombardment had begun.

"Lee's *chi* grows weak. He has little time." Uncle Moon's expression was cool. "As do we all. Come with us." It was not a question.

The Chinese highbinders didn't escort them back up the stairs, but farther into the basement. The ceiling continued to shudder. Dust slid off the protective bubble that Ingrid maintained around them. They dashed through a storage room and into a tunnel with a heavy metal door. After they passed through, one of the men lingered to secure the door behind them. It shut with a god-awful screech.

Ingrid couldn't sense Blum from the basement. Maybe the feeling was mutual. She could only hope so.

They emerged from the tunnel into another storage room. "He's not responding anymore," Cy murmured. He gently jostled Lee in his arms.

Ingrid couldn't cry, she couldn't scream, she couldn't be weak, not here, not with these men. She made herself look away from Lee to take in everything else around her. Chinese men and women in soiled cotton work clothes were sorting through the boxes as if looking for something particular, their calls to each other high and urgent. Even so, they paused to bow as Uncle Moon passed. He waved to them to continue.

Lee had described Uncle Moon as one of the most powerful and feared figures in Chinatown, and one of the most gifted *lingqi* physicians in the past hundred years. That respect and awe were evident even as the world crashed down on these people. Again.

Ingrid sweated profusely due to her fever and the confinement of the bubble. The thick cloth of her brassiere felt damp and itchy, her spine like a river of sweat.

The path narrowed into a canyon of wooden boxes. One of their guards bumped against the bubble and bounced off. He cried out to his brethren. Ingrid winced. Well, that secret was out. At the head of the pack, Uncle Moon glanced back. He didn't look surprised, just thoughtful.

"Mr. Moon, sir," she called. Her voice sounded dull, as if she were speaking into a jar. "Lee's dying. We can't walk forever."

"I'm aware of his tenuous condition. I must work on him in a place that allows us a quick exodus."

Through an open doorway, she spied a whitewashed laboratory worthy of a Pasteurian doctor. It reminded her of the similar space tucked away in San Francisco's Chinatown where Lee injected her with a substance he refused to identify.

As she watched, a man swept what were surely expensive microscopes onto the floor with a heavy clatter of metal and glass. Another man ripped charts from the wall while a third worked to open a can that was labeled OIL. Whatever had been made in the laboratory, the room was now going to burn in order to hide the evidence.

Their group passed through another doorway, and a dense metal door sealed behind them.

Ingrid's lungs felt strained as the supply of oxygen to them ran low, and she had to let the shield drop. She and Cy took in deep, ragged breaths. She pressed her fingers against Lee's face as they continued to walk; his faint breath warmed her skin.

"Do you smell something?" Cy murmured.

"Now that you mention it, yes. It smells moist. Are we entering a sewer?"

They rounded a corner and the tunnel opened into a

wide, grand space. The walls were brick, with grand arches over passageways and up to the ceiling on high. A platform some fifty feet in width and length was covered in boxes, canvas bags, and dozens upon dozens of people, as well as mounds of bricks and dirt. The edge of the platform seemed to drop into a dark abyss, but heads were ascending and descending from that far side. There had to be stairs, but to what? They were already belowground.

Uncle Moon conversed with some men in a torrent of Chinese. Others stopped to listen. A new concussive blast caused more dust to shiver from the ceiling; a brown fog shifted beneath the swaying pendulum lights.

Uncle Moon beckoned to Ingrid and Cy and pointed to his feet. "Bring him here."

Cy rushed forward, Ingrid right at his side. The highbinders stood on guard. Ingrid met their cool gazes. Cy knelt to lay Lee on the cold bricks, and as soon as he stood and stepped back, Ingrid formed a bubble around them. Heat trickled from her limbs.

"You can't keep doing that," Cy muttered. His torso was awash in crimson. "Think of the effect it's having on your body."

"Think of what'll happen to my body if I don't stay on guard."

"If you reach toward your pockets for kermanite, or I reach to mine, they'll fire on us for certain."

"All the more reason to keep the bubble in place." Her hand slipped into his.

Moon knelt down behind Lee. His face, so deeply wrinkled,

looked more like a caricature of an old man than reality. He clapped his hands. The sound echoed back, surprisingly loud, and even through the bubble Ingrid felt a flare of magic.

An older highbinder advanced, his bald scalp flecked by shiny ringworm scars. He uttered a string of words in Chinese, his face stoic, and dropped to his knees. He bowed forward as if to kiss the bricks, his fingertips mere inches from Lee. Moon's hands had frozen after he clapped, like in prayer. He lashed out a hand over the bowing man, palm open, as if to grab a handful of strings. Moon's red silken sleeve rippled as he brought his fist to his chest, then opened his fist over Lee. He manipulated the air, like he was strumming an invisible harp, and murmured indecipherable words.

The bowing man sank forward, his face completely on the ground; then he slumped to one side.

"Lord Almighty," whispered Cy. "Just like that."

Just like that, Moon had yanked the life from a willing sacrifice, and used it to try to save Lee. The man surely didn't even know who Lee *was,* but Uncle Moon had asked him to die, so he did.

Ingrid only realized her concentration had slipped when she sensed the full force of Moon's *lingqi.* Even then, realizing the bubble was gone, she was too stunned to reconstruct it. This magic was beautiful and horrible and utterly mesmerizing. Moon's artistry had the same effect on the others around them. Men watched, jaws slack, their expressions ranging from reverence to terror, most somewhere in between.

This was the second time Ingrid had witnessed a dark

healing. American society muttered that all *lingqi* was evil because it was Chinese and therefore inherently inferior. Ingrid knew better. Reiki and *lingqi* were different words for the same thing. Both involved manipulation of ki or *chi*, whether the sacrifice came from plants or animals.

Blum's Reiki had been both beautiful and insidious as she had snapped rabbit kits' necks to draw the energy to heal Ingrid the night before the earthquake. The stench of her unleashed power had been musky, wild, almost like an animal's scent, though Ingrid hadn't comprehended yet that Blum was a kitsune.

Moon wielded comparable power, with similar sinuous motions, but the sense of it was profoundly different. The potency of his magic prickled against Ingrid's face, as if she had come indoors to escape bitter cold. Each lash and coil of Moon's arms, like a martial artist practicing against a strong wind, sent new ripples over her. The smell of it reminded her of the herb shop they had just walked through, of unfamiliar yet not unpleasant spices.

Were Moon's practices different because his sacrifice was willing, unlike Blum and her rabbits? Had Moon used men like this to save Mr. Sakaguchi? Ingrid didn't want to know. There was something abhorrent about this on a fundamental level—that height of power, used to pull life from another human being with such ease.

Papa had wielded his magic in such a ruthless way, too. Ingrid had that same potential. Maybe that's why this sight appalled her in such a personal way even as she ached for Moon's magic to save Lee, for the sacrifice to be worthwhile.

"Why are you here, Ingrid Carmichael?" Uncle Moon's utterance of her name pulled at her senses, heavy as lead. Magic laced the syllables. He continued to work, his gaze never leaving Lee.

"We're here right now to save Lee, but we came to Seattle together to retrieve Mr. Sakaguchi. Lee intended to trade himself for our sensei."

"Why do you care about them?"

That took her aback. "I love them."

"Love is fickle. It changes by the season."

She felt Cy squeeze her hand. "Not always. Mr. Sakaguchi has raised me as his daughter. Lee is my brother. We don't look alike, but our bond is real." She knew that Chinese culture believed strongly in filial love and duty; surely that explanation would suffice for him.

A loud boom rang from above, followed by a resonant shudder. The ceiling groaned and powder filtered down. Chatter around them increased. A woman ran by, practically dragging a small child by the arm as she clutched a baby to her breast. Men began to grab boxes and dashed for the stairs down into darkness.

Moon clapped his hands again. The sound reverberated through Ingrid. A man in stained cotton work clothes stepped forward, said something in Chinese, and bowed beside the dead man. Ingrid looked away, but she still tasted the potency of Uncle Moon's magic, as if a pinch of ground cinnamon had been dropped directly onto her tongue. She resisted the urge to gag.

Gripping Cy's hand harder, she sidled toward the edge

of the platform. She didn't want to get too close, but she needed to see where so many people were going.

Brick staircases zigzagged down and down to another platform. It sprawled out as a miniature naval dock—but there were no boats. Instead, sleek and long black tanks were moored there, partially submerged in the water.

"Submarines," murmured Cy. "Amazing. China's whole naval fleet was said to have been destroyed over ten years ago. These look to be of Russian make and fairly new. Black-market deal, maybe, or commandeered."

There were six crafts below, and empty berths besides. Ingrid watched as the little girl was pushed to the top of a jutting tower and then grabbed by hands to be pulled inside.

"As long as airships don't see them out in the sound, it's a good way to escape," she said.

"We must be close to the water, but it was still a major construction feat to widen the sewer enough to allow passage for those submarines. How did they move so much dirt without it being noticed? The danger of collapse . . ." He shook his head in awe. "This is something they've worked on for a while."

Moon sang as he worked. The magic dug into Ingrid's flesh like kitten claws.

Cy glanced back. A few men had stepped closer to monitor them, but their weapons had been put away. "How are we going to make our own escape, Ingrid?" he murmured. "Even if we get out of here, we're running straight into a street battle."

"You said before that we control what we can. Right now, that's overseeing Lee to make sure he's taken care of."

"Not like we have a lot of say in that regard." He tilted his head to acknowledge their guards. "Can you sense Blum?"

"Not since we went belowground. I'm hoping that feeling is mutual."

Cy's dark expression didn't agree. "She said she tracked you from hundreds of miles away. You sensed her from hundreds of *feet* away. I don't think being underground will throw her off your scent. Foxes know warrens."

He was right. Being too optimistic would get her captured here. Ingrid backed away from the ledge and closer to Uncle Moon. Rat-a-tats of gunfire carried from up above, followed by another heavy boom.

A cluster of men ran inside the chamber and to Uncle Moon. Soot and sweat covered their faces and clothes. They cast odd looks at Ingrid and Cy, and then engaged in a rapid conversation with the physician. The men gestured to the submarines, to the ceiling and city above, and then back to the submarines, their expressions beseeching. Moon's hands and arms continued to work as he spoke, his expression remaining as stoic as ever. Three of the men dropped to the floor to kowtow. Ingrid stepped away, fearing another one of Uncle Moon's intense claps and more deaths in quick sequence.

"It looks like they're trying to convince him to leave," said Cy.

"Yes. They're trying to get Dr. Moon to bring Lee aboard

a submarine, but he's reminding them that he cannot work a healing while surrounded by so much iron."

A man spoke from behind them. "It distorts how a physician senses ki. Lee will die if they board, and the other men fear they *all* will die if they stay much longer."

A sob rose in Ingrid's throat as she whirled around. "Ojisan!"

CHAPTER 21

Ingrid flung herself at Mr. Sakaguchi. He wore the same sort of stained cotton work clothes donned by most of the Chinese, the sleeves short on his arms. The wrinkles around his eyes had deepened in the past week, and his combed-over salt-and-pepper hair had thinned to show more of his scalp. He opened his arms wide to intercept Ingrid.

She wrapped herself around him, squeezing him as she never had before. His head pressed against her shoulder as he shuddered in a sob. Mr. Sakaguchi had never been one to show physical affection; it was not encouraged in Japanese culture. Knowing this made his reaction all the more poignant.

"Ojisan," she whispered again. She seemed incapable of saying or thinking anything else. She pulled back to look him in the eye. They were of almost equal height. Tears streamed down his cheeks.

"How was Lee injured so severely?" Mr. Sakaguchi gripped her arms.

"Another *tong* held him captive just blocks away. The *qilin* came to me and told me where he was. It can see the places it's called on to guard," she whispered. "One of the rival highbinders shot Lee as we escaped."

"You saw the *qilin*. It spoke with you?" Mr. Sakaguchi's gaze was stiletto sharp. She nodded. "You know what this means, how it regards you . . ."

"I know what it's supposed to mean, yes, but in my case, I think I'm handy because of my powers. That's all." All she had wanted for her life was, in truth, to be accepted as a geomancer—to travel, fill crystals, and maybe teach the little ones at an auxiliary. She could never see herself as a wise ruler or sage worthy of a *qilin*'s attention. "I can understand why the *qilin* came to Lee, though. It should have gone to him even if he was of common blood. Lee . . . Lee has that way about him."

Ripples of magic, of life essence, thrummed against her skin as Moon continued to work on Lee.

"You know about his father, then." His voice was especially soft. Ingrid and Cy nodded, and Mr. Sakaguchi regarded Cy as he extended his hand. "I believe we met briefly amid dire circumstances at my home."

Cy clapped his hand heartily. "Yes, sir, I'm Cy Jennings. I'd just come to your house when you were shot. Ingrid and I have become close in the past week, sir." To his credit, he didn't blush as he said this.

"Have you?" Mr. Sakaguchi arched an eyebrow. A blast

shuddered through the ceiling. "Your presence here is telling in that regard. I'm honored to meet you, but I wish the two of you weren't here at all. What happened in the past week, Ing-chan? When I was told of what befell San Francisco, I thought . . ." His voice withered away.

He thought she had died. Or worse, that she had caused the disaster.

Ingrid struggled with finding the words to summarize everything that had happened. This was never how she pictured her reunion with Mr. Sakaguchi, and their conversation couldn't last long. Blasts continued in quick succession. The highbinders guarding them were looking more ill at ease by the minute.

A cluster of women ran through the chamber. Dirt powdered them into brown ghosts, their eyes large and white.

"I didn't cause the earthquake. Papa did," said Ingrid. "Thuggees somehow got hold of him and brought him from China. Mr. Thornton was part of the conspiracy. He set up the auxiliary explosion."

"No." Mr. Sakaguchi shook his head, his skin blanching. "That's not possible. That horror couldn't have been caused by one of our own."

"Sir, I'm sorry," said Cy. "Mr. Thornton confessed his guilt outright. He even arranged it so the Chinese took the blame. You lived through the explosion, so you looked all the more complicit."

Mr. Sakaguchi continued to shake his head, as if he could shift the whole world right again. "I've known him almost twenty years. He was a stalwart colleague, I can't—"

"Ojisan." Ingrid cut in like a scalpel. "We don't have time to argue over this. *He did it.* He confessed. He's dead." She took a deep breath. It felt wrong to interrupt Mr. Sakaguchi like that, as if their roles had somehow reversed. "The earthquake provoked a two-headed snake to emerge in Olema. I talked to it. Mr. Thornton had brought Papa there. I . . . talked with him. Briefly. He tried to kill me. The snake, it . . . well, it ate him. In my defense."

Mr. Sakaguchi seemed to accept this more readily than the betrayal of one of his fellow wardens. "Your mother and I, we thought to spare you . . ." He took a deep breath. "Abram was not a good man."

Ingrid wanted to tell him how deeply she knew this, how Abram had likely murdered his other geomancer children, but the vibrations from the explosions above shuddered through the ceiling and reminded her of the time more urgently than any clock.

"No, he wasn't," she said gently. She squeezed his hand. It trembled. How strange, to see him so frail, but she'd been so weak in recent days, too. If she sat to rest now, rising again would feel like moving a mountain. "T.R. helped us to get to Seattle. He's trying to retrieve that stolen kermanite. Papa partly filled it during the earthquake."

"The Thuggees were behind that theft as well? A full conspiracy within our ranks." He shook his head again, slower this time. The truth had begun to sink in.

"Warden Sakaguchi, sir," said Cy, voice low. "Ingrid's found she can pull in power already bound in kermanite—"

"Cy—" she hissed.

"Another skill inherited from her father." Cy spoke faster. "You've studied kermanite and fantastics. Ingrid's nature suggests a lineage that's not entirely human. These power fluctuations within her body have almost killed her more than once." She began to sputter a rebuttal and he motioned for silence. "Ingrid, I know, you've kept us alive by using your power, but I'm terrified about what it's doing to you." He faced Mr. Sakaguchi again. "Is there anything you know from your research that might help her to stay alive?"

"Yes." Mr. Sakaguchi considered Ingrid solemnly. "Tranquilizer darts."

"Ojisan!"

"Mr. Jennings, you have come to know her well in a short time. She's brilliant and obstinate. I wish . . ." He sighed heavily. "What I wish doesn't matter. I knew the threat of her own death wouldn't convince her to leave San Francisco, but I hoped that the potential she held to kill others might compel her to be prudent. Yet here she is." A particularly heavy boom acted as punctuation. Bricks clattered from the ceiling and walls close by. A wave of dust swept over them. Everyone hacked and coughed.

"I'm aware of the danger, Mr. Sakaguchi," Ingrid said, coughing again. "I'm also aware that I have the power to preserve lives. I'm not callous like Papa. I *care*. I take precautions."

"Carrying a bucket of water into an inferno only does so much, Ing-chan."

"Mr. Sakaguchi, I need the full truth now. What do you know about Papa's past? His childhood, where he is from?"

"Abram Carmichael was classified as a geomancer at age ten in a California orphanage. He refused to speak of his life before then. My best guess was that he was from somewhere in the Pacific, but I couldn't find proof."

"His tongue was looser in recent years. It seems that Pele is my grandmother." Ingrid studied him to gauge his reaction.

Mr. Sakaguchi slowly nodded, his brow furrowed. "Yes. Yes. That would fit with what little we know. However, you must keep in mind, Ingrid, that even though you may have inherited Madame Pele's unique affinity with the earth, you are still very much human. That is the one certainty."

Moon clapped again. The shock of his power dropped Ingrid to one knee, gasping as if she were being suffocated by both dust and thick magic. Cy's hand on her shoulder kept her steady as she glanced back. A third man stepped forward. He tapped his chest and spoke in Chinese, then knelt to join the row of bodies.

"He said, 'In twenty years I shall be another stout young fellow,'" murmured Mr. Sakaguchi. "In China, that was a phrase often uttered by criminals before execution."

"He assumes there'll be a Chinese baby born now for him to be reincarnated into," said Cy.

"When your current life is hopeless, you must look to the next," said Mr. Sakaguchi.

Uncle Moon's gestures were more urgent, more exaggerated, as he undulated his arms over the newly dead man and Lee. His loud, quavering voice was clear even through the cacophony that carried down from outside.

Ingrid wanted to feel hope, but when she looked at Uncle Moon and Lee, she felt only hollowness. How much longer until Moon gave up? How much longer until the ceiling collapsed, or UP soldiers poured into the chamber? She stood again, gently shaking away Cy's grip.

"There's another important matter," she said. "Ambassador Blum."

"*Her.* Yes. Do you know—"

"She's a kitsune with at least four tails. She practices dark Reiki that rivals his." She motioned at Moon. "She stabbed me and healed me as a test to see if I was like Papa. I escaped her during the earthquake but she can track me somehow. She's somewhere above us right now, hunting me."

Mr. Sakaguchi tottered on his feet. Cy and Ingrid reached toward him but he waved them away.

"Oh, Ingrid." He pressed a hand to his forehead. Ingrid had the terrible realization that he was mourning her death, even as she stood before him. "Just as geomancers act as a medium between the earth and kermanite, ki passes through a physician of Reiki as they heal someone. If they work with plants, it is common for botanical freshness to linger around the patient like a pleasant cloud. If they manipulate the cords of other lives, it creates a more perverse bond between doctor and patient."

"A stain," said Ingrid, thinking of what the Reiki doc in Portland said.

"Yes. A stain, one that lingers for weeks."

"Meaning, sir, that if you left with us right now, Uncle Moon here would sense your whereabouts over quite a distance."

"That is true, Mr. Jennings. This is not something commonly known about Reiki, and with reason, as it would alarm customers of even licensed franchises. Floral Reiki is far less potent, but a doctor can often recognize their recent patients by a trace of their own magic."

"My God." Horror formed a hard knot in Ingrid's gut. "I've been endangering all of you. Cy, Fenris, Lee, even Mr. Sakaguchi right now. I'm carrying part of her power inside me."

Ingrid had already known that, to a degree. Known that the potency of Blum's healing had kept her alive through overwhelming energy sickness in San Francisco and had assisted her recovery in the days since. That had been a major positive, no question, but Ingrid's regeneration skill couldn't offset *this*: that she was truly acting like a beacon, drawing Blum closer to everyone she loved.

"Ingrid." Cy cupped her chin and forced her gaze to his. "You weren't willingly healed, and sure as rain, you didn't know what all it entailed. This tracking ability might be part of why she stabbed you and healed you at all—"

Booms thudded through the ground directly above. All three of them dropped to the ground as Ingrid instinctively called up a shield. Chunks of masonry pattered against the bubble and slid to the floor. Cy and Mr. Sakaguchi looked around, their breaths rapid. Beyond the shield, the air was turbulent and brown as it flowed like a storm from the nearby hallways.

With a pang, Ingrid realized that she couldn't see Lee through all the dust. She ached to call up another shield over him, but he was too far away. And she wasn't sure if he was alive at this point to even need the protection. Her fingers curled as anxiety clogged her throat.

"You seem rather calm about this shield Ingrid can create," Mr. Sakaguchi said to Cy.

"I've been through this with her a time or two now, sir, including a rather memorable walk on the bottom of San Francisco Bay."

"I see. I think we could have an interesting talk about my Ing-chan, Mr. Jennings."

"I think we could, too, sir, and I heartily hope for that someday, but I think we're about out of talking time here. I reckon the fox is trying to flush us from our warren."

"I agree, Mr. Jennings."

The dust faded. The highbinders became visible first, like phantoms in a mist. They had bent over Moon to shield him. As Ingrid watched, they stepped back. Moon's arms continued their dance. The gestures no longer had grace. They lashed like angry whips, this way, that, as if he could beat Lee's *chi* into submission, into staying put.

Ingrid let the bubble fall again. She immediately coughed, as did Cy and Mr. Sakaguchi.

"I do not know what else to do," Uncle Moon said, voice rasping. His hands rested on his lap, still for the first time in ages. “I can’t sacrifice all of my most loyal men.” He gazed on Lee with fondness and despair.

Mr. Sakaguchi stepped forward. “I will give my life to save his.”

“Ojisan, no,” Ingrid broke in. This was a noble gesture worthy of one of his beloved operas like *Lincoln*. “You can’t—”

His focus remained on Moon. “I’m an old man. I’ve lived a good life. Lee must live.” He echoed the *qilin*.

Cy shifted uneasily beside Ingrid, and she whirled on him. “Don’t you dare volunteer,” she hissed. “Don’t you dare.”

At the same time, she knew she’d been willing to sacrifice herself for Lee, too, though not in *this* way. Not by willingly giving herself to dark magic.

“I would rather Lee die and China with him than have his *chi* tainted by Japanese ki.” Moon referred to the Japanese version of *chi* as if clearing phlegm from his throat. “Your teaching has corrupted him.”

“You knew who I was and what I represented when we reached our agreement five years ago. Lee is to be a bridge between our people.”

“Our bridges have been destroyed by your bombs and your Durendals. What remained was lost to earthquakes.”

Cy stood close enough that Ingrid could feel him cringe.

“The bombs are not mine, nor are the Durendals,” Mr. Sakaguchi said softly.

“Nor is this boy.” Moon’s fists formed hard rocks on his

lap. He said something curt in Chinese. Two highbinders picked up Lee.

Ingrid suddenly felt Blum's presence like the crackling pressure of a lightning storm.

Moon stiffly stood and hobbled toward the stairs. Ingrid looked around, her heart pounding in terror. Their guards had abandoned them. She, Cy, and Mr. Sakaguchi were simply being left behind.

Bullets were precious to the Chinese. Better to leave them to the Unified Pacific.

"Mr. Sakaguchi. You have to go with them. Lee needs you as his sensei now more than ever," she whispered, galled by her own words. "I can feel Blum getting closer. She can track *me,* and Moon can track *you.*"

Mr. Sakaguchi's eyes widened; she couldn't wait for him to respond. She rushed forward.

"Dr. Moon! Sir! Mr. Sakaguchi needs to go with you."

Moon stopped, and for the first time his face showed genuine surprise. "What? You're asking me to take him? You came all the way to Seattle to set him free, and now this?" He advanced on them, his strides growing stronger, his expression angrier. "He is a useless Japanese man. He has eaten our food, wasted my time. I shouldn't have saved him to begin with, but I did so for Lee's sake. There's no room for sentimentality now. You would have him breathe our precious air as we suffer his presence?" He motioned to the last submarine below.

The *tap-tap-tap* of gunfire rang out close by, somewhere

in the tunnels. The remaining hatchet men readied their guns, but instead of looking to the doorways, they looked to Mr. Sakaguchi. They seemed grimly eager, as if they had been starving for this opportunity to shoot him.

Ingrid held energy close to her skin, waiting. Her mind was blank. She couldn't refute Moon's argument. She even respected the presence of his hatchet men. They, at least, would shoot to kill Mr. Sakaguchi. Blum wouldn't grant him that mercy.

"You're right." Mr. Sakaguchi's whisper was so low she scarcely heard it. "Dr. Moon can track me. Even more, he now knows you possess peculiar skills, but he has higher priorities to address at the moment, and little room left on the submarine." Grief lined his eyes. "We make each other all the more vulnerable."

Mr. Sakaguchi stepped forward. "Take me with you. Allow me to help tend Lee, and I will fill kermanite for your cause."

Uncle Moon's gaze sharpened. He said something to the unburdened highbinders, and they jogged toward Mr. Sakaguchi.

"Ojisan!" she gasped. He couldn't do this. Supporting war went against everything he was.

"Dr. Moon is right. The war has changed. I can no longer play conscientious objector while the remaining Chinese are slaughtered. This mountain I climb may be insurmountable, yet . . ." His eyes took on a dreamy sheen. *"Yamaji kite—Naniyara yukashi—Sumire-gusa."*

Ingrid was taken aback as she recognized the Bashō haiku:

Coming along the mountain path
I am somehow mysteriously moved
by these violets.

"Continue to bloom, my beloved daughter," Mr. Sakaguchi whispered. Ingrid wanted to say something, anything, and couldn't form words. Mr. Sakaguchi's gaze shifted past her to Cy, to whom he gave a wordless nod. His guards prodded him, and he faced forward as they reached the stairs.

Ingrid advanced to the edge of the precipice. Lee was being lowered into the last remaining submarine. Uncle Moon stood atop the vessel, a brilliant figure in crimson. Mr. Sakaguchi and the other men ran down, down, their footsteps echoing in a mighty space that was now almost entirely empty.

Blum approached with reverberating steps. The world seemed quieter otherwise, the bombardment more distant. The airships had likely withdrawn as ground troops moved in with Blum.

Ingrid was tired of running. Grief made her feet adhere to the bricks, transforming her into a statue.

"Ingrid." Cy pulled at her shoulder. "Ingrid! We can't stand here and gawk."

She nodded and willed herself to wakefulness, willed the heat in her veins to stir. She still carried fever. If they could get far enough away, maybe the sylphs would be rested, maybe they could work dog sorcery again, anything to hide her long enough for them to reach the *Bug*.

Maybe, maybe, maybe. The word pestered her like a mosquito.

"Which way's she approaching from, Ingrid? Stay with me."

Ingrid pointed the way they had come. Blum trailed them the way a dog sniffs out a fox; maybe that role reversal was part of Blum's joy in the pursuit.

"You're wearing out like the sylphs were." He grimaced and pulled filled kermanite from his pouch. "You need this. We have to move, Ingrid."

He dragged her forward even as her body absorbed power from the crystals. Magic twined her wrists, coursed through her marrow, filled her lungs. Her fever soared; her exhaustion worsened. She forced away the weakness, binding magic into her muscles to make them stronger, emblazoning new energy into her brain as if she'd guzzled a full pot of Fenris's foul coffee.

Ingrid pushed away the ground as she started to run.

Blum loomed closer, her feral and magical presence exuding foulness worse than the decomposing animals along Chinatown's walls.

Ingrid had to run faster, faster. She gripped Cy's arm and pulled him along, up a staircase, through the broken shell of a building. Fire stretched into the night sky, blinding her for all of a second. She blinked away the eye strain. She clutched Cy's hand, and together they ran north along a razed street of Seattle.

CHAPTER 22

Brilliant red and black strokes colored the night, as if a painter had upended two pails onto a broad canvas. Cinders and ashes choked the air. Someone screamed nearby, the sound inhuman. A Durendal, maybe more than one, rumbled beyond sight. Ingrid looked to the sky. Smoke and clouds worked together to suffocate the stars.

The Unified Pacific airships had indeed withdrawn to the far west, over the water. Fear spiked in her chest: What if they spotted the submarines? What if they bombed them?

Control what we can, control what we can, she told herself with every thud of her feet. The submarines had a better chance than she and Cy. She needed to keep her focus here, not on the horizon.

Her attuned senses warned her of approaching soldiers. She pushed Cy down as she brought up a shield. Bullets pinged away as she and Cy rolled across the ground. He jumped to his feet and withdrew his gun as he ducked behind the shattered remnants of a brick wall. Ingrid let the bubble drop. Cy fired twice in succession. A yell and a thud came in reply.

"There's another soldier," he muttered, stopping her as she was about to shield them again. Ingrid pulled herself into a crouch behind the wall. Sweat soaked her filthy dress, the cloth weighed down as if by mud.

Cy peered around the top bricks. A bullet sang over his hat. He aimed, ducked again, then popped up to fire. Ingrid waited for a scream, a sign of a hit, but after a moment Cy tugged on her. They continued at a crouch.

"Death is like that sometimes." His voice was so low she almost missed the words. "Quiet. A snowflake falling in the dark. You don't know how the snow has accumulated until you see the drifts in the morning."

I'm sorry, she wanted to say. Sorry he was in the place, that she'd brought him here, that he had to kill again. That she knew each death killed part of him.

But she also knew that those words would have been as insufficient as the shopkeepers' aprons she had pressed against Lee's gut wound. Grief and guilt would have their time. For now, they had to survive.

"If we're separated, if anything happens, work north to meet Fenris in Edmonds," Cy said. Sweat and ashes smeared his face like camouflage.

"We're not getting separated. I'm not about to leave without you."

"Even if that's in UP custody?"

"We're not going to—"

She sensed the ordnance as soon as it departed the Durendal's gun. The air quivered in advance, like a pressure wave preceding an earthquake, the ripples striking her before the boom registered in her ears. She grabbed Cy again and pulled him down as the shield ensconced them. The skeletal wooden building to their left exploded. Shards of wood and bricks and belongings rained down on the bubble as the heat of the blast flared and dissipated against the glass-like sheen. Her contrived shield did nothing to mute the sound that dominated her senses for a matter of seconds. Ingrid screamed and scarcely heard it, though she felt her throat turn raw. Pain seared her eardrums then dulled, a fierce ache lingering.

She studied the firm mud beneath her hands. No reaction from Hidden Ones, no blue miasma. Ingrid's pulse ticked like an overwound pocket watch. God, if she was hurt here and now, an earthquake wasn't the only issue. A major seism could cause a tsunami. This whole area would flood, and those submarines out in Puget Sound . . .

"Ingrid?" Cy sounded distant and muffled, even though he was right beside her.

"I guess I need to make my bubbles block sound, too." She felt the movement of the Durendal a block away. The heavy tank created rumbles like a shallow tremblor.

"You're not hurt?"

She shook her head. "Just my ears. Everything sounds funny."

Debris flecked the dirt street around them. Bits of wood

flamed like torches while jagged shards of glass reflected nearby conflagrations like thin puddles of captured flame.

Cy helped her up. Her hands and legs quivered, her fingers and toes tingling almost to the point of numbness. Ingrid had power, though. She had to keep going.

Blum's presence stretched over her like a long shadow.

"How many bullets do you have, Cy?"

"Three more in chambers, more to reload."

She let the barrier fall so she could concentrate on safely navigating the debris as they ran forward. She couldn't use up her power unnecessarily; only a scoop of charged kermanite remained in her pocket. Once they found adequate temporary shelter, she could get more crystals from Cy.

"If we can't get away from Blum, you have to shoot me, Cy. It's a mercy. You know it is."

She didn't need to look at him to know the agony upon his face.

"Don't ask me that, Ingrid. Don't put that on my soul."

"How would your soul handle me being captive, a weapon?"

"Are you willing to shoot me, too? Or use your power to . . . ?"

It was only fair of him to flip the dilemma around, and she couldn't answer. The very thought made something in her chest wither.

She reached for his hand. Their fingers twined together, their holds desperate.

Blum approached fast, faster than they could run, her essence like the buzz of an angry wasp nest. Ingrid glanced back. A Durendal drove up the street behind them. Downed street poles crunched and shattered beneath its treads. Blum stood on the side rail, her fitted black coat billowing with an elegant flair.

Ingrid pulled Cy to run faster. They had to find a side street, they had to get away. The firebreak around Chinatown lay ahead, the intact buildings beyond like silhouetted black obelisks.

She spied a gap in the buildings ahead. They swerved around a fallen, flaming wooden pole only to see a knot of troops blocking the path some twenty feet distant. Ingrid brought up her shield as she spun around. A shattered building fully blocked the avenue toward the water. The Durendal's heavy shudders made rocks dance and clatter across the earth.

Blum had herded them right into a trap.

Hand in hand with Cy, Ingrid sprinted north. It provided a straightaway for the tank, but damn it, the way was mostly clear and they had to—

"Ingrid Carmichael!" The power embodied in the invocation of her name hooked her like a harpoon. She staggered to a stop, gasping. Cy dragged to a stop as well, his grip on her strong despite her clammy skin.

Heart skittering, body trembling, Ingrid turned to confront Ambassador Blum.

Ambassador Blum still wore her young, redheaded form. Against the backdrop of fire and destruction, she looked decidedly perky. Her tumultuous red hair was only partially braided up so that a cascade of curls fell over her shoulders.

The ashy smudges across her cheeks somehow managed to look artful. She wore the same black fitted dress as earlier, the mantled peacoat swirling about her hips as she hopped from the side rail of the Durendal to the ground. The tank leveled its gun at Ingrid and Cy as Blum ambled forward to one side. She motioned with a black-gloved hand. Boots pattered as soldiers deployed around them, the sound tinny and muffled.

"Ingrid Carmichael, Ingrid Carmichael! Fancy meeting you here."

Ingrid flinched at the repetition of her name. Blum's toothy grin made it clear how she relished that reaction.

Cy's hand was damp against hers. She felt the rapidness of his pulse, his terror. He had run for a dozen years to avoid this moment.

Ingrid licked her dry lips and blurted out the first thing that came to mind. "Moshi moshi!"

Blum stared at her in surprise and burst out laughing. It was a joyous, carefree sound, a full-on belly laugh. She clapped her hands together and did a happy little hop. "Aha! You figured me out! However, I hate to disappoint you. That trite test only works on young kitsune with scarcely a nub of a tail and no practice with spoken human language. I can say 'moshi moshi' quite well in person *and* on the telephone, thank you very much. I confess, elocution lessons helped."

Within the bubble, a waft of Blum's musky power somehow thickened the trapped, smoky air. Ingrid's shoulders heaved as she fought to breathe. It was as if Blum's very presence could suffocate her.

The ambassador strolled closer with a playful roll to her gait. "Tell me, Ingrid, how did you hide yourself earlier? I was quite impressed. I thought I'd snared you at the docks, and then it was like you vanished from existence until a short while ago. Have you been doing some research?"

"You told me before that you think I'm clever. Give me some credit."

"Oh, I grant you plenty of credit. You survived San Francisco. That would be quite impressive for any human being, but for a geomancer surrounded by such an intense flow of energy, it's downright miraculous." Blum tilted her head to one side. "Then you came here, to Seattle of all places. Let me guess: a rendezvous with your mentor, Mr. Sakaguchi?"

Ingrid didn't try to mask her grief at the name. *Please let the submarines get away. Please let Mr. Sakaguchi and Lee live.* "I don't know where he is."

"Oh, I believe you. He'd be with you now, if at all possible." Blum sighed and kicked the dirt like a petulant child. "I had reports that he was with a *tong* here. I imagine he's still about, somewhere. It'll likely take a week for soldiers to burrow throughout the underground of this slum, but maybe we'll find him. It's much easier to speak with the living than the dead, though. Spirits are always so . . . so . . . fixated on things and people and unresolved life issues and so on. They lose all conversation skills. It's worse than teatime with the president."

"You . . . interrogate ghosts?"

"If necessary. If possible. Ghosts are a rarity, in all truth.

A person has to die with a certain strength of will or an intense emotion that enables them to linger, and often people with magic embody that requisite tenacity. Maybe we'll get a ghost out of the Cascadian Auxiliary. It's horrific enough a scene. I should thank you for your assistance there, while I have it in mind." Blum looked oddly somber. "If you hadn't stepped in, those boys would be aloft over the Pacific now and forced into a lifetime of eating borscht. Of course, part of the credit for their rescue goes to Mr. Augustus as well. Oh, come now, Cy. No smile or 'moshi moshi' from you? No no, dearie. Keep the gun aimed downward. I know you're a crack shot, but you're also now aware that a bullet won't eliminate me." She waggled her pointer finger. Her black glove hid her ambassadorial ring.

"You're not immortal," Cy growled.

"No, and thank goodness I'm not! Part of the fun is in the risk. Immortality would be as dull as an imperial coronation. It *is* good to see you again."

"'Fraid I can't say the same."

Blum gazed on him with a fondness that perturbed Ingrid. "Tsk, tsk. You seem to have lost the ability to converse in complex sentences since you deserted. Twelve years is certainly a long time to evade the A-and-A. Lo those many years ago, I personally wrote the notice regarding your death in an airship crash. I arranged your funeral, too. It's surprising, really, how often deserters will show up at their own interment in order to see their family again, but you didn't take the bait. Alas. Your mother sang 'The Sweet By and By' in such a lovely soprano. You would have found it quite touching." Blum's grin was downright vulpine. "I arranged another such memorial for someone you know well."

Cy's rage rattled in his breath. Ingrid gripped his hand, both in support and to remind him to stay calm. He took a moment to regain control before he spoke. "You're referencing my father, Miss Blum?"

"Your father? Actually, no, but we can certainly talk about him. He's missing in San Francisco, did you know? He's old for a man. He's had a good life. To think, the two of you were so close to each other in the same city after so many years apart, and you didn't even know." She shook her head, her curls bouncing. "I was stunned to find you had been in San Francisco, too. Imagine my delight when I saw your name in Mr. Thornton's appointment book! The surname was different, but there are only so many engineers named Cy in this world. I had a hunch it was you. What astounding circumstances, to bring you and Ingrid together. I wasn't sure if you'd made it out of the city with her, Cy, but I'm ever so glad you did."

With a start, Ingrid realized that Blum didn't know they had indeed met with the elder Mr. Augustus. The chaos of the earthquake hours later had acted in their favor, in this small way. Cy seemed to come to the same understanding as he squeezed Ingrid's fingers.

"Let Ingrid go and I'll come with you," he said.

"What?" snapped Ingrid.

Blum burst out with more airy laughter. "Oh, Cy, Cy. How *noble*. You assume the A-and-A still wants you."

"They always need good engineers," he said.

"Cy, what the hell are you doing?" Ingrid hissed. He maintained a level gaze on Blum.

"Good *loyal* engineers. There's no denying that you're downright brilliant, but we also have a far better employee at work on our most vital project right now, and with this person we needn't worry about pesky things like sabotage."

Did Blum know about the flaw that Cy built into Durendals, or was she referring to something else?

"Don't expect loyalty from *me,*" snarled Ingrid. She pushed more energy into the protective bubble as she eyed the soldiers around them. They seemed to follow Blum's orders out of fear more than respect—a marked difference from how soldiers behaved around Mr. Roosevelt.

Another Durendal rumbled along somewhere close by. Someone wailed. Two gunshots rang out, followed by a distant flash of light. She wondered if it came from a flash grenade. Far, far in the distance, airships continued their low meditative hum.

Blum grinned and fidgeted with her skirt, the luxurious pleated fabric rippling in the indirect firelight. "My dear Ingrid, the advantage in working with *you* is that your best work can be done while unconscious. You don't have to be awake to transfer energy to kermanite, or for your pain to provoke geomantic yokai. It's really astonishing how medicine has advanced in recent years thanks to the war! Pain can be evoked through efficient and clean methods. We live in an amazing technological age.

"I would visit you often, though. I could even read to you, if you're incapable of holding a book on your own. Over the years, I have sought out books from the library of Alexandria, volumes no human has read in centuries. Some make for dull reads, mind you, but others are a delight." Blum's smile was bright. Hopeful. "I could bring tea as well. You do prefer tea, don't you? Not that American travesty that is coffee?"

Ingrid shuddered at the perversion of friendship Blum was describing. "As fond as I am of old books, I think I'd prefer to freely live my life and read more contemporary works."

"Live out your life . . . with Cy?" Blum shook her head, as if talking to a small child. "I'm afraid not." She motioned to her soldiers. Their gun barrels shifted to aim at Cy.

Ingrid squeezed Cy's hand to reassure him. His heartbeat quivered through his sweaty palm. She could protect him with an energy bubble, but she would rather not give up that secret to Blum. How could they slip out of this trap?

"You don't need to kill him," she said.

"What, are *you* going to offer to come with me willingly if I leave him alive? You're both willing to sacrifice for the other. How nauseatingly sweet." Blum laughed. "No, Ingrid. You must understand that hope is a kind of gangrene. A less smelly type, most assuredly, but a form of fatal rot nevertheless. You shouldn't waste your conscious hours on something as finite as *love*. Besides, if Cy's not in our employ, he shouldn't work for anyone else either." Blum shrugged and flicked her hand.

Five guns fired simultaneously, and Ingrid was ready. The bullets impacted on the bubble and formed brief, glass-like ripples in midair before ricocheting away. One pinged back at the tank with a metallic ding.

Blum lifted a hand. The soldiers froze. “Oh my. Ingrid, now *this* is a surprise.”

Ingrid gritted her teeth. “We’re going to have to run for it,” she quickly whispered, as low as she could, though her legs wobbled as she stood still.

“Can’t outrun the tank,” Cy muttered quickly.

“I’ve shattered a few walls tonight. I could run at the tank.”

“It’s made of enchanted orichalcum.”

She glanced at him. “We have to try *something.*” She couldn’t afford to dwell on doubt.

“What other tricks can you do?” mused Blum. “Can you really tear through orichalcum? That could come in handy. Oh yes, whisper away over there. I may be in human form but my hearing is—”

Through her heightened senses, Ingrid heard the soft, subtle click of a gun off to her right.

Unfortunately, Blum noticed it as well. “Take cover!” she shouted, waving to her soldiers as she ducked below the tank’s gun barrel. Pops erupted around them. Ingrid hunkered down with Cy as another bullet bounced off their shield.

Chinese men and women screamed as they jumped from the rubble and flung themselves at soldiers. The refugees’ arsenal ranged from rakes to planks to metal pipes to bricks. Only a few had guns.

“Banzai!” yelled a soldier, the word punctuated with a

gurgle. Screamed Chinese words melded into a cacophony of rage and desperation and pain.

"This is our chance!" Cy said.

A soldier lunged toward them, but a Chinese woman tackled him by the legs. His face impacted on the street with a harsh crack. Behind them, a soldier turned, gun barrel aimed at the woman. Ingrid gasped and slashed her arm through the air. The soldier flew back five feet to crash into the metal plating of the Durendal with a sickening crunch.

Fire erupted in Ingrid's thigh. She screamed as she collapsed forward and rolled to her side, hands pressed to her right leg. Heat burbled through her veins, a different heat than what poured over her fingers. She lifted a hand toward her face. Blood painted her palm dark.

Pain roared through her thigh, her blood pumping and gushing against her hands. The bullet had struck or passed through near her femoral artery—where Papa had been stabbed, the wound that would have killed him if the massive snake hadn't gotten him first.

Like father, like daughter.

Cy clutched her shoulders. "Ingrid. Oh Lord."

The earth shivered as it awoke. Blue mist crept across the muddy street to where Ingrid lay prone on her side.

CHAPTER 23

Ingrid soaked in earth energy with a ragged gasp. It felt good, even as she bled out. A pleasant distraction. Was this how Papa felt at the end, as his blood sizzled and boiled? He was powerful, even then—he'd almost succeeded in suffocating her, even at a distance. Ingrid was still powerful, too.

She willed her senses to dull the pain. It worked. In the absence of agony, she suddenly became aware of how hard she was breathing, how her heartbeat rampaged. She formed a shield around Cy and her again as a precaution and rolled to rest on her knees with a groan. Her injured thigh almost scooted out from under her. The miasma continued to thicken.

"You need to stay down, keep the leg elevated—" Cy said.

"No. It won't save me," she gently said as she held up a bloody palm. Energy coiled up her arm to form a writhing blue fireball within her cupped hand. She shook her head, dazed at her own magic—such power and powerlessness all at once. Her gaze was pulled south to where Mount Rainier stood. The earth still knew her pain, even if it was dulled in her brain. "And I'll be damned if I show weakness before Blum."

"You shouldn't be hurt, not here!" snapped Blum. She crouched in front of the Durendal about ten feet away. "I'll—"

Ingrid struck the air with her fist as she dropped the bubble for a scant second. Blum took the blue fireball like an uppercut. With a distinctively animal yelp, she flew back and landed just short of the Durendal.

The melee around them had already reached a quick end. Soldiers and refugees sprawled in the street and rubble, some dead, some whimpering, some escaping into broken buildings nearby.

"Your ring can't protect you from everything, can it?" Ingrid called to Blum. "You're not immortal, after all." Through the pulse of her blood, the pulse of the earth, she knew the weakness of the made ground beneath her. "A thixotropic reaction," she whispered to herself.

The textbook definition from her auxiliary flashed through her mind: *When viscous ground is shaken and liquefies.* She pushed power into the earth.

A crack spread outward from her palm and zigzagged toward Blum and past her, expanding as it went. Ingrid shoved harder. Metal twisted and wrenched as dirt gave way. The Durendal sank into the ground, back end first, then suddenly angled forward. The heavy barrel tipped down. A few injured soldiers yelled and dragged themselves away.

Blum tried to scamper away, too. Ingrid felt the compressions of her feet through the earth. Dirt crumbled beneath Blum and one of her legs sank to midcalf. Ingrid clenched her fist, and the earth clamped down as if with teeth. Blum screeched and twisted, but Ingrid willed the dirt to compress as hard as marble.

"Bring down the bubble for a second," Cy snapped. She did.

He fired his gun. Blum snarled and jerked back, a hand to her shoulder. Ingrid brought the shield up around them again.

"I aimed for her head," said Cy. His voice carried a coldness Ingrid had never heard before. "That ambassadorial ring distorts the shots. We can't kill her. You could bury her, and she'd dig her way out again."

"I could bury her so deep it'd take her centuries to claw her way free," Ingrid whispered, but knew without question that such a feat would be fatal to her. Nor would it conclusively eliminate Blum.

Oh God. What had become of them? Cy, the avowed pacifist, the man who hadn't even wanted to touch a gun. Ingrid, who would find moths indoors and try to cage them in her fingers to free them outside. She felt detached sadness as she realized how they had changed over the past week.

Why are you hurting me, cousin? The words were a whisper, but rang through Ingrid like a bell.

"Cousin?" she said aloud.

"Ingrid?" asked Cy. She limply waved him to silence and pivoted to look toward Rainier. Was this, really . . . ? There was no visible plume from an eruption and no earthquake, but the blue fog continued to thicken. Who else could this be?

Tacoma? Ingrid said within her thoughts. An overwhelmingly positive emotion surged in reply. Oh God, she was talking with a spirit bound with a fourteen-thousand-foot volcano. *My name is Ingrid.*

I'm trying to slumber, cousin-from-over-the-water-Ingrid. I promised my people I would stay asleep as long as possible.

The voice was neither male nor female. It simply *was*. Ingrid wondered if the people it spoke of were the native tribes now scattered to the winds, so many dead to disease or doomed to lives on remote reservations or coastal canneries, or people who lived here in a much more distant time. Rainier had experienced minor stirrings in the past few centuries, but geologists speculated that it had been thousands of years since there'd been a cataclysmic eruption.

Ingrid didn't want such an event to be her dying legacy. The fast-moving mud and debris flow of a lahar shouldn't reach Seattle, under normal circumstances, but she knew what Papa had caused in San Francisco. He had *attracted* more damage to his location. If she drew in lahars and lava, if seisms caused a tsunami, thousands upon thousands would die. The repercussions could be felt as far away as Baranov or even Japan.

She formed a bloody fist against her seeping wound.

Pain undulated from her thigh as agony tried to erode the barrier she had made.

I'm sorry, she thought. *I'm happy to meet you, but I don't want your mountain to awaken either. I'm hurt, and I'm so sorry that you feel my pain, too.*

You should return to your mountain. It's bad to be far from home. The voice was sleepy.

A mountain? Where would her mountain be? Her first thought was Mount Diablo near San Francisco, where she used to go on picnics with Mama. A sob choked out, with another spike of god-awful pain. Gritting her teeth, she forced the feeling to dwindle down, but she wouldn't be able to squelch the full sensation for much longer. She was weakening fast. The shield would fall soon, too.

The earth quivered in response. Rubble shifted.

"Cy," she gasped. "Cy?"

"I'm here."

"Tacoma's . . . waking up. Talking to me. Can't let that happen . . . volcano. Stop this."

"Oh, Ingrid."

Cy was hunched over her, his shoulders shaking, the pistol against his thigh. "I love you, Ingrid. I can't, I can't—"

"I'll die anyway," she whispered.

He closed his eyes, his lips moving as if he prayed.

Pain rolled through her like magma. Her concentration shattered as agony dappled her vision in red. The shield dropped, and smoke wafted over them.

"Finally!" growled Blum.

Ingrid's pain stopped. Not simply dulled, but *stopped.*

She looked at her hand, her darkened skirt. "Cy?" she whispered.

The normal tone of her voice made him sit up straight. He looked at Blum then back at her. "Ingrid? She . . . healed you?"

"Of course I healed her. I am *not* about to drown in boiling mud or water or be brained by floating debris. I have *plans,* and they do not include death. Not tonight." Blum bared her teeth. "Ingrid, I was worried that you wouldn't drop that fool blockade until you were actually dead." The kitsune had stretched out to grasp the leg of one of the downed soldiers. "I much prefer to heal while in my Masako body. *She* was the gifted Reiki doctor, after all. It's taxing to draw on that power while adorned in *this*." She motioned to her skin with a grimace. "But even if I was wearing Masako, it's always difficult to heal someone at a distance—and a near-fatal wound at that. I had to use three soldiers! Three! You should be grateful that the bullet passed straight through your leg. If it had struck your torso or head . . . well." She shrugged. "We wouldn't be having this conversation."

Three men had just died in order for Ingrid to be saved. She could see the bodies around Blum now. Young men, sprawled and still. Ingrid had been so deep in her pain, so overwhelmed by Blum's ever-present magical musk, that she hadn't even felt their ki tugged away.

Cousin-from-over-the-water-Ingrid, thank you. Tacoma's appreciation felt warm and fuzzy in Ingrid's mind. *I will sleep more.*

Sleep deeply and for many years, Ingrid replied in her thoughts. *Peace to you, Tacoma.*

Peace. With that, the heightened presence dwindled to nothing.

Ingrid didn't feel peace as she looked on the kitsune, still snared in the street. What if Blum changed to a fox now? Her leg wouldn't be trapped anymore. What would they do then? "You killed them to heal me." Rage shook her voice.

"It was that, or Rainier awakens, or your lover boy shoots you in the head, though he didn't seem quite up to that. That's romance for you." Blum looked at the bodies around her. "I'll be blunt. These men were already injured, one of them quite badly, so it's not as though I gave you their full measure."

Fueled by anger, Ingrid pushed herself to stand. She was wobbly as a newborn foal standing upright for the first time. Her knees knocked together and her injured leg gave out; Cy caught her and guided her down again.

"Good catch, Cy." Blum gave an approving nod. "Ingrid, do take it easy. Your artery is patched and the pain is frozen for now, but you still have anterior and posterior flesh wounds that could become infected, and you lost a dangerous amount of blood. You also have substantial muscle atrophy and nerve damage—it's a wonder you can walk around at all! My magic will help attend to your most urgent needs, but it needs *time.* You'll need considerable rest and hearty meals with lots of meat."

The sound of ripping cloth caused Ingrid to look over at Cy. He'd grabbed a shirt from a fallen man. "I need to bandage your thigh. It'll keep more filth off your wounds."

Heavy tapping sounds rang from the stuck Durendal. Soldiers were trapped inside. God, how had Ingrid done that? She shivered, cold despite her lingering fever. She brought up a shield around Cy and herself again.

"Speaking of wounds," said Blum. "It's curious how you are unable to bear children."

Ingrid gawked at her. "You can see that?"

"She's trying to needle you," Cy muttered. "And delay us while more soldiers come."

"Of course I am, Cy. And yes, Ingrid, I can read your body in *intimate detail* during a healing." She gave them a knowing smirk. "You haven't been spayed, as your ovaries are still present, but your body has been purposely altered in a way that prevents pregnancy. Judging by the scar tissue, I'm guessing it was done around puberty, most likely by a floral Reiki doctor working alongside a surgeon." Blum sniffed in disdain. "I suppose such an operation was necessary, considering the repercussions of your pain. A shame, though. I wonder what sort of children you could have produced?"

What kind of children *could* she have had? She'd never considered this before; since her teen years, she had known it was impossible. Her mind conjured an image of a brown-skinned little girl with spectacles perched on her nub of a nose, airship schematics clutched in a pudgy fist.

"Shut up," snapped Ingrid; even her mind was racing. Mr. Sakaguchi and Mama—they'd had her . . . *fixed*? She thought of when she was twelve, when she was told her appendix had to be removed, though she'd had no pain beforehand. Had this other surgery occurred instead?

Cy used his pocketknife to slice down the length of her skirt. Blood made her bloomers adhere to her skin. "Ingrid, don't let Blum get to you." Even so, she could see the anger in his eyes.

"I suppose it's a good thing I can't talk to Ojisan right now," she whispered.

"Yes." He wrapped her thigh and she gasped as he tugged the cloth tight, though she still didn't feel any pain. The thin blue sheen that remained on the ground was pulled toward her. "You have a legitimate reason to rage at him, but remember, she wants you to think these thoughts."

Ingrid nodded, and hated Blum all the more.

"I don't suppose you'd be willing to free my leg?" asked Blum. She sounded blasé. "I can summon medical aid for you. That gunshot wound isn't your only concern. These power fluctuations aren't good for you. If only you could see what you're doing to yourself, child."

Child. It set Ingrid's teeth on edge. "Can't foxes chew through their own legs to free themselves from traps?"

Blum made a face. "Certainly, but I've become well adapted to my human forms and the Western way of *cooking* red meat. I haven't worn my original body in *ages*."

Cy tied off the bandage. He'd wrapped her thigh so tightly that she barely had feeling down through her leg, but that was likely for the best. Blum might have saved her life—damn the yokai—but Ingrid's physical well-being still dangled from a precipice.

"While proper doctoring would be a fine thing, I don't

think Ingrid wants the chains that come along with your offer, Ambassador," said Cy. He stood, bringing Ingrid up with him. She wobbled but had the focus now to weave more power into her muscles.

If only you could see what you're doing to yourself, child. Ingrid didn't want to know, but she had a horrible feeling she'd find out soon enough.

Blum shrugged. "It was worth asking."

A man screamed close by. Ingrid turned to see a Chinese woman smashing a brick against a downed soldier. The soldier's skull crunched like a melon. Other Chinese people crept from the rubble. They eyed Cy and Ingrid with caution.

Ingrid looked between them and Blum. "I don't want to be cruel like my father," she whispered with a glance toward heaven. But she and Cy needed to survive. They needed to get away from this place.

These Chinese people had even more reason to hate Blum than Ingrid did.

"We're not a threat to you," Ingrid said as she looked at the refugees. She pointed at Blum as she and Cy started hobbling north. "That's an ambassador of the Unified Pacific. She's nigh impossible to kill, but for now, she's trapped in the street. Don't get too near her. She has very powerful *lingqi*."

"An ambassador?" a Chinese man asked. The words bubbled through a mouth of blood and broken teeth. The others stooped to pick up bricks. Ingrid pushed herself to walk faster.

"Good-bye for now, Ingrid Carmichael!" called Blum. "I'll remember this. Cy, I hope you make it to Atlanta soon so you can see your sister."

"She's buried in Wedowee, Alabama, not over in Atlanta!" he snapped. He kept his gaze forward.

"The only thing she's buried in is work, in her laboratory, as she completes my Gaia Project. Her genius will end this war at long last."

Cy's hold on Ingrid grew tighter. He practically carried her as he walked faster, his strides longer. Ingrid felt dizzy. Maggie was alive?

"Hope is a kind of gangrene!" Blum's high laugh was aborted by the crunch of a brick on flesh. She keened, high-pitched, bestial. Ingrid and Cy rushed onward and didn't glance back.

CHAPTER 24

"Maggie is alive." It took Cy several minutes to manage the words. "She's the gifted engineer that Roosevelt talked about, too. Lord help us. If anyone could create a flying citadel that would end the war, she could."

"Her death must have been faked like yours was," said Ingrid. Smoke billowed over them. Bricks and shattered wood crunched underfoot.

"Yes. Though I bet she did it willingly. In San Francisco, Father said he was grooming her to administer the company. She'd hate that. She needed to invent the way most folks need to eat. Oh, Maggie." The agony in his voice broke Ingrid's heart. She gripped his arm, and he looked her way. "I can't dwell on this now. Distractions will kill us." He took in a deep breath. "How are you feeling?"

"Like magic is the only thing that's keeping me conscious

and alive. I don't know how much longer I can keep going, though. I *should* be dead."

"Thank God I didn't shoot you." His voice was ragged.

"That's the most romantic thing I've heard all day."

His chuckle was dry, exhausted. "Quite the couple we make."

"I think we're a fine pair."

"I don't suppose you know where our friends the sylphs are about now? Soldiers are bound to have a perimeter established up ahead."

"I can see." Ingrid drew on the tingle of power in her skin. Blum's foulness still lingered on her senses. "Damn it!"

"What?"

"Blum re-created a bond between us when she healed me. No wonder she is so nonchalant about our escape. Well, the sylphs can temporarily help us hide from her, too."

"Right now, I imagine she has other things on her mind. Like *bricks*."

"Maybe they can manage to knock her unconscious. I don't know. I'm afraid to assume anything positive when it comes to Blum."

Ingrid motioned for Cy to be quiet. She stretched out her magic in a way she had never done before, deploying her awareness like dandelion puffs scattered on a breeze. She intimately knew the sylphs' distinct scent, their heat, and she let her awareness wander in search of it. It took a matter of seconds to get a feel for their presence. Her gaze shifted north.

"I found them. They really did stay close." Even more, the

eagerness of the sylphs flared at the caress of her power. They immediately began to fly toward her. She could have wept, but she couldn't let down her guard, physically or emotionally.

Ingrid felt other entities nearby, too. Of the mundane and deadly variety. "Soldiers are moving in on us. We must hide, fast."

"Here." Cy left the street and clambered through a gutted building. Ingrid followed a mere step behind. Some of the interior wood walls still stood to almost ceiling level. Debris dust shifted like a cloud underfoot. They found an alcove in a corner. Part of the roof had dropped to form a makeshift ceiling. "Will this do?"

"Yes. It should only take the sylphs a few minutes to get here," she whispered. She swiped a few scorched rocks aside to sit down, and was suddenly put in mind of how Fenris had labeled crates back in the skating rink. "Cy, I have an idea. I need your Tesla rod."

He arched an eyebrow. "What are you . . . ?"

"I can't feel any pain right now and soldiers are going to find and free Blum any minute. She might be hurt, but I'm not going to count her out. I need a more permanent ward against her."

He blanched beneath the filth on his face. "You're going to brand yourself."

"It's the only way. Her dark Reiki will heal a lot, but burn scars are about as permanent as you can get." Ingrid tried to sound upbeat about it, even as her stomach clenched in a knot.

"How will *you* feel about yourself, with 'inu' permanently on your skin?" he asked, brow furrowed. "It won't change how I feel about you or your body, but it's not . . . it's not a pleasant label."

She managed a small nod. Logically, she understood the anvil-heavy weight of what it meant for someone of her skin color to bear a brand. To be permanently labeled a dog, even willingly, even if it kept her alive . . . *no.* The symbolism within that mark would sear too deep. The whole concept was repulsive beyond words.

"You're right," she said, voice thick. "We need to think beyond the old stories about kitsune versus dog. There must be other antagonists."

Her thoughts traveled to the *qilin* and what it said to her: *You possess the heat of potential, of the very force of the earth.* She carried that heat and potential within her body right now.

"I will *make* myself into Blum's antithesis. I'm powerful. Pele is more ancient and incredible than Blum could ever hope to be, and I'm her kin." She nodded to Cy. "I'll go with tsuchi."

Earth. 土 Three strokes to write. Simple. Powerful unto itself. It was a positive character—literally, as it resembled a plus sign, and also a cross planted in the ground. The kanji was similar to that of the radical for samurai, too—for that, the upper horizontal stroke was longer.

She pushed back her coat and slashed skirt to bare the bloodstained bloomers on her uninjured leg. The activity of the evening had shredded her stockings, so it took almost no force to peel the cloth away to show the brown skin of her thigh.

Cy partially telescoped the rod and twisted it in a different way. The blue tip glowed. She swallowed dryly. By the time she could feel pain again, they had better be aloft in the *Palmetto Bug*.

"Do you want me to do this?" Cy asked softly. The voices of soldiers carried from nearby.

"I think there'll be more power in me making the strokes. More . . . meaning. But if you can steady my hand, that might help."

He sidled closer and planted a soft kiss on her forehead. The sorrow in his eyes caused her to blink back tears. He positioned her hands on the weapon, his fingers overlapping hers, and together they began the first stroke of the kanji.

There was something god-awfully abhorrent about burning her own body in such a way, even without the pain. She pressed as lightly as possible to leave a mark; her skin melted and scorched, brown turning to vivid pink and red. The smell was the stuff of nightmares, more primal nightmares than the ones of San Francisco she had repeated over the past week. Bile rose in her throat and she made herself swallow it down.

Cy's strong grip kept her shaking hands steady. She made herself work past her own revulsion to the well of heat in her chest, embedding power into every stroke.

Earth. *Tsuchi*. A force more timeless than Blum, more resilient. Foxes lived in warrens, but Ingrid embodied the power that *made* that warren. Magic trickled in, hot and cold in her bared and burned tissue. She imagined the invisibility offered by the sprites, but rendered it through earth magic. To Blum, Ingrid's essence was to be camouflaged like a wyrm in the dirt, like a clenched flower bud amid briars. It didn't matter that Blum's Reiki stained her; it was no longer a stain. It was bleached by Ingrid's greater power.

She made certain it was the greater power, too. The strokes of the kanji were short, but she put everything she could into them. Ingrid shoved out the same sort of power she had used to knock down buildings in the ruins of San Francisco, except now she funneled that energy into herself.

This would work. It had to.

Heat burned and roiled as it poured through her hands and down the Tesla rod. The blue tip glowed brighter. Ingrid's fever dissipated; she continued by pulling on her very life energy. If Blum caught her, she'd have no life, anyway. *This had to work*.

"Ingrid. Ingrid? Let go. It's done."

The kanji was complete in a matter of seconds, but in that time, Ingrid felt as if she had aged decades. Cy plucked the rod away and quickly shut it off. Ingrid's hands seemed stuck in their curved grip, and her trembling grew to full-body convulsions.

"I hate her." Her whisper rattled like the wind in an autumn oak tree. "I hate her for making me do this."

Cy stroked loose hair from her face and cradled her

close. "God Almighty, you've gone from a fever to freezing cold. What did you do to yourself?" His whisper was choked.

"I used the magic that I still held, and more. I had to. If I can't prevent her from tracking me, I'm as good as dead." She violently shivered.

"I can pull out more filled kermanite for you to draw from."

"That might be a good idea, just to bring up my body temperature."

Cy opened one of the bags at his waist. Ingrid accepted a pinch of kermanite and clenched her fist. The power filtered into her system, the warmth creating an especially intense shiver. She turned her hand to dump out the pulverized kermanite and her arm immediately fell limp to her lap.

"I have nothing left," she whispered. She could shift her arms and legs a bit, but everything felt rubbery, as if her extremities weren't fully part of her body.

What damage had Blum seen in Ingrid's atrophied muscles, in her very nerves? Could the dark Reiki blunt some of this new deterioration that Ingrid had undoubtedly caused?

"Don't worry about that now," he said, though worry shone in his eyes. "I carried you through San Francisco. I can carry you out of Seattle. Here. I saved more cloth. Let me bandage your leg."

The burn still didn't hurt, and she didn't even want to imagine how it would feel later.

Sylphs descended like fluttering lost stars, each one a

tiny spark of heat. Ingrid assessed them. They were still tired, but the short rest had done them good.

"They can hide us for several blocks, not much more than that," she whispered.

"Good. That's all we need."

The sylphs began to swirl around them as Cy helped Ingrid up. Their distinct magic slapped against Ingrid.

She staggered and leaned on Cy to make it through the rubble. Once they were in the street, he swept her up into his arms. The sylphs tightened their flight paths.

Dozens of soldiers marched along the street headed south, toward Blum. Another Durendal roared by. Cy and Ingrid remained utterly quiet as they reached the blockade past the dynamited firebreak. Scores of soldiers and police stood guard, as did dozens of citizens. Some still wore suits, while others clutched robes and nightgowns. Their gazes focused on the battle to the south, though fewer gunshots and explosions were ringing out now.

Cy dodged people, and they unknowingly dodged him in turn. A little boy in pajamas made airship noises as he wove between people's legs. He looped around Cy while making *putt-putt* sounds like automated gunfire then switched back to replicating engine rumbles. Ingrid numbly stared at the boy, too tired to even feel renewed rage toward Mama and Mr. Sakaguchi.

Cy's rhythmic walk lulled her. She hated that her weakness forced her to be such a burden to him, but at the same time, it was a relief to rest for the first time in hours. Her body, her mind, her spirit were utterly depleted.

The streets were almost vacant due to the curfew, though shadows shifted here and there as men dashed across the street. The *clip-clops* of approaching hooves echoed against buildings. It took another block for the wagon to fully come into view. A red cross emblazoned the side of the canvas cover.

"An answer to a prayer," Cy murmured. He ducked into the deep shadows of a doorway. Refuse shifted underfoot. "The sylphs can go. We have our ride."

The sylphs were almost as tired as Ingrid. This time, they weren't resistant to the idea of rest at the *Palmetto Bug*. They departed as a small cloud.

"How are you doing, Ingrid?" he asked softly as the wagon rolled closer.

"It's hard to keep my eyes open."

"Then don't keep them open. Your body needs to heal. Let it. You probably need to sleep three days straight and eat through the whole larder, and that's fine and dandy."

She snorted softly but her brain was so fuddled she couldn't think of a thing to say.

Cy emerged from the shadows, Ingrid in his arms, and dashed into the road.

"Thank God!" he called. "I have a woman here, badly injured."

"Whoa!" The woman driver reined up. She wore a white nurse's cap with a black outfit. "Where'd you come from? Police shoulda had you wait at the line for the other ambulance."

"Shrapnel hit our building," Cy said, not missing a

beat. "I've walked along, but no taxis are about, with this curfew—"

"I'm supposed to be off duty, but I can get you to Seattle General—"

"Ma'am, beg your pardon, but I have a doctor up in Edmonds who'll see her. She's worked in my household and grew up with me, and I know for a fact that hospitals won't treat a woman like her right." He lied so easily, so fervently.

The woman grunted but she didn't naysay him. "She looks like she's in a bad way. Hop in. I can get you out of downtown."

"I'm much obliged, ma'am."

Cy's politeness brought a faint smile to Ingrid's face as her eyes closed and consciousness slipped away.

"Damn it, but you had me scared. Those sylphs arrived hours ago. They flew right up inside the *Bug* and claimed a top rack, like they own the place, and I've been waiting and waiting for any sign of you."

Ingrid blearily jerked awake at the sound of Fenris's voice. To her surprise, her head was resting against Cy's chest as he carried her again. Had she really slept that deeply? A pink tint warmed the sky. It was *morning*?

"Hey." Fenris leaned close to her. His voice and demeanor softened. "You know we just cleaned this airship top to bottom. Are you going to bleed on everything again?"

"Fenris . . ."

"Yeah, yeah." Fenris backed off.

"Not bleeding anymore," she slurred. Her head lolled

so she could see Cy. "I slept all the way here?" More sleep sounded like a good idea, too.

A brisk wind billowed in her face. They stood at the top of a mooring mast. The view showed a variety of roofs, swirling birds, and plentiful airships at other masts. Crafts rumbled all around them.

"You did. Judging by how you slept, I'm guessing you still can't feel pain?" asked Cy.

"Not yet, no." The events of the night flooded through her brain. Lee, Mr. Sakaguchi, the submarines, Ambassador Blum. "No soldiers followed us?"

"Nary a sign of UP blue once we left downtown. Your sorcery seems like it successfully threw off the fox." His smile was faint, his concern for her obvious.

"Is the *Bug* ready to go?" she asked.

Fenris stuffed his hands in his pockets. The wind tousled his short hair. "Yeah, but is this it? I mean . . . no Lee?"

"This is it," Cy repeated softly. "I'll tell you more later."

"You don't have to protect me," Ingrid mumbled. "I was there, you know. Help me stand up. Your arms must feel like noodles after hauling me around again."

Cy hesitated. "Are you sure?"

"That your arms are worn out? Yes. Now let me down."

Her feet tapped on the steel grate of the mooring mast. Her body immediately sank. Cy hauled her close.

"I think you're the one with udon for limbs," he chided as he lifted her up again.

Ingrid remained quiet. Her legs hadn't even tried to work. That was new. She just needed to rest for a few days, that was all. She was no spring chicken when it came to recovery from power sickness. The flight aboard the *Bug* would give her the time she needed, and Cy had assuredly stocked the larder in anticipation of her appetite.

They boarded. Cy settled her in her usual bunk. The vicinity still reeked of vinegar. Fenris prepared the ship for departure as Cy scurried around to gather supplies to thoroughly clean Ingrid's injuries once they were in the air.

With the engine revving, Fenris returned. He leaned on the cabinets to stare down at her in the rack. "So, which way are we heading?"

"She still needs a doctor, but we need more distance between us and Seattle." Cy sat with his legs crossed in the hallway, his arm against hers. "Blum might not be able to track her now, but this city is a hive of soldiers, and it will be for a while yet."

"Let's fly to Portland," Ingrid said. "We need to send news to Mr. Roosevelt, and he has several contacts there. Maybe he'll even head north again because of everything that happened here tonight."

Cy looked up at Fenris. "How much laudanum do we have?"

He waved away the question. "Lots. I can't stand the stuff. Interferes with my focus. And my chest wound is healing just fine, thank you, so no one needs to nag me about that."

"I'll save my nagging for later, then. Do you need anything to eat now?" Cy asked Ingrid.

She shook her head. The movement made her feel dizzy. "No. I want to sleep more as soon as my wounds are clean."

Cy clenched her hand. "Promise you'll let me know when you're ready for the laudanum?"

"Promise."

Ingrid awoke screaming. Her legs were on *fire*. The vibrant pain shattered the world into black specks, her vision at pinpoint. Her full body ached and throbbed. Pain. Pain. Pain that would destroy the city, that would drown Lee and Mr. Sakaguchi in their submarine, that would bury Cy in a savage lahar—

"Ingrid! Ingrid!" Cy shouted. Broad hands gripped her shoulders and forced her down. "I'm here, calm down—"

"You have to shoot me, Cy! You have to! Don't let Tacoma wake up, not because of me!"

"Ingrid, sweetheart, we're not in Seattle anymore. We're flying to Portland. The city wasn't destroyed, just Chinatown, and that wasn't your fault at all." Her lungs roared with need for air. Her pulse pounded out a marathon as seconds ticked by. "Lie down. There, that's it."

She quivered as she settled down on the pillow again, reality slowly coming back to her. Seattle wasn't destroyed. Blum had healed Ingrid to save the city—to save her own life. Maybe Lee and Mr. Sakaguchi were alive, too. Maybe. Where would the submarines have gone? Some remote island off the coast? She brought a hand to her face and found her skin soaked with sweat. Oh God, but her legs throbbed like buckets of hot coals, the right one worse; the bullet had blazed a path straight through her flesh.

"It feels like my legs are going to burn off." She could

barely speak through the pain. "How close are we to Portland?"

"A few hours out. Skies are clear. No thunderbirds about." That was a reminder she didn't need to hear. "Here, sit up, let me get you some water."

He helped her to drink; her jaw and lips were so tight that half the water dribbled down to her chest. Every movement seemed to spur more agony. She wobbled at the edge of consciousness. Through it all, her stomach resounded hollow and needy and nauseous all at once. She wanted to eat, but she knew nothing would stay down.

"Laudanum?" Cy asked.

"Laudanum. But I need to use the facilities first." God, but she hoped he didn't have to help her with every little thing there, too.

She was vaguely aware of the warm presence of the sylphs in the rack above. They sent her a flash of acknowledgment even as they continued to rest. Their bellies were sated; good.

Ingrid gripped the edge of the bed as she pivoted her hips out. Her bare calves flopped into the hallway. Pain throbbed down their lengths, but it was nice to actually see them—confirmation that they still existed, even if the flesh felt as if it were immersed in a furnace. She wore an old nightgown that Lee had packed for her. Lee. Ingrid blinked back tears even as she inhaled with a hiss at another horrendous pulse of pain. She scooted her bottom forward. Her nausea worsened. Her feet dragged; her knees angled out in a very unladylike way.

"What the hell?" she gasped.

She stared at her legs—which looked alarmingly thinner than before—and moved them with her hands; both knees felt rigid, reluctant to bend. She could feel the pressure of her touch, so it was not as though her skin was numbed. The cool air had even caused her leg hairs to go prickly. She positioned her knees so that her feet were flat on the tatami.

She tried to scoot out again. Her legs didn't move, even as agony seared through most every nerve ending.

Ingrid understood power sickness. She understood fatigue. She knew what it meant to feel weak and wobbly, but this, this . . .

"Cy?" Her voice was unnaturally high. "Cy, my legs aren't working. They're not working at all."

CHAPTER 25

Thursday, April 26, 1906

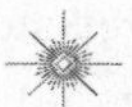

Nighttime. The shades were drawn. Ingrid was lying in a bed in a room that didn't reek of vinegar, but of antiseptics and lemon. Mr. Roosevelt's contact had secreted them in a manse somewhere in Portland. Truth be told, between her pain, her panic, and eventually, Fenris's opiates, Ingrid wasn't sure of the details.

Pasteurian and Reiki physicians had visited; no names were exchanged, as discretion seemed to be the rule within this household. The gunshot wound was healing well enough, thanks to Ambassador Blum's magic and Cy's ministrations. The burn on her other thigh had been treated with salve and no longer pained her.

She could barely see Cy through the cracked door. He was conversing in the hallway with Mr. Roosevelt, whose voice boomed here and there: "Sakaguchi, still captive!" "That fox!" "Fool's luck for certain!"

The door finally shoved open. "Miss Carmichael," said Mr. Roosevelt. He offered her a bow.

"Mr. Roosevelt, sir." She tried to sit up.

"Ingrid!" Cy scowled as he came alongside her.

She let her body drop into the sheets again. She had to try. She had to pretend that her legs might still work, wasted as they were. She had said nothing to the doctors about geomancy or power sickness. The Pasteurian analyzed her with his eyes and his instruments, while the Reiki doc studied her strangely stained life essence. Both agreed that her condition seemed to involve her brain and the nerve impulses to her extremities, especially her legs. The Pasteurian used the term "spasticity." He said some days might be better than others, and that she might show slow improvement over weeks and months if she worked to regain her muscle strength. Maybe. Not even the ki doc could do much to treat a brain and nerve injury. Such extensive, infinitesimal damage might even be too much for Blum to directly address.

"Don't strain yourself on my account, Miss Carmichael," said Mr. Roosevelt, his hands clasped behind his back. "I cannot visit for long. This is a quick stop as I make my way to Seattle to assess the scope of the damage there. I'm sorry to hear of your condition. My staff can offer several locations where you might quietly, covertly convalesce."

Home. She wanted home. She wanted to return to a city, to a time, that no longer existed. Ingrid thought back to what Tacoma had said—that she needed to return to her mountain for safety. If only she had such a refuge now.

Her grandmother had such a place, though: Kilauea, in the Hawaiian Vassal States. A volcano that did not sleep.

"Cy told you about Mr. Sakaguchi and Lee?"

"Yes, Cy did." Mr. Roosevelt's mustache twitched as he said the name. "I'll monitor any reports of submarines. Nothing has emerged—pardon the unintentional pun—thus far, so it's my hope that Ambassador Blum remains ignorant of their escape method as well. However, if these submarines are used to attack American forces, that changes everything. Our military will retaliate, regardless of who is on board."

To that, Ingrid could only nod. She knew Cy wouldn't mention the pact that Mr. Sakaguchi had made with Uncle Moon, which was good. Mr. Roosevelt wouldn't approve of his friend filling kermanite for the Chinese cause. It would make the pretense of their broken friendship into reality—and cost Ingrid and Cy their most powerful ally.

"Blum's method of tracking you disturbs me greatly," Mr. Roosevelt continued. "This sorcerous brand on your body seems to be working—and healing as well as a burn can, from the doctors' reports—but I suggest you travel far. Very far. Blum's powers aren't infinite, and the effects of all Reiki are known to fade in time. Again, my staff can assist with these travel arrangements."

"Thank you, sir," Ingrid said. She already had a certain place in mind.

"That said, there is one particular reason why I wished to see you both again. Our conversations this past weekend have lingered in my mind. About you in particular, Mr. Jennings." Roosevelt whirled on his heel. "You looked familiar to me, as did your mannerisms. It took me a full day to realize that you're truly Bartholomew Augustus."

Cy stood, fists balled at his hips. He met Mr. Roosevelt's cool gaze. "The deceit was necessary, sir."

"You're a deserter from the A-and-A, presumed dead in an airship crash."

"I did desert, sir, but I made no effort to fake my death. Ambassador Blum mentioned in Seattle that she arranged that deceit with the hope that I might foolishly attend my own funeral."

"Did she?" Mr. Roosevelt adjusted his glasses on his nose. "So you merely ran from your duties, is that it? Are you one of those white-livered copperheads?"

"Sir—" Ingrid pushed herself to sit upright. Her arms quivered from exertion. Her legs had taken the brunt of the magical-physical depletion, but her entire body had been damaged.

"My duties to God, humanity, and the good of my own soul took priority, sir." Cy stood at parade rest, his posture strong.

"Damned conscientious objectors," Roosevelt spat. "Well, you're no coward. You proved that much. I'd see you locked up, but you *do* hold another vital role now with Miss Carmichael in your charge."

Ingrid was now Cy's assigned duty? She would have laughed at the pompous statement, but she had no desire to make Mr. Roosevelt even more incensed.

Cy accepted the news with a cool nod. "Has there been any word of my father, sir?"

"No. Last I heard, George Augustus is still missing in San Francisco." Mr. Roosevelt sighed.

"While my twin sister is alive and well in Atlanta," Cy said softly. "My father doesn't know, does he?"

"Am I correct in guessing that Ambassador Blum informed you of this news?" asked Mr. Roosevelt. Cy nodded, and Roosevelt's thick shoulders sagged. "George does not know, and that has pained me greatly. I have come to call him a good friend in recent years."

"My family has known greater pain, sir," Cy snapped.

"This is what your sister wanted, Mr. Augustus," Mr. Roosevelt growled back. "She wanted to escape and invent again, and that never would have happened, not with the burden of Augustinian's management falling on her. I have seen her work on the flying citadel." His voice softened as he shook his head. "There is nothing like it in the world."

"I can believe that." Cy sounded so very tired. "She was always the smartest of us."

Roosevelt looked between Cy and Ingrid. "I must depart. My staff here will assist you, and I'll assist when possible. You know how to contact me again. I hope your recovery continues to go well, Miss Carmichael." He shook Cy's hand, somewhat grudgingly, and laid an avuncular kiss on Ingrid's knuckles, and then he was gone.

Cy stared at the door for a moment and then pulled a small, familiar box from his pocket. He triggered the mechanism inside of the invention that he had dubbed the radioflash; it emitted no sound as it neutralized any electronics within range. There were none in view—this domicile wasn't even wired for electricity—but Ingrid knew he was most concerned with whirly-flies left to spy on their conversations. He also physically checked her room several times a day, paying special attention to the vents.

Satisfied with their security, he pocketed the radioflash and sat beside her.

Ingrid reached for his hand, and he clung to her as if to a lifeline.

"I think it was easier to mourn Maggie when she was dead than to think of her working on that war machine. God help me, that's a horrible thing to say, but it's the truth." He stared into the paisley wallpaper. Tears stung Ingrid's eyes. She hated to see him hurt this way. She hated that Blum's parting shot had struck so true. "Death counts don't matter to Maggie. It's about creation. The fun of it. What happens after that . . ." He shook his head.

"We must stop the Gaia Project from going forward," Ingrid said. "It's Blum's pet scheme."

"One of how many?" Cy's laugh was curt. "You're right. We do. We need to go up against my twin sister to do it. Destroy the invention she likely loves more than anything else on this earth. God help me, but I want to save her. I want to save her soul before she causes so much destruction."

Blum's words echoed in her mind. *Hope is a kind of gangrene.* Ingrid shook her head to force the thought away. "It doesn't sound like Maggie'd welcome your intervention."

"No." His expression was grim. "She won't. But it's still

what needs to be done. Mr. Roosevelt said before that the citadel is almost ready to deploy." He released a huff of breath. "However, right now, Ingrid, you—"

"If you're about to tell me to go to some remote resort to convalesce while you head off to kill yourself doing some damn fool thing, I should remind you that my arms still work, mostly, and I can throw something at you."

That coaxed a small smile onto his face. He scooted closer, his grip becoming more tender, less desperate. "Or I could do this."

"That works, too." She stroked the veins down the back of his knuckles. "We need to stay together. Somehow, some way, an opportunity will arise when we can take down Blum. If not with the *guandao,* then by other means. Surely we'll find Lee again. Mr. Sakaguchi, too." Though she was unsure of how this second reunion with him would play out, knowing what she did now. Damn Blum and her foul truths.

Cy looked weary to marrow and soul. "We don't even know if Lee or Mr. Sakaguchi is still alive right now, Ingrid."

"I know, I know. But I have to think that we followed the course that the *qilin* thought was best. You'd think that divine beings would know more or be able to do more, but then, look at me." She snorted. "This body of mine is all too human—"

"I'm quite fond of that body, and I do intend to look at it as often as I can."

At that, she gave him a small smile. "This body does have its perks, but it's also decided that I can't walk right now. That . . ." She took a deep breath as her brain fumbled for words. "That won't stop me. I *refuse* to be weak. I need answers."

Cy's brow furrowed. Light gleamed off his pince-nez. "Where'd you think to find them?"

"Hawaii. I want to talk to my grandmother, if at all possible. If I can understand my heritage and my power, maybe I can do something to stop the Gaia Project. Something that won't cause more damage to my body."

Cy stared at their hands. His thumb stroked circles against her knuckles. "Hawaii is a prime place of harvest for Japanese geomancers. The energy always flows. That could kill you, Ingrid, or make this spasticity worse."

"Geomancers there take precautions. A trip there'd send us far from Blum, too, like Roosevelt advised. If you or Fenris have other suggestions, I'll gladly listen, but I'm not about to lounge in a feather bed while this war goes on. There's a line in the opera *Lincoln,* do you remember? 'The war is done but I'm a warrior yet.'"

"I remember." Cy's gaze met hers. "There's the line after that, too—'I'm a sinner, true, but eternal peace is what I hope to get.'"

"'What I hope to get, get.'" Ingrid spoke the refrain.

She clutched his hand with shaky fingers. The burned kanji character on her thigh ached, reminding her of its presence and of her own inherent power. Yes, she might be bed-bound for now, but she wouldn't stay down.

Somehow, she must fight on for the sake of peace.

Author's Note

The world shown in *Breath of Earth* and *Call of Fire* is grim, and it is based on historical truth. Japan's ambitions for the Chinese mainland began long before World War II. In America at the turn of the twentieth century, Chinese immigrants were persecuted and murdered, and justice did not prevail. The Geary Act and its "Dog Tag Law" in the 1890s truly did force Chinese residents to at all times carry photo identification cards as evidence that they were legal residents of the United States.

Some historical details in these books, such as the altered life spans of Chinese Emperor Qixiang and Abraham Lincoln, were deliberate. It is vital to note that in reality, the Qing Dynasty is remembered as ruthless, corrupt, and extravagant; men were indeed executed if they did not wear the queue style haircut. There was no declaration of equality between the Manchu and Han peoples.

Theodore Roosevelt is a brilliant, contradictory, and charismatic historical figure. In reality, he did indeed believe in the manifest destiny of America as a world power, and he rightly predicted that Japan's rising clout would bring it into conflict with America in the coming years. He was also a progressive for his time period when it came to matters of race and society. I found it bizarre, really, how well he fit into the altered history of *Call of Fire*.

The Old Chinatown of Portland, Oregon, was different from other Chinatowns in the United States. It was geographically the largest, due to extensive urban gardens, and was not segregated from the white population. This enabled these diverse people to come to know and understand each other. This is a marked contrast to cities like Tacoma to the north, where in 1885 the entirety of Chinatown was emptied by vigilantes and then burned. Hundreds of Chinese people fled to Portland and other cities.

Dog sorcery was truly practiced to prevent attacks by kitsune in Japan, with the character for "dog" written on the foreheads of children to guard against possession.

Russia and Japan have squabbled over territory for years—and still do. The real Russo-Japanese War took place in 1904 and 1905, with a peace deal organized by President Theodore Roosevelt; he later won a Nobel Peace Prize for his effort.

Other historical and cultural inconsistencies are the result of my undeniable ignorance. I beg forgiveness for any errors and omissions.

My goal in writing these books is not just to entertain through fiction, but to encourage people to read nonfiction about this time period—to confront the dark parts of American history that are dismissed and ignored.

The research bibliography I included in *Breath of Earth* incorporated many of the works I also used for *Call of Fire.* The following are additional books and articles that provided useful data for the series. This list can also be found at BethCato.com with links to available works online.

Japan, Its Mythology

Kitsune: Japan's Fox of Mystery, Romance & Humor by Kiyoshi Nozaki

Daughters of the Samurai: A Journey from East to West and Back by Janice P. Nimura

Early Twentieth-Century America (General)

Hard Drive to the Klondike: Promoting Seattle During the Gold Rush by Lisa Mighetto and Marcia Montgomery

"Airship-Mooring Masts of the U.S. Air Service," *Aerial Age Weekly*, Vol. XIV, No. 14, December 12, 1921

Native American Tales

A Guide to B.C. Indian Myth and Legend by Ralph Maud

Myths and Legends of the Pacific Northwest by Katharine B. Judson

Totem Tales: Indian Stories Indian Told by W. S. Phillips

Theodore Roosevelt

Honor in the Dust: Theodore Roosevelt, War in the Philippines, and the Rise and Fall of America's Imperial Dream by Gregg Jones

China, Its Mythology, and Chinese in America

The Man Who Loved China: The Fantastic Story of the Eccentric Scientist Who Unlocked the Mysteries of the Middle Kingdom by Simon Winchester

Hawaii

A Military History of Sovereign Hawai'i by Neil Bernard Dukas

Pele: Goddess of Hawaii's Volcanoes by Herb Kawainui Kane

The Burning Island: Myth and History in Volcano Country, Hawaii by Pamela Frierson

"Pele's Journey to Hawai'i: An Analysis of the Myths" by H. Arlo Nimmo, *Pacific Studies,* Vol. 11, No. l, November 1987

"Pele, Ancient Goddess of Contemporary Hawaii" by H. Arlo Nimmo, *Pacific Studies,* Vol. 9, No. 2, March 1986

Shoal of Time: A History of the Hawaiian Islands by Gavan Daws

The Hawaiian Revolution (1893–94) by William Adam Russ Jr.

The Hawaiian Republic (1894–98): And Its Struggle to Win Annexation by William Adam Russ Jr.

Stories of Hawaii by Jack London, edited by A. Grove Day

Pau Hana: Plantation Life and Labor in Hawaii, 1835–1920 by Ronald Takaki

Mark Twain in Hawaii: Roughing It in the Sandwich Islands, Hawaii in the 1860's by Mark Twain, foreword by A. Grove Day

Kokoro from the Heart: Cherished Japanese Traditions in Hawai'i by the Japanese Women's Society of Honolulu

"Some Transportation and Communication Firsts in Hawaii," by Robert C. Schmitt, *Hawaiian Journal of History,* Vol. 13, 1979

Hawaii, the Big Island Revealed: The Ultimate Guidebook by Andrew Doughty

Acknowledgments

Tackling a project of this historical depth has been an enormous challenge. I'm grateful for every bit of emotional and intellectual support that has come my way. I have done what I can to make this work as historically accurate as possible, even with certain timeline shifts. Errors are aggravating and unavoidable, and I beg forgiveness for my ignorance.

The community at Codex Writers assisted me with Japanese translation questions and other historical and medical queries. I count the people there among my dearest friends and I am so grateful we have such a strong community. Thanks for making that happen, Luc Reid.

My writing career would not exist without the inspiration I continue to draw from the video game RPGs I loved in my youth. Dragon Quest/Dragon Warrior IV first showed me the use of a dog against fox magic. I first saw kirin as an esper in Final Fantasy VI. Final Fantasy Tactics made geomancy a cool thing. I could go on and on. The fact is: video games are not a waste of time. They saved my life as a teenager. They brought me and my husband together. They made me the storyteller I am today.

I quoted Basho's verses from *Zen and Japanese Culture* by Daisetz T. Suzuki. This is proof that college textbooks do indeed come in useful years later!

My first readers for *Call of Fire* were Rachel Thompson and Rebecca Roland. Thanks for reading so quickly to allay my fears!

I'm grateful for the constant support of my agent, Rebecca Strauss at DeFiore & Co. She's my superhero.

Oh, Harper Voyager. You wonderful, sloth-loving people. Much gratitude to David Pomerico, Caroline Perny, and Pamela Jaffee. Special thanks to my new editor, Priyanka Krishnan, for helping me to make *Call of Fire* a cohesive and shiny novel.

Last but not least, there is my family. My parents. My brother. My husband, Jason. My son, Nicholas. My cat, Porom. I love you all.

About the Author

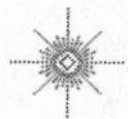

Beth Cato is the author of *Breath of Earth* and the Clockwork Dagger fantasy duology, which includes *The Clockwork Dagger,* nominated for the Locus Award for Best First Novel, and *The Clockwork Crown,* an RT Reviewers' Choice finalist. Her Clockwork Dagger–set novella *Wings of Sorrow and Bone* was nominated for a Nebula Award. A native Californian, Beth currently writes and bakes cookies in a lair outside of Phoenix, Arizona, which she shares with a hockey-loving husband, a numbers-obsessed son, and a cat the size of a canned ham.